The Golden
Pagoda

The Golden Pagoda

Ashleigh Bingham

ROBERT HALE · LONDON

© Ashleigh Bingham 2004
First published in Great Britain 2004

ISBN 0 7090 7670 3

Robert Hale Limited
Clerkenwell House
Clerkenwell Green
London EC1R 0HT

2 4 6 8 10 9 7 5 3 1

Typeset in 10/13 pt Times
Derek Doyle & Associates, Liverpool.
Printed in Great Britain by
St Edmundsbury Press, Bury St Edmunds, Suffolk.
Bound by Woolnough Bookbinding Ltd.

CHAPTER ONE

After four days, the howling whiteness of the blizzard passed as quickly as it had struck, leaving the sky so blue it looked as if it had been enamelled.

The man on the ledge, huddled into a depression in the massive wall of black rock, lifted his head and forced his eyelids to open a crack, then closed them quickly against the painful brilliance of the crown of white mountain peaks towering around him, tier upon tier.

Silence. The silence of death was in his ears. He tried to move his swollen fingers and the agony made him gasp. His feet had lost all feeling, but the days of clawing, gut-twisting hunger no longer persecuted him if he allowed his consciousness to drift.

He sank again towards the edge, where gentler times and places beckoned. Tennis on the lawn with his sisters, and his mother pouring tea on the terrace; the pretty, laughing faces of the young ladies who flirted with him at the hunt ball. There was one girl in particular – what was her name? Louisa? Every detail of her porcelain features passed before his mind's eye, and recollections of her affected shyness made his cracked lips twitch. Was it Lucinda? Leticia?

He should remember her name, because his mother had been most insistent that she was a *very suitable* girl and that it was high time he became engaged. 'She only came out this season, and she's sure to be snapped up before the year is over. You must make her an offer before you leave England.'

Dear God! Surely he had done nothing so damn stupid? The last thing a serving officer on the North-West Frontier needed was a wife, but he had a faint memory of drinking too much champagne the night before sailing for India. He'd dropped to one knee in front of her, but surely she hadn't taken his proposal seriously? And now he couldn't remember the girl's name. All he could see was the image of his mother turning away from him in tight-lipped exasperation. 'Oh, Richard, why aren't you more like your brother?'

He drifted deeper. Peace was coming closer. If he let go now it would all be

5

over, all the pain and desperation. He imagined his mother and sisters receiving the news of his death and rushing into the library to spin the globe, searching for the mountains marked *Pamir*. He doubted they would know where to begin to look.

Of course his mother would immediately order a memorial tablet in the best Italian marble to be erected in Winchester Cathedral. He could see it in the nave, decorated with a splendidly carved laurel wreath surrounding the name of Captain Richard Eldridge. The lettering would be in gold, listing his family connections.

Near death, alone on a rock ledge that straddled the imperceptible border somewhere between India, China and Russia, Richard Eldridge was suddenly gripped by a deep concern regarding his memorial. His mother would never be satisfied simply with names and dates. She'd find a long, sentimental verse, then add some totally inaccurate platitude that his life had been 'sacrificed for the glory and honour of Queen and Empire'.

Damn it! He hadn't suffered the punishment of frost-bite and starvation for Victoria and her territorial possessions. He'd been sent up here to discover why Alastair Mottram had been murdered somewhere in these mountains. And what had happened to the information he carried.

Eldridge felt his heart pump faster and pain swept back into his extremities. The pleasant memories that had carried him away from his wretchedness refused to be rekindled and he heard his father's booming voice informing members of the Cavalry Club of the death of his youngest son.

'Of course Richard should have taken up the job I'd arranged for him on General Gordon's staff, but would he listen to common sense? No. Insisted on packing himself off to India.' Richard saw his father draw deeply on a cigar and shake his head. 'He always was a headstrong young fool. Went off alone on a hunting trip and got himself lost in some godforsaken place over there. Froze to death when his bearers ran off and left him.'

Captain Eldridge struggled for breath and began to cough. 'Lies!' he wanted to roar at his father, sitting in the warm comfort of leather and cigar smoke in London. 'They didn't abandon me, damn you. Three of my men are down there in the ravine with the pack animals. My jemadar carried me until he could barely walk himself and now he's gone on to find help. He'll come back and he'll find me alive, because I'm damned if I'll allow you or anybody else to slander the men who have given me nothing but absolute loyalty.'

He rasped the thoughts aloud, aware his anger was now verging on madness. Lucinda, Louisa, Leticia . . . whoever you are, come back again and take me away from this place. Or Barbara, Beth and Beatrice. Do you remember me? Cassandra, Caroline. . . . Pain stabbed under his ribs when he coughed.

Another night alone on the mountain ledge passed and dawn had barely kissed the tips of the icy peaks when he heard voices close by. It took a great effort to lift his eyelids and squint into the broad, grinning face of the fur-hatted Kirghiz nomad leaning over him. He didn't understand the man's language, but the message was clear when his head was lifted and a kid's skin full of thick yak's milk was put to his parched mouth. He sucked a little, then a little more, as he peered up into the ruddy, weather-worn faces of his four rescuers.

He could make no more than a grunt to express his gratitude, then clenched his jaws as he was lifted on to a rough litter and covered with a wolf-skin rug.

All movement was agony on the journey through the mountains, but he resisted the temptation to fall into oblivion. His mother must not have an excuse to erect any damn mawkish memorial on the cathedral wall. Besides, if he died now his sisters would be forced to go into mourning and miss the London season. They both looked most unattractive in black.

He lay on the litter, occasionally opening his eyes to squint at the landscape of peaks and glaciers shining like mirrors in the sunlight. The Kirghiz men carried him along treacherous paths scratched into the sides of mountains, through slides of heavy snow, across unstable slopes of grey scree.

On the second day, he became aware that the narrow path was dropping, and the next afternoon they were met on the high meadows by horsemen, one with a falcon on his wrist. Amidst a noisy jostle, they slung his litter between two thick-coated mountain ponies for the descent towards the tree line.

He was warmer now under the rug, and that increased the pain in his frost-bitten hands and feet. Gangrene. He knew what treatment the army surgeons would offer, and the image of their scalpels sent a wave of panic through him. What would these nomads do? Now he was sweating, and the pain under his ribs was more intense when he coughed.

He lifted his head and a wide valley far below came into his hazy view, with the scattered yurts of the Kirghiz encampment looking like a dozen brown felt mushrooms growing out of the grass. Blue smoke from the cooking-fires drifted from the holes in their roofs.

The rescuers fired rifle shots into the air to announce their arrival, and this brought a rush of horsemen along the valley floor to escort them through the herd of grazing horses, yaks and fat-tailed sheep.

Daylight had faded as the litter was unslung and, accompanied by the sound of high-pitched, excited female chatter, he was carried into the smoky interior of a yurt that stank of boiled mutton and fermented milk. Several chickens and two bleating kids were booted outside and his litter placed on the floor.

Immediately he found himself surrounded by inquisitive, broad-faced women. Disoriented by pain and exhaustion, he coughed and struggled to make these hovering, almond-eyed Kirghiz understand that they must not cut off his fingers and feet. He could force nothing more than a croak from his throat as he tried to order them away. Someone lifted his head and he drank greedily from the bowl of warm, buttery gruel put to his lips. He wanted to laugh. He wanted to weep. Above all, he wanted to live with his body intact.

Suddenly lamplight appeared, and from the entrance of the yurt came a firm, clear voice speaking words that had the effect of clearing a space around him.

The women shuffled back as the light moved closer, and he struggled to focus his clouded sight on the face of a pale-skinned woman whose hair, untidily pulled up on to her head, was the deep shade of red that Titian had painted on a portrait hanging in his mother's drawing-room.

He closed his eyes to shut out the hallucination, but they sprang open again when he felt the rug pulled aside. The woman was kneeling beside him and when she reached for his hands he gave a grunt of apprehension, but could find no strength to pull them away from her.

'My name is Georgina Larssen, Captain Eldridge. Let me see what I can do for you.' She spoke English, and he questioned his own sanity. An Englishwoman here? The pain was excruciating when she began to ease the glove from one hand.

'Your trooper was brought in several days ago, Captain. He gave me your name.' She spoke matter-of-factly and turned his hand towards the lamplight; her frown of concentration deepened as she sniffed the skin. 'The herdsmen found him in the mountains and fortunately he was able to tell them where he'd left you on the Mingteke Pass. I'm glad they located you.' She hesitated while she examined his fingers one by one. 'He was in a very weakened state when he arrived here, and – I'm sorry – I was unable to save him. He died this morning.'

Richard looked at her blankly and wished he could weep. He owed his life to Jahig Ali's loyalty. Perhaps the young man would still be alive if he hadn't given his last ounce of strength to save a British officer. Let that information find his father. Let him dare speak another word against a native recruit.

The red-headed woman – he couldn't remember her name – remained silent while she held his swollen, discoloured fingers and examined the skin, watching him flinch at her lightest touch. Then she wrapped the hand in a shawl before she began to ease the glove from his other hand. Her face came close to his as she peered at his ears, his lips. The faint scent of English violets wafted about her, and that confused him even more.

A circle of inquisitive eyes watched her actions as she took off his boots and examined his feet.

'Don't . . . I order you, no knife . . .' Fear made his tongue fight to rasp the words.

She shook her head slowly. 'I can't be sure until I see your skin in daylight, Captain, but I see no signs of gangrene yet.'

She bewildered him, this woman who was unapologetically touching his body in a way that no English lady of his acquaintance would ever do. He coughed and was overcome again by the sharp pain under his ribs.

She signalled a Chinese attendant to come to his side while she felt his hot forehead with her palm. 'My servant will try to make you comfortable,' she said and, while she remained crouched beside him, the man opened the front of his jacket and removed the leather pouch strapped to his wasted body. The woman leaned across him and put her ear against his chest, listening to the rattle in his lungs.

Frowning, she sat back on her heels and regarded him for a moment. 'I'll do what I can for you here, Captain Eldridge, but I must try to get you down to the hospital in Kashgar.'

'Kashgar?' Shock ground the word from his raw throat.

'You're in China now – or rather, Chinese Turkestan. You crossed the border two days ago.'

She picked up his pouch, climbed to her feet and turned away, rubbing a finger across her bottom lip. The Chinese servant began to strip his damp clothes, to wash and dress him in thick native garments while she stood a mere three feet away. He grunted his outrage at her lack of propriety. And he wanted his papers back, too. That pouch contained information that was for the eyes of the British Intelligence Office in Simla, and no one else.

She sank to her knees beside him again when he was covered. 'I'll do what I can for your frost-bite, Captain, but I fear you've developed pneumonia.' Her tone was blunt. 'The nearest doctor is my stepfather at the Swedish Mission Hospital in Kashgar. But that's a three-day journey, and you're far too ill to risk travelling all the way down there with the Kirghiz pack animals.'

He tried to speak, but began to cough. She raised his shoulders and held him against her until the spasm passed. 'I'll send a message down to the hospital and ask Doctor Larssen to send up our covered cart – but that's going to take time.'

9

He closed his burning eyes and knew he had little strength left. He swallowed whatever nourishment she put to his lips, and tolerated the agonizing touch of her fingers as she stroked a salve into his hands and feet repeatedly through the night. To ease his pain she put a small wad of opium under his tongue.

And always lingering about her was a faint, disturbing scent of violets that reminded him of his mother's garden parties. He sweated and tossed and worried. It was outrageous for an Englishwoman to wander around a nomads' camp at night and stroke oil into the hands and feet of a man to whom she hadn't been introduced. This wasn't the sort of woman his mother would invite to lunch.

Helpless, he lay through the night, drifting in and out of sleep, listening to the heavy breathing and snores of the men and women whose yurt he was sharing. From outside came the occasional sounds of a lowing animal and clanking neck-bells, and once he heard the howl of wolves, followed by a rifle crack. He had no idea how many times pain and spells of coughing dragged him into consciousness. And he couldn't comprehend if the screaming woman was part of his conscious or unconscious state.

When morning came, he lay on his back looking up at the circular wooden framework of the yurt, at the strips of rawhide tying the structure together, and realized he had survived the night, although his hands and feet were useless and pain stabbed under his ribs.

The people of the yurt woke, stretching and scratching and rolling up their padded sleeping-quilts. Richard felt a rush of icy air when the heavy flap over the doorway was lifted and the baby animals brought in for the night were pushed outside to their waiting mothers.

Ruddy-faced children came to peer at him, grinning when he opened his eyes a crack and they realized he was still alive. The men followed the animals outside, and the women built up the central fire, chattering as they squatted around a big iron cooking-pot.

The Englishwoman entered the yurt and the women's laughter stopped, though they smiled shyly at her, and one of them filled a wooden bowl. She spoke to them as she took the food, but when she turned to bring it to him, Richard saw the looks the women threw to each other behind her back. They were laughing at her, in a gentle way.

'Good morning,' she said, propping a cushion under his shoulders, then blowing on the wooden spoon before she put it to his lips.

He watched her face as he forced himself to swallow the greasy mutton soup, and noticed how the circles of fatigue under her blue eyes were even darker this morning. Blue eyes that he suspected had been weeping. She dipped the spoon into the bowl again. 'Try just a little more.'

He swallowed each time, because she insisted. 'I want you well on the road to recovery before we set off for Kashgar, Captain.' She looked across to the women around the cooking-fire, and he saw her lips tighten. 'It's important to let these people see me perform at least one miracle before I leave.'

CHAPTER TWO

Georgina Larssen left her Chinese hospital attendant with their patient and, pulling her thick woollen cloak tightly around her, walked outside the yurt.

She blinked at the brightness of the blue sky and the white peaks framing the valley. The placid life of the Kirghiz camp had already fallen into its traditional morning rhythm, and the valley echoed with the sounds of neck-bells clanking as the children brought in the bellowing and bleating animals for milking.

With rifles slung across their shoulders, men were riding out, and boys were herding a flock of sheep to pasture on the far side of the stream. After last night's tragedy, she could see no hint of grief expressed amongst the Kirghiz this morning.

Emotion balled in her throat and she didn't pause until she reached a clump of high rocks on the far side of the valley. Here, sheltered from the wind and away from the curious eyes of the nomads, she sat huddled with her head resting on her drawn-up knees, and let her frustration and disappointment dissolve into private tears.

Her stepfather had tried to warn her. 'Go, of course, my dear, and do what you can,' Doctor Larssen had said, 'but don't allow your expectations to ride too high. In my twenty years out here, I doubt I've ever changed any of the old customs and superstitions.'

Her own stubbornness had convinced her that these tribal women would welcome the skills she came to teach them about safer birthing methods. Their culture prohibited any contact with Doctor Larssen himself, and while spells, talismans and potions did no harm when a birth was progressing normally, any complication usually meant disaster for mother and baby.

The Kirghiz had welcomed her into their camp as an honoured guest, but for these mountain people giving birth was a normal life-cycle event, not a medical procedure. Everything in their lives depended on the will of the powerful gods who lived in the mountains, the women explained.

Could she have prevented last night's horror if she had been there when the fifteen-year-old went into labour? If the women had called her away from the English officer, could she have turned the baby before that delivery turned into disaster?

She felt ill when she recalled the image of what had confronted her when she'd walked into the yurt, crowded, hot and noisy with women chanting spells above the girl's screams. They politely brushed aside her protest when the mother's jaws were forced open and a broth of snakeskin poured into her mouth.

'It is good,' they insisted, 'for does not a snake slip with ease from its skin?' When the mother and child died an hour later, a senior woman touched Georgina gently on the shoulder. 'Honoured Sister, it was a bad baby to do this to its mother. Better it dies quickly, for no mother desires a cursed baby that will bring evil to the family.'

After that, the women went about the rituals concerned with a death in the camp, but there was no wild outpouring of grief. When Georgina wept, women clustered around her, offering comfort. 'It is the way of nature, Honoured Sister. The gods of the mountains decide our fate.'

And that was what they'd said to her when they watched her fight for two days to save the life of the young Indian soldier found dying of exposure on the high pass. They'd watched to see if her European brand of magic could change the inevitable, and she'd failed.

Her last chance to prove herself was to keep Captain Eldridge alive. If he survived and was well enough to travel down to Kashgar in the hospital cart, the Kirghiz people might understand that Doctor Larssen's medicine was sometimes stronger than the will of the mountain gods.

The days and nights passed slowly as Georgina and Ho Sung, her Chinese attendant, hovered close to their patient and waited for the hospital vehicle to reach the camp.

Eldridge rallied some days, and she was convinced his fever was gradually dropping, despite the lingering cough. Ho Sung washed and shaved him, and her mixture of oils and ammonia applied to his hands and feet had kept gangrene at bay. The skin remained unbroken, although he was in constant pain, but every day she saw signs of improvement. He slept less, he was less disoriented, and when at last he began to complain, Georgina heaved a sigh of relief.

'If anyone ever tries to serve me a dish of mutton swill when I leave this place, I'll run him through with m'sword!' he muttered as she put the spoon to his lips. His grey-blue eyes looked up at her, squinting as he tried to focus. 'Who are you? Where are my papers?'

'I'm Georgina Larssen, and your papers will leave here with us, I assure you.'

'But what—?'

'What am I doing here?' She brushed a sweep of fair hair from his forehead and wiped his face with a cool cloth. 'It's a long story, but ten years ago Doctor Erik Larssen went to England on leave. He met my mother, they married, and we all came back to live at the Swedish Mission in Kashgar. I've been working at the hospital with him ever since.'

She watched him frown as he struggled to absorb those facts. His face was at last losing its hollow-eyed look of starvation; it was actually a very good-looking face, with high cheekbones and a strong chin.

'You're a doctor?' he asked. 'A nurse?'

'No, Captain, I have no qualifications at all.'

Doctor Larssen looked up from his desk in the dispensary when he heard the sound of hoofs and wheels entering the mission compound and, holding his lantern high, he hurried to the door leading out on to the hospital veranda. Natasha, Georgina's mother, was already running from the house on the other side of the Mission compound to greet her as she swung down from the weary little horse.

'My dear, my dear.' Emotion choked Erik's voice as he held his arms out to his stepdaughter, and she flung herself into them.

'He's still alive, Father! See? I've kept him alive.' There were rare tears of excitement on her cheeks. She brushed them away before she turned to Natasha. 'Oh, Mother, please don't look so concerned. I'm perfectly fine.'

Doctor Larssen quickly blew his nose and pushed his spectacles back into position as he went to their patient, barely conscious on the floor of the cart. 'You've done well, Georgina,' he said. 'I'm truly proud of you.'

The three middle-aged Swedish missionaries, Mr Frederik Hakvin with his wife and sister, came hurrying from their house, and stood in a group by the cart. 'Thank God you're home safely! What a brave girl you are.' The trio clapped their hands, nodding and smiling at her, and servants clustered around them as Richard Eldridge was carried into the hospital.

'Welcome to Kashgar, Captain Eldridge.' Richard opened his eyes to the pleasant male voice beside him, and looked into the face of a grey-haired man whose steel-rimmed glasses were slipping down his nose. 'I am Erik Larssen, and you're here now in my hospital, so let me see what I can do for you.' Two attendants stood by while he began his examination, occasionally uttering little murmurs of satisfaction.

'Good, yes. Very good, Captain,' he said at last, straightening. 'I'd say it was a truly fortunate coincidence that my daughter happened to be in the mountains to provide help when you were found. Surely an act of Providence.'

Richard looked around wildly, trying to orientate himself, trying to find the woman who had refused to let him die. 'Where is she?' he gasped. 'My papers – I must have my papers.'

'Your papers will be quite safe at the Mission,' said the doctor, signalling the attendants to lift him into the waiting bed.

Richard wanted to make a strong protest about losing possession of the confidential report he'd been carrying, but his strength failed him. In the morning he'd demand . . . demand that she. . . . He gave a wordless murmur and closed his eyes.

When Erik returned to the house, he found Georgina still awake and waiting for him with her mother in the sitting-room.

'So,' she said, as he sank into his chair, 'what is your opinion?'

'Captain Eldridge should do well now. You've done splendidly to keep the circulation in his hands and feet, my dear, but he's going to be with us for some time.'

'Who is he, darling?' Natasha slanted a mother's glance at her daughter. Georgina raised an eyebrow. 'I have absolutely no idea. He's been barely alive for the last two weeks.'

'But he *is* alive,' Erik said, 'and he has you to thank for that.'

'Yes, I'm glad, but oh, Father, I couldn't do anything to convince those tribal women that they could save lives if they at least *tried* to understand what I was showing them. Do you know—?'

'All I know, Georgina,' he interrupted gently, 'is that those hardy people who move with the seasons can't afford to be sentimental, so they ensure that only the fittest of their tribe will survive. You've read Mr Darwin's views on this. Is he wrong?'

She pushed herself from the chair and her shoulders sagged as she walked towards him. 'I really don't know how Mr Darwin's theory applies to the human race. I simply found the Kirghiz attitude unbearably heartless when they made little attempt to fight for a life.' She shrugged. 'But you were absolutely right, Father – they're not prepared to change any of their old ideas.' She bent to kiss his forehead.

15

'Perhaps not yet, but I'm sure they were impressed when you kept the Englishman alive. That's given them something to think about.'

A little later, when Natasha lay close and warm in bed beside Erik, she thought about Georgina alone on her crusade in the Kirghiz camp, and wondered what impressions of her beautiful, strong, determined daughter had been formed by the young Englishman now lying in the hospital.

Natasha had the fire lit next morning, and stood behind Georgina, brushing dry her long, freshly washed red hair, and struggling against the waves of guilt she felt at times like this.

Georgina would be twenty-four next birthday, and where did her future lie? Ten years ago, Natasha had been angry when she'd been called a selfish and inconsiderate mother to bring her child to this ancient, alien land. It was the urgency of her own need to marry Erik Larssen which had made her discount the disadvantages for Georgina to grow up in a country where she would have few opportunities to meet other Europeans.

Natasha had been thirty-four when she married Erik Larssen, a man she had known for only two weeks. It had been an unlikely match – the slight, dark-haired Russian ballerina and the tall, shy, middle-aged Swedish mission doctor. But it had been a true love-match ten years ago, and it was still.

She looked fondly at him now, sitting by the window, reading a Swedish newspaper that was three months old. From the day they'd met, Erik had accepted her – and her illegitimate, red-headed daughter – and he'd never questioned the circumstances that had driven her from the Imperial Ballet in St Petersburg to the thankless secretarial work she performed in Bradford.

She refused to let herself think how far her ballet career might have soared, had life taken a different turn. But never for one moment did she regret marrying Erik Larssen. Was it too much to hope that one day her daughter would find her own security and happiness with such a man?

He put down his paper and looked across the compound at the people already coming through the gate. 'Come up to the clinic as soon as you can, m'dear. I think we have a busy day ahead of us.'

'Wait for me, I'm almost ready.' Georgina stood quickly and lifted the thick hair from her shoulders, swept it up on to her head and anchored it with combs and pins. A few minutes later, Natasha watched her husband and daughter talk earnestly as they strode across the compound towards the hospital.

Right at their first meeting, a bond had formed between Erik and Georgina, and as soon as they'd all arrived in Kashgar, she had followed her new step-father into his clinic. There had been no discussion about it; the fourteen-year-old simply became his shadow. She observed and questioned; he explained, and she learned. After a time, he laughed and called her '*my assistant*'. As she worked beside him, her skills grew, and so did her confidence. By the time she was eighteen, a trickle of women had started to visit the clinic, asking to see her – women whose culture did not permit them to be touched by a male hand.

Even though her hair was the colour of a devil's, the doctor's daughter was welcomed into the houses of the local Kashgaris and the Chinese in the city, and in villages scattered along the old Silk Road that skirted the desert.

'Erik, darling, we must think of Georgina's future,' Natasha said often. 'She won't be able to remain at the Mission when you have retired.'

'Retire?' he said to her just last month. 'I have no plans to retire for another ten years at least, my love. I'm only sixty.'

Any concern about Georgina's future lay entirely with Natasha. In another ten years, Georgina would be thirty-four.

'I'm perfectly happy here, Mother,' Georgina said each time Natasha hinted that she should consider finding a post as governess with some English family living in India. 'Go down there and join the fishing fleet to catch a husband? No, thank you! Besides, Father needs me here.'

The one thing Natasha could not share with Erik was his faith that the Lord would watch over Georgina's future. That was a mother's duty.

That evening, soon after dinner, when Erik had gone back to the hospital to visit his new patient, Georgina stretched and gave a weary sigh.

'Those weeks up in the mountains exhausted me more than I realized, Mother. I must go to bed; I simply can't stay awake any longer.'

Natasha sat alone, sewing, trying for as long as possible to ignore the sound of an unlatched gate banging in the wind. At last she put down her work, picked up a lamp and went out to fasten the gate leading into the vegetable garden behind the house. As she passed Georgina's window she saw her, still dressed, sitting at her writing-desk, surrounded by maps and papers.

Natasha stepped closer and recognized the British officer's leather pouch which Georgina had carried back from the Kirghiz camp. Now it lay open on the bed while she was apparently making notes of its contents spread around her.

What was the girl doing? Natasha felt a familiar surge of frustration. She loved her daughter dearly, but there were times when she didn't know her at all.

Natasha walked back into the house and picked up her sewing. Georgina had been only four when she'd been sent to boarding school, and visiting one day a month over the next ten years had never been enough to forge strong links between them. While she'd worked as secretary to a grim, wealthy woman in Bradford, Natasha had seen Georgina develop the capacity to slip behind a façade of cool indifference to shield herself from the taunts of being the only 'charity child' at the school, and to deal with unhappiness by denying it.

On their days together they'd spent much of their time talking like casual acquaintances about Georgina's schoolwork, and sometimes Natasha had told her a little about the Imperial Ballet School in St Petersburg. Their strongest link grew in the Russian tongue they used when they were together.

Only once had Georgina asked about her natural father, the red-headed Scotsman who had gone long before she was born. Even then, Natasha had lied.

She dropped her sewing again and sat staring with unseeing eyes at the patterns on the floor rug. How little about herself she had been able to reveal to Georgina. Those secrets would go to the grave with her; not even her beloved Erik could be told about the events in St Petersburg twenty-five years ago.

Richard Eldridge had no idea what day it was, or for how long he'd been lying in the hospital. He remembered Doctor Larssen frequently being by his side. He remembered Miss Larssen's voice, too.

His spirits lifted. This morning the pain in his chest had almost gone, though his bandaged hands and feet still throbbed at times. And he had an appetite that would put a hungry wolf to shame. Ho Sung appeared at his side and adjusted the pillows so that he was able to sit and look through the window at the morning activity in the Mission compound.

His bed was screened from the rest of the small hospital ward and he was grateful for the privacy. He needed to muster his thoughts and make plans. At that moment he caught sight of Miss Georgina Larssen walking from a house at the far end of the compound; it reminded him that the first matter to be arranged was the return of the documents she'd taken from him in the Kirghiz camp. He watched her approach the hospital building and instinctively steeled himself to confront her.

But she looked straight ahead as she walked along the veranda past his window, and he twisted his head on the pillow to see her enter a room built at right angles to the little hospital building. She came out a few minutes later, tying the strings of a white apron and smiling as she spoke to the people waiting on a long bench.

Richard's neck ached as he strained to watch her, but an attendant appeared with towels, scissors and a razor, and within a few minutes he was once more clean-shaven with his sun-streaked fair hair trimmed. The terror of the mountains was behind him. Against the odds, he'd survived, and soon he'd be away from here to resume his search for information about Alastair Mottram's murder.

He looked at his useless, bandaged fingers. How long would it be before he was fit to travel again? Two weeks? Three? There were no telegraph lines to get a message back to Simla, but he knew there was a British Consul here in Kashgar who would help him.

Ho Sung came to the bed with a dish of scrambled eggs and spooned them into his mouth.

'Excellent,' said Doctor Larssen when he came into the room and saw the empty plate. He felt Richard's pulse. 'You are young and your body will repair itself in time, but only if you observe my instructions to the letter and refuse to allow yourself to be carried away by impatience.' He had the strong, Nordic features and blue eyes of his Viking ancestors, and a Scandinavian lilt in his speech.

Richard gave him a guarded smile. 'I have my orders to follow, Doctor. I must be on my way as soon as I'm able.'

Erik Larssen frowned at him over the top of his glasses and shook his head uncompromisingly. 'Be grateful you still have some circulation in your fingers and feet, young man. In time the pain will ease, but if you attempt to walk too soon you run the risk of skin damage and infection. If that should happen, you might see me yet having to sharpen my knife.'

Richard's stomach tightened. 'How long will I be here?'

'Until you are ready to leave.' The doctor placed a fatherly hand on Richard's shoulder. 'Have patience, young man.'

When he'd gone, Richard drew a slow, deep breath, and tried to swallow his frustration. Out there amongst the vast, uncharted mountains was information to be gathered, while the diplomatic rumblings between Westminster and St Petersburg grew increasingly ugly. It was no secret that the Russians wanted to take England's place in India. The British Army was ready for an attack across Bolan Pass into the Punjab, or down the Khyber Pass, but should the Russians discover a viable route through the northern mountains, and gather the support of the local rulers, the British Army would be faced with a major problem on the North West Frontier.

What had Alastair Mottram learned before he was murdered?

Richard blew a hiss of frustration, but he was quickly distracted by the sound of chattering children straggling across the compound to a small building on the opposite side. Two middle-aged European women – one short and plump, the other tall and thin – stood waiting on the doorstep.

So, he deduced, the Mission also runs a school. How much more appropriate it would be for Miss Larssen to be employed there, instead of kneeling, as she was at this moment, beside a man wrapped in a dusty, frayed cloak, who had apparently collapsed at the door of the clinic. As Richard watched, she called two attendants to carry him into the building, while she picked up his long jezail musket and followed.

Richard felt unreasonably angry. How could a girl like that be permitted to do this kind of thing? She had a ladylike appearance, and yet she behaved in a way that would be unthinkable to any young lady of his acquaintance.

Well, it was no concern of his what Miss Larssen did, he thought and closed his eyes to contemplate the weeks of boredom stretching ahead of him.

He woke later with a start to realize he had slept away the whole morning, and blinked to focus his sight on a slight, dark-haired woman standing at the foot of his bed. She was not young, but her features were exquisite.

'I'm so sorry if I wakened you, Captain,' she said in a softly accented voice. 'I am Doctor Larssen's wife.' She came to sit beside him. 'My daughter has told me of your terrible experience in the mountains, and we are all delighted to see you making a good recovery.' Her smile was enchanting.

'Thank you, ma'am,' he said, and found it difficult to pull his thoughts into order. The dainty Mrs Larssen was the mother of the red-headed sergeant-major?

'I'm here, Captain, to ask if you would like me to write to tell someone at home that you are safe. Your wife? Your sweetheart?' As she spoke she held her head to one side, and he noticed a sprinkling of grey at her temples.

'No wife, Mrs Larssen, and, if I remember correctly, no sweetheart.' He forced himself not to grin at her gentle inquisition. Mothers of unwed daughters often did that at a first meeting. 'But, thank you, I'd like to accept your offer. I do have a mother in England who should be reassured I'm still alive, as well as my Commanding Officer, if you would be so kind.'

'Of course,' she said, and called for a small table to hold her writing-slope and ink-well.

'Oh, and I need to speak with the British Consul here as soon as possible. Could he be informed that I. . . .'

'Mr McCallum is away on official business and I hear he's not expected back in Kashgar for at least two weeks.' Again she smiled engagingly. Lord, she was a beautiful woman. 'We are a very small community of Europeans here, you see, Captain, so news gets about.' She dipped her pen in the ink, then wiped it and put it down again.

'You understand, of course,' she said in a low voice, and leaned towards him, 'the Swedish Mission holds itself apart from any of the – er, shall we say political *tensions* that are currently in the air between the British and Russian Consulates.'

'And do you also have acquaintances in the Russian Consulate, Mrs Larssen? Am I right in detecting a Russian accent in your speech?'

Natasha quickly lowered her eyes and dipped the pen into the ink again. 'My daughter sometimes plays tennis with the Russian wives there,' she said dismissively, 'but the Russians here rarely mix with anybody outside their own Consulate.' She held the nib poised above the paper. 'Shall we begin?'

Richard had no difficulty in dictating a brief report to his Commanding Officer, and the letter to his mother was scarcely less formal. He concluded his message with a light-hearted reminder to her that it was not yet time to erect a memorial to him in Winchester Cathedral.

Natasha threw him a look of mock disapproval. 'You must not joke about such matters,' she said, then laughed. 'Now, Captain – or may I call you Richard?' Her hazel eyes sparkled captivatingly. 'Now, Richard, I am going to add a little postscript to your letter' – she pursed her lips and lifted her shoulders apologetically – 'and quite shamelessly suggest that your mother might care to make a donation to the work of the Mission Hospital.'

He threw back his head and laughed. 'Absolutely, Mrs Larssen. Tug as hard as you can at her heartstrings.' Considering the property his mother had inherited, she could afford to be generous. He was caught by a sudden spasm of coughing. Natasha put a glass of water to his lips, and he lay for a few minutes struggling to catch his breath.

'I take it, Mrs Larssen, that you don't work beside the doctor, as Miss Larssen does?' he said at last.

Natasha looked startled by the suggestion. 'I fear I don't have my daughter's strong stomach.' Then she laughed. 'My only talent is in letter-writing – and reading.' She nodded towards his bandaged hands lying on the blankets. 'Would you like me to come and read to you? I imagine it will be a little time before you are able to hold a book.'

'Yes indeed, thank you. I'm—' He was cut short by the sudden appearance of Georgina, bearing the battered leather document pouch he'd carried for weeks under his clothes.

'Good afternoon, Captain,' she said crisply. 'Where would you like this to

21

be kept now? Here beside you? Or would you prefer my father to continue to hold it under lock and key?'

He noticed the sharp glance Mrs Larssen threw at her daughter.

'Until the bandages come off Richard's hands, the pouch should be kept safely in this cupboard beside the bed,' Natasha said, with a touch of ice in her tone. 'We wouldn't want prying eyes to read any confidential papers, would we?'

He noticed Georgina's surprise at her mother's intervention, but she nodded, then turned to him with her hands clasped in front of her, and tilted her head. He was quite unconvinced by her efforts to appear demure.

'My father is concerned that you're going to find difficulty with the tedium of a long stay in hospital,' she began, and he immediately had the impression that what he was about to hear would be entirely Miss Larssen's own ideas.

'And his suggestion is. . . ?' Richard was unable to prevent the ghost of a smile from creeping across his lips.

'We've found an old chair in the storeroom and that could be repaired to allow you to leave your bed when you're stronger, and be moved about a little.'

'Yes, and as soon as you are ready to visit us,' Natasha added, throwing her daughter a no-nonsense look, 'we would be most happy to have your company at dinner, wouldn't we, Georgina?'

'Yes, of course, Captain Eldridge,' Georgina said gravely. 'And after dinner I can entertain you with my vast collection of fossils.'

'So, you're a fossil-collector? How fascinating,' he said with studied politeness, though he guessed she was teasing him. 'And, while you were out hunting fossils, Miss Larssen, I suppose you didn't stumble across the cave of the Golden Pagoda, by any chance?' It was a joke, but she didn't laugh.

'The Golden Pagoda? What have you heard of the Golden Pagoda?' Her tone was cool.

'Only what everyone heard one night in the Officers' Mess. Something about the legend of a wall painting in a cave out here in the desert, if I remember. I thought it was another version of the "pot of gold at the end of the rainbow" myth.'

'You're probably right,' Miss Larssen said, and closed the conversation with an abruptness that made Richard aware he had somehow touched a nerve.

CHAPTER THREE

Richard had the staff angle his bed so that he was able to look straight through the window and observe the daily comings and goings of the Mission. As eager as he was to fight his way back to health, there were days when his body refused to co-operate and he could do nothing but lie back on the pillows and look at the mighty sweep of snow-topped ranges in the distance, and the high, crenellated mud-brick walls of Kashgar city a mile away. Out of sight, and some distance to the south, Natasha had told him, was the smaller, walled city the Chinese overlords had built for themselves.

Each day, through the open gateway of the Mission compound, Richard watched a constant noisy stream of people passing along the road, donkeys and carts loaded with melons, camels and pack horses almost hidden under sacks of rice and bales of cotton.

Across on the far side of the river-bank he could glimpse the cotton dyers stretching their long, bright strips of cloth on to the grass to dry in the sun. Every now and again a strange, drawn-out note sounded through the general hubbub. These were calls from the millers along the river, Natasha had told him, blowing through rams' horns to signal they were ready for more grain to grind.

Adding to the noise was the mullah's call to prayer five times a day from the great mosque, and the sound of gunfire and blowing horns when the four big iron gates to the city were closed at sunset and opened at sunrise.

It was a different world out there beyond the Mission compound, where the vast desert of stones and sand to the east was tamed by the rivers that rushed down from the melting snows and glaciers to feed all the fertile oasis cities along its rim.

Despite the other distractions, Richard found the enigmatic Miss Larssen constantly drifting in and out of his thoughts. He told himself that it could only be this enforced boredom that made him grow restless each morning while he waited to see her leave the house at the far end of the compound and walk towards the clinic. He glanced at his half-hunter lying on the table beside him, and felt his anticipation rising. At any moment now she would close the door of the house, cross the compound and come past his window.

It irritated him to acknowledge that his pulse increased its beat as she approached, but he reasoned that was simply due to the pleasure of watching the way she carried herself with an elegance that would not have been out of place in a London ballroom. She moved like poetry. She was taller than his sisters, more handsome than his mother. Georgina Larssen confused him. His own feelings towards her confused him.

Actually, he was peeved by her avoidance of him. She rarely spent time at his bedside, but when he watched her moving about the Mission during the day, talking with other people, he saw her drop the air of lofty reserve, and he heard her laugh – a deep, gurgling laugh, natural and absurdly fetching.

When the day was over, he often watched her leave the hospital with her stepfather, their heads close in conversation, her arm through his. Or sometimes his arm was thrown affectionately around her shoulders.

Each time he saw them together, Richard Eldridge was reminded of the depth of his own lifelong loneliness in a family where generations of privilege had failed to breed the kind of affection that Georgina experienced every day with her stepfather. It occurred to him that never once had his own father thrown an arm across his shoulders. And even when he was six years old and ill with scarlet fever at boarding school, his mother had gone off on her holiday to Italy. Was it any wonder that what he'd lacked in affection while he was growing up, he'd made up for in the mischief that had brought his tutor's rod across his backside more times than he could remember?

He tossed on the pillow and made up his mind to let the matter rest. Boredom, he told himself, was at the root of his growing fantasies about Mrs Larssen's cool and distant daughter. As soon as he was away from here, his mind would be kept busy with all his unfinished work. Right now it would be madness to allow his embarrassingly foolish preoccupation with Miss Larssen to become transparent. There were young ladies a-plenty waiting for him just over the horizon.

Natasha came to read to him each afternoon, and the middle-aged Swedish missionaries – Mr Hakvin, Hilde, his plump little wife, and Birget, his tall sister – who ran the school, announced themselves as keen chess-players when they came to visit. They brought a little set that Mr Hakvin had carved himself, and one lady moved Richard's pieces while he played the other.

Richard had considered himself a skilful player, until he faced the Hakvin ladies across the board, and frequently lost.

'Your game will improve once you are well again, dear Captain,' Birget said consolingly as she packed up the pieces and put them in the cupboard beside Richard's bed, while Hilde uncovered a dish of her preserved fruit and fed it to him.

Erik Larssen presented himself as a chess-player, too, and although he was not in the class of the Hakvin ladies, Richard enjoyed playing an occasional game with him. Most of all he enjoyed the doctor's company – his sly, dry wit, and his occasional willingness to chat about his stepdaughter.

'Georgina shows no aptitude – no patience – at all for this game,' he said, frowning as he concentrated on a move, which then resulted in the loss of a knight. He tut-tutted at his blunder, then laughed. 'My daughter says there are as many archaic rules in the game of chess as there are in this country.' He peered at Richard over the top of his glasses. 'Georgina finds it difficult to accept rules, you know, especially the ones that cultures impose on women.' He leaned forward, the chess game suddenly forgotten. 'She has a vision that she can persuade these people to change the rules they live by, but very few are ready to listen.' The corners of his mouth turned down. 'Georgina has such determination! At times I feel she is in need of protection from her own courage.'

'Miss Larssen is a remarkable young lady,' Richard agreed, and inwardly winced at his own patronizing tone. *Remarkable?* When the chess set was put away and he lay in the dark, waiting for sleep to come, Captain Eldridge thought of a dozen other adjectives he could use to describe the doctor's daughter, and every one sent a surge of heat through his veins.

Natasha was not involved in any work at the hospital or the school, but once a week she and the cook went into the city to buy provisions for the Mission.

'The servants don't like to be seen with me when I bargain with the shop-keepers,' she told Richard with a laugh. 'The cook says it lowers his dignity, but I find it lowers the cost of running my household when I go to the markets myself.'

After he watched her leave, mounted sideways on her horse with her skirt arranged about her, Richard lay for a time wondering how a woman with the beauty and refinement of Natasha Larssen lived – with every sign of content-ment – in this strange, remote land. She was devoted to her husband, of course, but was marriage itself enough in life to keep such a woman happy?

Marriage certainly hadn't kept his own mother happy, nor his father, despite the refinement of their surroundings – and her money. As a small boy Richard had witnessed their misery – the blows, the angry threats. He discovered that marriage had not stopped his father from loving other ladies, and he'd listened in disbelief when his mother had told his father that she was glad he was being sent off to the war and that she hoped he'd make her a widow. He'd seen a flame of murder in his father's eyes as he knocked her to the floor and stood over her.

But Hugo Eldridge had come back after that war, and they'd lived apart for more than twenty years now, still married, and still unable to speak to each other. And yet at every opportunity his mother badgered her sons to find *suitable* wives!

Well, marriage was quite out of the question now he was with the Intelligence Service. Permission to marry was never granted to serving officers.

He looked out the window at that moment and saw Georgina Larssen laughing as she ran across the compound to join a little group of children turning a skipping-rope outside the school. She lifted her skirt and jumped with them, joining their sing-song, off key voices in a Kashgari version of *Jack be nimble, Jack be quick, Jack jump over the candlestick.*

He exhaled a long breath. What if he'd met a woman like that in England? Would he have found some way to break the rules for her? His family wouldn't approve; the Regiment wouldn't approve, but. . . . He coughed. Dear God! This forced inactivity was clearly turning his brain. He called loudly for tea to be brought and asked for the dampness to be wiped from his forehead.

A little later he saw her ride out of the compound with a tennis racquet, on her way to play with the ladies at the Russian Consulate. He closed his eyes and struggled to recall the faces of all the lovely, well-born, refined young women he'd held in his arms – the delightful females who had successfully won their way into his heart for a month or two.

Damn! This idleness was softening his brain!

'I hope you have had a comfortable day, Captain.'

The sound of her voice woke him and he saw her standing at the foot of his bed. It irked him that she would never engage in the kind of inconsequential social chit-chat that young ladies of his acquaintance usually did with apparently little effort.

'Quite comfortable, thank you, Miss Larssen,' he said, and she seemed about to turn away. He fought for something to say that would keep her with him. 'Tell me, apart from tennis and your dedication to fossil-collecting, how do you amuse yourself in Kashgar?'

She made a show of weighing up his question, though he caught a movement at the corners of her mouth. 'Once you are no longer confined to this bed, Captain, I'm sure you'll discover that Kashgar can offer all kinds of interests.'

He raised his eyebrows in a theatrical show of scepticism.

'Why, quite recently when I was passing the Russian Consulate,' she continued, as if she was speaking to a child, 'I saw the old company of Cossacks leaving, and the new one taking over. There was a great ceremony on the parade ground, and the band was playing.'

'Remarkable! You saw a changing of the guard!' He aimed at sarcasm, but missed, floundering. Because as she stood there, looking down at him, he became aware that the rays of the afternoon sun were slanting in and touching the edges of her dark red hair, giving it an ethereal halo effect, as if she had stepped straight from a page of some gloriously illuminated manuscript.

The breath caught in his throat. Every masculine instinct in his body woke with a jolt to realize that standing a few feet away from him was a woman whose unique beauty was suddenly unleashing the powerful tiger of lust into his veins.

Her blue eyes held his gaze for a moment, then, as if she had read his thoughts, she looked away shyly, and took in a deep breath. That movement emphasized the roundness of her breasts, and he swallowed hard.

'Good evening, Captain,' she said, and turned to hide her face.

'Good evening, Miss Larssen,' he said gruffly. God! He was teetering on the brink of making a complete fool of himself. He hadn't even felt this way about Lucille. Hah! Now he remembered that name. Lucille. Lucille Mountford, the *very suitable* girl his mother said he should marry. Lucille, the pale, pretty little creature who had dimpled at him so charmingly when they'd strolled into the shrubbery and who had allowed him to kiss her after three waltzes at the hunt ball.

He rolled his head back on the pillow and groaned. Georgina Larssen. He must never allow himself to imagine leading Miss Georgina Larssen into the shrubbery for one sweet kiss. They might never emerge.

Little happened to break the monotony of Richard's daily routine until Doctor Larssen at last gave permission for the bandages to come off his hands, and he was given cotton gloves to wear. He tried to ignore the sight of the damaged skin on his stiff fingers and began to coax movement slowly back into them.

Now was the time to plan a course of action for when he was fit enough to walk out of hospital and get back to duty. And the first thing to be done must be to put all visions of Doctor Larssen's daughter right out of his head. That was made a little easier for him when she was called away and spent several days in an oasis village treating a badly burned woman.

Mr Hakvin made him a stand to hold a book, and though he no longer needed Natasha to read to him, she maintained her afternoon visits. The Hakvin ladies continued to beat him at chess, and when Erik Larssen pronounced him fit enough to leave the bed, he was presented with a unique chair.

'See how the footrest can be removed when no longer required?' Mr Hakvin said eagerly.'And look, here are carrying-poles to be slipped out when the chair is brought indoors. And little wheels on the legs so it can be moved about a room. Most useful, don't you think?'

'Thank you, Mr Hakvin,' Richard said, not sure whether to laugh or weep at his new mode of transport. 'I'm sure there is not another like this anywhere.'

'My pleasure, sir, and here come Birget and Hilde now with the cushions they've made for the seat and the back.'

Natasha came to watch as the ladies bustled in and tied the red-striped cushions into position, then all stood back with smiles of anticipation. He couldn't disappoint them. 'I do appreciate your kindness. I wonder if a couple of porters might be available to take it for a trial straight away?'

The ladies hurried for their hats and coats and Doctor Larssen arrived to see his patient placed in the chair. He gave a nod of approval as Richard, wrapped in a sheepskin coat and with a rug around his legs, was hoisted up by two young men and carried ceremoniously out through the Mission gates.

The road towards the city was lined with willows and poplars, and Natasha, Mr Hakvin and the two Hakvin ladies walked alongside him, cheerfully pointing out a holy spring, wayside shrines, a prisoner in chains, a camel caravan coming from the desert. The noise coming from one house, Mr Hakvin explained casually, was the sound of an exorcist ridding the place of an evil spirit.

Richard felt like a schoolboy being taken out on a holiday treat. A dozen rosy-cheeked, chattering schoolchildren trailed behind him, and the cavalcade was soon joined by two little boys riding donkeys, a woman leading a goat and an old man pushing a handcart filled with melons. People along the way turned to stare at him with friendly curiosity. They came out of their houses and shops, and some called greetings to the missionaries.

If only the Eldridge family in Mayfair could see me now, he thought, and his grin widened. This scene would shatter their sensibilities beyond repair. The Mountford girl – he'd forgotten her name again – would no doubt have an attack of the vapours if he told her about the lives led by the extraordinary women who had befriended him in Kashgar. Hilde, Birget, Natasha – and Georgina. Especially Georgina. How could he ever explain a woman like Georgina to his mother and sisters? This land was not just another country; here was another world.

On their return to the hospital, Richard's chair was put down on the veranda, the carrying-poles removed and stood up against the wall, and Erik came to ensure the outing had gone well. Then it took some time for everybody to fuss about and be reassured that he was comfortable and needed nothing further. 'Thank you – every one of you – for everything you've done – are doing – for me.'

The ladies took turns to kiss his cheek before they left, and the men patted his shoulder, and everyone spoke at once to reassure him they were happy to have been of help.

There was one person he had not yet thanked for all of this. She was in the dispensary now. He waited, and shortly Georgina came out on to the veranda, untying her white apron and draping it over an arm.

'I'm glad to see the chair has passed its first test,' she said, and came towards him almost shyly.

'I think, Miss Larssen, it's high time I thanked you properly for many things,' he said. 'First and foremost for keeping me alive up there in the mountains.' The catch in his throat surprised him.

She paused momentarily, as if deciding what to do. Then a flush crept into her cheeks as she crouched beside him and put a hand on his arm. 'It was you who fought the truly hard part of the battle, Captain.'

Her strong, capable hand had touched him many times, but never like this. Companionably? He looked into her eyes and for one moment saw a chink appear in her usual impenetrable, protective poise. The muscles in his abdomen clenched. He needed to touch her, but his fingers were gloved, so impulsively he leaned forward to brush her cheek with his lips. There was an infinitesimal pause in her breathing, but she didn't pull away.

'If I won a victory, Georgina, it's only because I was lucky enough to have you as my commanding officer.' Her scent teased his senses and thickened his voice. It was the first time he'd used her Christian name.

Then, to his surprise, she angled her head and lifted her chin so that her lips, parted slightly, were invitingly close to his. Her effort was artless, somewhat awkward, and yet when he felt her breath mingle with his, a raw need slammed into him.

He lowered his mouth slowly and watched her eyes widen as she gave a silent gasp, then her lids closed. She pressed her lips against his and her hands slid up his arms, behind his neck. His heart hammered and his arms circled her, pulling her nearer, deepening the kiss. Her lips parted further and she responded with a need that seemed to equal his own.

At last she pulled away from him, breathing fast, flushed and smiling nervously. She brushed a strand of hair back off her face; it was a gesture both defensive and disarming, and made her seem very young.

'Oh,' she said unsteadily, 'I suppose that was to congratulate you on your recovery.'

He smiled back at her. 'Thank you, indeed. Please congratulate me any time you feel like it.'

They studied each other silently for several moments while she reclaimed her outward calm, though he noticed a pulse still throbbing in the hollow of her throat.

'My father thinks you'll soon be able to leave here, Richard.' After all this time, his name came hesitantly to her lips.

'Will that be long enough for me to know you better?' He was well aware that up until two minutes ago he had sworn to himself never to think about that, let alone to speak those words.

'Oh, I fear getting to know me would take far too long,' she said with a laugh, standing to smooth her skirt. 'I doubt you'd have the patience.'

'Then teach me about patience, Georgina. Surely that wouldn't be beyond the ability of a woman who worked a miracle and kept me alive in the Kirghiz camp.'

There was challenge in the glance she slanted at him. 'Yes, but you very much *wanted* that miracle to happen.' She pursed her lips. 'I doubt you really want to learn anything about patience. What would you do with patience back there in the world where you belong?'

'I'm a long way from that world now.'

'You're a traveller, Richard. Travellers don't stay. Eventually they move on.'

'Surely, here in Kashgar, we're all travellers. I don't believe you'll stay here for ever. Not you. Not here, Georgina.'

'You might be right, you might be wrong.' She stared reflectively across the city to the high, white peaks of the mountains, and then back to him. 'I don't think I want to leave this place. Few women in the outside world are allowed the kind of freedom I enjoy here, and I don't want to lose that independence.' She shrugged her shoulders and pulled down the corners of her mouth. 'If I went to live anywhere else, I'm afraid I'd always make life difficult for the people around me.'

He bit back the challenge that was on his lips. Their banter was fast developing an undertone that threatened to sweep him into saying something that might snap the flimsy bond that was starting to materialize between them. So he grinned and gave a noncommittal shrug that put an end to the discussion. He'd have to teach himself patience because, by God, he was going to *need* patience if he was to find a way through Georgina's wall of reserve and rekindle the warmth she had revealed briefly today.

Georgina ate dinner slowly that evening and contributed little to the conversation. Richard Eldridge was in her thoughts and she was trying to put a name to the unpredictable feelings which had surged through her that afternoon. Every feminine instinct had wanted him to kiss her, and that warm urge had momentarily evaporated all her reliable, cool restraint. This afternoon, on an impulse, she'd issued a tiny sexual invitation and straight away he'd understood her message. She'd surprised him; and she'd surprised herself. But not for one second did she regret it, though now she was left with a strange restlessness.

She swallowed, steadied her breathing, and put another spoonful of jellied peach into her mouth, savouring the moist softness and the shape of the fruit against her tongue. A tingling warmth grew in the core of her, and she understood its source. She might be a virgin, but she wasn't a child. She knew the attractions that drew men and women to each other.

Georgina looked across the table at her mother and Erik. What would Natasha say if she told her about the wild confusion which the handsome English officer had roused in her this afternoon? Up until now it had always been Erik she had turned to for advice. But this was not something she could discuss with him, and after all these years she didn't know how to begin sharing intimate matters with her mother.

Erik smiled across the table at her as he reached for more peaches. 'You've been deep in thought, my dear. Are you worried about the little Chinese girl? They say she begged to have her feet bound like her sisters, you know.'

His voice cut across her thoughts and she nodded quickly to him. 'Yes, I've had her on my mind since I heard about it. The message said something had gone terribly wrong, but they won't bring her to you.'

Natasha clicked her tongue in sympathy. 'Can you imagine any man being seduced by the *Golden Lotus*? Preferring to marry any girl with tiny, deliberately deformed feet rather than a girl with a pretty face?'

'There are a lot of things I don't understand, Mother,' Georgina said on a sigh.

31

'I think perhaps you should ride over to the Chinese city tomorrow, m'dear,' said Erik. 'Remind the mother that the girl might yet be saved if we unbind the feet and treat the infection without delay.' His face was grave. 'Pay an informal call – and at least let them know they are in our prayers.'

The next day, Georgina rode into the Chinese city and stayed with the wailing mother and her wailing kinswomen around the child's bed, listening to the wailing women crowded into the courtyard outside the window. The seven-year-old died in the afternoon, and that put an end to her agony. Somewhere under the tight bindings around the cracked and bent bones of the tiny feet was the source of the infection that took her life.

The mother had politely resisted all Georgina's persuasion. Whether Erik Larssen could have changed the outcome was questionable, but the family had refused to give the child even that slim chance of life.

Georgina swallowed the bitter, strangling despair in her throat and paid her formal condolences to the weeping women who had obviously loved this little girl, but allowed her to suffer and die.

On her way to the outer gate as she was leaving late in the afternoon, she saw the father in his long black robes, standing in the garden. She walked to him along the gravel path between the flower beds, and they bowed respectfully to each other. When she looked into his face she was too angry to speak; all she could do was to shake her head sadly.

'You honour our house by sharing our grief, Madame,' said the father gravely. 'But you think that Heavenly Blossom's feet should have been unbound to let her run about freely. What would have been the good of that? No one would want to marry a girl with big feet, so she might as well be dead.' His face was drawn with sadness. 'Please understand, Madame, a father worries greatly to know which of the two evils to choose.'

Georgina acknowledged his statement wanly. 'I think we must agree, sir, that one culture always has great difficulty understanding that of another.' They bowed to each other politely again before she left.

With a heavy heart she rode home slowly as the sun dipped behind the mountains. The cries of the dying child were still in her ears, and it was impossible to sort through her impressions of the day and put them into neat little mental boxes. It seemed that whatever she tried to do in this ancient land, she was never able to scratch far below the surface of the culture. Erik Larssen had long ago developed the patience to accept that limitation. Would she allow herself to mellow if she stayed here for another ten years?

CHAPTER FOUR

Natasha always carried a degree of anxiety about Georgina's independent forays around the city on medical matters, although the Kashgari people had never shown resentment towards the small European presence amongst them. The Swedish missionaries had been a curiosity when they'd first arrived, but little ever ruffled the surface of placid, simple Kashgari life, apart from occasional arguments over a trading matter, or water for a farmer's fields, or a woman.

When Georgina set off to the Chinese city, Natasha rode to the market as she usually did each Thursday morning, with the cook beside her, pushing the handcart.

She dismounted at the city gate and was greeted with noisy good humour by people in the great square in front of the mosque, the stallholders in the bazaar and tradesmen working cross-legged in their dark little cave-like shops. She spoke enough of the language to enjoy an occasional conversation as she and the cook wove their way along narrow streets.

In the main square, they skirted the crowd gathered around the storyteller sitting on his platform, and stopped for a moment to watch the money-lender in the doorway of his establishment, clattering the beads of his abacus.

When they entered the food market, the cook's handcart slowly filled with flour and sugar, tea, meat, rice and other staples for the Mission, and with the shopping completed, he started for home. Natasha then liked to spend an idle hour alone, wandering among the displays of exotic carpets and embroidered silks, jewellery and jade.

People from the British Consulate sometimes shopped in the city, but it was rare to see Russian ladies there. There was a little group ahead now, easy to identify in their elegant, lace-trimmed gowns, with parasols held aloft to protect their soft complexions. Several Cossack officers escorted the ladies who, at that moment, were forced to gather up their skirts and flatten themselves against the wall as a caravan of heavily laden Bactrian camels passed along the twisting lane, giving way to no one.

Natasha hung back, watching an ivory-carver at work, until the ladies had turned a corner and were out of sight. They were likely to be wives of the officers who'd arrived recently with the new Cossack guard, she decided. The novelty of the native market, with its dust and distinctive odours, rarely lasted long with Russian newcomers.

As she turned away from the ivory-carver, a movement caught her glance. What she saw on the other side of the lane made the world around her sway precariously, like a slowly spinning top.

Standing there was a handsome figure in a Cossack uniform, languidly leaning against a wall, watching her. For a quarter of a century her nightmares had been filled with this moment.

'The years have treated you with the utmost kindness, Natasha Luboff.' He straightened his shoulders and sauntered towards her, the smile on his long face as dangerous as it was dazzling. 'You are just as beautiful as ever.'

She froze like a hare caught in a beam of bright light, remembering that deep, honeyed tone in St Petersburg the night he'd accused her of murder.

'Why are you here?' Suddenly she was nineteen again. Alone and terrified.

'Why am I here in this flea-bitten city of Kashgar? I've been sent to serve my country, of course,' he said, with the sarcastic edge she remembered so well. 'But today I'm here in the market simply to meet you again, Natasha.' He lifted one eyebrow knowingly at her.

'How   how did you know I'd be here?'

'Chance? Destiny? Who knows what forces were at play when I caught sight of you last week here in the city?' He clicked his tongue at her and slowly shook his head. 'Poor Natasha, the missionary's wife, who comes shopping in the market each Thursday. What a predictable pattern your life has developed, my darling; so unlike our wonderful days together in St Petersburg.'

Her mind spewed images of that last terrifying night there. Of the gaiety and music in the ballroom providing an incongruous backdrop to her flight through the palace. Of finding Tatiana lying crumpled on the snow below the balcony. Of Gregori Suvorov's voice beside her, accusing her of pushing Tatiana to her death.

'I want nothing to do with you.' Natasha's voice was a dry whisper. 'Go away. Leave me alone. Please, *please* Gregori, turn away now and forget you saw me, I beg you.' Trembling threatened to overwhelm her. 'It was all so long ago.'

'How could I forget you now, Natasha, when I've remembered you with such warm affection for the last twenty-five years? Come, let's spend a little time quietly recalling the old days.'

She sucked in her breath as he took her arm, but she had no strength to resist when he led her along a narrow, winding street lined with songbirds hanging in their wicker cages, to a teashop where a blind musician was entertaining on a mandolin.

'You know, my dear Natasha, the Ballet took years to recover from the loss of its two rising stars – you and Tatiana – on the same night,' he said, as they sat at a table in the corner. He looked into her eyes and slowly pulled off his gloves, finger by finger.

How well she remembered those big, hairless hands; the long white fingers; the polished nails. She recalled the touch of them on her body, their skilled seduction as she lay on warm silk sheets while the deep winter snows of Russia muffled all sound from the outside world.

Her heart thundered. When he reached across the table for her hand, she snatched it away and sat with them both tightly clasped in her lap. The old cynical smile curled the corners of his lips, and chilled her blood.

'Impetuosity was always your downfall, Natasha, my dear,' he said. 'Please don't try anything impetuous now.' He ordered tea, and until it was brought to the table, he sat studying her with cold blue eyes that had once looked at her with the heat of lust.

She fought to contain her panic. 'You must believe, Gregori, that I did *not* kill Tatiana. She was dead when I found her. I swear before God I was innocent.'

He leaned back in his chair and paused for dramatic effect before he spoke. 'God and I both know you were innocent, my dear, but nobody else believes it.'

She gave an audible gasp. 'Are you saying. . . ? Do you mean you know who did kill her?' Her eyes widened. 'Oh, no! Was it you who pushed – who threw Tatiana over the balcony?'

'What a fool I would be to admit that, my angel.' His smile failed to reach his pale eyes. 'Unlike you, what motive did I have to kill her?'

'And you think I had a motive?' All the old, choking bitterness welled in her throat.

'Of course, you had every reason for wanting Tatiana dead, my darling, and who would blame you? After all, she clearly engineered that scandal involving the Grand Duchess's diamonds. Tatiana was always jealous, and she simply wanted to ruin your prospects of becoming prima ballerina.' He shrugged nonchalantly. 'Obviously she stole the necklace and told the police where to find it, in your dressing-case, so why wouldn't you wish to see her fall off a balcony and break her neck?'

A wave of anger hit Natasha. 'You knew all along I didn't take the necklace?' She trembled. 'You knew it was Tatiana who stole it, when we were invited to dance that night at the Shuvalov Palace?' Her voice rose. 'You knew Tatiana had me falsely accused, and yet you were willing to stand by and do nothing to help me?'

'How can you say I was not willing to help you, my darling?' His voice was low, his eyes hooded. He looked like a cat waiting for a songbird to perch in front of him.

She fought to calm her pounding heart before she could speak. 'Did you think you could help me by throwing Tatiana over the balcony?'

His lips curled. 'Oh, indeed I was ready to help, Natasha, but as I've just reminded you, impetuosity was *your* downfall.' She frowned, unable to follow his drift.

'Your great mistake, my dear,' he continued, with exaggerated patience, 'was in running off to that red-headed merchant, the idiotic Scot who had been scampering at your heels like a lapdog for weeks. Foolish, foolish girl – if only you'd come to me.'

A chill ran through her. 'But – but it was you who accused me!'

He gave her a bemused smile. 'I think, Natasha, that had you stayed in St Petersburg you would very soon have found the opportunity to persuade me otherwise.' His gaze held hers meaningfully as he rubbed his fingers across his chin. 'Think of the path your career would have taken you, if you had run to me instead of choosing to escape on that merchant's ship.' He clicked his tongue at her. 'Unfortunately, it means, my darling, that the police files in St Petersburg are still open with the name of Natasha Luboff, who is wanted for the theft of a diamond necklace from the Grand Duchess Katarina, and for the murder of the ballerina Tatiana – what was her name?'

Natasha's eyes burned with resentment. 'Oh, don't torture me again, Gregori. Why can't you allow it to rest? What good would it do to open it all again? Who, apart from you and me, would remember now?'

One eyebrow rose and he looked at her with a supercilious calm while he sipped his tea. She could see how much he was enjoying her misery.

'You may be right, Natasha. Perhaps they *have* all forgotten you in St Petersburg, but can you imagine what the reaction would be in Stockholm if the Missionary Board heard that Doctor Erik Larssen's lovely wife has unanswered charges of theft and murder in Russian police files?' He clicked his tongue and wagged his head as if she were a wayward child. 'You have never told your husband about that little matter, have you, my lovely one? Or your beautiful daughter?'

Oh, God! He knew of Georgina! Natasha's desperation turned to anger. 'You always were a sadistic swine, Gregori. Is there some point to this torture, other than your own entertainment?' Her voice hardened. 'What reason do you have now for doing this, apart from shattering a good man like Erik Larssen, who has spent twenty years giving his life to help these people here?' She bit her bottom lip to stop its tremble. Georgina! Whatever else happened, she must ensure that Georgina was kept away from Suvorov's machinations.

'Ah! Now I see a little of your old spirit, my darling.' He gave an approving smile and brought his palms together several times in applause. 'Now you are beginning to sound more like the little Natasha Luboff I remember so fondly,' he said. 'She always fought for her own interests.'

She waited with a pounding heart while he eyed her speculatively.

'I think you could still be swayed to protect your own interests,' he said at last. 'Along with your husband's and your daughter's.'

Knots twisted in her stomach as he lifted the cup to his lips and watched her over the rim. Slowly he lowered the cup. 'Your Russian ties may have vanished, Natasha, but you certainly owe no loyalty to the British.' His fingers began to drum the edge of the table. 'There is an English officer in your husband's hospital,' he said, and his eyes narrowed. 'I want you to tell me all about him.'

CHAPTER FIVE

Georgina rode home slowly from the Chinese city with all the unanswered, bruising questions of the unhappy day hanging like a weight around her heart. The stars were out before she entered the Mission compound and saw the lights shining from every window of the house. The unusual sound of voices and laughter met her as she dismounted.

Natasha, wearing her best pink silk gown and a radiant smile, opened the door and, as Georgina crossed the threshold, she made a surreptitious gesture for her to smooth her hair before coming into the sitting-room. 'Darling, I have a lovely surprise for you,' she said animatedly. 'We have guests for dinner.'

'Oh, Quentin, you're back at last!' Georgina said with obvious pleasure as the British Consul stepped towards her with his hands outstretched.

He kissed her on both cheeks. 'Your father has just been telling us about your mission to the Chinese city. Futile, I suppose?' Quentin McCallum, still under forty, was a slight man with seemingly boundless energy. His pleasantly unremarkable face creased as he smiled at her. 'And see who I've brought with me, Georgina.' He moved aside so she had a clear view of the strikingly handsome, middle-aged man whose dark hair carried only a few streaks of grey. He had climbed to his feet, and was looking down at her with an approving gleam.

She flushed. 'Mr Davenport, er – Simon. How nice to see you again—' And then she caught sight of Richard sitting somewhat tight-lipped in his chair on the other side of the room. The bandages had gone from his feet and he was wearing the soft felt slippers the Hakvin ladies had made. Her flush deepened. 'Oh, Richard, I'm so glad—'

Natasha fluttered to Richard's side. 'Yes, isn't this all a wonderful surprise?' She gave a little laugh and gestured expansively at the visitors.

Her mother's uncharacteristic brittle gaiety made Georgina exchange a puzzled glance with Erik.

He crossed the room and put a comforting arm around his stepdaughter.

'Indeed, it is a long time since we've had the pleasure of three guests on one evening to dine with us,' he said. His grip tightened and Georgina leaned against him. She didn't need to tell him she had spent a miserable day with the dying child. He was always able to sense her feelings.

'You see, Georgina,' Natasha said with a girlish giggle, 'while you were out today we arranged for Richard to come for dinner tonight, and then' – her fingers fidgeted with the velvet ribbon around her neck – 'when we had news that Quentin had just arrived back in Kashgar, and Mr Davenport was visiting, we decided it would be lovely to have a little party.' Her skirts rustled as she swept towards her daughter and led her away from Erik. 'Dinner will be ready soon, so do make haste now and change, darling.' At the door she whispered: 'Wear the cream taffeta. Brush your hair and let it hang loose.'

Georgina was grateful for the excuse to escape briefly to her bedroom. What had happened today to put her mother into this strangely agitated mood? Usually Natasha was a relaxed hostess on the rare occasions they had guests to dinner.

The houseboy knocked on the door with a basin of warm water, and Georgina slipped out of her clothes and began to wash. Was it Simon Davenport's unexpected reappearance that was making her mother suddenly behave like a character in a Sheridan play?

She unpinned her hair and brushed it vigorously. Four years ago when he had passed through Kashgar on some kind of archaeological work for the Royal Geographical Society, the urbane Mr Davenport had left no doubt that he enjoyed her company.

At the time, Natasha must have noticed it, too, because she'd found all sorts of ways to remind Georgina that Mr Davenport was already over forty, and had warned her that he was a *man of the world*. Whatever was meant by that, Georgina found him charming and very easy to like. And in his company she had never been overwhelmed by her usual tongue-tightening shyness.

She took the cream taffeta dress from its hanger. Her mother had made it with a low-cut neckline to flatter Georgina's figure – a fact she'd gauged from the admiring looks it had attracted on the few occasions she had worn it.

She held it against herself for a moment, then suddenly felt unsure about wearing it tonight. Unsure about the dress, or unsure about herself? she thought ruefully as she quickly reached for a high-necked one in deep blue. And neither was she prepared to leave her hair to hang freely as her mother had instructed. As a compromise, she brushed it away from her face and clipped it behind her neck with an ivory clasp given to her years ago by an Indian trader.

She dabbed a little of the violet scent behind her ears and on her wrists, then looked at her reflection in the mirror before she left the room. She was dressed as a missionary's daughter.

All eyes turned towards her as she rejoined the party, and she saw a flash of irritation on her mother's face when she recognized the blue dress.

'Now we can serve dinner,' Natasha said, quickly indicating that Simon Davenport should sit beside Georgina, with Quentin and Richard placed together on the opposite side of the table.

After Erik had said grace, the conversation flowed easily amongst the men. Georgina would dearly have liked to question Quentin about the outcome of his official visit to the northern khanates, but that would have to wait. Tomorrow she would call at the Consulate and give him the information she'd gleaned from the Kirghiz tribesmen while she was with them in the mountains, and he'd pass on any matters of interest to the British Intelligence Service in Simla.

Richard, she noticed, though he still wore the cotton gloves, needed no assistance from the houseboy to cut his meal. He looked at her often, and each time he smiled she looked away because, as pleasant as it was to be reminded of their brief interlude yesterday, she knew those warm looks would change to outrage as soon as she made her confession about tampering with the information in his pouch. She'd have to tell him before his fingers regained sufficient movement to open the clasp himself, and discover the forgery she'd substituted.

She should have told him about it before she went away to see the burned woman. In fact, she had steeled herself to face the moment of truth yesterday; but that was before he'd kissed her and blown every sane thought from her mind. Perhaps the opportunity for a few moments alone with him would present itself later this evening.

He smiled at her again and she felt herself flush. Of course he'd be discreet when she warned him not to compromise the Mission's neutrality by revealing anything about her information-gathering activities for the British. Especially when she told him that his original report was still safely locked in a drawer of her dressing-table. If the Consul had not been away when Richard first came to the hospital, she would have taken the pouch to him immediately. She had always been very clear about where her loyalty lay, and in these times of suspicion and intrigue throughout the region, it always paid to be overcautious, Quentin had repeatedly warned her.

Natasha ate little at dinner and, although from time to time she joined in the laughter around the table, she appeared distracted and contributed only a few words throughout the meal.

Over the rim of his glasses, Erik watched her closely. When she had come home after her visit to the markets this morning, Natasha's white face and racing pulse had alarmed him. He'd given her a draught for the headache she said was causing her to feel unsteady, and his advice was for her to spend the afternoon in bed.

Instead, she had gone straight to Richard Eldridge and invited him for dinner tonight. And, as if that wasn't enough, when she heard an hour later that Quentin McCallum was back in Kashgar with Simon Davenport as his guest, she sent a porter off immediately with an invitation for them to come and dine as well.

Now, despite her apparent excitement this afternoon while she was organizing the dinner, she gave few signs of enjoying it.

Erik looked around the table and his gaze rested on Georgina. No wonder the other men in the room couldn't take their eyes away from her. Her cheeks were flushed and the simple blue dress she wore heightened the colour of her irises; tendrils of her hair, which was pulled back from her broad forehead, were slipping from the ivory clip to curl waywardly on her neck.

As he watched her with shrewd, fatherly eyes, Erik acknowledged that Georgina was glowing tonight with the sort of provocativeness that only the utterly innocent possess. And two apparently eligible men at the table were in tight competition to win her smile. He could see she was shyly enjoying their attention, and when he looked to Natasha sitting at the other end of the table, Erik wondered why she wasn't also showing an interest in this turn of events.

As the meal progressed, Richard felt increasingly irritated by Simon Davenport's efforts to impress Georgina. He brushed away the notion that a little kernel of jealousy was glowing green just under his heart.

Surely it was merely Georgina's polite attempt to sound interested that was encouraging the fellow to keep talking about his expeditions for the Royal Geographical Society? Who cared about Davenport's story of the British Museum's enthusiastic acceptance of the crates of frescos and rare manuscripts that he'd taken back from his last expedition along the Silk Road?

'How much of this stuff is going to be left out here if the museums in London and Berlin and St Petersburg keep up this rate of plunder?' Richard asked, attempting to hide his personal pique under a smokescreen of professional disparagement. One more tale of Davenport's archaeological adventures and Richard thought he might find himself damaging his fist against the man's chin. It might even be worth it to put an end to his grandiosity.

41

'Don't worry, Richard. What we've unearthed is a mere drop in the ocean,' Simon said, unruffled. He turned back to Georgina. 'Anyhow, it's usually the local people who lead me to some remote site – a tomb, a buried city out in the desert, a cave in the mountains.'

'Good Lord!' Richard persisted. 'Surely that means you're taking advantage of simple people who have no concept of the value Europeans are placing on their artefacts?' He raised the point merely to be argumentative, and saw Georgina flash a stern look towards him.

'Quite a moral dilemma, isn't it?' Simon's lips twitched. 'What should we do? Walk off and leave these treasures to deteriorate completely, or take them away to be preserved?'

Richard's hope of discrediting the ethics of archaeological work was undermined by the laughter in Davenport's eyes, and he was about to throw in another challenge when Simon posed his next point: 'Suppose one day we found the legendary cave of the Golden Pagoda and simply left it to deteriorate. Would we be thanked if. . . .'

Quentin McCallum stiffened and Richard wondered what was behind the warning frown the Consul shot at his guest. What made him uncomfortable about the mention of the Golden Pagoda tonight?

'Did I tell you, Simon, that my wife wrote from London saying she'd been to one of the lectures you gave at the Society?' Quentin said, changing the topic.

Simon looked surprised. 'I wish I'd known she was in the audience. Yes, the lectures have been well received, I'm happy to say, and so are my journal articles about the Silk Road.' He paused and turned to Georgina with a lazy, engaging smile. 'I've just had a marvellous thought,' he said. 'From what Doctor Larssen has told me about your work in this region – especially your contact with the tribal women – I must insist you write an article about them for the Royal Society's journal.'

Georgina gave her head a vigorous shake. 'Sorry, that's out of the question. I'm afraid that anything I wrote at the moment about women in this country would be far from objective. I thought I could go out to them and show. . . .' To steady her voice, she laughed. 'Of course, I could write about the Russian ladies who come out here with their beautiful complexions, and insist on playing tennis with a parasol held aloft in one hand the whole time.'

'Then I take it you easily win every game you play against them?' There was affection in Simon's grey eyes when he smiled into hers. It was a point not missed by Richard.

'Perhaps we actually spend more time drinking tea than running about on the tennis court.' Her colour deepened under Simon's gaze. 'The Russian ladies love to gossip because they don't often go outside the grounds of the Consulate, and they're always so homesick. They're never happy when their husbands are sent out here on duty. A new company of Cossacks arrived just a couple of weeks ago, you know.'

Natasha was overcome by a spasm of coughing, and from the other end of the table Erik looked on with concern while Quentin filled a glass with water and passed it to her.

Richard shifted impatiently in his chair and spoke before Simon had a chance to continue with the topic of the new Russian arrivals. 'Georgina, don't forget you've promised to show me your vast collection of fossils,' he said, willing to endure anything to claim a share of her attention tonight. 'I've been looking forward to it.'

She rewarded him with a warm chuckle. 'Oh dear! I'm afraid I might have raised your expectations too high.' Her forehead puckered. 'At the last count, I think my total collection amounted to three.'

'Well, three is an interesting number,' he said banteringly, 'although I expect you would like to add more to it.'

She inclined her head a fraction.

'Perhaps now that I'll soon be permitted to use my legs again,' he continued with a straight face, aware of Simon Davenport's amused interest, 'you and I could arrange to go on a fossil-hunting expedition one day soon?'

Erik smiled to himself as Georgina lightheartedly agreed, and he was about to draw Natasha into the subject when there was a loud, insistent rapping on the front door. The company around the dining-table fell silent, listening as the houseboy opened it to the sound of loud, agitated Chinese voices.

Georgina left the table to follow Erik to the door, and together they returned to the dining-room with one of the hospital attendants.

'Dreadful news, Richard,' Erik said, shaking his head in angry disbelief. 'I'm afraid someone has climbed the wall and stolen that dispatch pouch you kept beside your bed in the ward. The little chess pieces lying on top of it were knocked out on to the floor and Ho Sung said he heard the noise, but when he got there' – the doctor spread his hands – 'not a sign of the thief.'

He clicked his tongue and glanced at the expressions on the faces around him. The three Englishmen frowned as they muttered together. Georgina stood apart, silently watching them, biting down on her bottom lip.

Natasha stared at the tablecloth. She was ashen-faced and breathing fast, her lips slightly parted. Then her head fell forward.

Alarmed, Erik ran to her. 'What is it, my darling?' He felt for her pulse, and then with a hand on her waist, he urged her from the chair. 'Forgive us, gentlemen, I'm afraid my wife is unwell.'

'I'm sorry, Quentin, I must go with my mother,' Georgina said, moving to follow Erik. 'Will you see yourselves out?' She lowered her voice so the others wouldn't hear. 'I have something important to tell you. I need to talk to Richard first, and then I'll come to the Consulate tomorrow morning.'

CHAPTER SIX

'Your mother slept badly, my dear,' Erik whispered, when Georgina knocked on her parents' bedroom door the next morning. 'I've persuaded her to stay in bed today.' His weary eyes showed that he'd had little sleep either. 'Sit with her; look after her for me,' he said as he brushed his tousled hair at the mirror and adjusted his glasses. 'There is no urgent surgery waiting at the clinic. We'll remove that tumour on the Afghan's leg tomorrow.'

Georgina nodded and looked at her mother asleep on the pillow amidst a tangle of bedclothes. She moved to straighten them while Erik watched and shook his head.

'I don't know what has caused this,' he said, scrubbing a hand wearily across his chin. 'She seemed well enough when she set out for the market yesterday. I'm always in fear of some exotic disease coming in with a caravan from the east, but she has no symptoms that I can see.'

Georgina kissed his cheek. 'I'll let you know if I notice any change, I promise.'

Shortly after Erik left the house, Birget and Hilde Hakvin called to Georgina from the front door.

'Dear Mrs Larssen, she is not well we hear,' Birget said, thrusting a jar of preserved apricots into Georgina's hands. 'Please tell us if we can be of help.' Hilde offered a pot of custard.

Georgina spoke with them on the veranda and considered asking one of the ladies to sit with Natasha while she ran up to the hospital and immediately faced Richard with her confession. There was no doubt in her mind that the theft of his notes had been arranged by the Russian Consulate. A number of times Quentin McCallum had expressed a wonder about how far they would go in this race for information. Now she had shown him.

It was gossip from the tennis ladies that had alerted her months ago to the interest that Petrovsky, the Russian Consul, was taking in the arrival of any English traveller who came through the mountains. She always discreetly passed on to Quentin McCallum the interesting snippets she overheard on her social visits to the Russian compound. After her mother's collapse at the table last night, there had been no opportunity to reassure Richard and Quentin that the thief had got away with nothing more than the notes she'd falsified. This morning she was left wondering who on the hospital staff had been paid to tell where Richard's pouch was kept. However, the sooner she broke the good news to him that his original papers were safe, the better. Better for him, if not for her.

But while she and the Hakvins were talking, she saw Quentin McCallum's sturdy little carriage pull up at the steps of the hospital. Richard, as well as his chair, was loaded into it immediately and driven through the gates.

She bit her lip. Richard must have arranged this early visit while she was helping to settle Natasha into bed last night. If she could get to the Consulate while Richard was there, she could explain her reason for tampering with his information, and Quentin McCallum could act as mediator. Or bodyguard.

'Could I ask one of you ladies to come and sit with my mother for an hour or so?' she asked the Hakvins.

'Of course, Georgina dear,' said Hilde. 'Just give me a little time to arrange the lessons, ya? Ten o'clock?'

The houseboy was working quietly to put the house in order after last night's dinner party when Georgina carried a breakfast tray from the kitchen and soundlessly opened Natasha's door.

She was surprised to see that her mother was no longer in bed. With her hair already brushed, she was dressed in a wrapper, sitting tight-lipped in a straight-backed chair, her hands resting along its arms.

'Father wanted you to stay in bed today, Mother.' As usual when they were alone, they spoke Russian. 'He said you needed to rest.'

'It's not rest in bed that I need, Georgina.' Natasha shot her a look of accusation. 'The only *rest* I need is *rest* from the anxiety about you and your persistent refusal to take responsibility for your own future.'

Georgina had been about to put the tray down on a small table, but she froze and stood with it in her hands, blinking in confusion.

'You're almost twenty-four years old, Georgina. Surely you realize that a woman in your position must shape her own destiny. If you do not, circumstances will do it for you, and you will find yourself with nothing but a life of poverty and uncertainty. What is to be your fate if you persist in clinging to

Erik and his work here? You must go. You must take charge of your own future!'

Georgina clattered the tray on to the table and sank on to the foot of the bed, facing her mother in the chair. She waited several moments before she was sufficiently in control to speak. 'You're confusing me, Mother,' she said coolly.

'Then open your eyes and look honestly at your position. Surely you have learnt *some* lessons from observing the course of my life?' Natasha raised her hand to halt Georgina's interjection. 'You must remember how bleak my life was before I seized the opportunity to make Erik Larssen fall in love with me.'

'You *made* him fall in love with you?' There was a deep note of incredulity in Georgina's voice.

Natasha tossed her head. 'Of course I did. Many men fell in love with me when I was young because I used every feminine device provided by the Good Lord for such a purpose – soft smiles, warm looks, sweet scents, the occasional touch of skin. . . .' She clicked her tongue. 'You weren't raised in a nunnery, my dear.'

Georgina could only stare wordlessly at her mother.

'All the men who said they loved me sent me pretty trinkets and flowers, and took me driving in their carriages. I should have chosen one while I had the opportunity, but I naïvely thought I could wait.'

Georgina's chin lifted. 'You chose my father. You must have loved him once.'

'No!' Natasha shot her an odd look. 'I was never in love with him, though I was forced to leave St Petersburg with him because of circumstances I was unable to control.' Her knuckles were white as she grasped the wooden arms of the chair and leaned forward. 'Don't you see? That is just the point I want you to appreciate now. Don't wait until it is too late; find a man who will provide for you and let him know you are ready to give yourself to him.'

'That's not what I. . . .'

'Good God, Georgina, are your emotions so frozen you're incapable of understanding what I'm telling you? Shape your own fate, girl, before someone else does it for you. Reach out now for an opportunity that will take you far away from here. None of us can stay in this place for ever.'

'I'm not an imbecile, Mother!' Tempers were now raw. 'I assume you and I are having this discussion today because both Mr Davenport and Captain Eldridge were facing each other last night like stags in the rutting season, and you're convinced that either one of them is ready to take me if I simply lift my skirts.' Her tone rang with cynicism. 'And I'm sure you assume that as they are both gentlemen, the one I choose to lie with will take my virginity and then feel obliged to marry me?' The heat of anger burned up her throat and across her cheeks.

Natasha shrugged. 'In Russia we had a saying: "When you cannot get what you want, it is sometimes wiser to want what you get." '

'Oh dear, in that case, which man do I want? The stunningly handsome, middle-aged Mr Davenport, whose background is a total mystery?' Her words carried a harsh, mocking edge. 'Or Captain Eldridge, who, from what you've told me, is the irresponsible, indulged youngest son of a family of wealthy snobs who would never accept a woman like me?' She made an impatient gesture. 'God's name, Mother, why would I want to throw myself at either?'

Natasha made no comment, apart from a heavy sigh that carried her displeasure. When at last she spoke, her voice was flat. 'I'm simply warning you, Georgina, to remember that you are a penniless woman, so unfreeze your emotions and weigh up the opportunities that are presently here in front of you.' Her fingers began to drum on the arm of the wooden chair. 'I'll tell you now that your stepfather and I are planning for him to retire – as soon as possible. He'll be provided with a small annuity and we'll be able to live with his sister in her little house in Stockholm. I'll take in sewing, or find work somewhere with my pen, perhaps. But the Missionary Society won't permit you to stay on here without us, you know.'

For the second time this morning Georgina stared, slack-jawed, at her mother. 'Father has never ever even *hinted* to me anything about leaving Kashgar. *You're* the one pushing him to retire. Why? Why? He's not ready to go yet.'

Natasha raised her perfect brows. 'This is my life – my life with Erik, and I feel no necessity to discuss it.' She held Georgina's gaze unwaveringly. 'Experience has taught me that each woman must choose a path and follow it, or she finds herself washed up somewhere like flotsam on a beach.'

She narrowed her eyes. 'I was very young when circumstances in Russia overwhelmed me, and I was in a state of panic when I ran away with the man who was your father. I was impetuous, and very foolish not to have discovered he already had a wife and three children living in Liverpool, less than half a mile from the little rooms where he installed me when we arrived from St Petersburg.'

Again, Georgina was speechless.

'And I was carrying a child.' Natasha's fist came down hard on the arm of the chair. 'When he said he was sending someone to – deal with – me—'

A bitterness, so sharp she could almost taste it, rose in Georgina's throat as she sat rigidly watching her mother's ashen face.

'Listen to me, Georgina! Listen and learn! I decided at that dreadful moment to take control of my own life. The time had come at last for me to make my own decisions! I left Liverpool straight away and went to Bradford, because I'd heard of work there in the mills.' For a moment she paused, staring at the faded pattern on the carpet.

'Yes, mill work was grim, but I earned the money to rent a bed in a house where other girls lived. Of course, my pregnancy couldn't remain a secret for long.' She crossed her hands across her stomach. 'I was determined that my baby would not be delivered in the workhouse, so when the time drew close, I deliberately presented myself to the local vicar as a *fallen woman*, deeply repentant and in need of forgiveness. And, more importantly, in need of a safe place to have my baby. I played my part well, and his unmarried sister was a dear lady who took me in to her little house, though she was quite ill herself and as poor as a church mouse. Afterwards, when I went back to work in the mill, I stayed on with her and she looked after you – she loved you very much – but a few years later she died.'

It was several moments before Natasha could continue. 'The vicar's sister had told him of my fine handwriting, so he took me to meet a woman who agreed to employ me as her secretary. But, of course, she refused to have a small child in the house.'

'So I was sent off to school,' Georgina said, in a barely audible voice. 'Then, after ten years, Doctor Erik Larssen came to Bradford and you made sure he fell in love with you.'

'Yes. And I have ensured that not once has he ever had reason to regret our marriage,' Natasha said, with renewed intensity. 'Nothing in my life is more important than his wellbeing. And yours. Absolutely nothing!'

There seemed to be no more words left after that. They were both white-faced, sitting in silence, shaken by the eruption of anger that had pushed them even further apart.

'I'm sorry, Mother,' Georgina said at last across the emotional gulf. 'If only I'd understood. . . .'

'It matters little now that you have never understood me,' Natasha said wearily, 'because I'm afraid there is much I don't understand about you, either.'

The moment was interrupted by a knock on the front door and Hilde Hakvin could be heard cheerfully telling the houseboy she had come to sit with

Mrs Larssen while Miss Larssen went out.

Georgina shrugged apologetically. 'I won't be away long, I promise, but there's something important that I must attend to now.'

Natasha's face was expressionless and for a moment Georgina hesitated, then left the room to greet Hilde. When she returned a few minutes later, she was surprised to find that Natasha was back in bed, turned to face the wall with the covers pulled up tightly around her.

'Ah, good! She sleeps,' Hilde whispered and, settling into Natasha's still-warm chair near the window, she took her sewing from her basket and smilingly waved at Georgina to leave.

Lying with her eyes tightly closed, Natasha heard Georgina ride out of the compound, and silent tears came to dampen her pillow. Tears of frustration; and hatred. And fear. Fear that she did not have the strength to outwit Gregori Suvorov; fear of his power to hurt Erik. Fear that he would find a way to persecute Georgina also, if she remained in Kashgar.

She hated the Colonel now, just as she had hated him in St Petersburg twenty-five years ago. She hated him for forcing her to drive Georgina away, but if her daughter did not escape now, it would surely be only a matter of time before Gregori Suvorov began his old sadistic games with her.

Georgina would resist him, of course, and that was where the real danger lay. The Colonel did not take kindly to being thwarted, as she'd discovered in St Petersburg when she'd first tried to avoid his advances. Georgina needed a husband to take her far away from the evil that stained everything touched by the tentacles of Gregori Suvorov. Natasha wept. If the only way of saving her daughter was to send her out of Kashgar and out of her life and Erik's – then so be it.

The patch of damp on Natasha's pillow spread. It was frustrating to recall how dull-witted she had been yesterday when Suvorov had taken her to the teashop. Fear had frozen her brain. She should never have told him where Captain Eldridge kept the papers beside his bed.

She forced herself to lie still as a stone under the bedclothes so that dear little Hilde Hakvin would not be concerned, come to her side and find her in tears.

What would the missionary say if Natasha revealed the very un-Christian thoughts that were flying into her mind at this moment? How would Hilde react if she knew that Natasha was considering one solution that would solve all the problems presented by the Russian Colonel?

Her attempt this morning to shock Georgina into considering marriage to either Simon Davenport or Richard Eldridge had achieved nothing but to make them both angry. And her all-night discussion with Erik about leaving the Mission and retiring to Stockholm had upset him deeply.

That was why she could see only one solution to the threat of Gregori Suvorov's presence in Kashgar. She would have no peace of mind while the Colonel lived. What could possibly bring about his death?

CHAPTER SEVEN

Georgina's insides churned with tension as her little horse trotted out of the compound with Richard's notes in a satchel slung across her shoulders. She could think of no reason for her mother's sudden outburst. Why had she chosen *this* morning to reveal the story of her life for the first time?

Perhaps tomorrow, when they were both calmer, she and Natasha could have a rational discussion on the subject of marriage, though it wasn't going to be easy, she thought, as she rode along the busy road skirting the city walls.

Take responsibility for your own future, Natasha had demanded; shape your own destiny or circumstances will do it for you. Georgina had to admit that, ever since arriving in Kashgar, she'd deliberately side-stepped the reality that one day her work with Erik must come to an end. Her mother had been right about that this morning.

But Natasha had been wrong to accuse her of having frozen her feelings towards marriage. Agreed, she was shy and sexually inexperienced, but the instincts that nature had planted were very real and very warm indeed. It made her warm now, just remembering how she'd enjoyed the utterly feminine sensations racing through her last night while she watched Simon and Richard jousting for her attention at the table.

Her thoughts were interrupted when she saw the road ahead blocked by people pouring out of the city through the north gate. From inside the walls came the blare of horns, and the crowd scattered quickly to clear a pathway for the entourage of the Tao-tai, the Chinese commander of Kashgar.

Georgina strained to glimpse him sitting statue-like in his elaborate sedan chair, dressed ceremoniously in bright brocades, with the long tassel on his black satin cap swinging with the movement of the chair. He was followed by a shambling line of Chinese soldiers from the garrison stationed within the old city walls.

Coming along the road to meet the Tao-tai's procession was the full company of Cossack guards from the Russian Consulate, one hundred horses gleaming, their harnesses jingling. They were led by a powerfully built officer who halted his men with parade-ground precision and rode forward alone to greet the Chinese commander.

Georgina watched the proceedings with interest. This must be the new Colonel the ladies at tennis had gossiped about. They said he'd been at the centre of a scandal in St Petersburg with a niece of the Tsarina, and been banished to Kashgar for five years. It was only the plea of the Princess, the tennis ladies tittered, that had prevented his exile to Siberia.

She tried to position herself to see his features more clearly. He was a heavy, good-looking man, and he moved with assurance as he performed the military formalities with the Tao-tai, apparently impressing not only the commander, but also the crowd. When he eventually wheeled his horse, Georgina caught a scornful curl at the corners of his mouth. Intuitively she disliked the man.

At that moment, the Colonel's eyes swept the faces of the crowd, and before Georgina could look away, their glances met. She tensed, and turned quickly, with no idea why he should produce a prickle of unease in her veins.

She hung back behind the procession and rode in their dust until they turned into the road leading to the Russian Consulate. Then she pushed her little horse to make up time, and was hot and wind-blown when Quentin McCallum's Indian servant announced her arrival.

Quentin, Richard and Simon, gathered around the desk in the Consul's office, looked up in surprise as she came into the room, then, speaking almost in unison, they asked after Natasha.

'She's much better this morning, thank you,' Georgina said, immediately removing her hat and throwing it on to the hatstand. 'But my father has ordered her to stay in bed, so I must hurry back to sit with her.' She dropped into a chair and dragged in a lungful of air while she pulled off her gloves. Then she put her satchel on to the desk. 'Gentlemen, I think you should sit while I tell you why I'm here.'

Her well-rehearsed confession was heard in silence until Simon Davenport threw back his head and hooted with laughter. Richard clamped his jaws and glared before he fumbled for his notes in the satchel.

'You have every right to be angry with me, Richard, but frankly, in the beginning you were so weak there seemed little point in telling you what I'd done.' He looked unconvinced. 'In any case,' she added, 'I've always been told to pass information directly to the Consul himself. As he wasn't here at the time. . . .'

After a quick glance at the notes, Quentin interrupted her and leaned forward to speak, his elbows on the desk.

'Will the Russians be convinced by what you've substituted, Georgina?' He always thought like a diplomat. 'If their intelligence people suspect us of playing games with them, we'll have to watch out for political repercussions.'

'I did a *very* good job, Quentin,' she said. The gleam of mischief in her eye undermined the gravity in her tone. 'I'm sure the Russians will simply come to the conclusion that the observations were taken by an incompetent, blundering amateur.'

Simon's grin broadened, and Richard seemed about to protest, until a twitch crept into the corners of his mouth. Quentin's serious expression didn't lift.

'I hope your prediction is right, Georgina,' he said, 'because I've just been telling Simon and Richard that while I was away I saw evidence everywhere of the Russians using a great deal of gold to ensure the khanates would throw their support behind the Tsar if trouble comes this way.' He got up and walked heavily to his map on the wall, sweeping his hand across the names of little kingdoms lining the Silk Road. 'Oh, I was received politely enough everywhere and feasted by the khans, but it was clear that Petrovsky's inducements had already dissuaded them from offering any support to the British.'

Georgina nodded thoughtfully. 'On my way here this morning I saw the Cossack guard escorting the Tao-tai and his soldiers to the Russian Consulate.' The men looked at each other. 'Nobody who saw that performance would doubt that the Russians have the Chinese here right under their thumb.'

'That must have been the new fellow, Suvorov,' Quentin said. 'I haven't met him yet, but from the reports I've read, he comes with something of a reputation for trouble.'

'I think the Russian ladies here are looking forward to a little of the so-called *trouble* his reputation brings,' Georgina said with a touch of acid. 'They're saying he was banished for having an affair at court.'

'There's probably an element of truth in that version,' Quentin said bluntly, 'but I understand that Suvorov was playing a political game in St Petersburg last year when he took the Tsarina's niece to bed.'

Simon steepled his fingers and tapped his chin. 'Why wasn't he sent to exile in Siberia?'

'He should have been, but he got himself posted to Kashgar instead,' Quentin said with tight-lipped emphasis. 'We'll have to watch him closely because he's going to do everything he can to get himself back in favour with the power-brokers in St Petersburg by making life difficult for the British here.'

'Petrovsky must be delighted to have a man like that posted to his

Consulate,' Richard said with a raised eyebrow. 'Do you think the Colonel was behind the theft at the hospital last night?'

Quentin nodded. 'And I'm sure his public performance with the Tao-tai today was another reminder that if the British are seen to be a nuisance, the Russians could have the Chinese withdraw permission for our presence here.' He crossed to the desk and resumed his seat. 'So, you see how delicate the situation is for our Intelligence people in Simla. This little outpost is the northern eyes and ears for British India, and it's imperative we tread very gently and avoid doing anything that would get us thrown out.'

'I can't imagine anyone treading more gently than Georgina on her mercy missions,' Simon said, in a tone that made Richard's eyes turn quickly towards him.

She gave a self-deprecating smile as she stood and walked to the map on the wall. 'I was up here for three weeks,' she began, finding the position of the Kirghiz camp. Beyond that mapped area, the vast expanse of mountain ranges through Tibet, Kashmir and Afghanistan contained only sketchy detail.

'I'll be brief,' she said, 'but during my time up there with the Kirghiz, they told me they'd heard – probably third-hand – of a British officer being killed on the Afghan border.'

'Good God, Georgina, that was Alastair Mottram!' Richard said. 'Why didn't you tell me they knew about him?'

'I'm sorry,' she said, 'but there was no point, when you were fighting for your own life.' Her no-nonsense tone put an end to his argument. 'Please understand that all I heard was tribal gossip, but the Kirghiz did say that the British officer was killed after he had met up with a Russian man and his wife who came from the direction of Ferghana.' She pointed to the horse-breeding plains north of the Pamirs.

Quentin blew a low whistle and raised his eyebrows. 'They must be the Russian botanists you've heard about, Simon. What are they up to?'

'You think they are agents?' Georgina asked, and he nodded.

'Every expedition travelling around this country is sending back information to one government or another,' Simon said matter-of-factly.

A servant knocked and came into the office, carrying a tray of refreshments. Georgina poured the tea and passed the cups to the men.

'My only other scrap of news from the mountains,' she said, when she had taken a sip from her cup, 'is about a monk – I think from Tibet – who arrived all alone one night at the camp. From the little I could understand, he told the Kirghiz he was on a pilgrimage to visit some of the holy places along the Silk Road.'

The men around the desk listened, but her news was not unusual. A trickle of devout Buddhists still made long pilgrimages like this. 'He only stayed one night, just sitting there counting his beads and spinning his prayer wheel, but I heard him ask the men in the camp about the cave of the Golden Pagoda. The Kirghiz knew nothing, and the next morning he'd gone long before the sun was up.'

The men exchanged glances.

'For years I thought the story of that cave was a myth,' she said, 'but now I'm not so sure. On two occasions I've been shown talismans – just little pieces of gold-painted plaster – which families said had come from the cave years ago.'

Simon locked his hands behind his head and tipped his chair back on its legs. 'Hmmm,' he said. 'The legend of the Golden Pagoda is about its power to bring hope. Nice thought, but from an archaeologist's point of view, any talisman chipped from it means the fresco has been damaged.'

Quentin interrupted them. 'Georgina, I'd like to know one more thing about that priest. Exactly when did he leave the Kirghiz camp?' He reached for his pipe and filled it from a tobacco jar while she made a calculation on her fingers.

'He probably left about six weeks ago,' she said. 'Why? Have you had news of him?'

Quentin seemed deep in thought as he struck a match and held it to his pipe, sucking the stem until the tobacco caught light.

It was Simon who answered. 'Unfortunately, I think I saw your priest recently,' he said, righting his chair and leaning forwards. 'I was there when a man's body wearing dark red robes was found blocking one of those ancient underground water-channels – called karez wells, aren't they?'

'Was he quite elderly, and very thin?' she asked apprehensively.

'I imagine he was even thinner when I saw him,' Simon answered, pulling down the corners of his mouth. From their expressions, she realized that the other two had already heard this news.

'I'm afraid your priest has been deliberately put down one of the maintenance shafts into a water-channel a few miles outside Khotan. He was sealed in.' His voice dropped. 'Whether he actually died of starvation or suffocation I couldn't say, but I saw no signs of cuts or bruises on his body.'

'How dreadful! He owned nothing but his prayer wheel and beads and a begging-bowl.' She narrowed her eyes at Simon. 'Were those things found with him?'

'He still had his beads around his neck, and I brought them back here.'

Quentin reached into his desk drawer, pulled out a carved, wooden rosary and swung the strand from his index finger 'It's not a Buddhist string of one hundred and eight beads,' he said, giving her a significant look, 'but one hundred exactly.'

She understood. 'So he was a British agent?' The Intelligence Office in Simla recruited and trained pilgrims – code-named *pundits* – to move through the mountains gathering information, and to calculate distances in their survey work, they reduced the number of beads on each Buddhist rosary to one hundred.

'Did you find his prayer wheel, Simon?' The agents carried coded messages along with written prayers in the wheels.

'I'm afraid not,' he said. 'The only thing he had in his hand was a sharp rock that he'd apparently used in the dark to scratch a few marks on the wall beside him before he died.' He held her gaze. 'It looked to me as if he was trying to write *Golden Pagoda*.'

Georgina frowned. 'How – I mean, were you digging in that area or. . . ?'

'No, nowhere near it.' Simon picked up a pencil and drew a rough map on the blotting paper in front of him on the desk. 'The information was sent to me at my site, and by the time I got to the karez well, the body had been uncovered. I just had time to scramble down to see where he'd been lying. I noticed the scratches he'd made on the wall before the workmen covered the channel with the stone blocks again and got the water flowing.' His pencil drew a wavy line back to the city. 'That was the end of their interest in the matter. They buried the body in the desert, and nobody appeared to give a damn about his murder, or his scratchings on the wall.'

'Had that Russian couple been seen working around there at the time?' Georgina asked the obvious question, but Simon shook his head.

'I heard nothing of them in that region.'

'So we're left with the riddle of the Tibetan's marks, which might be simply the wanderings of a poor, sick mind.' Quentin voiced what the others were thinking. 'Was the Golden Pagoda his last vision? The hallucination of a dying man?'

'Or' – Richard said, staring reflectively at the empty spaces on the wall map – 'was he trying to leave a message about the location of the information he'd gathered out there?'

Quentin appeared doubtful. 'I'm usually advised if one of our agents is sent to work in this region.'

'Yes,' Richard said, 'but suppose he was unable to communicate with you, or perhaps for some reason he had to bypass Kashgar because of the Russian

couple? Forget about hallucinations and think what could have been so important about the cave of the Golden Pagoda that the poor fellow used his last
moments in the well to scratch those words.'

'I think Richard has raised an interesting point,' Simon said quietly. 'We
should give it some thought.'

For a few moments they sat in silence, then Georgina reached for her
gloves. 'Excuse me, gentlemen, I must go now. Perhaps I'll be able to call
again in a day or so.'

Simon was the first to stand. 'I'll ride back with you, if I may, Georgina.'

'Thank you, but perhaps if Richard is ready. . . .' She sounded far too eager.

'Oh, but I'm not going back to the hospital,' he said, scratching his neck
and looking at her with a somewhat abashed smile. 'I'm sorry, Georgina, I
assumed Doctor Larssen would have told you that he's agreed I'm fit enough
to move in here with Quentin. He's given me permission to take ten steps a
day. . . .'

To prove his point, he gripped the edge of the desk and hauled himself to
his feet, attempting to control a wince behind his smile. 'It won't be difficult
for the houseboy here to look after me,' he said, waiting for her response.

Her expression was unreadable.

'I'm sorry,' he said, 'but after the fiasco with the thief at the hospital last
night, and with so many official matters to discuss with Quentin now that he's
back. . . . Well, we thought it would be more convenient if I moved into the
Consulate.'

His news had sent a surprising and unwanted jolt of emotion through her,
but she hid it well under a flurry of activity.

'It sounds an excellent arrangement,' she said, while she pulled on her
gloves with exaggerated care. 'My father and I had been concerned about
where you could be sent to recuperate, now that we can do no more for you at
the hospital.' She lied smoothly. 'And as you and I have already discussed,
Richard, you'll soon be fit enough to be on your way again.' She reached for
her hat and stabbed the long hatpin through it to anchor it on to her hair,
annoyed to find anger was making her fingers fumble.

She turned to Simon with a smile that was too bright. 'Thank you for your
offer; I'd be delighted to have your company on the ride home. Shall we go
now? Goodbye, Quentin. Yes, I'll remember to give your good wishes to
Mother. Goodbye, Richard.' She turned and left the room with a swirl of
skirts.

'Well done,' Simon said quietly, bending so that his voice was near her ear
as they walked to their horses. 'Always make sure you have the last word.'

She glanced up at him and caught the amusement in his eyes. 'Oh dear, why did I suddenly sound like a shrew just because Richard said he wasn't coming back? Was I as rude to him as I think I was?' She felt Simon's hand on her elbow tighten.

'Yes, you certainly were, and it was no more than his discourtesy deserved. After all you've done to restore him to health, he should never have walked away from the Mission without a word of thanks to you.' He smiled wickedly. 'Preferably while face down in the dust, kissing the hem of your skirt.'

She gave a snort of laughter. 'I think I might have acted a little unreasonably back there, but he did surprise me with the news that he had already moved into the Consulate.' *Disappointment* was what she'd felt, but she would never admit it. She took several deep breaths and felt some of her tension subsiding. 'Of course, with Quentin's wife and children away there's lots of room, so it's logical for Richard to go there. After all, he was at the hospital for nearly a month, so if my stepfather thinks he's ready. . . .'

'No, no, no, Georgina! Don't climb down yet from your high horse. You look glorious up there, my dear. Let Richard stew in guilt for a few days and see what he does to repair his reputation for discourtesy.'

She looked at him sceptically and gave a laugh. 'Why would he care what I think of him?'

'Believe me, he cares very much indeed. Men always care how they are regarded by lovely ladies like you.' He sent her a tiny wink. 'I'll guarantee that, within a day or so, Richard will be knocking at your door with profuse apologies for his ungentlemanly behaviour.'

She slanted him a sideways glance and allowed herself to smile. 'Perhaps he should be warned that if he does knock at my door, the first person to answer it will be my mother.'

'Then she would simply be doing what all concerned mothers of beautiful daughters have been doing since time began.'

He spoke teasingly, but she saw something gentle in his eyes. It was deeper than mere politeness. It didn't matter. He wouldn't scold her, and he wouldn't judge. She felt he understood her, and she was glad he did because that made her comfortable with him.

'Never, never make apologies for any man's behaviour, Georgina.' He pursed his mouth in a play of disapproval. 'Believe me, a discourtesy of that kind would have the perpetrator instantly cut from polite circles. Richard's mother, Prudence Eldridge, is the self-appointed guardian of English society's standards, you know.'

'You know the Eldridge family?' The question sounded like idle curiosity.

'Very few people can claim that privilege,' he laughed. 'I've probably danced once or twice with the sisters, and I've played cards at the club with his brother, Albert.' He tried, but failed, to smother a snort. 'The one thing you can say in Richard's favour is that he's not a bore. You don't find him a bore, do you?'

She shook her head. No, Richard didn't bore her at all. Quite the contrary. 'Richard doesn't approve of women like me,' she said, with an attempt at flippancy.

'He doesn't yet *understand* a woman like you. You've broken the shackles of convention that he's grown up with, and your thirst for independence terrifies him.'

She glanced at him and pulled a doleful face. While they talked, the gait of their horses had slowed to a steady plod.

'Oh, Simon, you know very well that my so-called independence is nothing but an illusion. The day I leave here it will all disappear like the mist and' – for the first time she admitted her only viable option – 'and I'll probably go back to my old school and ask for a teaching post, and try to remember how to conform to all those conventions the English demand from ladies who wish to appear respectable.'

'Stepping back into the past is never as easy as it seems, m'dear. Nothing is ever the same after you leave. People change, perceptions change.' His voice was soft with kindness. 'Sometimes it's better to risk the future, even with all its unknowns.'

'I don't know what to do for the best. For the first time ever, Simon, my mother and I had a most appalling set-to this morning,' she said with a calmness that surprised her. 'She thinks I need a strategy for my future. I know – everybody knows – she has good reason to be concerned about me.'

He said nothing and she looked at him cautiously.

'What would you do if you had a daughter of twenty-three, who was unmarried, untrained in any useful occupation, and blighted by a determination to remain' – she searched for the right word '– *unrestrained*?'

'If such a daughter were mine, Georgina Larssen, I would treasure her beyond life itself.'

His voice was velvet-edged, and behind his deep grey eyes she sensed a sadness that surprised her with its intensity. She had a sudden impulse to reach out and touch his hand, but their horses were too far apart. So she did nothing, and they said nothing more as they rode towards the Mission.

CHAPTER EIGHT

Gregori Suvorov woke slowly and opened his eyes to meet the soft almond ones that were looking knowingly into his from the exquisite oval face beside him on the pillow. Christ Almighty! He barely had the strength to lift himself on one elbow and reach for the thin gold cigarette case on the bedside table. The Tao-tai had promised that she was exceptional, and she had proved him right.

He lit a cigarette and lay back, drawing on it and letting the smoke curl from his lips, watching it dance in the early ray of sunlight lancing the shutters on his bedroom window.

The girl slid her body like a weightless silken sheet across his, and her tongue began again to flick warm, sweet sensations around his nipples while her soft, knowing fingers played their magic between his legs. In God's name, where did this tiny, milk-white body find the stamina to deliver such a night of erotic amusement?

It was clear to see why the Tao-tai had called her his favourite concubine, and lending her to the Cossack colonel was a clear acknowledgement of the Russian-Chinese political understanding that had been reached yesterday. The Tao-tai's gift would have held more significance, of course, if the Consul himself had accepted the gesture, but Petrovsky was far too politically wily. But there was no reason why she could not be sent to entertain and delight Colonel Suvorov of the Cossack Guard, and Gregori had found the night's visit a unique experience.

But now he was becoming bored with her repertoire. She was too practised, too perfect. She wasn't a woman; she was a porcelain doll who performed when her spring was wound. And besides, she was Chinese, and he despised the whole inscrutable race. He rolled on to his side and pushed her away from him, then smiled at the fear in her eyes as he held the tip of his glowing cigarette close to her nose. The girl whimpered in confusion and terror. Somehow she had displeased the foreign devil, and she had no understanding of why that should be so when she had performed perfectly the full cycle of Heavenly Mysteries. If the Tao-tai heard that his gift had failed to please this man, she would be punished. Yet why had he now become so angry when all night he had moaned and gasped with the pleasure she had given him?

Her eyes filled with tears as she slid from the bed and stood, wordlessly, pleadingly, beside him. The eunuch appointed to escort the Tao-tai's concubines on their rare excursions from the house, was waiting for her in the adjoining-room. Surely he would have heard the Russian's groans of ecstasy throughout the long night and would report the white man's satisfaction to the Tao-tai. With her palms together, the girl bowed lower and lower to the large, exhausted figure on the bed.

Gregori waved his hand dismissively, and turned his head away. She had spent too much time on top of him, controlling him, rousing him, teasing, playing with his urges. All through the night his role had been a passive one while she'd performed her countless well-rehearsed skills on his body.

It had been an interesting experience, but that style of sexual game had left him with a strangely depleted sense of his own manhood. The performance of the Tao-tai's little Chinese goddess, he realized, had taken his power away from him; it had been too easy to lie back against the pillows and simply let her exhaust him with her tricks. That sort of thing might be the ultimate experience for a Chinaman, but what Gregori needed for complete sexual satisfaction was to be in control of any woman he took to bed. He liked nothing better than the sense of male victory that came when he lay with a supposedly *unattainable* woman, felt her fighting under him when he entered her, and listened to her mounting cries of pleasure as he tamed her, before she shuddered in ultimate surrender after their battle.

A long time ago, Natasha Luboff had given him that kind of satisfaction. No, not Natasha now, but it would be interesting to meet her daughter and see what she had inherited from her mother.

He stubbed his cigarette in the ashtray and lay with his hands clasped behind his head, watching the dust motes dancing in the rays of light hitting the far wall.

He'd find out more about Natasha's tennis-playing daughter from the ladies at the Consulate. In the mean time, the pretty little rosebud wife of the Second Secretary seemed ready for plucking.

Georgina assisted Erik during his surgery to remove a bullet from the stomach of a tribesman brought in from the desert, and spent the rest of the morning at the dispensary bench, mixing elixirs and vigorously grinding the ingredients for her father's prescriptions.

She was reaching for another brown bottle on the shelf when she heard the sound of carriage wheels. They stopped at the steps of the clinic, and Erik's voice called a greeting.

Through the window she saw Richard being helped from the Consulate vehicle, and a prickle of pleasure ran over her skin. She smiled to herself, but kept at her work, filling jars and labelling them until, thirty minutes later, a shadow fell across the dispensary bench. She turned slowly and tried to give the impression she was surprised to find Richard standing in the doorway, leaning on two sticks.

She pulled out a chair for him and perched herself nonchalantly on the bench, saying nothing, swinging her legs while she eyed him, and managing to hide her delight that he had come as Simon had forecast.

'Miss Larssen,' he began, with straight-faced formality, 'I am here this morning to offer abject apologies for my appalling behaviour in running off yesterday without a word of farewell to you.'

She inclined her head. 'Hmmmm.' The tone was non-committal, her smile tepid. She was enjoying the moment.

He studied her, apparently deep in thought. 'Of course, you must accept that the fault was not entirely mine,' he said, and his mouth quirked, seeming to anticipate her look of surprise. 'The whole incident could have been avoided if you had taught me the art of patience when I pleaded for your help not long ago.'

Her smile was like a burst of sunlight. 'Who in this world could ever train a man like you to be patient? You should be careful, Captain, about requesting too many miracles.'

'Maybe you're right,' he said, and held his almost-healed hands towards her, opening and closing hem to demonstrate the mobility in his fingers. 'I shouldn't ask for more than this. Walking is still painful, but I'm ready to mount a horse again.'

For a moment they fell silent and sat studying each other awkwardly, like strangers in a railway carriage.

'Believe me, I'd never willingly do anything to upset you, Georgina.' His hair had fallen across his forehead again, giving him a boyish appearance.

She shrugged, but a flush crept into her cheeks. 'Say no more. Anyhow, now that you're almost fit again, we'll all be saying goodbye to you soon.'

'Actually, I'm not sure about that,' he began, then stopped, as a man carrying a boy limply across his arms paused uncertainly and peered in the doorway, before Ho Sung's voice called for him to come into the clinic.

When the man had gone, Richard continued in a low voice, 'My commanding officer in Simla has sent an order for me to wait here with Quentin and perhaps—' There was obviously more he wanted to tell her, but Ho Sung burst in with a message that Doctor Larssen wanted to see Georgina in the clinic straight away.

She slid off the bench. 'Excuse me, I must go, Richard,' she said. 'Would you like someone to help you across to the house? You'll stay to lunch, of course.'

He struggled to push himself to stand. All she did was to step forward and put out her hands to steady him. But the next moment, her arms were around his waist and she was holding him tightly, her forehead against his chin.

For five long seconds she stood there, unwilling to surrender the dangerous pleasure of his body close to hers. She looked up at him and they searched each other's eyes. Her thoughts were reflected in his.

'May I?' he whispered, and she smiled.

Quickly, lightly, he brushed her lips with his, as she hoped he would. As she knew he would. She took a breath and moistened her lips, opening them and raising her hands to his face, pulling his mouth hard against hers with an urgency that compelled him to respond. He held her shoulders and she could feel his heart hammering as they clung together briefly. His hands slid down her arms and their fingers touched and twined, while he kissed her again.

They pulled apart. 'Oh, Georgina,' he said on a sigh, and his smile widened.

He seemed about to kiss her once more, but she shook her head. 'Not now, I must go to my father. I'll ask Ho Sung to walk to the house with you.' She picked up his sticks, and put them into his hand. 'Tell my mother I'll be home as quickly as I can.' Her face remained gloriously flushed.

He grinned good-humouredly after her as she hurried away, calling for the attendant to accompany him across the compound. Dear God! And to think that once he'd worried that breaking through Georgina Larssen's air of untouchability would be impossible. He'd spent hours lying on his back in hospital, wondering what lay hidden behind her reserve, and now he knew that just below the surface was a tantalizingly eager, responsive woman. He could feel the smile, unstoppable, spreading across his face.

One touch, simply one touch of their lips was all it had taken to melt that icy exterior and unleash the rush of pleasure he'd felt heating her body when she pressed against him. Miss Larssen was indeed a lady of many surprises.

Oh, God! The genie was out of the bottle now. Even to consider having an affair with her was madness, but irresistible.

*

Natasha was delighted when she saw Richard standing on her doorstep.

'How well you look,' she said, and quickly brushed aside the apologies for his abrupt departure. 'Think nothing more of it, my dear. It was my silly little dizzy turn at the dinner table that put everyone off their stride, but I'm perfectly well again now.'

She fussed about him, settling him in a comfortable chair and bringing a foot-stool. When lunch was ordered, they sat talking of small, inconsequential things while her gaze kept drifting towards the window, waiting for sight of Georgina.

It was obvious that Natasha was as anxious as he was to have her here, but for different reasons. Natasha couldn't hide the fact that she was ferociously keen to snare a husband for Georgina, and somehow he'd have to give her a clear message that a permanent attachment – to anyone – was not an option for him.

'Tell me, Richard, have either of your sisters lost their hearts yet?' She was determined to keep the topic of romance flowing.

'They're both still young, Mrs Larssen, but I've lost count of the times Eleanor and Sophie have fallen in love. However, I haven't yet heard of any of their suitors gaining the approval of my mother and elder brother.'

'Naturally,' Natasha said smoothly, 'all families want the best for their daughters.' She laced her fingers and lay them in her lap. 'And has your brother found a young lady who measures up suitably?'

'No, I don't think so,' was all Richard said. Bertie might be middle-aged before he found a lady who could match Prudence Eldridge's expectations. It was fortunate for the family that Bertie was the first-born, because he invariably saw eye-to-eye with their mother.

From an early age Richard had been labelled a 'tearaway', and Prudence had scolded him often for slipping through the social barriers to associate with the wrong class of people. 'You must remember the family's position in society, Richard,' she had cautioned a thousand times.

Bertie had found no difficulty in limiting himself to suitable acquaintances, which predictably dulled his social life, but Richard's powers of discrimination were never so finely tuned. His capacity for enjoyment often raised eyebrows in polite circles.

But his activities were regarded differently when he joined the army. In London society, his mother had called him a 'harum-scarum'; in the Regiment, his fellow officers said he had 'dash'. What Prudence Eldridge saw as 'recklessness', the Colonel had called 'courage', and he'd been given a medal not long ago for charging a Pathan position that had a British company pinned down on the road to Kabul.

The chime of the clock on the mantel cut across his thoughts and Natasha gave a little sigh of relief. 'Ah, here comes Georgina at last. What could have taken so long this morning at the clinic?'

Through the window, Richard saw Georgina running towards the house. She moved as lightly as a dancer, and as she came closer he could see excitement in her expression. Because he was here, waiting for her? His heart picked up a beat. He and Natasha smiled at each other as the front door flew open and Georgina rushed into the drawing-room.

'Oh, Richard!' Her hand flew to her mouth. 'I'm so sorry, but Father and I are to leave immediately. I've come home to pack a change of clothes.'

Natasha bristled. 'Don't be ridiculous, Richard has called on us. Where is Erik?' Anger thinned her voice. 'Lunch is waiting, Georgina. You can't go anywhere now!' Then she caught sight of the travelling-cart leaving the stables, heading towards the hospital steps, and stamped her foot.

Georgina's eyes were bright as she turned to Richard. 'Remember the man you saw carrying the child into the clinic this morning?' He inclined his head. 'Smallpox,' she said, 'but Father says the boy has a very mild strain.'

He looked baffled; Natasha shook her head warningly.

'Father says we've been presented with a marvellous opportunity to use this boy's mild illness to vaccinate everybody in his village. But we must do it quickly.'

'Oh, must you go too, Georgina?' Natasha sounded defeated. 'Just for once, can't you try – try to be less enthusiastic?'

Richard wisely held his tongue.

'Mother, you know how dreadful it is when smallpox sweeps through a district, and everybody shrugs and says it is either the will of Allah or some god of the mountains,' she said. 'The man who brought in his sick child this morning is the headman of Jaikin – that little village along the western road – and he has agreed to let Father vaccinate everybody there. But I'm the only one who'd be permitted to touch the women.'

'Doctor Larssen must have been very persuasive with the fellow.' Richard's remark helped to stem Natasha's next objection, and won him Georgina's smile.

'Yes, it took a long time to make him understand that if we use swabs from his son's skin, we could transfer his mild sickness to a scratch on the skin of other people, so that they'd also catch the mild sickness, which, in turn, should stop them getting a full-blown case of smallpox in the future.' She gave her mother a reassuring nod. 'There's nothing new in this idea, you know, although it would carry fewer risks if we had the cow-pox vaccine they use in England. But as we don't, we must do the best we can – and Father says this is the mildest case he's seen in years.'

If anything, Natasha looked even more dispirited.

'Don't you see, Mother, this is just the first step. When word gets about that Jaikin has accepted Doctor Larssen's help, other villages might follow.'

While she was talking, nobody noticed that Erik had come home and was standing in the doorway. When Natasha saw him, he held out his hand to her.

'I'm sorry, my love, but we should be away no more than one or two nights.'

Her sigh was one of resignation. 'Lunch is ready. You must eat before you go,' she said, and led them to the table. 'I'm sure, though, that Richard will be disappointed to lose the pleasure of Georgina's company this afternoon.'

They sat at the table and Geogina picked up her fork. 'Never mind, Richard,' she said in a low voice, 'I promise that when I come back I'll take you to explore all the excitement that Kashgar offers.'

'I'll keep you to that promise,' he said, and sent her just the ghost of a wink.

Gregori Suvorov's palm was damp on the handle of the door as he closed it behind him and walked from the Consul's office. Tactfully, the Second Secretary and his clerk kept their heads bent over their work as the Colonel strode through the outer office, looking neither to the left nor right, his face a mask of white fury.

Petrovsky's loud-mouthed, scathing reprimand had carried clearly through the building. Probably the news was already on its way back to St Petersburg that Colonel Suvorov had allowed himself to be caught by a British joke.

Somehow Natasha had found a way to trick him and make him appear an incompetent fool before his superiors. It had taken Petrovsky and his intelligence officer less than a week to recognize that the British information which Gregori had acquired by stealth and presented with such flourish, could not possibly be taken seriously.

By God, Natasha was going to be made to pay for this humiliation. He called for his horse to be brought to the steps and stood slapping his riding crop hard against his boot as he waited. How was he going to punish her? By using her police records to crucify her husband at the hands of the Swedish Mission Board? Yes, he would certainly put that in motion, but how much time would it take? Too long. What he needed at this moment was to feel his hands around her throat. Or to throw her from a balcony.

He mounted his horse, wheeled it towards the gates and dug the spurs into its flanks, sending up a cloud of dust behind the flying hoofs. What would cause most pain to that sow, the creature who had made him the object of ridicule? Not just her husband's downfall – it must be her daughter's as well. He whipped his horse faster, and the surge of power in the muscles of the animal beneath him sent a heat into Gregori Suvorov's loins and brought a thin smile to his lips. The breath expelled from his nostrils grew louder and faster as he envisaged a scene that would for ever shatter any peace of mind Natasha Luboff thought she had.

He would ride Natasha's daughter with the whip, as he was riding this horse now. He would ride her to exhaustion and deafen himself to her cries for pity. And all the time Natasha would know about it; perhaps somehow it could be arranged for her to watch her daughter's degradation, and be helpless to come to her aid. How he would enjoy that!

Ah, yes, the lovely Natasha was going to regret the day she dreamed she could outmatch Gregori Suvorov. Subtly, slowly, he'd make her aware that he was edging ever nearer to her secure little world. He would stalk her, stalk her daughter, watch her torment when she recognized his old game-plan, enjoy her growing terror, knowing that she could never call for help without revealing her St Petersburg secrets.

The daughter would wonder. The mother would know, and never dare to disclose that knowledge. Then, some time, some place, he would make his move, and the girl, too, would learn that Colonel Suvorov was not a man to be taken for a fool.

To avoid another meeting with Gregori, Natasha no longer went shopping in the city markets with the cook. She told Erik she hadn't completely recovered from her recent mysterious indisposition. The cook couldn't conceal his delight when he was sent off alone with a shopping list and a purse of money, but Natasha felt it was the price she had to pay for her own security.

She looked up from her writing-table at the window and saw Gregori on his horse, blocking the gateway while he stared towards the house. She held a hand across her mouth to stop from crying out. Was he coming into the compound? It made no sense. She had told him about the documents Richard had kept beside his bed and he had sent someone to steal them. What did Gregori want from her now? There was nothing more she could tell him.

Her fingers played distractedly with the pen on her desk. Flowers had come yesterday for Georgina, and naïvely Natasha had assumed that Richard must have sent them to wait for her return. Fool! Fool! her mind screamed. This was the old game Gregori had played in St Petersburg when he'd first tried to intimidate her. He'd left flowers, then would later appear silently outside the apartment where the dancers lived, stalking the object of his obsession, like a hunter stalking a doe. Until he was ready to strike. This was his message to her this morning. He was doing it again! The breath caught in her throat.

The flowers yesterday had been sent to Georgina! Was he mad to think her strong-willed daughter would allow herself to be seduced by such a ploy? In God's name, Gregori hadn't even met her, had he?

When he turned his horse and rode out of view, Natasha put her head in her hands and tore at her hair, shaken by silent sobs, confused by the implied threat in his appearance at their gate. She remembered him too well not to understand that for some reason she, Natasha, was the target of this performance; Georgina was simply to be the sword used for her punishment. Terrifying, monstrous spectres rose in her mind. What unspeakable revenge might he take on Georgina when she refused to be seduced?

Natasha stood quickly and took his flowers from the vase. She ran from the house and threw them on to the pile of rubbish smouldering behind the stables. Georgina would never know about them. More flowers were sure to come in the next day or so, and she would do the same before Georgina saw them.

Whatever malevolence Gregori Suvorov was planning, it had to be stopped. Stopped before Erik and Georgina became aware of his vile intentions. Gregori must be stopped before he had an opportunity to expose the secrets of St Petersburg, and Natasha could see only one solution.

CHAPTER NINE

Georgina took Richard's arm and tugged him away from the carpet-seller. Over her shoulder she made a comment to the man left standing in the middle of his shop, and he laughed good-naturedly.

'I don't know what you said to the poor fellow,' Richard said as he limped to the silk merchant a few doors away, 'but it sounded to me like an insult.'

'Oh, it certainly was,' she said off-handedly. 'And he loved it.'

'I take it he was quoting me an outrageous price?'

'Absolutely ridiculous,' she said. 'Of course, if you'd really wanted to buy that huge carpet I could have kept bargaining and got the price down even further.'

'So why didn't you? What makes you suppose I wasn't genuinely interested in buying it and having it sent down to India?'

She gave him a no-nonsense look. 'That was a drawing-room carpet if ever I saw one, and you've always made it very clear that you have no intention of leaving your army life to settle down in a house with a drawing-room – or a wife. . . .'

She stopped herself from saying more. This was foolish territory to enter, because since her return to Kashgar she'd discovered that Richard Eldridge had become far too important to her, and she spent altogether too much time thinking about him. And she wasn't thinking calmly, either.

'Will you at least help me to buy a shawl for your mother?' he said when they paused outside the silk merchant's display. 'Let me see you beat this poor man down to a rock-bottom price.'

One and a half hours later, following several cups of tea and a display of apathetic head-shaking over the man's entire stock of glorious silk shawls, they selected four. By this time, Georgina and the merchant had struck a bargain that delighted them both, although neither party would dream of acknowledging it.

When they rode back to the Mission, Richard ceremoniously presented the Hakvin ladies, Natasha and Georgina each with one of the shawls. 'With my thanks for all your kindness.'

Again Richard stayed to dine with the Larssens, as he had the previous evening after Georgina had taken him to visit the old walled city; and also the evening before that, when they'd returned from the great Sunday camel market on the other side of the river.

Since she had arrived home at the end of the vaccination work, they had ridden out together each day. They were both aware of the attraction growing between them, both unwilling to put it into words, both reluctant to lose the occasional opportunity for physical contact that always seemed to be accidental, and never was.

There was definitely nothing accidental about the embrace they had shared last night as she walked with him to his horse. He thought it was she who had initiated it, but he wasn't sure. A mutual desire seemed to have exploded out of nowhere, once they stood alone together under the stars. Her hand brushed his; he held it, lifted her palm to his lips, heard her sharp intake of breath.

There was always an odd mixture of innocence and passion about her. When he pulled her close, her mouth was ripe and trembling, then her whole body became alive, heated, nerves afire as she moved against his arousal as they clung together and a mutual desire flared. He groaned and at last they'd pulled apart, gasping, hearts pounding, terrified that words would escape – forbidden words that once said could never be recalled. Then he had sprung on to his saddle and spurred his horse through the gates.

Tonight, Georgina, in her simple blue, high-buttoned dress, smiled politely at him across the dining-table as the family chatted about inconsequential matters. Natasha was cheerful, Erik wryly humorous.

But tonight it was impossible for Richard to ignore the underlying sensuality that hung in Georgina's every look. He returned her smile involuntarily, and felt his own body responding with alternating messages of delight and concern that she enthralled him so. It was foolish to allow himself to feel this way about her; but then, he had never before met a woman like Georgina.

He looked back across the table to Erik, and tried to glue his attention on the anecdote about something amusing that had happened years ago to old Father Paul, the Jesuit missionary, on the road to the Three Springs waterfall. Richard had missed the point of the whole story, but he joined in the laughter at the end.

'It's very beautiful up there at the Three Springs Falls,' Georgina said without lifting her eyes from the dinner plate. 'I think Richard and I should

71

take a picnic there tomorrow, while this pleasant weather holds.' She looked innocently towards Erik. 'Do you mind if I don't come to the clinic, Father?'

'Of course he doesn't mind, darling,' Natasha interrupted before Erik could speak. 'A picnic – yes, we'll pack you a lovely picnic and – and actually, Erik, I've been thinking for a long time now that I should be of more help in your work.'

She ignored the looks of startled disbelief that Erik and Georgina threw to each other, and smiled at him appealingly. 'I know, my darling, I'd be quite useless beside you in the hospital, but I'm sure I could do something in the dispensary – grinding up all those mysterious things you put in bottles and jars.' She made an expansive gesture with her hands. 'Surely even *I* could learn to do that.'

'Thank you, my dear,' Erik said gently. 'Perhaps we can discuss it later. At the moment we're not busy, and there's nothing there that Ho Sung and I can't manage.'

'Then surely that is a perfect opportunity for Ho Sung to teach me what is safe – and what is dangerous – on the dispensary shelves.' Her lowered lashes hid her eyes.

More flowers from Gregori were presently smouldering on the rubbish pile behind the stables, and the gatekeeper had become convinced that the Russian officer who sometimes stood silently at the gate must either be mentally afflicted or under the spell of an evil spirit. In either case he should be neither spoken to, nor spoken about.

Erik and Georgina remained totally unaware of the Colonel's visits, and only Natasha knew what lay behind his strange behaviour.

The next morning, Georgina and Richard set out early for the waterfall. They talked little as they rode towards the mountains, but they were both aware that they were approaching a moment that would for ever change the course of their relationship.

'Do you want to turn back?' Richard slid a sideways glance at her when they were halfway there, and she shook her head, outwardly calm and apparently unaware of the flush of nervousness spreading up her throat.

They continued to follow the river past cotton fields and vineyards, through a tiny whitewashed village where the flat roof-tops were covered with apricots and peaches drying in the sun, and the looms of the silk weavers clattered in their courtyards.

All around them, the snow-capped peaks and glaciers glistened as the sun climbed higher and the road grew steeper, leaving behind the farms and houses, and winding its way into the hills where the air was heavy with the scent of pines. The roar of rushing water grew louder around every bend in the trail, until at last they reached a green knoll facing the foot of the falls.

They dismounted and watered the horses, and after Richard had hobbled them and left them to graze, he came to stand behind Georgina, resting his hands lightly on her shoulders as they watched the unstoppable cascade plunge from the top of the falls and crash in a flurry of white water on to the rocks below.

It seemed to him a fitting metaphor for their visit here, and before his last ounce of restraint was swept like a leaf over the top of the falls, he put his lips to her ear.

'Are you sure?'

She turned slowly and looked at him with an irresistible mixture of innocence and passion. 'Yes, Richard, I'm quite sure. I want you to be the first man to love me.'

His lungs seemed suddenly deprived of air.

'I want you to make love to me, Richard, nothing more. No promises, no tomorrows. Just give me today to remember.'

Her hands slid up his arms, across his shoulders, and when her fingers stroked the back of his head, his heart thundered. He wrapped his arms around her, and crushed her tightly against him, kissing her ear, her neck, her hair, running his open hands across her back.

'Georgina—' His mouth found its way to hers, already eager and open, and he kissed her deeply, gasping as he drew back. 'Georgina – I want you, oh God, how I've longed for this moment – but you must understand, please understand, that any day now I'll be ordered back to the work I've sworn to finish. I can't take you with me.'

She stroked his face. 'It's all right. I know we can have only a little time together. It's today I want, nothing more, I promise.' She looked deeply into his eyes. 'Please have no worries, Richard, it will be all right. I promise I know what I'm doing. After all, I *am* a doctor's daughter.'

It took a moment for her message to register, then he smiled and embraced her, pressing his lips into the warm, white curve of her neck, while his head swam with the scent of her. He reached for her hand. Her fingers clasped his tightly, and he felt the nervousness she was trying to hide declare itself in the dampness of her palm.

While he took a blanket from behind his saddle and spread it, she pulled the pins and combs from her hair. A cascade of burnished copper fell around her shoulders; he stroked it, marvelling at the softness of the glowing strands that slid through his fingers. Excitement and desire lit her face, and she looked suddenly and wonderfully wanton as they fumbled with their buttons and laces, laughing at the clumsiness created by their own haste, until at last they sank naked on to the ground, lying a little apart, on their backs, and now silent as they studied each other, both breathing heavily.

Like strangers approaching a strange land they waited, as if for some sign that permission had been given for them to cross the border and enter unknown territory. A bat's-squeak of uneasiness crossed his mind. This was destined to be a dangerous journey.

At last it was she who gave the signal. He saw it in her guileless smile when her fingers slid across the space between them, entwined with his and held them tightly, invitingly. Her blue eyes looked into his, and the tip of her tongue moistened her lips. It was too late then for hesitation.

Delight rushed through him as he raised himself on one elbow. She watched expectantly as his gaze drifted slowly from her face, across her breasts and stomach to her legs, and back again.

'You're truly exquisite,' he murmured.

'So are you,' she said, and put out a hand to touch his tanned, sinewy forearm, as she would have touched some piece of porcelain or a sculpture, just for the pleasure of feeling its shape and curve beneath her palm. She ran her fingers up his arm, sweeping over the soft golden hairs, and when her touch reached his shoulder, his neck, his jaw, then brushed gently across his cheek and along the curve of his ear, he could hold himself back no longer.

He drew her against him and he heard her soft gasp of anticipation before he kissed her, sliding his tongue inside her mouth and feeling her body arch instinctively in response. He willed himself to keep the fever from his touch. Nothing he did must hurt or alarm her. This first experience of lovemaking was one she would recall always, and it must be as perfect as he could make it.

But, dear God, he was only human, and the sensation of her body moulding itself invitingly into his was akin to setting flame to tinder. The kiss became primal and ravenous, tongues sliding sensuously together, hands stroking and exploring as his yearning flesh hardened. Her passion rose to meet his; they kissed and played, warmed by the sunlight, gasping, panting. She moaned and dug her fingertips into his back when his fingers slid into deeper intimacy, tenderly teasing her desire, until her wet, silky warmth rewarded his touch and she groaned, pleading.

His lips played over her face, her breasts; her teeth nipped his neck, his ears, his nipples, until he could hold himself back no longer. He sank into her warm flesh with a low cry, driving into her, stroke after stroke. A power – elemental, passionate, primitive – raced beween them. Again and again she lifted to him, seeking her pleasure in his silky hardness as their mutual hunger and need came together in a firestorm of sensation, until they reached the threshold beyond which the world fell away, and nothing existed but their plunge into the white heat of the void.

Afterwards she lay entwined with him, half sleeping, half waking, smiling, not speaking, the scent of their rapture clinging to her warm body. She reached out and laid her hand against his cheek. He put his own hand over it, cradling it for a moment, then turned his head and gently kissed her palm. The tug on his heart was slow and tender and very real when she rolled towards him. Then, in the deep peace of passion spent, she sighed her contentment and drifted into sleep with her head on his shoulder, one arm flung across his chest.

He stroked her tenderly and felt the rhythmic rise and fall of her breast against his chest. His breath was caught in a sweet, melancholy ache, shafting deep into his gut, twisting like a dull dagger. Today he'd willingly thrown himself from the top of the waterfall with Georgina Larssen and lied to himself that he'd be capable of walking away from her without a backward glance.

He had just proved to himself that he was the greatest fool since the dawn of time. He snuggled her closer to him and buried his face in her sweet-smelling hair. Walking away from this woman was going to be the most difficult thing he'd ever had to do. Now, lying with her in his arms, he longed for nothing more than for her to become part of his life for ever. And that was impossible.

The sky was purpling into night when Georgina and Richard returned to the Mission, and the darkening shadows made his features indistinct. But she didn't need to see his face to read his feelings. They were akin to hers, she was sure.

The day had been overwhelming in its intensity. When she had woken and they had eaten the picnic, they'd again made love. Together they had drifted playfully, languidly kissing and caressing, until their heat flared and swirled, sucking them again into its glorious flame.

Repleted, he had slipped into sleep with his leg wrapped around hers and his head against her breast. His warm breath teased her nipple and she'd begun to weep because, when he woke, this day would come to an end, and she knew now that she had lied to them both when she said she wanted nothing more than this. Before today, she had never understood that once the door of love was opened, it would refuse to close again.

'Goodbye, Richard,' she said at the doorstep of her parents' house. 'I think it will be easier for both of us if I don't invite you in.' She reached for her well-worn mantle of reserve and wrapped it tightly around herself. 'It would be foolish for us to meet again, but I'll treasure the memory of today. Thank you, from the bottom of my heart.'

When she touched his arm, she felt him tense defensively, and knew that he was floundering as deeply as she was. This whole day had been a mistake. Her mistake.

'I agree that it would be wiser if we didn't meet again,' he said, in a voice so low she had to strain to hear. 'My orders will come any day now and. . . .'

'God's speed, Richard,' she said and spun towards the door, opening it without a backward glance. Once inside, she closed it and leaned her back against the stout wood, listening to him ride away and battling her wild, irrational sense of loss. She held her knuckles between her teeth and refused herself permission to weep.

It took several moments to steady her breathing, and her composure was as fragile as a wren's egg when she walked into the drawing-room to face her parents' expectant looks.

'It really was a perfect day to visit the falls,' she said, far too brightly, before either Erik or Natasha could speak. 'There was a wonderful flow of water coming over the top, and I caught sight of a spotted deer further up the mountain.' She pulled off her gloves and threw them on to a chair. 'There was a bird with a yellow throat that I couldn't identify, but it had a beautiful call.'

She saw Natasha's face sag with disappointment. She had expected that, but it was the mistiness in Erik's eyes that was almost her undoing. He, too, must have had high hopes for this day.

'Richard is expecting to be called back to duty any day now, you know. I don't think we will see him here again.' Her voice started to shake with the emotion that refused to be repressed any longer.

Erik came towards her with his arms open, and like a child she flung herself into his comforting strength. With her head nestled into his shoulder, the tears began to flow.

'Father, I don't know who I am any more,' she whispered. 'Help me.'

CHAPTER TEN

Simon sat at a table in the corner of Quentin's office, quietly revising his catalogue, while the Consul and his First Secretary sorted the official mail that had just arrived from India.

Richard wandered into the room, picked up a book and left again. Quentin and Simon raised eyebrows at each other. It was clear that something had happened last week to stop his visits to the Mission, as well as producing this irritating restlessness.

Quentin opened a letter marked *Confidential*. 'By God, I wish we had a telegraph line across the mountains,' he said, frowning. 'It seems that the war party in St Petersburg is gathering strength, and is being egged on by – of all things – talk of a revolt by the Sikhs in the Punjab.'

Simon looked at him sharply and shook his head. 'Not the Sikhs. I don't believe it. They stood firmly with the British in the Mutiny of '57.'

Quentin was too preoccupied to notice the colour leave Simon's face. 'Well, the Mutiny was thirty years ago, and here's the confirmation that Maharaja Duleep Singh is at this moment in Moscow, and offering to start a revolt amongst the Sikhs. He wants to help the Russians invade India, if they'll promise to restore him to the throne in Lahore when the British have been wiped out.'

Quentin sat quietly drawing on his pipe for a few moments.

Simon leaned back in his chair, locked his hands behind his head and closed his eyes. 'Many of us still have memories of the atrocities thirty years ago during the Great Mutiny,' he said quietly. 'Nothing like that must ever be allowed to happen again.'

Quentin gazed through the window. 'Well, I can tell you that this news has raised alarm along all the Western borders here. Our intelligence-gatherers are being sent out in force.'

He opened another envelope and scanned the contents. 'Good! At last

Richard has been given something to do. He's ordered to find the Russian botanists and see what they're really doing here.'

He sent for Richard to come to the office, and while they waited, Quentin looked at Simon. 'Can I persuade you to embark on another expedition straight away?'

Simon gave a wry grin. 'You're thinking that an archaeological trek would provide a perfect cover for some intelligence-gathering? Of course, and I'm sure nobody would be surprised to see me take on an assistant named Eldridge.'

When Richard joined them, he found Quentin and Simon at the desk, already surrounded by open maps and intelligence reports.

'Your orders have just arrived, old chap,' Quentin said, handing him the letter. 'Pull up another chair, and give me your thoughts on an idea I've been talking about with Simon.'

The trio discussed the expedition and traced routes from the mountains to the desert. They estimated the number of porters, camels and horses that would be needed, the equipment for an expedition, and provisions. It was destined to be a long, rough journey.

Quentin could see Simon's interest growing as he studied the maps.

'I know for certain that no archaeological work has ever been done anywhere around that area.' He looked at Quentin with a question in his eyes. 'I'm sure it would add authenticity to our expedition if I had permission to do a little digging along the way?' He noted Richard's frown, but Quentin gave a nod of agreement.

'I'll leave that to your judgement, gentlemen,' he said. 'But, when you catch up with the Russian couple, they might find the expedition more convincing if you have a few genuine antiquities to show them. They're not fools.'

'Well, I'm sure we could spend a day or so digging somewhere,' Richard said without great enthusiasm. 'When do we leave?'

'Ah.' Quentin cleared his throat, looking from one to the other. 'There is one more important addition to the party, gentlemen.'

'I can't see anything we've overlooked,' Simon said.

Quentin shuffled through the pile of orders on his desk until he found the one he was looking for, and passed it to Richard. He read it and frowned.

'They want a Russian interpreter to go with us. Who's it to be?'

Quentin lifted his shoulders in a show of helplessness. 'I have no interpreter here, apart from Georgina Larssen.'

Richard's jaw dropped. 'Good God, Quentin, you can't ask her! Her – her parents would never allow it!'

'Oh, I doubt they'd oppose anything Georgina had set her mind on,' Simon said. 'But perhaps it's the lady herself who should first be consulted.'

Quentin already had a pen in his hand. 'I'll send a note and ask Doctor Larssen if we may call at the Mission this evening. After dark.'

Erik Larssen frowned when Quentin voiced his request for Georgina to travel with the English party. Natasha almost skipped with excitement, and Georgina remained glacially calm, avoiding eye-contact with the three Englishmen.

'I appreciate your wish to remain non-aligned in political matters, Doctor, and I can promise that if this wasn't a matter of the greatest urgency, I wouldn't be here,' Quentin said in official tones. He looked towards Georgina. 'There is nobody on my staff who understands Russian as you do.'

'Yes, yes, Georgina is most fluent.' Natasha couldn't hide her enthusiasm for the venture. Georgina's expression gave away nothing.

Erik shook his head again. 'I'm not happy with your plan,' he said. 'There is every chance of my daughter being recognized by someone along the way, and that would be most embarrassing for the Swedish Mission.'

Quentin pursed his lips thoughtfully for a moment. 'Yes, of course, I do appreciate that,' he said, and his eyes darted around the five faces watching him. 'If, however, Georgina was seen to be travelling in the company of someone to whom she had just become engaged – say, for instance, er – Richard – it would be perfectly natural. . . .'

'No! Absolutely not!' gasped Georgina.

'Ridiculous suggestion!' Richard growled. 'Impossible.'

The vehemence of their united protest produced an emotionally charged silence in the room. Then Georgina took a deep breath and looked at Erik.

'Quite frankly, Father, I'd like to be useful on this expedition,' she said matter-of-factly, 'and I think it could be done without implicating the Mission.'

They all waited.

'Quentin, your idea would certainly answer any questions about the Swedish doctor's daughter travelling with two British archaeologists. And, more importantly, the Russian man and his wife might be less suspicious if there was a woman in the party.' There was no sound in the room but the ticking of the clock on the mantel. 'So – if Simon has no objection – I'd agree to be his fiancée for however long the journey takes.'

She tilted her head at him questioningly. He drew breath as if to speak, but for a moment seemed surprisingly frozen by indecision.

'Oh, yes, yes, how splendid!' Natasha laughed and clapped her hands. 'And Richard will be your chaperon, of course.'

Richard struggled unsuccessfully to formulate a logical protest to fling into the arena. He looked at Simon's drawn face. Discomfort? Why was the man not instantly accepting Georgina's proposal?

At last Simon took a breath and smiled. He crossed the carpet and, with a charade of courtly manners, took her hand and raised it to his lips.

'I am honoured, Georgina,' he said, 'and tomorrow I'll produce an engagement ring for your finger.' His voice was surprisingly unsteady, and Richard had to remind himself that what he was watching was nothing more than a pantomime. There was no reason why he should experience this gut-wrenching misery.

Tears of delight sprang to Natasha's eyes, and she wanted to run next door immediately and invite the Hakvins to come and join in the congratulations. Georgina threw her a stern look, but Quentin agreed. 'Why not add a little authenticity to our plans?' he said.

'I was very presumptuous, Simon,' Georgina said later as they stood together sipping Birget Hakvin's heady apricot brandy. 'I hope you don't mind too much about this engagement business. I should have asked you about it first, but the idea suddenly popped into my head.'

'Because you feel safer with me than you do with Richard?' His observation made her flush. 'And, of course, you're quite right to feel safe with me, my dear. My dangerous years are long gone.'

'Oh, no, that's not it at all. I'm sorry. Oh, Simon, if you don't like this arrangement—'

'I have a feeling the only part I'm going to regret will be the day we come back to Kashgar, and you tell me you've changed your mind about our engagement,' he said, keeping his voice low so they couldn't be overheard. 'But, never fear, I'll insist you keep the ring.'

Natasha could see that Erik's enthusiasm for Georgina's journey didn't match her own. Erik wanted Georgina safely home with him; Natasha wanted her as far away as possible from Gregori Suvorov.

For the next few days, while Quentin studied fresh reports on the sightings of the Russian couple, Simon and Richard went openly about the business of organizing a permit from the Tao-tai for their expedition. Then horses, camels and porters were hired, and tents and provisions bought, along with timber to be made into packing-cases for archaeological finds.

After dinner, Richard and Simon sat smoking on the unlit veranda while

Quentin worked in his office. They lay back in their chairs, both deep in thought, watching the blaze of stars above them in the blue-black night sky.

At last Simon stirred and stubbed out his cigar. 'I think, old chap, we should clear the air between us before we set out into the desert with Georgina Larssen.'

'I really don't want to talk about her,' Richard said, drawing deeply on his cigar. 'We had orders to take a Russian translator with us, and she was the only candidate. That's the end of the matter, as far as I'm concerned.'

'Lie to me if you must, Richard, but don't lie to yourself,' Simon said gently. 'It's very clear you have strong feelings towards her.'

Richard bit off an expletive.

'Very well, we won't mention it again after this,' Simon said, 'but right now I have two things you're damned well going to hear.' His voice was husky. 'Firstly, I'm aware of the rift that's developed between you and Georgina, and I think you're the greatest fool on God's earth to be turning your back on a woman like her. And secondly, while I have the deepest affection for Georgina, you have my assurance that throughout this whole charade, I have no intention of taking advantage of the position I've been placed in. Ever.'

'Please keep out of this, Simon. We don't need your concern because Georgina and I have come to a very clear understanding that whatever – whatever—' There was a catch in his voice, and he stood up to throw his cigar over the balustrade, keeping his back to Simon while he watched the glowing stub fall into the garden. 'Of course I have strong feelings towards her, damn it, but she and I both know that once this business is over, our lives will inevitably move in different directions.'

Simon rose from his chair and came to stand beside him. 'I'll say it again, Richard: you're a fool. What's holding you back? Your army career? Your family? Marry the girl and hang the consequences.'

Richard leaned forward to rest his elbows on the balustrade. 'You have my assurance that the kindest thing I can do for Miss Larssen is *not* to marry her.'

'What are you so afraid of?'

Richard gave a sigh that was almost a groan. 'All right, yes, Georgina and I have been very close, but it was her decision as much as it was mine to take the affair no further.'

Simon made a sound of astonishment spiced with disbelief that instantly raised Richard's defensive hackles.

'Tell me,' he said, straightening, 'why is it that men who choose to remain bachelors inevitably think they're qualified to pontificate on the necessity of shackling every love affair into a marriage that would probably end in making

81

both parties miserable? I assure you, I know what I'm talking about.'

Simon held his tongue, pulled his cigar case from a pocket, opened it and offered one to Richard. He accepted it wordlessly, and the time it took to prepare and light them presented an opportunity for heated feelings to cool. The two men perched themselves side by side on the balustrade, and for a time sat silently with their own thoughts.

'Actually, Richard, I'm a widower,' Simon said at last. 'But I've been one for so long it's easier to maintain the bachelor-image, than to be reminded that once – briefly – I had a wife called Anne.'

'Oh, God, Simon, my apologies for being such an offensive idiot. I had no idea – I mean— How long ago?'

'She was killed in front of me during the Mutiny in '57. I'd come out to India to marry her a month before, and we'd just arrived back from our honeymoon in Kashmir when the Mutiny broke out, and hell erupted right across the country.'

They both drew deeply on their cigars for a few moments. 'You were in the army?' Richard asked.

Simon shook his head. 'Lord, no. I was certainly no warrior, but Anne's father handed me a rifle when the sepoys stormed the house and, I can assure you, I learned a lot about marksmanship that day. I wanted Anne to stay beside me. British women and children were being massacred on the road in front of us as they tried to escape. I thought I could keep her safe.'

Richard gave a wordless murmur, and waited, sensing that Simon had more to say.

'D'you know, I've always felt that Georgina Larssen is very like Anne. Not in appearance – far from it. Anne was small and dark-haired, but Georgina has the same kind of determination – stubbornness – recklessness – that I loved so much in Anne.'

Richard felt his throat tightening. 'Doctor Larssen once told me he thought Georgina sometimes needed protection from her own courage.'

'That's it exactly! It was Anne's courage that killed her.' He gazed with unseeing eyes across the dark garden. 'She must have seen the little girl under the upturned cart.' He had to stop and clear his throat. 'We'd just witnessed the mother's death – the sickening frenzy of her mutilation – and before I realized what she was doing, Anne was running from the house, trying to reach the child before the sepoys found her and hacked her to death, too.'

The words were coming fast. Richard had heard enough, but Simon couldn't stop now.

'The buildings around us were burning, and I saw Anne run through the smoke. I tried to stop her; I saw the bayonets close in around her, saw her fall under them – heard her screams. . . .' He stopped momentarily and swallowed. 'A bullet hit me and I went down at that point.' His voice was under control again, and after he had thrown away the stub of his cigar, he stood and brushed an unseen ash from his jacket.

'So, there you have it, Richard, and I'd be glad if you'd keep all that to yourself.'

'You can count on it,' Richard answered, and extended his hand. 'Perhaps between us both, we can make sure that Georgina is delivered safely back to her parents when this job is completed.'

CHAPTER ELEVEN

Now that Miss Larssen was away travelling, Ho Sung, the Chinese attendant, was delighted with the new order of seniority at the hospital. He felt great pride to be standing beside Doctor Larssen and assisting him during surgery. He spent less time now in the dispensary, for the doctor's wife had taken his place each morning to grind compounds and mix syrups.

Ho Sung had been surprised when Mrs Larssen first came to stand beside him at the bench, wanting to learn his skills, eager for him to explain what each bottle and jar contained. She had followed his instructions precisely, and now she was able to prepare many of the doctor's prescriptions without calling for help more than once or twice a morning. She also talked with the herb-sellers when they delivered medicinal plants and roots collected deep in the mountains. She wanted to understand all about their properties, she'd told Ho Sung. Wouldn't it be shocking if one day she made a mistake and unknowingly included some poisonous herb in a bottle?

Simon's caravan turned east to skirt the desert where the sandhills curled one after the other like fossilized waves on some vast yellow ocean. Away to their right stood the great, snow-capped line of the Kunlun mountains, the daunting barrier to the mysterious kingdom of Tibet lying beyond.

The weather was still cool enough for them to travel all through the day, and at night Simon and Richard huddled over maps in their tent.

Initially, Georgina and Richard had each tried to ignore the other's presence, which amused Simon, and he cheerfully paid no attention to the stiffness between them. As the days passed, they found it impossible to remain aloof, and good humour began to creep out at unexpected times, until a comfortable, easy companionship at last settled into the daily routine.

The deeper they travelled into the remote region, the harder it was for Simon to contain his glee, and his enthusiasm was infectious. 'Lord knows what might be waiting to be found out there in the desert,' he said at least once a day. News of his progress along the Silk Road filtered ahead through the scattered villages, and people came out to see the English archaeologist, offering to sell antiquities they'd found.

While Simon bargained, Richard and Georgina spoke to the local people. Had a Russian lady and gentleman come this way? The villagers shook their heads.

Their camel-drivers gossiped, and word spread that travelling with the expedition was a woman with strange red hair, who was said to possess great healing powers. Men and women with aches and fevers sometimes came to ask her help, and she dosed them with quinine and aspirin. Once she was called to visit a passing westbound caravan to set a camel-driver's broken femur, and sometimes she produced a bottle of elixir for a coughing child.

Richard looked across at her now, standing beside the campfire with her hands at her waist, stretching to ease an aching back. She was dusty and untidy, and dark rings of weariness circled her eyes, but never once on their journey had she uttered a complaint. Simon was right. He was a fool not to tell her how deeply he felt.

'Bring your lamps and come in here quickly,' Simon called from the door of his tent. He was standing beside a broadly grinning youth. 'Look what this lad has brought.'

On the folding table, Simon had spread several faded and flimsy sheets of birch bark covered with a strange script. 'This is absolutely marvellous,' he said, and slapped the man on the shoulder. 'They're clearly dated from the seventh century, and all about mundane matters such as who has failed to pay taxes, deeds of loans and – look at this one! – it appears to be a petition for the recovery of a donkey that had been hired out and not returned.'

'Are there more where these came from?' Georgina asked, and Simon nodded. 'Richard, I must detour, just for a couple of days.' He was as excited as a boy on Christmas morning. 'These scraps show that a civilization flourished somewhere here more than a thousand years ago.' He rubbed his palms together. 'Let's go and see what's there, and if I find it's worth serious digging, I'll come back another time.'

'Oh, I'm looking forward to this,' Georgina said. 'I take it we'll leave at dawn?'

But it was well before first light when the camp was woken by the noisy arrival of a young man on a camel, pleading to talk with the red-haired healer.

Georgina listened, and her heart sank. 'I must go with this man,' she called as Simon and Richard appeared from their tents. 'He's come from a caravan camped just beyond those hills, and he says a woman there has gone into labour and she's in difficulty. And there are no other women.'

Georgina went to dress and pack what she needed, and when she left the tent, Richard was waiting with their horses saddled. Simon was beside him, and they were deep in conversation.

'It's settled, Georgina,' Richard called, shoving his compass into a pocket. 'Simon is going ahead, as planned, and after you've done whatever has to be done, we'll follow him out to his diggings. I've got the bearings.'

'Thank you,' she said to them both.

'Take care.' Simon helped her mount.

Stones flew up from the hoofs of their horses as Richard and Georgina followed the man to the caravan camped beyond a line of hills five miles away. Dawn had brightened into day by the time they reached the young woman, the wife of the head camel-driver. The men stood about helplessly as Georgina knelt beside the girl, with the distraught father hovering over her shoulder, watching in horror.

'Richard, he's making things more difficult for me here,' Georgina called. 'Can you persuade him to light a fire? Find more water? We're going to be here for a long time, I fear.'

Richard and the men moved to the other side of the rocks, and stayed there until at last Georgina called for the father to come and greet his new son. As well as thanking Allah, she told him, he must thank his wife for her strength and determination to stay alive throughout the ordeal. The exhausted girl smiled.

'If we travel fast, we might be able to meet up with Simon before dark,' Richard said as they set out. He checked the compass bearings and they rode hard towards a line of red cliffs in the distance. The sun stood high above them; the air was still.

'Is it much further?' she called as the sun slid westwards. He followed her glance over their shoulders at the farway horizon to the east, where the sky was becoming an ominous shade of yellow, and he let out an oath.

'Ride like fury into that gorge, Georgina! Don't stop for anything. We're going to be hit by the *kara-burhan*!'

Georgina had never experienced the black hurricanes of the desert, but she'd heard tales of them. She swung her horse and kicked it into a gallop across the stony ground, and they were almost to the shelter of the cliffs when quite suddenly the air began to move. An explosion crashed around them, and the light flickered unsteadily, shading down from clear yellow to dark umber, which grew still darker.

The horses, sensing the danger, stretched themselves to the limits, stumbling occasionally as they raced over the open ground, until the appalling violence of the storm burst in to them. The darkness deepened as sand and pebbles were lifted up, whirled and dashed down around the horses, accompanied by the howl and roar of the storm.

Georgina was struck by a force of wind so violent she felt herself pushed sideways from the saddle. Terrified, she threw her arms around the horse's neck, but it was impossible to keep a grip on the mane and stop herself from being plucked off by the screaming blast. It blew the breath back down her throat till she thought she would suffocate.

Crouching low to the ground, she covered her face with her hands, and a moment later, Richard was beside her, struggling to take off his jacket, wrapping it around her head. They struggled – sometimes crawled – to find shelter against the red cliffs where they lay with their backs to the wind, his body stretched protectively behind hers. The terrified horses disappeared into the boiling darkness.

After an hour, the wind dropped to gale-force and he dragged her to her feet. 'Come on!' he shouted close to her ear, 'the *burhan* will come again. We need to find a safer place before the next one hits.'

The light in the sky changed minute by minute – yellow, green, yellow again, black suddenly, when they could see nothing, then yellow once more. They followed the contours of the red rock walls of the gorge before the next blast struck with the shriek of a thousand banshees, and the desert rose up to flail and suffocate them again.

In the darkness, Richard pulled her into an opening in the rock wall, and together they struggled into a defile which was angled away from the main force of the terror. They crept further along it until the twisting cleft surprisingly ended in a wide, bowl-shaped opening. By the yellow light of the storm they saw a line of caves cut high into the rock wall facing them, and scrambled to a worn flight of steps. He was behind her, holding her when she stumbled, dragging her when her strength faltered. They struggled up the steps leading to the caves, fingernails breaking as they clawed their way on hands and knees, fighting the force of the wind, until they reached the relative shelter of the first cave and sank on to the floor, panting from exhaustion and terror. He pulled her to him; she lay huddled in his arms, trembling, occasionally letting out a deep sob. He could feel her heart pounding hard against his ribs as the roar of the *burhan* echoed around the cave.

'We could have died out there,' she said again and again as she clung to him. 'I pray Simon and the men are safe.'

'Tomorrow we'll find them,' Richard said, 'but now, while there's still some light, we must find a more sheltered place.' He brushed the dust and sand away from her face and helped her to her feet. They moved deeper into the temple complex, too exhausted to do anything more than glance at the paintings that covered every wall and ceiling.

They groped their way into a dark, protected corner and fell to the floor. All sense of time was lost as they lay together in a place where the *burhan* no longer threatened. Whether night had fallen, or whether it was still the storm that ruled the outside world, was immaterial to them during those long hours of darkness.

She lay in his arms; his closeness gave her comfort, and carried them deeper into a dark velvet haze where the rest of the world no longer existed.

'I love you, Georgina,' he said thickly, with his lips against her forehead. 'I'm empty and incomplete without you; I want to make you part of my life for ever.'

She made a sound of surprise.

'Believe me, I've never felt like this before.' The pressure of his fingers on her arm tightened. 'Perhaps one day—? Would you wait?'

'Richard, nothing has changed. We agreed to be lovers, but we didn't pretend we would ever have a *tomorrow*.' The roar of the wind outside had dropped to a moan, and a sense of peace infused her. 'Of course I'll wait for you.'

There was a flagrant promise in the way her body arched against his, and she sensed his instant response. Her fingers fumbled in the darkness to undo their buttons, and the heat spread under her skin. She was filled with a hunger for him as she lay on him and kissed his face, traced the outline of his lips with her tongue and surrendered completely to the moment, to all that she was, to all that was him. Her hands slipped between his legs to caress his yearning flesh, then she sighed as she unhesitatingly guided it home.

For a moment he forgot how to breathe; his heart thundered and pleasure rushed and rose through him like a tide. It swept him up, caught him, spun him, then flung him high – and he shattered in her hands.

She kissed him again. 'I love you, Richard. I'll wait till the end of time.'

They lay locked together, scarcely stirring, until they woke to find a yellow light had crept into the sky and the air outside was silent. They stretched cramped muscles, and smiled at each other as she brushed back the sweep of hair on his forehead; then they sighed and climbed to their feet, straightening their clothes. Richard looked up and peered through the gloom towards the far wall of the cave.

She heard his sharp intake of breath and followed his gaze to a huge, golden shape looming down on them. She stared at it incredulously and moved closer. He came up behind her and wrapped his arms around her waist. 'So, the Golden Pagoda isn't just a myth,' he breathed against her cheek.

A tremble ran through her. 'Is this merely a coincidence, Richard, or were you and I meant to find it?' She gripped his arms tightly. 'Can't you feel something happening inside you when you look at it?'

They stood in awed silence, looking up at the details of the majestic seven-storeyed image slowly emerging in the growing light. She leaned her head against his chest; she felt giddy with the joy of love. This would have been the perfect moment to tell him she was sure now that she was carrying his child. For all her clever calculations that promised there would be no risk of falling pregnant when they'd made love at the waterfall, nature had laughed and played the trump card.

She was well overdue now, and absurdly happy about it.

What would Richard do if she told him? Marry her immediately to preserve her honour, and walk away from his duty, then carry into their married life a burden of guilt, or resentment, because she had forced him to leave his work unfinished?

'I'll wait, Richard, I promise, however long it takes,' she'd said. If she loved him less, she would have told him now. But, loving him as she did, she kept silent.

They stood at the foot of the Golden Pagoda as the sun rose and light crept further into the cave, bringing a unique luminescence to the painting on the wall.

'So, now we know the message Simon found in the well wasn't just the hallucination of a dying priest.' He kissed the top of her head and dropped his arms. 'What else is to be found here?'

She stayed numbly in front of the pagoda while he moved about the cave, searching in dark corners, under drifts of sand until, with a crow of victory, he swooped on a well-worn prayer wheel lying behind a fallen rock.

'Look! Here's our confirmation that the priest was here a few weeks ago.' He carried it into the rays of dusty sunlight slanting in to hit the floor of the cave, and with some difficulty, unscrewed the top. Packed inside the simply decorated cylindrical copper base were sheets of tissue-fine paper, all closely written in a spidery hand. He scanned some quickly.

'These ones look like prayers written in Tibetan,' he said, more to himself than to Georgina, who was still transfixed in front of the golden wall painting.

'We must bring Simon back to see this,' she said without turning her head.

'Yes, but first look at what we've got here.' She saw the papers in his hand. 'They're written in British code.'

The light in the cave grew brighter each minute as Richard stood leafing through the papers, his frown deepening. 'It's difficult to decipher, but I think there's something about a Russian force in Ferghana – a gathering of horses – no, a gathering of Mongol horsemen on the plains – thousands? – being trained by Russian officers.' He gave a huff of disbelief. 'Mercenaries being trained by Russian officers to invade India from the north?' He shook his head and shoved all the papers into an inside pocket of his jacket. 'I'll have to put these in order and work through them later.'

'Doesn't this place infuse you with the most wonderful feeling of serenity?' she said, and reached out tentatively to touch the base of the painting where pieces of plaster had been chipped off. The paint felt rough under her fingertips; the plaster crumbled. She caught a piece as it fell, and held it on her palm for a moment before she slipped it into the pocket of her skirt. If anyone ever needed a talisman, she did right now.

'Are you ready to leave?' Richard asked. 'I'm afraid it's going to be a long walk to reach Simon's camp. And we need to find water.'

They stayed a moment longer, taking one last look at the golden image. 'We must always remember this place, Richard. The Golden Pagoda heard our promise, it knows our secrets.'

He stroked the back of his hand across her cheek. 'How could I forget the promises we've made here? You're mine, and always will be, Georgina.'

CHAPTER TWELVE

The reality of their situation asserted itself once they left the cave and faced the desert. The yellow sky hung heavy with the dust from yesterday's *burhan*, and everywhere on the ground, sand and stones were piled in drifts against the cliffs.

Richard took regular compass readings once they were back in the wide gorge. Georgina had lost all sense of direction during the storm.

He drew her a rough map in the sand. 'We're here,' he said, 'and Simon should have reached his site – about here – before the storm hit yesterday.'

'How far?'

'Far enough,' he said, 'and without horses, we won't reach it today.'

They kept to the shady side of the gorge, but walking through the sand was tiring, and the glare hurt their eyes. Their hats had been lost when the *burhan* struck, and the food and water bottles had disappeared with their horses.

Her throat was dry; neither of them tried to speak. They trudged on, side by side, surrounded by the high wind-carved walls of red rock, hearing no sound but the crunch of their own boots on the floor of the gorge. Each hour, Richard declared a halt and they rested for ten minutes, with their backs propped against the rocks. It wasn't difficult to ignore the hunger, but as her thirst increased her tongue swelled, and she picked up a pebble to suck.

By late afternoon her head was swimming. Occasionally she staggered, and it was Richard's arm around her waist that kept her knees from crumbling. His own lips were dry and cracked, and when he called the final halt for the day, she slid from his grasp to stretch, exhausted, full length on the stones. He lay beside her, holding her hand. 'Tomorrow,' he croaked. 'We're doing well. We'll find Simon tomorrow.'

She could do no more than grunt her relief, but just when she thought he'd fallen asleep, he suddenly raised himself on one elbow. 'Listen!'

She heard nothing.

He scrambled to his feet, and pulled her with him. 'Listen! Can't you hear it?'

His arm was around her again, urging her to stumble another hundred yards to a cleft in the wall where a spring of clear water bubbled from the rock and ran into a pool below. They dropped to their knees, cupped their hands and splashed the water into their mouths, on their faces, necks, heads. They pulled off their boots and paddled into the cool, shallow water, splashing, laughing with relief, turning in circles as they hugged each other.

They slept beside the spring and drank deeply from it again the next morning before Richard judged the direction of their march, and they climbed out of the gorge turning north before the sandhills began. Here, the heat became fiercer, and the glare brighter. She stumbled and he carried her in his arms when she thought she could go no further. Shade was harder to find, mirages appeared and disappeared as the sun crept higher. Shimmering visions of green oases, cities of tall buildings, whole caravans—

Now there was a rider on a horse and two men with camels coming towards them out of the mirage ahead. The horse was travelling fast, the camels lagged behind. A voice was calling; Richard gave a cracked laugh, put Georgina down, and waved his arm.

The horse reached them, and it was Simon who flung himself from the saddle. 'Thank God you're safe, Anne. Thank God.'

'I'm all right, Simon. Truly. Richard looked after me.' Simon pulled out his water-bottle and put it to her lips.

Emotions were high, and it was only Richard who heard Simon call her *Anne*.

'We've found the Golden Pagoda, Simon! It's magnificent,' she said, and wiped the back of her hand across her cheek. 'We hid in the cave when the *burhan* hit yesterday. Are you and the men all right? Did you find shelter?'

'Yes, thank God. We'd reached the site before it struck, but I can't tell you how relieved I am to see you both, Richard,' Simon said, reaching for his hand.

The two camel-drivers pulled up beside them and the animals sank, grumbling, to the ground.

'Our camp is only about five miles on,' Simon said as he helped Georgina to mount his horse. 'And I had news this morning that the Russian couple has been seen at an oasis just a day or two ahead of us.'

Simon had made camp inside the crumbling mud-brick walls of a vast city half-covered by sand. 'Just look at it! This is every archaeologist's dream,' he said with an expansive gesture as they rode in. 'It was called *Niya*. There's no

time to linger now, but I'll come back and dig with a full team one day. Look!'
he reached into a bag near his tent. 'See what I've already picked up – these
coins and shards of pottery show remarkable Greek and Persian influences.
Who knows what else is waiting under the sands?'

Georgina went to her tent and the canvas bath was erected. With the desert
grit and sand washed from her body and hair, she lay dozing on her bedding,
listening to the men outside discussing the priest's coded reports as Richard
deciphered them.

'There's something going on here that gives me an uncomfortable feeling,'
she heard him say. 'Can all this be true? It's almost as if the old priest has seen
too much to be believed. As you know, Simon, it's usual for one agent to
gather no more than a few threads of information for Headquarters to eval-
uate.'

'This fellow seems to have discovered the whole Russian strategy for an
attack by horsemen through the Pamirs,' Simon said in a tone of disbelief.
'And then he was murdered.' His voice softened. 'Could this have happened
to your friend, Mottram, too?'

She heard Richard shuffling the papers. 'Lord knows,' he said. 'There's a
lot I'll have to clarify, and I'm hoping that when we meet up with the Russian
couple Georgina will discover something to throw light on the puzzle.' He
gave a grunt of frustration. 'This all seems just a little too obvious, and it gives
me a feeling that we're being led by the nose.'

There was a long silence and Georgina again drifted to the edge of sleep,
until Simon spoke. 'Now, tell me about the Golden Pagoda.'

'Well, that's certainly something more positive to talk about,' Richard said,
'and I can show you the location on a map. Every cave is covered with remarkable wall paintings, but the pagoda itself is truly spectacular. It must be nearly
thirty feet high, and the colour positively glows. There's a bit of damage to
some of the lower parts, but in the main it seems intact.'

'I gather you were impressed,' Simon said, and Georgina heard Richard's
answering chuckle.

'Oh, I was certainly impressed. In fact, I'll never forget the time I spent in
that cave.'

Georgina smiled as she listened. She reached for the talisman she'd taken
from the Golden Pagoda, and circled it over her flat stomach. She would never
forget that time in the cave, either, any more than she would forget the day at
the waterfall with Richard.

Georgina knew that Natasha was going to be furious when she heard there
was a baby on the way. But Erik Larssen would understand. Erik was compas-

sionate and strong, and he would help her, love her, love her child. She held her talisman tightly. One day Richard would come, and his child would be waiting.

'You'll be pleased to know our horses were found this afternoon,' Richard said, when she joined the men for dinner beside the camp fire. 'My animal has a cut on his foreleg, but the other seems sound. They'll be ready to travel in the morning, if you are.'

'I feel perfectly well, thank you,' she said quickly. 'So, tell me, what am I to do when we meet the Russians?'

'First of all, I want you to be careful.' He was no longer smiling. 'The most important thing is for you to be accepted by them, Georgina, and try to gauge what they're doing out here.'

Erik Larssen's face was tight with concern as he stood quietly in the doorway of the dispensary watching Natasha sitting at the bench and lethargically grinding a compound. He was aware how little she'd been sleeping; the dark circles under her eyes were testament to that. Even Quentin McCallum's recent news from Richard, reporting that Georgina was well and they would all soon be on their way home, had not helped to calm her. Actually, it had even increased her tension.

At that moment she looked up, and her expression tore at his heart. What had happened to put this fear into the eyes of the woman he loved beyond all else? He crossed the floor now and took her hand. 'Listen to me, Natasha. I can't bear to see you like this. Tell me what is worrying you. Let me help you. Anything. . . .'

'Don't concern yourself, my dearest,' she said. 'I promise it will soon be over.'

Two days of fast travel into a landscape of barren hills and waterless gullies brought Simon's party to an insignificant oasis where, in the shade of a clump of tamarisk and artemisia trees, a man and woman sat near the entrance of a tent, almost as if they'd been anticipating guests. On the other side of the water six horses grazed, and two natives with rifles slung over their shoulders lounged not far away, smoking long pipes.

At the approach of Simon's sizeable caravan, the woman rose and helped the man to his feet where he stood leaning on her arm.

The woman was aged around forty, with a square, thin-lipped face and thick blonde hair that was cut short. Her baggy native trousers were tucked into long boots and she wore a high-necked Russian blouse.

'Good evening,' Simon called to them with his easy charm. 'I hope it will not inconvenience you if my party shares this location for a few days?'

'We leave soon,' the woman said curtly. Her accent was thick, and she was obviously uncomfortable with the English language.

The man beside her smiled and nodded as the party dismounted, and Simon led Georgina, with Richard two paces behind, towards the couple. The grey-haired man was probably about the same age as the woman, but so thin and ill-looking it was hard to judge. He wore European clothing, none too clean, and rimless spectacles on his long nose. Before he was able to speak, he had to draw in several shallow breaths.

'Parvel Levka, sir. And my wife, Irena.' He offered Simon his unsteady hand.

'Delighted to meet you, Mr and Mrs Levka.' Simon bowed. 'Please allow me to introduce my fiancée, Miss Larssen, and my assistant Mr Eldridge.' The party acknowledged the introductions with a formality that seemed more than a little incongruous in the circumstances, Richard thought wryly.

'Your reputation precedes you, Mr Davenport,' Parvel Levka struggled to say. 'Even in St Petersburg, we have read for many years of your discoveries along the Silk Road.' He began to cough from the exertion of talking and held a handkerchief to his lips. 'Apologies,' he gasped.

'No more talk, Parvel,' his wife said sharply, and with a strong arm around his waist, she turned him towards the door of their tent. 'Make your camp far on the other side,' she said over her shoulder to Simon. 'My husband must have rest, not noise.'

'We will do our utmost not to disturb you, Madame Levka,' he said, signalling the camelmen to move to the other side of the oasis where the Levkas' two servants were sitting.

'We'll have to work quickly,' Richard said as they sat talking while their tents were erected and the cooking-fire started. 'Irena is obviously uncomfortable about our presence here, and I wouldn't be surprised if they simply disappeared into the night. They're travelling light. Four riding horses and two pack animals could get away quickly.'

Georgina shook her head. 'She can't travel with poor Mr Levka in that condition. The man is very ill indeed; I think he has consumption.'

When the sun had dipped beyond the horizon and dusk settled over the desert, Richard watched Irena Levka on the other side of the oasis. She was alone and sitting by a meagre cooking-fire; there was no sign of her two servants.

'Somehow I have a feeling that Mrs Levka's cooking skills might leave much to be desired,' he said, turning his head to catch a waft of their own savoury hare stew simmering in the pot. 'She and her husband might like to share some of our food tonight.' He threw Georgina a questioning look.

'What a kind, thoughtful man you are, Mr Eldridge,' she said, straight-faced. 'Yes. I'll knock on their door, bearing gifts, and they'll invite me in. I believe the Greeks perfected that tactic.'

'Remember to tread carefully, Georgina,' Simon added. 'We know what these people are capable of doing.'

CHAPTER THIRTEEN

As she carried the bowl of hot food towards Irena Levka on the far side of the oasis, Georgina slipped into her new character. With each step she became more and more an uncertain Englishwoman, overwhelmed by the harshness of this land. Miss Larssen was now someone starting to question the wisdom of her engagement to a man whose life's work was based in the desert.

'Madame Levka?' she called softly as she approached the Russians' camp and Irena looked up in surprise. She made no response.

'I have brought a little food for you and your husband,' Georgina said tentatively. 'Our men trapped a number of hares last night, and – and I thought, perhaps, in view of your husband's health—' She put the covered bowl on the ground next to Irena.

The woman lifted the lid and nodded dismissively, lowering her head again. 'Madame,' Georgina began, then sat down to face her across the dying fire, 'as we are alone, may I take this opportunity to speak with you, woman to woman?' She formed the English words slowly and carefully, but even so she noticed the Russian struggled to comprehend them.

'Woman to woman?' The Russian's accent was thick.

'Yes, Madame. Forgive me, but I am so desperately confused about – I mean, I think I may have made a terrible mistake in promising to marry a man who expects me to spend much of my life in a land that is so hostile to women and all that women want – need. He says I will learn—' She reached for a handkerchief and twisted it around her fingers. The Russian woman kept her gaze on the embers of the fire. 'Please tell me, Madame, how did you learn not to be afraid out here?'

She waited several long moments for Irena Levka to respond, and when at last she lifted her head, Georgina recognized two things: the Russian was very angry, and quite drunk.

'Go far away from me; I despise females such as you.' Her lips curled and her pale grey eyes blazed. 'You look a healthy woman and maybe even they have given you an education, yet you hide behind your skirts, determined to be useless.' After her first few words spoken in broken English, Irena had lapsed into Russian and Georgina pretended to look suitably bewildered.

'And you will continue to be useless all your life, because you have no *passion*. No passion for a man, no passion for making some meaning out of your own life. You float like a jellyfish. Passion, passion. Find passion and you'll overcome all fear.' With surprising agility she scrambled to her feet, left the food untouched, and went to the man who was coughing again.

Shadows on the canvas showed Irena moving about the tent, tending to her husband, crossing and re-crossing the floor. Occasionally, the man and woman spoke softly to each other, too softly for Georgina to catch their conversation.

She stood, picked up her lamp and walked away heavily past the embers of the fire, towards Simon's camp. In the shadows of the trees she stopped, put out the lamp and returned silently to lie in the dark, close beside the back of the tent. Parvel's voice was an indistinct whisper, but from Irena's passionate comments, Georgina caught the drift of their conversation. They were discussing botany.

The desert plant specimens they had collected and packed for exhibition in St Petersburg would by now have reached the rail-head at Samarkand, Irena's strong voice was reassuring her husband. 'They will be on next week's train, my darling, and soon your name will be known around the world. No one will ever be able to surpass the Levka Collection.' Alcohol slurred her words, but her passion was undimmed.

He made a comment which Georgina couldn't catch.

'Don't worry, Parvel, I'll personally oversee all the cataloguing. What's that? Of course I know where to find a specimen of it tomorrow.'

His whispered words were cut short when his cough overcame him again.

'Yes, yes, I'll ride up to the Shirgar Valley in the morning, and find the little *torenia*,' her voice faltered, 'and from now until the end of time, it will be known as the *torenia levkaii*, my love.'

He said something and Irena began to sob, seemingly as passionate in her grief as she was in everything else in her life. When her husband had settled, the lamp in the tent went out and Georgina heard Irena climb into bed beside him.

She moved silently away. It was difficult to reconcile the tender episode she'd just overheard with the fact that this man and woman, who expressed their love and shared a passion for exotic plants, had also, in all probability, played some part in the murders of a British officer and a Buddhist priest.

'I'd hardly rate my visit a success,' Georgina said when she rejoined Richard and Simon. 'Madame Levka didn't like me at all, and the food didn't interest her. All I overheard them talking about was collecting another specimen tomorrow, and discussing a shipment that's already on its way to St Petersburg.'

By the time she had dressed and presented herself for breakfast the next morning, the news had already reached Richard that Madame Levka and one of her servants had ridden out to look for plants growing between rocks in some valley to the south. The camelmen were always ready to pass on camp gossip.

Georgina and Richard looked at each other and raised their eyebrows. 'Perhaps this would be a good time for me to visit Mr Levka with a little of Doctor Larssen's famous cough elixir,' she said, delving into the box of medicines. 'It might at least soothe his throat.' She hesitated for a moment and looked at Richard. 'I've seen my father sometimes add a little extra laudanum at this stage of an illness.' Her words sounded like a question and he nodded slowly.

'Take care, sweetheart.'

A servant with a rifle across his knees sat idly by the door of the Levkas' tent when Georgina approached carrying the medicine bottle in a satchel slung over her shoulder.

'May I come in, Mr Levka?' she called, and his faint voice answered. She wasn't at all sure how to go about the business of gathering information. 'Look for the unlikely,' was all Richard had said.

Parvel Levka's head on the pillow was damp with sweat, and his red-rimmed, sunken eyes were ringed with dark circles. He blinked and strained to focus on her figure in the doorway. 'Please,' he said breathlessly. 'So kind of you.' His English was more fluent than his wife's.

'I've brought some cough elixir that you might find soothing, Mr Levka.' She smiled and put the bottle and spoon on a box beside him.

His sallow skin was stretched tightly and looked as thin as tissue paper; he lifted a veined hand and weakly indicated a chair. 'Do sit with me for a little.' He reached for a blood-splattered handkerchief and held it to his lips.

Every surface in the tent was strewn with boxes, papers and books. She stepped around the clutter, pulled a folding chair close to him, and resumed the role she'd adopted last night with Irena.

'Your wife is searching for specimens again this morning, Mr Levka? She seems to fear nothing in this terrible country. I doubt I'll ever learn such courage.'

His eyes were dark and bright, watching her sharply. His body might be near death, but she could tell his mind was alert still. She adopted her best bedside manner and when he returned her smile, she had no idea why those dark, watchful eyes in the helpless body should send a chill down her spine.

'Last night I heard you come to visit my wife, Miss Larssen,' he struggled to say. 'Understand, please, that Irena has always much passion – for love, for my work, for her work. Especially for *her* work. Her passion has always fired her to great heights.'

The speech brought on a paroxysm of coughing and blood-spitting. The servant came into the tent, but Georgina waved him away and tended to Parvel Levka herself. She wiped his lips and bathed the sweat from his face, propped him up on the stained pillows again, while all the time his hard, penetrating gaze remained fixed on her face. She put her ear near to his mouth to catch his whispered question.

'The time, Mr Levka? Why, it's already ten o'clock.' This information appeared to excite him and had the strange effect of causing his pupils to dilate. The eyes watching her movements now seemed as black as a reptile's.

'Would you like to sleep again?' She reached for the bottle of cough elixir. 'A little of this might help to make you more comfortable. Will you take a dose?'

He smiled thinly. 'I have no doubt it will ensure my sleep, Miss Larssen.' He opened his mouth and swallowed the laudanum-laced measure she slipped on to his tongue. 'I do hope you will stay in here with me until my wife returns. She, too, will be most grateful for your kindness, your compassion.'

He fought to find breath for the words that would have been entirely appropriate, if Georgina had not detected a sliver of sarcasm in the barely audible speech.

'Sleep peacefully, Mr Levka,' she said, struggling to hold a beatific smile. 'Of course I'll be here beside you when you wake.' She watched his lids drop slowly over the sharp, lizard-like eyes and gave a sigh of relief when she was no longer under his scrutiny.

She reached into her satchel for a notebook and pencil and moved quickly to examine the first stack of papers on the cluttered table. Richard needed information. What information? She skimmed through sketches, descriptions, locations of hundreds of plants discovered and classified by the Levkas during months of work. There was no doubting their professional dedication.

And now, while Parvel lay dying, his wife was out there somewhere, collecting more specimens. He'd said that Irena was a passionate woman, but surely at this moment her passions were ranked in an odd order.

Georgina looked through the disordered notebooks and correspondence and sheets of pressed flowers. She searched amongst clothes and in boxes of drying bulbs and roots. She glanced at her watch, then across at the man sleeping quietly. It was already midday; the search was taking her far too long. What was she looking for? What was concealed in this vast accumulation of botanical data?

Frustration mounted and the knot of anxiety in her stomach tightened as she reopened the first bulky notebooks, looking at them more closely, listening all the time for the sound of Irena's return. Parvel stirred and gave a cough, but his eyes remained closed and he settled again. Some of the pages she studied were neatly presented and illustrated, others had margins scrawled with rough calculations and dates. The tidy pages, she noted, were tightly written in one hand; the untidy ones were in a bolder script, which she intuitively felt belonged to Irena.

She flipped through the pages she had previously read, willing them to reveal the answers Richard needed. Only Irena's pages had notes in the margins. Georgina held her bottom lip between her teeth and frowned. It appeared that Irena had calculated the exact location of certain specimens. Perhaps the date noted beside each was the time of its flowering? The puzzle was, if Irena had given such detail on some plants, why was Parvel not following a similar system on the ones he described?

She went through Irena's entries again, listing the locations marked in the margins and the dates on those pages. She wrote them down and an interesting pattern started to emerge, although its significance was beyond her. Richard would know—

She heard no movement from the bed, but something made her turn to look at the Russian. He was awake and watching her, his eyes wide and bright. Her heart gave a leap, but she held his gaze and made no apology.

'You and Madame Levka have travelled far,' she said in Russian, and he laughed soundlessly. 'I've been reading about the plants that were collected in the Pamirs, after you arrived there from the Ferghana region.' Frustration boosted her audacity. 'By the way, when you were on the plains, did you see the army of Mongol horsemen being trained there to invade through the mountains? It seems to have been a poorly kept secret.' She came to stand beside his bed, looking down at his disease-ravaged body and feeling no pity.

'Oh, well done, Miss Larssen,' he breathed, 'there *is* passion in you after all.' His hard, black eyes shone with amusement and Georgina's gall rose.

'Indeed, Mr Levka,' she said, determined not to drop her poise. 'I always become passionate when good men are murdered: an officer named Mottram, a Buddhist priest. They can't have been the only ones to have seen the horsemen at Ferghana. Why did they have to die?'

'. . . more useful dead than alive,' was all she could comprehend of his whisper. His cough again overwhelmed him, and this time Georgina called in his servant to attend to him.

As she watched the Russian gasping, spitting blood, her loathing of the Levkas and their work swelled in her throat. She looked again at her watch. What passion for botany was keeping Irena from her husband's deathbed? This morning the men had said she'd ridden out before six o'clock with one servant and a packhorse. It was now almost seven hours. . . .

Irena had no intention of coming back! The realization burst upon her. And, of course, the woman would have taken with her whatever information was truly important. The confusion she'd left behind here in the tent had been designed to delay any search.

Georgina rushed to the door of the tent. Richard and Simon were sitting together in the shade of the tamarisk bushes, and the moment she appeared they were on their feet and running towards her with their rifles at the ready. When they entered the tent, Levka was lying back on the pillows, without even the strength to lift his hand to the corners of his bloodstained lips. He watched them with eyes that looked like polished onyx; and he was smiling grotesquely.

'Save your concern for him, gentlemen.' Georgina's tone was frigid, and they halted at the sight of the pitiful figure on the bed. 'He's known all along that Irena won't be returning here to play the loving wife.'

'She left him alone in this state?' Simon's tone was disbelieving.

'Oh, yes, indeed. Mr Levka described Irena as a passionate woman, and said her greatest passion was *her* work. It's clear now what work he meant.'

Parvel struggled to lift his head from the pillow. 'By now, Irena is well on her way to the Kunluns.' He forced out the words on a thin hiss of breath.

'She'll never get across the Tibetan border—' Richard began, but Georgina put a hand on his arm.

'Wait a moment,' she said. 'Last night I heard Irena promise to collect a plant specimen from the Shirgar Valley this morning. Which direction is that?'

'Nowhere near the Kunluns, I'll guarantee,' Simon muttered as Richard pulled a map from his inside pocket. She cleared a space on the table and they stood around it while Richard located the Shirgar Valley and with his finger traced a route westward from there towards the Tian Shans and into Russian territory.

He whistled. 'It's a possibility, I suppose.'

Levka lay silently, watching them with wild, half-closed eyes.

'Don't put the map away yet, Richard,' Georgina said, flipping through her notebook to find the list she'd made of Irena's calculations and dates. 'Do these figures make any sense to you?'

He studied the Russian's survey-readings closely and marked the positions on his map. They ran like tributaries of a river across the Pamirs into India. High mountain passes. Narrow and treacherous. No way through for heavy Russian artillery, but quite possible for the superb little Ferghana-bred Mongol horses to negotiate.

'What do the dates beside each one relate to?' she asked, and Richard shot a stony look into the eyes of the man on the bed.

'I have a suspicion about that, but when I catch up with Madame Levka I'm sure I'll find the confirmation I need.' He tore the page from Georgina's notebook and put it into his pocket along with the map.

'She will kill you!' Levka's words spat like venom from his mouth.

'Then I'll simply have to make sure I kill her first,' Richard snapped, and strode to the door of the tent. Georgina ran after him; Simon hung back by the side of the coughing man.

'What are you going to do?' asked Georgina.

'I'm going after her, sweetheart. It's possible that the dates you noted might relate to supply depots she's calculated to get those massed horsemen into Indian territory for an attack on the North.'

'And catch the British by surprise?'

He took her by the arms. 'I have no evidence yet, but I suspect that our Russian friends here might have been used by their masters in St Petersburg to create the illusion of an attack coming through the mountains. Just an intuition, but I must make sure it's been planned merely as a feint. Murdering Mottram and the priest might have been arranged just to focus British interest up here.'

His grip on her arms tightened and he swallowed hard while his eyes searched her face. 'I don't have the answers, but it's imperative I get this information about the situation back to my Colonel as fast as I can. I feel in my bones that if the British army and its artillery are sent up here, it would clear the way nicely for the Russians to bring their heavy guns into the south.'

'You think those dates in Irena's notes could be the key?' Her voice was tight and strained, but there was no crack in her composure. It was her heart that was shattering. At any moment he would leave her and go to face God knew what danger, still knowing nothing of his child inside her. Her own cruelty shook her.

He took her face between his hands, put his thumbs beneath her chin and tilted her face up to his. 'I love you, Georgina. I swear I'll find a way for us to make a life together. Thank you for everything. Simon will take you safely back to Kashgar.'

He kissed her, urgently, and then he was gone. She stood by the Russians' tent and watched him on the other side of the oasis, making his swift preparations for travel, then he swung into the saddle. A moment later, with a wave to her across the water, he and one of their men galloped towards a line of barren hills.

Her fingernails dug into her palms as she stood staring numbly at the cloud of dust raised by the flying hoofs. Simon came to her, and he was about to speak when they both heard Parvel Levka's cough stop suddenly and other sounds come from inside his tent.

They exchanged frowns, and she followed Simon back to the tent. On the bed, the Russian lay motionless with the soiled pillow over his face; the servant had an oil-lamp in each hand and was methodically splashing the contents on to Levka's body and everything he owned.

'Orders of Madame Levka,' the man said stonily. 'I follow her orders only.'

'Christ!' Simon said under his breath, and after a stunned moment, he took Georgina by the arm and dragged her away from the tent, and back to their own camp. They stumbled in their haste to leave the scene of the Levkas' final obscene act, and paused only once to look around when the smell of the burning tent and its contents reached them.

'It's nothing to concern us,' Simon called to their own men, who were rushing to the fire. 'The Russians have gone, and in the morning Miss Larssen and I will start back to Kashgar – with perhaps just one deviation.' He looked at her questioningly. 'Do you mind adding a few days on to our journey? Richard has given me the position of the Golden Pagoda.'

'Oh yes, you must see it.' The thought of going back to the cave without Richard was almost her undoing, and she needed to resurrect all her old skills to create an impression of sang-froid.

Simon seemed unconvinced by her performance. 'Come in here, my dear,' he said, and led her into Richard's tent, ignoring her half-hearted protest. 'Sit on that bed and drink this.'

Perched stiffly on the side of Richard's bed, she sipped the brandy Simon poured. He watched her silently, but with Simon, silence was a comfortable state. She finished the brandy, and he poured her another. Her insides were no longer shaking, and when she looked up at him he smiled.

'Right at this moment,' he said gently, 'I think you need to lie down and have a jolly good cry. Go on; try it.'

'Oh, no! No. Absolutely not! Please don't think. . . .' No further words were possible because suddenly her face was buried in Richard's pillow and deep, shuddering sobs drained the air from her lungs.

'Good,' whispered Simon, crouched beside her. 'Let it all out. Everything. And later, if you like, you can tell me about it.'

He pulled off her boots and covered her with a blanket. She heard him get up and leave the tent while she lay weeping with her arms wrapped around Richard's pillow and her face pressed into the lingering scent of him on the linen.

CHAPTER FOURTEEN

All the way back to the cave of the Golden Pagoda with Simon, Georgina struggled with her fears about Richard's confrontation with Irena Levka. Simon offered no useless platitudes of reassurance; he encouraged her to keep voicing her anxiety, until she invariably circled back to the point of reassuring herself that a highly trained British Intelligence Officer would certainly outmatch any cunning Russian woman.

'You may think this strange, Simon,' she said, as they rode together, 'but I feel almost sad to think that Richard probably had to kill a woman like Irena Levka.'

He looked at her in astonishment. 'Why?'

'I spent only a little time talking to her, but I think in some way – as women – we might have had ideas in common.'

He gave a scornful huff. 'You're joking, surely?'

'No, I'm not. I've always thought that life is so unfair to women who enjoy an education and are then left – in Irena's words – to float like useless jelly-fish through life, simply because they are not men. Despite everything, Irena did prove to be a powerful woman in a man's world. Her husband said he was proud of her passion.'

Simon looked at her thoughtfully. 'You could never be like Irena, thank God. She might have been clever and capable, but she was driven only by passion. History shows that passion becomes dangerous if it's not leavened with a good handful of *compassion*. No, believe me, Georgina, you had very little in common with a woman like Irena Levka.'

She allowed herself a grin. 'You have a remarkable way of putting things into perspective for me. You're the only person in the world I feel I can talk to openly about – oh, about everything. I do love you for that, you know.'

He looked at her quickly, and didn't answer.

*

The full moon was up before the caravan made camp in the gorge near the steps leading up to the ancient monastery. Simon was far too impatient to wait till daylight to visit the Golden Pagoda, and in the bright moonlight, Georgina led him up to the caves. Once inside, they held their lamps high, and his enthusiasm soared as they passed the decorated walls and ceilings on their way to the central chamber, where the image of the seven-storeyed Golden Pagoda glowed.

Again its effect on her was overwhelming. It had listened to the promises she and Richard had made as they lay together; and it knew the secret she had kept from him. She half-closed her eyes and could feel him standing behind her again, his arms around her waist, whispering words of love into her ear. She cried without tears for Richard who was now far away. She cried for the baby growing inside her because this child did not know the man who was its father. She cried for her own loneliness in the time ahead.

Please, please let him come back to me soon, her heart whispered.

Simon was beside the painting, scraping at some of the surrounding plaster with a penknife. 'I could get this off easily,' he said to her over his shoulder.

She barely heard his words for the wave of nausea that overcame her. 'Simon, I must go,' was all she managed to say before the bile rose in her throat. She'd had the same experience early this morning. And yesterday morning.

'What is it, Anne?' He was beside her in three paces. 'Are you ill?'

His arms were around her. He put his cheek against her clammy forehead. 'Dear God! You are ill!'

'No, please, please, Simon. I'm not ill, I promise.' She put her hand over her mouth as he helped her down the steps towards the caravan, then stood with his arm around her while she threw up on to the sand.

'Please don't fuss, Simon; this sickness is quite normal. I'm just a little dizzy now.'

'Protest as much as you like, my dear Georgina, but nothing is going to stop me fussing. Come and sit down.' He settled her on to a rug and gave her some cushions, then brought tea laced with brandy. 'So—?' he said with a smile, and raised his eyebrows at her as he settled himself at her side.

'So,' she said, 'now you know.'

'Does Richard know?'

She shook her head. 'How could I tell him in the middle of all that business with the Russians?'

'When will you tell him?'

'When the right opportunity comes.'

He frowned. 'What will you do until then?'

She heaved a long sigh and looked up into the night sky. 'I don't have many alternatives. I'll go back to the Mission, keep working alongside my father and have the baby. My mother will be furious with me, and the Hakvins will be rather shocked at first, but they're full of forgiveness.' She spoke with a tone of resignation. 'Whatever happens, I can always depend on Erik Larssen to look after me. He's the one person who won't stop loving me because I've become a fallen woman.'

'Georgina, let me give you—'

'No, Simon! Never. Thank you for whatever you were about to offer, but I won't accept help from anyone but my father.' She'd spoken more sharply than she intended. 'I've thought it all out: I'll stay to help him at the Mission until he retires, or until my son or daughter' – at this point a quaver crept into her voice – 'until my child reaches school age, and then, if I have to, I'll go to England and take up a teaching post.'

'What about Richard? If he had the slightest idea about this— Oh, Georgina, he must be told what has happened. After all, he did have a part in – I mean, he must take responsibility for. . . .'

'For seducing me? No, Simon, it was quite the opposite.' She smiled to herself as she looked down at her fingers teasing the tassel on the cushion. 'Eight weeks ago I begged him to make love to me. And I *promised* him there was no risk of my falling pregnant.' She lifted her eyes to Simon. 'I miscalculated badly.'

'I know Richard loves you, Georgina,' he said with a touch of impatience, 'and he'll be furious if you keep this from him.'

'And I'm just as sure that this isn't the time for revelations. Of course I want to spend my life with Richard, but with sabres rattling and bugles starting to blow all along the borders, who can tell where he'll be sent or what circumstances will keep him in India? The baby won't wait, so I'll do the waiting, and when the time is right, he'll come for me.'

Simon propped himself on one elbow. 'Richard Eldridge is a lucky man.'

'It's funny how people find each other and fall in love, isn't it?' she said idly. 'My mother has a theory about that, but tell me, Simon, were you once in love with someone called Anne? You've called me by that name on a few occasions.'

He seem startled, and for a moment his gaze remained locked with hers, then he looked away to stare into the flames of the camp-fire. 'Anne was my wife thirty years ago, and in many ways you remind me of her.'

She remained silent, while he repeated the account he'd given Richard about Anne and her horrifying death. The tears that welled in Georgina's eyes began to slide down her cheeks. When he finished his story he looked at her again and frowned.

'For God's sake, please don't cry, Georgina,' he said, and reached out to wipe away the tears with his fingers. 'Anne has been at peace for a long time now, and nothing can turn back the clock.'

She put her hand over his and brought his fingers to her lips. 'No, Simon, let me weep for Anne, and for the life that was stolen from her, and for all the years you should have had together.' Emotion overwhelmed her. 'If I am like Anne, then I know how she must have loved you.'

For a moment he remained frozen, then a tiny nerve jumped near the corner of his eye. He was breathing hard as he climbed to his feet, and seemed about to turn away when he hesitated and looked down with an expression that tore at her heart.

He held out a hand and she took it. She wanted to offer comfort, but suddenly his arms were around her and his face was buried in the curve of her neck, his breathing ragged. They held each other tightly and she could feel his loneliness.

Gradually his lungs fell back into a steady rhythm. 'My abject apologies for that impertinence—' he started to say as he dropped his arms from her and stepped back.

She gripped his shoulders and looked him steadily in the eye. 'You are my dearest friend, Simon. Here—' Before he could pull away she stood on her toes and kissed him lightly, swiftly on the mouth. 'There, that's a friendship kiss.'

Initially he was startled, then she saw a tiny tremor cross his lips. He lowered his head and hesitantly returned the kiss. 'Friendship,' he murmured.

Simon's work to remove the wall paintings from the caves required painstaking accuracy. He estimated it would take him seven days to remove and safely pack the Golden Pagoda and some of the other astonishing works of art in the caves, but Georgina could see it was going to be longer.

'Take whatever time you need,' she called to him as he climbed the bamboo scaffold his men had erected against the wall. 'It will give me a few more days to prepare the announcement I'll have to make when I arrive home.' She fingered the talisman in her pocket.

'Another four or five days, that's all,' he said from the top rung. He had already cut around the Golden Pagoda with a sharp knife, dividing it into sections, with incisions that penetrated the clay, camel dung, chopped straw and stucco on which the painting was made. Now he reached for his fox-tail saw to continue the delicate work of removing each panel, which his men were waiting to pad and bind, and pack into the crates they'd made for the long journey to England.

She enjoyed watching the confident way he went about his work and she could tell he enjoyed her company. They talked randomly about all kinds of things. Simon, she learned, was acquainted with a number of very influential people in England, and he taught her a lot about current political concerns and social reforms, as well as art and the theatre, and the world of London society. That was the world in which Richard had grown up. The world that Simon moved in and out of with ease. It was a world that was unlikely ever to accept a woman like Georgina Larssen.

There was only one aspect of Mrs Larssen's work in the dispensary that did not please Ho Sung: the doctor's wife no longer bought their medicinal herbs exclusively from their usual herb-gatherer. He could see her at the gate now with a bent old man who was known to collect rare herbs from the mountains, and money was passing hands.

This was a vexation to Ho Sung because for many years he and the hospital's regular herb-gatherers had a very satisfactory agreement, and out of each payment made by the hospital, a most moderate sum was passed back to the dispensary attendant. It was the way business was traditionally done, and if Mrs Larssen continued with this new arrangement, it would mean a loss of face for the Chinese attendant, as well as the money.

Later in the morning, Ho Sung saw Mrs Larssen at the dispensary bench working fiercely with the mortar and pestle. Curiosity drew him in to peer over her shoulder at the root she was pounding to a soft grey paste. He was about to ask her about this unfamiliar substance, when Doctor Larssen called for him to come to the ward.

It was more than an hour before Ho Sung had an opportunity to go back to the dispensary, and by this time Mrs Larssen had cleared the bench and her grey paste was in an unmarked jar on the shelf.

This was too much for Ho Sung. She had broken the first rule, the most important rule of his dispensary. 'Madame!' he said, snatching the unidentified jar and twisting the tightly closed lid. 'Most dangerous not to have label put on immediately!'

'Don't open it!' Then she laughed and put out her hand for the jar. 'I'm sorry, Ho Sung. Yes, of course, I never fail to put labels on everything used in here, but this is my little secret – and I don't want you to say anything to my husband about it.' She leaned closer and dropped her voice. 'This is just for me, you see, and I'm taking it home immediately.' She whispered into his ear. 'It's a special preparation for the skin of a lady who is growing older and who wants to keep her youth, to please her husband.'

'Ah,' he said, nodding sagely. 'I will keep your secret.' He hoped the treatment would be a success for the doctor's wife, because he'd noticed how very tired and lined her skin was becoming. He gave her the jar.

'Thank you,' she said, and turned to go. 'I'm so glad you didn't open this, Ho Sung. It is a preparation for ladies only. It can do the most unspeakable things to any man who uses it.'

Relations between the Russian Consul and Gregori Suvorov had deteriorated further after the débâcle surrounding the forged British intelligence report. These days the two men made little attempt to disguise their mutual dislike, and the Colonel found himself increasingly excluded from discussions that took place behind the closed doors of Petrovsky's office.

Suvorov's boredom was suffocating him. He was bored with the tittering wives at the Consulate and with the Persian prostitutes who came through Kashgar with the caravans. He was bored with the regular ceremonial parades to impress the Chinese with Russian power. He was even growing bored with the games he played to keep Natasha awake at night.

Suvorov still had one informant in Petrovsky's secretariat, and a trickle of news reached him from time to time. Today he'd heard something that lifted his spirits. It was of no interest to him that two intelligence agents from St Petersburg had died somewhere in the desert, but he was excited by the news that the caravan of British archaeologists was now on its way back to Kashgar.

Colonel Suvorov linked his fingers behind his head and leaned back in his chair to grin at the ceiling. At last! He ran his tongue across the backs of his teeth as he thought, then he sprang to his feet. From his desk he took a sheet of official Consulate notepaper with its emblem of the imperial double-headed eagle, then called for his horse to be saddled.

The ivory-carver in the market listened to Suvorov's instructions, and kept the glee from his expression as the Russian officer made little attempt to beat down the inflated price he'd quoted for making it.

'It will take many, many hours to make an article of such beauty, lord,' the craftsman whined. 'This eagle will be most difficult to carve, but I shall not sleep until it is done. Please call at this hour in two days.' He bowed low, and the Colonel left the market smiling, no longer weary with boredom.

Natasha's daughter was on her way home, and the time for the biggest game of all was drawing near.

Natasha confessed to Erik that she had been neglecting her domestic work in recent weeks.

'Just look at that pile of sewing waiting to be done! Would you mind very much if I remain at home today?' she asked over breakfast, and waved a hand towards a half-finished petticoat lying on top of the basket.

'Darling, I'd prefer you to have a day of complete rest,' he said. 'Georgina will scold me if she arrives home and finds you looking so weary.'

She sighed. 'Yes, Erik. I'll be perfectly well again very soon.'

After he left the house, Natasha felt suddenly cold. She walked restlessly from room to room, unconsciously wringing her hands while she thought. At last this day had arrived, the day she had planned so meticulously and dreaded so deeply. Could she bring herself to carry through the plan that had kept her from sleep on countless nights?

She paused in front of the hall mirror to look at the drawn, ageing face staring pitifully back at her. Had her courage suddenly faded, like her youth? She bit down hard on her knuckles. If she permitted herself to weaken now, the consequences for Georgina and Erik would be devastating.

Curse you, curse you, Gregori Suvorov! she silently screamed. Again she went to her dressing-table and opened the little drawer where the ivory comb lay. She picked it up and ran her thumb over the imperial Russian eagle carved on the top of it. It was a signal to her that his presence was coming closer. The comb had come yesterday; with it was an unsigned message: *In anticipation of a daughter's return.*

She took a deep breath and steeled herself. There was no going back now. She took a sheet of paper from her writing-case and quickly penned a note which she instructed the houseboy to deliver into the hands of nobody but Colonel Suvorov at the Russian Consulate.

From her drawer, she took the unmarked jar of grey paste and held it to the light. Her hands grew moist and her throat dried as she stared at the crushed root of the mountain-growing wolfsbane plant. It was the poison once used by Chinese archers to tip their arrows, and would serve her own purpose perfectly.

When Mrs Larssen gave the cook a shopping list and sent him to the

112

market, he was surprised and more than a little pleased to have been given an opportunity to visit a certain spice-seller whose husband was never at home on Tuesdays.

'Please light the oven before you leave,' the doctor's wife called. 'I want to bake some currant cakes this morning.'

CHAPTER FIFTEEN

Colonel Suvorov threw back his head and let out a roar of laughter when he opened the unsigned note in Natasha's well-remembered script, and read her invitation to meet him on the river-bank.

There is much to be discussed, she'd written. No, there is nothing whatsoever left to be discussed, he chuckled to himself. The time for discussion had long passed; soon it would be time for Natasha to witness exactly how Gregori Suvorov dealt with any woman who humiliated him.

Natasha's invitation today was intriguing. For weeks she'd been a virtual recluse, rarely venturing outside the security of the Mission compound, and that had defeated his hopes of seeing her panic as he stalked her through the city. What was the woman planning for today, he wondered as he stood at his mirror and brushed his sleek, dark hair? Natasha was surely about to beg for some favour, plead for sympathy.

She had chosen a secluded meeting place on the river-bank, and as he rode past willow trees that were just starting to burst into leaf, he saw her sitting on the grass, with her skirts spread around her, watching a duck and her ducklings waddle in line to the water. Natasha's face was hidden under a wide-brimmed hat and her hand rested on a small basket by her side. She made no move as he dismounted and walked to her side.

'How delightful of you to arrange this meeting, Natasha,' he said, sprawling on the ground a few feet in front of her. 'Is your husband aware of your whereabouts this afternoon?' He looked directly into her eyes with a practised flinty, unblinking stare, designed to chill her to the bone.

Her smile surprised him. 'I'm merely resting here for a few moments on my way to visit poor old Father Paul.' Her fingers flirted with the handle of the basket; her hands were still smooth and delicate. 'I wanted to meet you again, Gregori, but not in the city, where we would be recognized.' Her eyes, bright and challenging, held his, and he was momentarily nonplussed.

'You see, I was so shocked when we first met in the market, I was unable to gather my thoughts together,' she said with a coquettish shrug. 'Now, I do believe you planned it all just to meet and court my lovely daughter.'

Her remark astonished him. 'Oh, yes, I'm certainly looking forward to the day I meet that particular young lady,' he said, making no attempt to stifle a laugh.

'Yes, I'm sure you are, Gregori, but there are certain conditions I insist upon before you seduce her. Georgina is no longer in the first flush of youth, and I must have your assurance that you will provide well for her in the future, otherwise I'll refuse to introduce you.'

His shoulders shook with mirth. 'You have my word of honour, Natasha, that your daughter will receive much, much more than she expects.'

'Good.' Natasha gathered up her skirts and seemed about to stand when he put a restraining hand on her arm.

'Don't hurry away, my darling. Surely Father Paul can wait a little longer for whatever charity you are about to deliver? He lifted the lid of the basket and gave a crow of delight to see a bottle of cherry brandy lying in it. He reached for it and pulled the cork to sniff the contents, then put it to his lips. He sipped, and nodded approvingly.

'Would you like to try one of these?' She lifted the lid of a box, and the aroma of small, freshly baked raisin cakes rose to tempt him. On top of each cake, three plump raisins were visible; only one cake was topped with four raisins.

He reached in and selected one, and put it straight into his mouth. Natasha also chose a cake, but took three bites to finish hers. He watched her closely. Her sudden air of self-confidence was amusing, but puzzling.

She smiled at him with a touch of mischief, and wiped a crumb from the corner of her lips. 'I'm sure Father Paul won't mind if we each have another one.'

And again he took a little cake and threw it straight into his mouth, talking as he chewed. 'Has your husband received his reprimand from the Swedish Mission Board? It's some time since I sent them a detailed report on Natasha Luboff's activities in St Petersburg.'

He took another swig from the brandy bottle while he watched her face and saw a flash of fear replace the twinkle in her eye. Oh, yes, this was more like it! What game was she playing today?

She chose another cake, then picked up the cakebox and was about to replace the lid, when he snatched it. 'Oh, no, my dear. I haven't finished yet,' he said. There were three cakes remaining. One of them had four raisins on top.

She tut-tutted. 'Now I'll have to bake more tomorrow for poor Father Paul.' She watched the Colonel take the one topped with four raisins, throw it into his mouth, chew and swallow it.

'Your daughter is on her way home, I hear,' he said, with a provocative lift of one brow. 'What a foolish mother you are to allow her to roam the country with two single men to ravish her nightly.'

She watched him closely as his tongue cleared the remains of cake from his teeth. A sudden aftertaste made him grimace.

'You're not to leave yet,' he started to say as she snatched the box, replaced the cork in the bottle and put them back into her basket. 'I haven't finished with you – haven't—' Now there was a sharp, bitter taste in his mouth, his tongue tingled and began to roll outside his mouth. He couldn't control it to speak. His hands were becoming numb; terror gripped him.

All colour had left her face and she had scrambled to her feet, watching him, wide-eyed. The bitch – what had she done? She was staring down at him as he struggled to signal with his arms for her to help. She made no move. There was a crushing pain in his chest and he felt his heartbeat falter, then it raced as he struggled for breath. Nausea. . .

This was her work! No! No! The little whore was backing away from him now, leaving him to die! She was going to pay for this! The obscenities he struggled to hurl at her were no more than desperate, strangled cries, and suddenly she was no longer there to hear them. He was alone.

She ran like a deer along the river-bank, half-blinded by tears of relief. She had done it! The wolfsbane had worked just as the old herb gatherer had promised, and Georgina would now be safe from whatever vile design Gregori had planned. Dear God, he was going to die and now they could all live without fear. She stopped running, suddenly breathless, and leaned weakly against the trunk of a tree while she uncorked the cherry brandy and sipped a mouthful. Her shaking hands had difficulty holding the bottle to her lips.

Even if Gregori had already sent his information about her to the Swedish Mission Board, as he'd claimed, she'd be able to deflect the damage before it hurt Erik. If the Board challenged her husband about his choice of a wife, she would simply deny that she was the former Natasha Luboff, and say that the late Gregori Suvorov must have been mistaken. There was no evidence to prove otherwise.

She almost skipped for joy. Single-handedly she had saved her daughter and her husband from whatever debased intentions were fermenting in Gregori's mind. Perhaps one day she might be pricked by guilt, but at this moment she felt nothing but elation. When the body of Colonel Suvorov was found, the community would express surprise to hear that such a fit man had been struck so suddenly by a fatal heart attack, for that was the effect the wolfsbane would produce; and she would be seen to agree with them.

It was a long walk back to the Mission. Natasha slipped past the hospital quickly, left the basket in the kitchen and went straight into her bedroom. Emotional exhaustion overcame her the moment she put her head on the pillow, and she was still asleep when Erik arrived home.

'I'm glad to see you took my advice and spent a quiet day,' he said, as he kissed her forehead. 'I do believe you look better already.'

Natasha insisted on returning to work in the dispensary the next day, and almost immediately Ho Sung noticed how fresh and clear her skin was becoming. He wondered if she might share with him the secret of the special preparation she had used to bring youth back to her skin. A shrewd man could make money in the markets with such a thing, he said, but she smiled and said the secret was not hers to share.

On the evening of the fourth day after her meeting with Gregori on the river-bank, Natasha and Erik sat quietly after dinner, she with her sewing, he reading a Swedish newspaper.

'So much news from Europe!' he said, looking at her over the top of the paper. 'And so little of it concerns us here.'

She made a murmur of agreement. Most information in Kashgar was passed from mouth to mouth, or in official announcements nailed to the gates of the city.

Erik sighed and re-folded the paper neatly, then smiled at her. 'I think the only news you and I really want to hear, is that Georgina will soon walk through that door.'

She looked up and nodded with a smile.

'Quentin McCallum told me he had a message saying that Richard has dashed back to India, and Simon has found an interesting cave to investigate somewhere.' He reached for another newspaper. 'The only other local news from Quentin was that the Colonel of the Cossack Guards was found half-dead on the river-bank a few days ago.'

Natasha kept her eyes on her needlework, her fingers steadily stitching. 'How sad,' she murmured.

'Oh, don't be concerned, darling, he's recovering,' Erik said. 'They thought at first he'd suffered a heart attack, but now it seems likely that he'd been poisoned.' Natasha's hand flew to her throat and she gave a cry. Her eyes filled with terror and her sewing slid to the floor as she sprang to her feet. 'No! No!

He can't be alive! No!' she screamed. Her hands flew to her hair and her fingers dug into it, dragging at the pins, loosening the strands. She stood swaying, all colour leached from her face. 'No . . . no. . . . Oh, God! No . . . no . . . no!'

Erik rushed to her, but she pulled away and ran into the bedroom, looking about her wildly. Erik followed, stunned, watching her fling open drawers and cupboard doors. 'I must go. I must leave immediately. You must forget you ever knew me!'

'Natasha, what madness is this? Stop it! Tell me what has happened!'

She panted loudly as her hands raked through her belongings, tossing them mindlessly on to the floor, until he came up behind her and pinned her arms to her sides. She wailed and fought against his strength, twisting, this way and that, until he lifted her bodily and threw her on to the bed and held her down.

She shrieked and thrashed and tried to push him away, but his fingers tightened around her arms. 'Tell me, Natasha! Tell me now, and I will help you!'

'Erik, let me go! You can't help me. I'm far, far beyond any help.' A rigor swept through her. 'I must go before he comes for me!'

Erik brought his palm swiftly against her cheek and silenced her. She looked up at the agony etched on his face and she slumped on to the bedcovers. 'Send me away, Erik. I don't belong in your life any longer. I was the one who poisoned Colonel Suvorov, and he'll soon come here looking for vengeance.'

For a moment he looked at her, stunned and disbelieving, then he shook his head. 'Oh, my poor darling,' he groaned, and lay down on the bed, close beside her. His eyes were squeezed shut and his head spun. 'What has that man done to you? Natasha, I demand you tell me everything.' Fear dried his mouth.

'Everything?' She nestled her head against his chest and wept.

No detail was omitted from her long story.

'Promise me, Erik,' she panted, 'I beg you to promise, that you will never reveal any of this to Georgina.'

'As you wish, my love,' he sighed.

On and on through the night she talked, and sometimes wept, as, one by one, she dragged her dark demons to the surface for Erik to meet. And all the time he stroked and comforted her, and held her fast.

When day dawned, he roused her gently. She looked around wildly, madly, terrified. 'He is coming for me! Listen. I can hear him coming!' She trembled violently and Erik forced another sleeping draught past her lips. He kissed her face.

'You mean more to me than anything in heaven or on earth, Natasha, my beloved, and I swear I'll not let anything hurt you again,' he said. 'I know exactly what has to be done.'

CHAPTER SIXTEEN

Signs of spring could be seen in the fields as Simon and Georgina approached Kashgar. She was weary of travel, though morning sickness worried her less.

'This has all been quite an adventure, hasn't it?' she said, stretching as she came out of her tent to join Simon for their last breakfast beside the camp-fire. 'Tomorrow morning we'll be waking up in real beds and eating from a table with a real tablecloth.'

'I've enjoyed your company, Georgina. I'm going to miss you when I set out again.'

'Yours is a lonely life, Simon,' she said fondly. 'Don't you ever yearn for something more?'

'More, my dear? How could I ask for more?' He laughed dryly. 'When the Golden Pagoda is unpacked in London, the Royal Geographical Society will award me a gold medal, and the name of Simon Davenport will be in every newspaper in the land. I'll be bombarded with invitations to dinners and weekend house parties, and I'll find myself booked to give long, erudite lectures on the Indo-Grecian influence on the treasures of the Silk Road.' He picked up a small stone and skimmed it across the dust. 'Then it will be time for me to leave England again, and find some other remote location to dig.'

There was an underlying bitterness in his banter, and Georgina thought it better to make no comment. She could only imagine how different the pattern of his life would have been, had Anne lived.

He looked at her, and his handsome face creased into a smile. 'And I have no doubt that you're going to be busy, too. I'm sure that once your parents recover from their surprise, they'll be delighted to welcome their grandchild. I envy them.' He studied her for a moment. 'Come, m'dear, it's time to mount up for the last twenty miles.'

Those miles seemed to stretch endlessly through the day. Home was coming closer, and she hadn't yet settled on the best way to tell her family she was pregnant.

'Are you concerned about your parents' reaction to the news?' Simon asked.

'You must be a mind-reader.'

'Yes, I think there are times when I *can* read your mind, Georgina.'

She pretended to look shocked, and he gave her a teasing grin.

'Fear not! I find your thoughts most intriguing.'

They shared a good-natured laugh. 'Oh, Simon, I'm really going to miss your company,' she said.

'Not nearly as much as I'm going to miss yours,' he said affectionately. 'Just keep wearing the ring, and remember me sometimes.'

It was some hours later that their caravan was met by two Indian guards from the British Consulate, riding out to intercept them before they reached Kashgar.

'Davenport-sahib,' one said, throwing a salute, 'I have a message for the memsahib to accompany us to the Consulate before returning to the Swedish Mission.'

'Why?' Georgina asked. 'Why shouldn't I go straight home?'

Simon called an order for the camel-drivers to take his treasures to wait for him in the caravanserai. 'Come along,' he said. 'Let's see what this is all about.'

They followed the guards to the British Consulate, and Quentin came out on to the veranda to greet them as soon as they rode through the gates. His expression was tense. 'Come inside,' he said, ushering her into his office and calling for refreshments to be brought. 'I think you should sit down.'

While Simon pulled a chair for her, Quentin placed himself behind the desk and took an envelope from the top drawer.

'Do you want me to leave?' Simon asked.

'No. Please stay,' she said, and he stood leaning against a window-frame, watching intently.

Quentin hesitated and drew a deep breath. 'I'm afraid there's no easy way to tell you this, Georgina, but your parents left Kashgar very suddenly about ten days ago. Er – for your mother's health, I understand.'

She had an odd sensation that she was peering at him through the wrong end of a telescope, and he was miles away, his voice far off. 'What? Why? When will they be back? I can't believe—' A nervous knot tightened in her stomach.

Quentin handed her the letter. 'Your father left this for you. He said it explains everything.'

He looked across to Simon and rolled his eyes in an expression of dismay, while she tore open the envelope and quickly scanned the two scrawled pages, frowning.

'It can't be true!' All colour left her cheeks, and her fingers tightened around the pages, crushing them as she held them against her breast. She stood, and Simon took a step towards her, then hesitated.

'I must have time to think.' Her voice was raw with emotion. 'Please, I want to be alone – excuse me.' She brushed past the men and ran into the terraced garden. They watched her walk aimlessly to and fro, then perch on a stone bench with her head in her hands.

Simon's hand on the doorframe was white-knuckled. 'What's the story, Quentin? For God's sake, out with it, man!'

The Consul looked at him helplessly. 'Erik Larssen came to say that Natasha had been taken ill again – I think he mentioned something about her *nervous disorder* – and he had to take her to a kinder climate immediately.'

'Where? Up to the mountains?'

Quentin scratched the back of his neck and pursed his lips. 'That's the rub. Apparently, they packed a couple of suitcases and hired a guide to take them over the Khunjerab Pass into India. Erik has sent a letter of resignation to the Mission Board and said goodbye to the Hakvins, who are quite distraught, I can tell you.'

'He's walked out on a lifetime's work? Good God! Do the Hakvins have any idea what's behind this?' Simon looked quickly across the garden at Georgina, sitting desolately under the trees.

'None whatsoever. Everyone at the Mission says that Natasha had been looking radiant recently – then suddenly...' He spread his hands, palms upwards. 'But that's not the worst of it.' He nodded towards Georgina.

Simon looked thunderous. 'What has he proposed for her?'

'I couldn't persuade Erik to explain his reasons for any of this, you understand. He simply begged me to tell no one that he and Natasha were leaving that day, and that they intended to travel straight down to Bombay. He said he'd be able to cable his bank in Sweden from there, and get them to send funds for a passage – not to Stockholm or London, mind you – but on the first ship sailing for either Cape Town or Australia!'

Simon groaned. 'What about Georgina? What provision has he made for her?'

Quentin dropped into his chair. 'Well, a new doctor will be sent out from

Stockholm, of course, so Erik wants her to live with the Hakvins at the Mission until he sends for her to join them.'

Simon groaned, and rested his forehead against the doorframe. 'No, no, no! I should have brought Georgina straight home as soon as that business with the Russians was finished.' He thumped his fist against the wood, and stood motionless for several moments. Then, breathing hard, he turned to Quentin. 'I'm going out to talk to Georgina now. See that we're not disturbed, will you?'

Simon walked to where she sat on the stone bench, and she looked up when he settled at the far end. He'd expected to find her in tears; instead the eyes that looked into his blazed with anger.

'Quentin has given me the gist of what has happened,' he said, studying her ashen face. 'What are you going to do?'

Her expression was tight with indignation. 'Well, I certainly can't stay on at the Mission in my condition, can I? Just imagine what the Board would have to say about that!'

She stood suddenly, and with her arms folded tightly across her chest, started to pace up and down in front of the bench. 'I can't understand why my parents have acted so impulsively. What made them rush off and abandon me like this?'

'Georgina, you're not abandoned!' Simon said sharply. 'You have me. I'll see you have enough money to do whatever you decide.'

She swung on her heel to face him. 'Well, that's most generous of you, Mr Davenport, but do you have any idea how – how *humiliating* it is for a woman of my age to find herself in this situation?'

'Of course, I know exactly why you're angry.' He felt his own frustration also escalating into anger. 'Listen, I'm saying that I want to help you. I thought – in the name of friendship – I would be the first one you'd turn to.'

Resentment glowed in her eyes. 'Actually, you're the *only* one now whom I can turn to for help, and I – and that—' She dropped back heavily beside him on the stone bench. 'Simon, it makes me so furious that, here I am, strong, capable, well-educated, but, because I'm a woman, I'm left here, floating like a helpless jellyfish!'

He started to say something, but she interjected impatiently: 'You laughed at me once when I mentioned that I shared Irena Levka's thoughts about women who accepted the view that they must go through life being simply useless because they were born female. Look at me now! Irena would never have found herself in my position.'

'Of course not! Irena has, no doubt, found herself dead!' he snapped.

Georgina had no quick response, and her breasts rose and fell rapidly as her gaze locked with Simon's. 'Well, you have certainly made it clear to me now exactly where I stand.' Her tone was brusque. 'I have been quite abandoned, so, thank you very much, I have no choice but to accept your money until I can make other arrangements.' She pulled the ring from her finger. 'I'll start by selling this.'

'Excellent. Now you're being sensible,' he said, just as brusquely.

'Oh, I'll be sensible indeed! I'll simply follow the course laid down by all *sensible* ladies caught in my predicament: take myself off to a quiet little hotel at the seaside, tell them my name is Mrs Brown, then walk up and down the beach every day, counting the stranded jellyfish, until the baby is delivered.'

His lips were as thin as hers. 'Good!'

'And, after that, perhaps my baby and I will decide to take a little cottage in the country for a few years.' She narrowed her eyes at him. 'I'm afraid your expenses will not be light, Mr Davenport! I have no intention of leaving my child to be raised by a stranger while I find work in the mills, as my mother was forced to do.'

'Have no concern that your expenses will ever be beyond my means, Mrs Brown.' His temper was mounting. Oh, dear God! This was a situation he'd tried for years to avoid.

'Please accept my most humble thanks for the generosity that will keep me out of the workhouse.' Georgina's words carried a brittle edge. 'I only pray that if you do remarry some day, your new wife never discovers you have a kept woman somewhere in a cosy little cottage.'

His expression startled her. There was hurt as well as anger in his eyes as he stood, and indicated for her to do likewise. 'Enough, Georgina!' he rasped. 'Come and walk with me.'

Dusk was gathering as she followed him obediently to the steps leading into the orchard planted on a lower terrace. They walked between the rows of trees, and when they reached the far wall and were no longer visible from the house, he stopped and leaned against the trunk of an apple tree. His gaze was on the brilliant sunset over the mountains while he fought to contain his emotion.

Georgina, herself, was now close to tears. 'Oh, Simon, forgive me for being such an idiot. I said all kinds of stupid things that I didn't mean. Please. . . .' She made a move towards him.

'Stand where you are, Georgina, and hear me out,' he said sharply, turning to her. 'I have something to tell you, and you alone. When I've finished, just give me a simple yes or no, and it need never be mentioned again.'

She propped herself against the next tree in the row.

He stooped to pick up a twig and rolled it between his fingers, watching the movement while he gathered his thoughts.

'You have every right to feel angry and frustrated at finding yourself thrown into this predicament, Georgina. Obviously, staying on at the Mission is out of the question, so let's look at the alternatives.'

'I refuse to throw myself on Richard's sympathy!' Initially, there was defiance in the look she threw at him, but her lips quivered and tears swam into her eyes. She wiped them away with the heels of her hands and sniffed. 'Oh, Simon, I'm terrified.' She wanted him to offer her words of comfort, but he didn't speak. 'It won't be long before it becomes evident that I'm carrying a child, and I know I have to face the possibility that perhaps' – she had to stop and swallow hard – 'perhaps it might *never* be possible for Richard to come back.'

'Yes, m'dear, given the nature of his profession, I fear that is something that has to be considered.' Simon snapped the twig he was holding and threw the pieces away before he looked at her. 'I love you, Georgina,' he said quietly. 'I'm thirty years older than you are, and I've loved and admired you since the day we met.' A shadow of sadness crossed his face. 'At this moment, nothing would give me more delight than to become your white knight and fall on to one knee, beg you to become my wife.' His voice dropped. 'However, life isn't quite so simple.'

He took a deep breath, and kept his gaze locked with hers for several long moments before he spoke again. 'I've already told you the circumstances of Anne's death during the Mutiny, and how I was shot and left for dead by the sepoys.'

She inclined her head, and again he had difficulty continuing. He forced himself not to turn away from her, and scrubbed a hand across his chin. 'As you probably know, it's the practice of the natives to mutilate the bodies of their male enemies—' His voice faded, and he gave her a significant nod. 'Unfortunately, I somehow survived their mischief, and I've spent the last thirty years wishing that either those bastards had gelded me totally, or that the damn bullet had killed me outright.'

A flash of understanding hit her like a body-blow. Her heart went out to him, and ignoring his warning look, she went to him with her hands outstretched. Her fingers wrapped around his and she lifted them to her lips. 'Dearest, dearest Simon. How can I help?'

'Help?' he repeated bitterly. 'Dear God, how can I explain their slipshod work to you—? Their knives made sure that I was – was left with no hope of ever being *helped*. . . . Oh, the *desire* still rushes through my blood when you're near me, the longing – the aching – to lie with a woman, to make love. . . . Oh, sweet Jesus, why do you think I spend so much of my life alone out here in the desert?'

She dropped her hands and stood biting down on her bottom lip while they faced each other for several agonizing moments, both breathing fast, both fighting to regain control of their rioting emotions.

'Nobody else on earth knows what I have just revealed to you, Georgina,' he was able to say at last.

'Nobody else will ever know, I promise.'

He kicked at a tuft of weed with the toe of his boot. 'I have a suggestion. Just hear me out.' His gaze settled on her fingers, nervously twisting the engagement ring he had given her. 'If you were to marry me immediately, I'd take you back to my house in London, and your baby could be born there, away from gossiping tongues.' He lifted his gaze to her eyes. 'I've warned you that I can never offer you the comfort of a true husband, but my name *can* protect you and your child.'

She struggled to speak, but he halted her. 'When Richard returns— No, Georgina, hear me out! When Richard comes back and you want to build a life together, you have my word that I'll step aside and make it possible for you to divorce me.'

Now it was impossible for her to speak at all. She could only stare at Simon, while the significance of his offer filtered through her tumbling thoughts. Her fondness for him had grown deep in the weeks they had travelled together, comfortable in each other's company. Now her heart swelled in gratitude, and she was aware of her lips stretching into a smile as she gave a faint nod.

'Yes?' he asked, and she nodded again, suddenly enveloped in a great rush of relief.

'Good, you're being sensible,' he said quickly. 'Now, let's get on with the arrangements and, if we hurry, we might be able to reach Bombay and find your parents before they board a ship.'

CHAPTER SEVENTEEN

'Did I hear you correctly, Simon? You and Georgina are to be married?' Quentin looked in astonishment from Simon to Georgina and back again. 'Well, I never! This is a delightful surprise. Why, I had no idea—' He thrust his hand into Simon's and shook it hard, then turned and kissed Georgina's cheek.

She gave a shy smile and looked up at the handsomely distinguished man who, in just a few minutes, had changed her whole view of the future. 'I'm truly most fortunate,' she said, then added lightly, 'and I'm still a little dazed by Simon's courage in offering to take *me* as a wife.'

'Never fear, m'dear,' he said in the same light tone, 'your independence is something I wouldn't dare tamper with.' There was eagerness in his expression. 'I think you and I will get along splendidly together in London, just as we did in the desert.'

'Yes, I'm sure we will,' she said, and a look of understanding passed between them.

'So,' Quentin said, rubbing his palms together briskly, 'what plans do you have?'

'I have matters in Kashgar that must be dealt with immediately,' Simon began, then turned to Georgina. 'Correct me, dear, if you have other suggestions.'

She trusted Simon completely, but there was an unsettling air of unreality about this impending change in her life. Her name would change, her home would change, and she wondered how much of herself would have to change when she left Kashgar with Simon Davenport.

The only constant thing left in her life was her love for Richard, and his child. She reached into her pocket to touch the fragment of gold-painted plaster that had become her link to him. Was there some other course she could have taken at this point, rather than rushing into a marriage with Simon?

Should she have thrown her predicament at Richard? But what of her parents' predicament?

She looked gratefully at Simon. His offer was the only solution possible.

'Now,' he said, rising from his chair, 'I must take Georgina home to see Mr Hakvin, and arrange for him to perform the wedding ceremony tomorrow afternoon.'

'I hope I'll be invited, too,' said Quentin. He stopped abruptly and cleared his throat. 'Pity Erik and Natasha won't be there.'

'Yes,' Simon said, looking at her quickly, 'but if we're married tomorrow, and leave immediately, we might be able to catch up with them in Bombay. Georgina, will that give you enough time to pack, and do whatever needs doing at the house?'

The thought of what might face her at home was frightening, but she nodded.

When they rode into the Mission, Georgina and Simon were met by the three Swedish missionaries, all solemn-faced and tearful, and all speaking at once.

'Your father has resigned, you know, and asked the Board to send a doctor to replace him!'

'Oh, I fear your poor, dear mother has quite lost her mind!'

'She was unable even to speak a goodbye to us!'

The reality of her parents' flight from Kashgar struck her when she walked into the empty house. The bewildered houseboy and the cook hovered awkwardly in the hall, awaiting instructions. Ho Sung and the other Chinese hospital attendants had gathered on the veranda, listening for scraps of news.

'It's all right, Mr Hakvin, and ladies,' Simon said with calming firmness, 'I'll see to matters here.' He took Georgina's arm. 'First, we have a very important request: Miss Larssen and I would like you to marry us tomorrow afternoon. We plan to leave immediately afterwards, and perhaps catch up with Doctor and Mrs Larssen in India.'

Frederik Hakvin beamed and rushed to shake Simon's hand. 'Of course, of course! Delighted, splendid!'

Hilde and Birget gave excited little cries and kissed Georgina. 'Your dear mother will be overjoyed. I'm sure it will help her recovery.'

Georgina tried to show a confident smile. 'Thank you all for your concern.'

'If you will excuse us now,' Simon said, with exquisite tact, 'I think Georgina needs time to see to her packing.'

He bowed to Hilde and Birget, and the three Hakvins bustled to the door. 'Do call on us to help in any way we can,' they said in unison.

Frederik paused beside the small table in the hall where several letters addressed to Doctor Larssen lay on top of a Swedish newspaper. 'Your father gave us no forwarding address, you understand,' he said to Georgina. 'Actually, he asked me to burn any mail that came for him, but I thought it best not to do so before you returned.'

'Splendid, Mr Hakvin,' Simon said, standing by the front door. 'Thank you; I'm sure Georgina will want to attend to it herself.'

When the visitors had gone, Georgina sat down wearily at the table and Simon handed her the letters addressed to Erik, then called for the houseboy to bring a meal for them. Most envelopes contained small accounts to be settled, and these Simon slipped into his own pocket, while Georgina opened an envelope bearing the crest of the Swedish Mission Board.

She gave a groan as she read the two closely written pages, then pushed them towards Simon and, with her elbows on the table, sat with her head in her hands. 'Good God!' Simon gasped several times as he read the letter. 'What madness is this? These claims made against your mother in St Petersburg can't possibly be valid. Charges of theft and murder? What idiots on the Board in Stockholm could have believed this about Natasha, and then dared to address Erik in this tone, dismissing him on the gossip of some informer, sending a replacement immediately? I'm damned glad he didn't see this letter before he left Kashgar.'

'You won't mention any of this to anyone, will you? Not even Quentin?'

He crushed the letter and threw it into the grate, then lit the paper and stood behind Georgina with his hands on her shoulders while they watched the pages reduce to ashes.

'Oh, Simon, I'm so glad that you and I have no secrets,' she whispered.

'No, there will never be secrets between us.' The pressure of his fingers on her shoulders tightened. 'Now, can I help you here with anything more tonight?'

'Thank you, no. I must see to my packing.'

'Fine,' he said. 'We'll have to travel light until we get to Peshawar, I'm afraid, but everything else can go with the caravan when it sets out with the collection.' He gave a wry smile and added: 'I'm afraid we're not likely to see any of it in London for months.'

She walked with him to the door and leaned wearily against it. 'Thank you, from the bottom of my heart, for carrying me through this awful time, Simon,' she said simply, 'and if I sometimes make mistakes – please tell me, and I promise I won't make them again.'

He stroked the back of his hand down her cheek and along her jaw. 'It's going to be all right, Georgina. You and I will never do anything to hurt each other.' A slow smile crept across his face. 'Let's both make a promise to find all the happiness we can, in whatever time we have together.'

He rode out of the compound, and the enormity of the decision to marry this man struck her with a new clarity. There was no regret in her mind, just the uncomfortable thought that when she made her wedding vows to Simon the next day, they would both know it would always be Richard who held her heart.

She turned back into the house that had been her home for the last ten years, and which was soon to be lived in by a stranger arriving from Stockholm. Her heart ached for her father who had been so savagely swept aside in some terri-fying avalanche of unexplained events.

She called for the houseboy to bring packing-boxes into her parents' bedroom, and her throat tightened as she opened the cupboards and saw the garments hanging there. She made quick decisions, then opened the drawers of her mother's dressing-table and continued to consign most items to the charity box. Then, ignoring the lateness of the hour, she packed her own belongings.

She owned little of value to take from Kashgar. The most important was the fragment of gold-painted plaster she kept wrapped in a handkerchief, the frag-ment of hope that one day Richard would come back into her life and meet the child who would be waiting for him.

Quentin McCallum had engaged the services of a photographer to record the wedding of Georgina Larssen to Simon Davenport. The simple ceremony was performed in the cluttered sitting-room belonging to the Swedish missionaries, with only Quentin, Hilde and Birgert as witnesses. Later, the group assembled on the veranda for photographs.

The Hakvin ladies, after working all morning to help Georgina pack the last of the Larssens' possessions, produced a celebratory luncheon before the couple left Kashgar.

With his usual grace and charm, Simon raised his glass in a toast to Erik and Natasha. Then Georgina watched him subtly mine scraps of information from the missionaries about events in Kashgar before her mother became ill – particularly about Natasha's recent work in the dispensary.

There was an artificial mood of celebration about her wedding day that tested her self-control. Several times she felt herself faltering emotionally, and was grateful for Simon's clear head and boundless energy, which ensured the ceremony, and later their departure, progressed smoothly. She had no idea of the size of the donation he made to the Mission, but judging from the width of Frederik Hakvin's smile, it was a generous one.

No attempt was made to stem the tears misting the eyes of everyone watching Georgina ride out of the compound with her new husband. 'If only dear Erik and Natasha could have waited to see the day Georgina became Mrs Davenport,' sniffed Hilde, fluttering her handkerchief.

Simon had seen Georgina's struggle to keep her emotions under control throughout it all, and was careful not to intrude into her thoughts as they rode south. Sheer strength of will had carried her through the last twenty-four hours. Dear God, how her every mood reminded him of Anne. He slanted a sideways glance at her youthful profile and vowed that he must never allow his yearnings to damage the delicate balance in their easy, affectionate friendship.

He had no doubt that one day Richard Eldridge would return, if a benevolent Fate decreed he remain alive through whatever difficulties lay ahead.

Until that day came – the day he'd promised to produce grounds for a divorce – he would have the joy of protecting her, and her child. Was it expecting too much to hope that this enchantingly sensual young woman would also find some measure of happiness in playing the role of Mrs Davenport in their borrowed time together? A few months? A few years? Would his financial and social position be sufficient to compensate for everything else he'd never be able to give her?

He tried not to think of the dangerous situation he had created for himself and his own sanity. He was already deeply in love with her.

They crossed the border into India, and another week's travel through the scattered settlements of the Hunza Valley brought them to the big British fort at Gilgit. Here, they were given the news that two weeks previously a Swedish couple had passed through on their way to Bombay.

'Are you sure you don't want to rest here before we set off again?' Simon asked. She was touched by his constant concern for her welfare – and the baby's.

'No, thank you, we mustn't delay. I feel as strong as a lion,' she said.

The jagged, snow-capped peaks dropped behind them as, for the next week, they followed the course of the Indus River down on to the dusty plains of Peshawar, where the gentle spring weather of the mountains was already simmering into summer.

As they approached the garrison city close to the Afghan border, the solitude of the sparsely settled North-West Frontier Province changed dramatically.

Now they shared the road with the donkeys and ox-wagons, camel-trains arriving from the deserts of Rajasthan, horse-drawn artillery and columns of marching British infantry, accompanied by their commissariat wagons, all heading towards Peshawar.

Simon had sent a message ahead to his friend, Sir Henry Pelham, the District Commissioner, who ordered his own carriage to meet them for the last few, weary miles to his bungalow on the outskirts of the army cantonment.

'This is like heaven on wheels,' Georgina said with a sigh, as she settled into the comfort of the well-sprung coach.

'You'll enjoy Sir Henry's hospitality, and I know Lady Pelham will be delighted to take you shopping in Peshawar for whatever you need to buy.' He cut her off before she could speak. 'My darling Georgina, don't argue. You are in desperate need of – well, frankly, everything, from a dinner gown to under-garments.'

'Have I no secrets at all from you, sir?' she said with a laugh.

'No secrets,' he said, and pretended to frown at her sternly. 'Remember also, Mrs Davenport, that I can still read your mind, and I forbid you to enter-tain any thoughts of spending less than one hundred pounds on this particular shopping expedition with Lady Pelham.'

'Oh, my dear Simon, how absolutely splendid!' Cynthia Pelham cried, when he introduced Georgina to the Commissioner and his large-hearted, large-busted wife. 'Married at last! Oh, you are a clever young lady, Georgina. We've spent years watching almost every woman in the country throw herself at Simon. I'm delighted.'

Simon adroitly altered the thrust of Lady Pelham's enthusiasm by mentioning the urgent need for new clothes to be ordered for Georgina.

'Oh dear! If you are determined to catch Saturday's train, that leaves us barely three days to see you outfitted!' Lady Pelham rubbed her plump little white hands together gleefully 'Georgina, you and I must leave for the city immediately after breakfast tomorrow. I know a very reliable tailor on Shahid Road. Lal Singh will not disappoint us.'

She and Georgina withdrew into her sitting-room after dinner and, with a dozen ladies' magazines to examine for fashion styles, began to draw up a list of essential garments to be made.

'Before we become too enthusiastic, Lady Pelham, I must tell you that I won't be able to wear these tight-waisted skirts for much longer. I'll soon be four months—' Her hand stroked the slight bulge in her stomach, and Cynthia Pelham's eyes filled.

'Oh, Simon is a lucky, lucky man to have married you, my dear. Children are always such a blessing to a couple. Sadly, Henry, and I have none.'

While the ladies talked of babies, Simon and Sir Henry lingered at the table with their port and cigars, discussing the latest news of Russian movements in the region.

'You saw the 66th Bengal Infantry coming into Peshawar yesterday?' Sir Henry lifted his glass and twirled it by the stem.

'We certainly saw a lot of troop movement along the road. Where are they heading?'

'Good question. The only thing that seems clear at the moment is that a Russian attack from the north now seems unlikely. Fresh intelligence came through recently that all the activity on the other side of the Pamirs was apparently designed as a feint.'

'Interesting,' Simon murmured, raising the glass to his lips and taking a sip. Tempted as he was to reveal Georgina's role in uncovering the Russian tactic, he kept his silence.

'Now,' Sir Henry said with a weary sigh, 'we've just heard that a Russian envoy has been very warmly received by the Amir of Afghanistan – who'd assured everyone he would remain neutral – so now Britain is demanding diplomatic representation at the Afghan court also.' He poured another glass of port. 'The Amir has recently been making rumbling noises about closing us out of the Khyber Pass, so General Roberts is heading off to Kabul with a sizeable delegation – as well as a sizeable chest of gold to match what the Russians have already presented to him.'

Later, when Georgina lay alone in her bed, Simon came to her room and told her what he had learned from Sir Henry.

'Richard's report – your information – played an important part in British plans, m'love.'

She lay quietly, aware of the life fluttering in her womb. 'So at least we know Richard arrived back safely in Simla,' she said, when she trusted her voice not to break.

Simon took her hand. 'I'm afraid, though, I have no news of your parents. They weren't sighted here, but perhaps they caught a train immediately. In any case, tomorrow I'll telegraph a friend in Bombay and ask him to make enquiries at the shipping agents there.'

'Simon, you're wonderful. Where would I be without you?' She sat up quickly and put her arms around him to reach up and kiss his cheek. 'Do you know, a funny thought just came to me,' she said on a quiver of laughter. 'I have become an utterly useless jellyfish, and I'm finding it a surprisingly pleasant experience!'

She slid back on to her pillows and he gave her a boyish grin. 'Good, I'm delighted to hear it. Keep floating, and I'll see to it that your sea remains calm.'

Their banter had stirred a sudden undercurrent; for a moment she saw a new depth in his eyes as he looked down at her. For a moment he seemed about to kiss her, but then he stood quickly and walked to the door connecting their rooms. He turned, and a lingering look of understanding passed between them before he closed the door.

CHAPTER EIGHTEEN

The Officers' Mess at Peshawar had every piece of its magnificent regimental silver displayed on the long mahogany table when General Roberts and his staff were invited to dinner on their last evening there.

'It's a great honour to have you here, General,' the Colonel said, 'and we wish you every success with your negotiations in Kabul.'

'Amen to that!' grumbled a grey-haired officer sitting opposite Richard. 'We've had two utterly futile wars with Afghanistan in the last forty years, lost rivers of fine British blood trying to put some order into the country, and what good has it done? Not a scrap!'

Richard nodded. His own private prayer for the mission was that he would complete his intelligence assignment, hand his report to the General and get back to Simla before any real trouble might erupt. How much longer now before he was able to tell Georgina that his army days were over?

'By God, Eldridge, you'll have ridden some miles by the time you get back from this trip!' muttered the major sitting beside him. 'All the way north into China, then down into Persia, now you're off to Afghanistan. Ever calculated the distance?'

Richard shook his head. 'Too busy to add them all up, but, you're right, I've certainly been kept busy in the last few months. In fact, it's hard to remember many occasions when I've slept in the same bed two nights running since I left China.'

'I hear General Roberts was particularly keen to have you along on this expedition,' remarked the officer sitting on his right. 'It seems you've made quite a name for yourself, old boy, dealing with those Russian agents in the Pamirs the way you did.'

Richard sliced into his roast beef and reached for the horseradish. 'I can't take all the credit for that. I was fortunate to have been given a lot of valuable local help in Chinese Turkestan,' he said, and smiled to himself as the image

135

of Georgina came to him, as it did a dozen and more times each day.

'By the way, gentlemen,' he said, when they all left the table at the end of the port, 'I have precious little time to spare tomorrow, but I'd like to buy a gift – perhaps some lace – for a young lady. Can you suggest where I could find something very special?'

Amid a few ribald comments, Richard was given the names of several reputable merchants. 'I'll be pressed for time, so which one is the closest?' he asked, and noted the address of Lal Singh on Shahid Road.

Over breakfast the next morning, Lady Pelham and Simon discussed the matter of hiring servants to travel with the Davenports on the long train journey to Bombay.

'I can highly recommend a man and woman who worked very well for friends of ours before they left India,' Cynthia Pelham said, and she sent a message straight away for the servants to present themselves.

By the time Georgina and Lady Pelham were ready to set off in the carriage an hour later, a pleasant middle-aged Indian woman named Chandra had arrived to attend her new mistress, and joined the ladies on their shopping expedition. Simon waved them off with strict instructions to buy only the best of everything needed to equip Mrs Davenport for her journey to England.

Chandra, Georgina soon discovered, had served several fashionable English ladies in recent years, and knew far more about the clothing needs of a memsahib than she did herself.

When they reached the premises of Lal Singh, they began the exciting business of choosing silks and cottons, buttons and laces and ribbons.

Lal Singh called for assistance from his workroom, and Chandra firmly stated the various undergarments and outergarments, for day and evening, warm weather and cool, that were essential for a stylish memsahib to travel all the way to England. A cheerful chaos developed when Lal Singh and his assistants began to unfold bolts of fabric to hold against Georgina, choosing shades. This new venture into the realm of ladies' fashion became even more bewildering when Lady Pelham and Chandra moved on to the problem of deciding styles for a woman with a rapidly expanding waistline.

The moment came at last when final choices had been made and Lal Singh's youthful nephew was sent to look after the shop, while the memsahib was escorted to the workroom for her measurements to be taken. Georgina stood patiently behind a screen while Chandra moved a tape around her body and called measurements to the tailor's assistant, and all the while Lady Pelham's ideas continued to flow.

*

Richard's patience was stretched as he wound his way through the narrow streets of Peshawar looking for the premises of Lal Singh. His venture into the city this morning had been delayed by an order to attend a meeting between General Roberts and the garrison commander, and he was now left with precious little time to find the perfect gift for Georgina.

Each time she entered his thoughts he felt his lips stretch into a smile. It would not be long now before her violet-scented body was in his arms again. In his arms for ever.

Damn, he'd taken another wrong turn. No sign of a street-name anywhere. 'Shahid Road?' he questioned a spice-seller, and the old man pointed. 'Lal Singh?' he asked in the next narrow street, and turned a corner in time to see a carriage pull away from the store he was looking for.

When he stepped inside, he found himself in a flurry of activity with what appeared to be the entire Singh family rewinding bolts of material and replacing boxes of trimmings on to shelves. 'We are honoured by your presence, sahib,' the little man said as he bowed deeply to Richard. How may I be of service?'

'Lace,' said Richard, and felt himself smiling again. 'Show me your best lace. I want a bridal veil for a very beautiful lady.'

'Oh, Simon, what a morning we've had!' Georgina laughed when they arrived back at the Commissioner's bungalow. 'I don't know how we're ever going to load all my new clothes on to the train.' She dropped into the white cane chair next to his on the veranda.

'That is why we've hired servants, Mrs Davenport,' he said drily. 'My new man has already been out to buy a trunk for your wardrobe.' He gave her a tiny wink. 'You're a jellyfish with no responsibilities now, remember? Learn to float, m'love.'

She shook her head at him and smiled.

'By the way,' he said, leaning towards her so as not to be overheard, 'when I was in the telegraph office this morning, I sent a message through Lahore to Simla, to ask about Richard.'

She held her breath while he pulled the reply from his pocket. '*Captain Eldridge away on duty. Return date uncertain,*' she read, and swallowed hard as she looked quickly at Simon.

'So, there you are. He's obviously fit and well, and busy again in some remote area,' Simon said, smiling as he stood to offer his arm when the brass gong sounded to announce luncheon.

'Thank you for being undoubtedly the nicest man God ever placed on this earth,' Georgina said, squeezing his arm lightly as they walked into the dining-room.

Richard returned immediately to the Officers' Quarters at the garrison, declined several invitations to join others for drinks in the lounge, and ran up the stairs, two at a time, to the solitude of his room. He unwrapped the slim parcel in his hand and fingered the gossamer threads of the lace imagining it one day soon covering Georgina's Titian hair as she made her wedding vows.

Whipped by impatience, he threw his helmet and jacket on to the bed, rolled up his shirtsleeves, settled himself at the desk and dipped the nib of the pen into the inkwell. At last! At last he could write the words he'd been burning to say to her. He was forced to pause a moment, to steady the tremor in his hand.

My darling Georgina,

It seems a hundred years since we said goodbye at the oasis; and yet it seems like yesterday. Leaving you that day was the hardest thing I have ever been forced to do, and in my heart you have travelled with me every day we have been apart; you have lain with me every night and filled every dream.

All I need tell you about Irena Levka is that she supplied the key to the cryptic notations you discovered, and – as you see – I am the one still alive. I'm afraid, my darling, the whole Kashgar business boosted my reputation to such a degree that the Colonel decided my experience was far too valuable to the Service at the moment to allow me to hand in my commission. As soon as I'd presented our report on the Levkas, I was sent south immediately to gauge what was happening along the Persian border, and now I'm on my way into Afghanistan with General Roberts's diplomatic mission to the Amir's court in Kabul.

We have spent the last two days in Peshawar, only a few miles from the Khyber Pass, which we'll be using tomorrow to reach Kabul. I have told my Commanding Officer in Simla that I am determined to leave the army as soon as this duty is completed. He's not pleased at my decision to marry, of course, but I can assure you, dearest Georgina, that my soldiering days will soon be over.

Warn your parents that I am about to snatch you away, because in a few weeks I'll be free to devote my life to your – to our – happiness. I'm not a wealthy man, but we'll live comfortably enough, whether you want to stay in England or go abroad.

Keep this veil in readiness for the day you and I stand together and confirm the wedding vows we have already made in our hearts. We both know, my dearest, that no signature in a marriage register, no vicar with a book of prayers, no bishop in a cathedral with bells and a choir of angels, could bind us more closely than our love has done already. The Golden Pagoda was our witness.

I am yours, utterly and completely, as you are mine. For ever.

Richard

PS I send my greetings to your parents and to the Hakvin family, as well as Quentin McCallum. I suppose Simon has long since gone on his way.

He folded the fine lace carefully and wrapped tissue paper around it again, then eased it into the thick brown envelope addressed to Miss Georgina Larssen, Swedish Mission, Kashgar, Chinese Turkestan. From Simla it would be carried safely over the mountains in the diplomatic pouch destined for the British Consulate. Quentin would have it delivered to the Mission.

As Richard wrote his own address in Simla on the back of the envelope, he tried to estimate how long it would take for her reply to reach him. Difficult to know. A month? Six weeks?

The Colonel's reaction on hearing Richard's single-minded determination to leave the army to marry a missionary's daughter had been choleric. But Richard knew that would be nothing compared to the outrage of the Eldridge family when he presented them with the *fait accompli* that he had wed the only woman he could ever love: Miss Georgina Larssen, the illegitimate daughter of a Russian ballerina.

His mother would never understand a woman who was not afraid to take her compassion to people with strange, un-English faces and strange, un-Christian beliefs. Would his sisters like her? Probably not. Her ideas would be sure to terrify them.

His grin was unstoppable as he ran down the stairs to leave his envelope with the Adjutant's corporal for posting.

At dawn the next morning he fell in behind the General, and rode into a high, harsh, barren land, where hawk-faced men with long jezail muskets were waiting on rocky heights.

He'd slept restlessly in the night, and had been woken several times by nightmares of Georgina wandering alone across a desert. Today he'd risen with an unaccountable feeling of despondency, and it deepened as the company rode up through the high passes, into a land notoriously hostile to the dreams of lovers.

CHAPTER NINETEEN

The Bombay hotel where Simon and Georgina stayed was a grand one on Malabar Hill, overlooking Chowpatty Beach, and their suite caught a welcome sea breeze. From the veranda, Georgina watched the parade of people and animals and vehicles passing below, and wondered how Simom would ever find her parents in this swarming city.

He'd gone out this morning to make enquiries at a shipping office, and learned that last week Doctor Larssen had booked passage to New York, but his funds from Stockholm had not arrived before the ship sailed. At the bank, Simon was told that Erik came each day to enquire if his money had arrived, and a clergyman said he'd heard of a Swedish doctor and his wife staying in a shabby boarding-house in the native quarter.

It was late in the afternoon when a carriage pulled up at the hotel, and Georgina saw Simon and Erik step down. Natasha seemed hesitant to leave the vehicle, looking anxiously about at people near the steps of the hotel, before she brushed Erik aside and ran ahead into the entrance.

Simon had reserved the suite next to theirs for the Larssens, and Georgina watched in horror as her mother, looking ill, shabby and distraught, was half-carried into the bedroom. Her eyes widened with astonishment when she recognized Georgina, and with a cry, she stumbled towards her.

'I did it for you, don't you understand?' Her voice rose in a thin wail. 'I did it for you and Erik. You! You! You!' Her fist thumped into Georgina's shoulder with each word, before Erik reached her and held her in his arms, rocking her to and fro, murmuring as he would to a frightened child. 'It's all right, my darling, we're safe. We're all safe now.'

She twisted her head towards Georgina, and her eyes were wild. 'Be careful, he is following! Don't ever let him know where you are.' A tic began in her cheek.

Georgina looked at Erik in dismay, but he shook his head. 'Leave us now, my dear. I have something to calm her. Tomorrow—' His expression tore at her heart.

'Oh, Simon, she's terribly ill, isn't she? What has my father told you?' Georgina dropped into a chair, and took the brandy he'd poured for her.

He sat beside her. 'Erik has said very little, actually. But' – he swirled the liquid in his glass – 'from what I've seen today and what I gleaned in Kashgar, I think Colonel Suvorov is behind this whole business. Natasha was terrified he would harm you. And Erik.'

'That's ridiculous!' Her glass trembled. 'I've never met the man!' Then she caught her breath. 'The letter from the Mission Board? You think Suvorov was the one who gave them that information?'

He nodded, and reached for her hand. 'For some reason, I think Natasha held great fears for your safety in Kashgar, and she tried to kill the Colonel.' His fingers increased their tension. 'But her poison didn't do its job well enough, and now she's terrified he's following her. And you.'

Speechless, Georgina clung to his hand as if she were drowning, and fought to regain her faculties.

'Now,' he continued, 'Erik is convinced that for her mind to heal, he must take her right away from the East. So, I've suggested they come to London with us.'

She felt giddy with relief. 'Oh, Simon, where would we be without you? How can we ever thank you enough?' She raised his hand to her cheek.

He gave her a bemused smile, and stood to pour himself another drink. 'I'm glad I've been able to do something for you.' He had to admit that these past months with Georgina – despite the Larssens' drama – had undoubtedly been the happiest period he had known in the last thirty years.

'Simon,' she said, with a thread of tension in her voice, 'as we have agreed to be open with each other, I want you to know that I've grown to love you very much. Um – this is difficult to put into words – but I realize the time will come when you'll go back to work in the desert again.' She rolled the stem of her glass between her fingers. 'Tell me, how can I live in your home and accept your kindness and feel as fondly for you as I do. . . I don't want to drive you away. . . Oh dear, am I making any sense at all?'

'You're making perfect sense, as usual,' he said, with his old good humour. He took her hands and drew her to her feet. 'As we have no secrets, Mrs Davenport, let me tell you that I find you a dangerous woman, but I'm delighted that you've agreed to live under my roof, and that – for the moment – I can call you my wife.' He kissed her nose. 'Separate beds, and days filled with purposeful activity, will ensure my sanity.' God help me to remember that, he said to himself as he left her.

As she lay alone in bed that night, Richard's baby moved inside her. *Richard.* Dear God, where was he now? Her feelings for him, which had once filled the very air she breathed, now seemed a memory, sharp-edged and vivid, like photographs neatly framed on a wall, to stir thoughts of what might have been, had she made different decisions.

Unbidden tears came to her eyes. If Richard was her past and Simon was her present, God alone knew what the future held for them all.

As soon as General Roberts led his party into the Khyber Pass and across the Afghan border, they entered the wild and mountainous territory where the Pathans jealously guarded their lands, recognized no law, and held allegiance to none but their own tribes.

Captain Eldridge took his scouting party ahead of the main body, to keep lookouts posted against attack. The men in the hills would be well aware of the gold that this one-hundred-strong escort of British soldiers was carrying to the Amir in Kabul.

Richard knew the tribesmen were up there now, hidden amongst the rocky ledges and crevices, watching the redcoats slowly make their way through the passes. He heard a whistle, in imitation of a kite. Sixty yards away it was repeated, and the signal was picked up by a third.

Even with binoculars he could see no sign of men hidden up in the rocks, although he knew they were there, waiting for a chance to attack. Once, the slanting rays of the afternoon sun glinted momentarily on the barrel of a musket high above them, and Richard's party swung their Enfields in that direction, but could find no target to line up in their sights.

Each night, after he had posted the pickets, he threw himself down on to the ground for a few hours' sleep, and sent up a prayer of thanks that another day had passed with no shot from a musket to claim his life; thanks that he was another day closer to the moment when he could turn for home and Georgina. He rigidly prevented any thought of her to distract his attention while they were on patrol, but at night, wrapped in his blanket, he allowed his dreams of the future to take flight.

On the seventh day of travel, the British party approached Kabul and entered the massive gateway of the citadel of Bala Hissar, built on the steep slopes dominating the city. The Amir's palace lay securely within the walls, and General Roberts and his senior staff were received by Amir Yakub Khan with flattering cordiality and every sign of friendship.

143

While the lengthy, formal negotiations were taking place, Captain Eldridge slipped into the intelligence work he had been assigned and mingled freely with the Amir's men.

Each day, while other officers were busy, he changed from his uniform to visit the bazaar coffee-shops, to smoke a bubbling hookah and listen to the gossip of the marketplace. And what he heard everywhere was an undercurrent of unrest throughout the city.

The negotiations with the Amir dragged on, and late each night Richard made his report in private to General Roberts. 'I'm hearing, sir,' he said, 'that Amir Yakub Khan is rapidly losing support outside Kabul itself, and even his popularity here is unreliable.'

'Is it his brother, Ayub Khan?'

'He's up to something in the south, I'm sure, sir,' Richard said. 'I'd like your permission to ride towards Kandahar to see if I can gauge what's going on.'

The General nodded thoughtfully. 'Be as quick as you can, Captain. The Amir is becoming very keen to see the colour of our gold, but we'll slow the negotiations until you bring some word on whether he's likely to be toppled by his brother.'

As soon as Richard left the General, he sent for two men he felt were trustworthy to ride with him to Kandahar He blackened his hair, stained his face and arms with walnut juice, and dressed in the clothes of a Persian trader – one whose wandering forebears had left him with a legacy of light-coloured eyes. Nothing to raise suspicions there, especially when this Persian trader had a purse of gold, and was looking for good-quality hashish to buy.

His escorts were familiar with the route to Kandahar, and provided sturdy horses for the long journey south. In the scattered towns and villages where they paused, the same air of fearful uncertainty underlay the gossip he overheard, as it had in Kabul. The army of Ayub Khan, the Amir's brother, was coming from Herat, travellers had reported, and was gathering strength.

Richard and his escort were still fifty miles from Kandahar when they met the first of the refugees fleeing from Ayub Khan's surprise attack on that city. He'd come across the desert like a whirlwind three days ago, they said, and they had seen the fighting in the city, the savage slaughter and pillage, with Ayub Khan's soldiers running amok, raping, mutilating men, women and children, day and night.

Richard turned his horse back towards Kabul, to reach General Roberts with his report before Ayub Khan had time to re-muster his debauched army in Kandahar and mount an assault on the capital.

'I suspect the Amir has been afraid that his brother was going to try this,' General Roberts told Richard. 'I wouldn't be surprised if the Amir makes a hasty exit from Kabul tonight, and takes the content of the Treasury across the border with him to Tehran.'

The British delegation, with appropriate diplomatic formality, left the appointment of a Resident in Kabul to remain an unresolved issue for the time being. At dawn the next morning, General Roberts led his company out of the citadel, and with the chest of gold untouched, rode back to India.

Quentin McCallum sat in his office attending to the weekly diplomatic pouch that had just arrived from Simla. He already had several reports ready to go back with the runner when he set out at dawn tomorrow. What should be done with this bulky brown envelope that Richard Eldridge had sent to Georgina Larssen?

Quentin pursed his lips, frowning as he recollected the events that had happened here in the last two months. Richard, he realized, must still be unaware that the Larssens had left Kashgar, and that Georgina was now Mrs Davenport.

Frederik Hakvin had told Quentin confidentially, of Erik's request for all Larssen mail to be burned, but surely not his one. Quentin's fingers played a tattoo on the desk as he pondered. As Simon had left no forwarding address in London, the only thing to be done was to return the envelope to Richard, together with a letter of explanation.

With his mission completed, Richard rode directly back to Simla. At Headquarters, weary and travel-stained, he reported to the Adjutant, then went straight to his quarters and soaked in a hot tub. He surprised himself by bursting into song as he scrubbed off the remains of the walnut-stain from his face and hands while his servant laid out his best uniform and rubbed a mirror polish on to his boots. Richard grinned. An officer who was about to hand in his commission must look his best when facing his irate colonel.

'My mind is quite made up, sir,' he was going to announce. 'Nothing will stand in the way of my marriage to a most remarkable young lady.'

He shaved and dressed. His servant helped him on with his boots and was about to hand him his sword, when there was a knock on the door and his mail was delivered. There was one letter addressed in his mother's familiar hand, and another large envelope carrying the insignia of the Kashgar Consulate.

He quickly dismissed the servant while he sat on the end of his bed and, with fumbling fingers, tore the letter open.

His own brown envelope, the one he'd sent to Georgina from Peshawar, slipped into his hand and his heart sank as he turned it this way and that. It had not been opened! He unfolded Quentin's letter and read it quickly, disbelievingly. He read it again, trying to make sense of the events Quentin described so meticulously.

Erik and Natasha had left the Mission, and Georgina had married Simon Davenport as soon as they'd arrived back in Kashgar. Sweet Jesus! Quentin had also included a photograph of the wedding day, with Georgina and Simon standing arm in arm, smiling into the camera lens.

How could she have done this? Richard felt a hammer pounding in his head. Simon! Simon had known damn well that Georgina had promised to wait until duty left him free to come for her. What a laugh! Apparently, she had waited for him no more than a few weeks before marrying Simon.

The correspondence slid from his hand to the floor as the pain of her – treachery? deceit? infidelity? stabbed at him as savagely as any enemy sword. He sat with his head in his hands, elbows on his knees, shaken by the white-hot, scalding anger rushing through him. Why, in God's name, had he thrown every scrap of caution to the wind and fallen so utterly in love with Georgina Larssen, who had just proven herself to be as fickle as other women? What a joke his mother would make of this if he told her.

Stupid, stupid fool, he castigated himself repeatedly, until he was overcome by a great need to get up and do something physical and destructive, to lash out, to smash his fist painfully against something – preferably against Simon Davenport's perfect features.

He paced the room, fighting his despair, while the hands of the clock crept around the face. No, he concluded at last, this was just another of life's lessons to be learned by the world's greatest fool. He stiffened his jaw and steadied his breathing. No one must suspect the blow he'd been dealt. This searing anger sweeping through him must now be used to cauterize the wound Georgina had inflicted, so that no evidence of his idiocy would ever raise sniggers in the Mess.

He arranged his features into a mask of impassivity, lifted his brandy decanter, poured a large drink and tossed it down. He squared his shoulders, picked up his helmet and strode to the door of his commanding officer.

'Well,' said the Colonel, narrowing his eyes, 'sit down.' He indicated the big leather chair across the desk. 'General Roberts informs me you're to be commended on the work you did for him.'

'Thank you, sir,' he said flatly, and watched the Colonel's moustache twitch. He was waiting to pounce like a tiger when Richard made the expected announcement about leaving the Service.

The Colonel cleared his throat noisily. 'The General has recommended you for a promotion.'

'Thank you, sir,' he said again.

'Well, *Major* Eldridge, I could do with a man with your field experience based here. Need someone who understands what's going on in the country, a man who can work with our network of agents.'

'Thank you, sir.'

The Colonel waited and his face grew redder. 'Dammit, m'boy, I can't go appointing you if you're going to pack up and clear out in a month or two! Have you still got a notion in your head to go runnin' off to marry some young lady?'

'No, sir. I've no plans to marry.'

'Good. Good.' The Colonel blew a long breath from under his thick white moustache. 'Plenty of time for that sort of thing later. *Much* later.' He nodded. 'I don't mind telling you that a man with your steady head is likely to go far in the army.' They both stood and the Colonel gave him a brief, rare smile. 'Come into the Mess now and we'll drink to your promotion, *Major*. This is a memorable day for you, eh?'

'Indeed, sir,' Richard said stiffly. 'This is one day I'll never forget.'

Upstairs, Richard's bearer was busy unpacking his master's travel-stained clothes to be sent to the washing-ghats. He brought fresh towels to the room, filled the water-jug, straightened the bedcovers and picked up the letters that had fallen to the floor. He had been trained from boyhood to be excessively tidy when working for an English officer, so he simply put all the correspondence away, out of sight, in the drawer containing the Captain-sahib's clean shirts. As convenient a place as any.

CHAPTER TWENTY

Simon booked their passage to England on the next P&O steamer leaving Bombay: two suites of staterooms on the upper deck, starboard side. It gave Georgina time to arrange for a tailor to make new clothes for Natasha, and for Simon and Erik to attend to business matters, particularly the transfer of Erik's moderate funds from Stockholm.

Georgina stayed beside Natasha, who refused to leave their suite. 'I did it for *you*,' the woman said a dozen times each day.

'Simon won't let anyone hurt us now, Mother. We're all going to England, and do you remember I said that you were going to be a grandmother?' Natasha always brightened at that. 'Let's talk about all the things the baby will need.'

As the steamer slipped out of Bombay a week later, they stood at the rail watching the city and its heat haze gradually fade to a thin, indistinct line on the horizon.

Once the passengers began to mingle, Georgina became aware of how well-known the name of Simon Davenport was. As they steamed across the Arabian Sea and into the Red Sea, it seemed that everyone on board wanted to meet the renowned archaeologist, and his wife.

'Simon, have pity on me. I'm hopeless at small-talk,' she muttered. Conversations stopped, and heads turned when the Davenports approached.

'Leave the talking to me,' he said. 'Just smile and look beautiful.'

But the whispered appraisals were often difficult for them to ignore.

'No wonder the old boy couldn't resist *those* blue eyes.'

'Ho ho! What I'd give to have a stunning figure like *that* waking up beside me each morning!'

'That glorious colour of her hair, Maude. D'you think it's natural?'

Simon showed nothing but a gentle amusement. What he felt inside was a fierce, possessive pride, and a dangerous delight, as they drifted together through the lazy shipboard days. He tried to remind himself that what the passengers saw when they admired his beautiful bride, was akin to viewing a mirage in the desert. Tonight they saw Georgina as his wife, but perhaps next month, next year, or the one after, the man she loved would come back into her life, and this illusion would disappear.

He sipped champagne now, watching how the rise of her breasts was delightfully displayed in the low cut of the new peacock-blue silk dress she'd worn to dinner. Increasingly his awareness was filled by the closeness of her. He sipped more champagne, and as they stood talking with passengers in the saloon, his hand slipped along her bare arm until his fingers met hers and entwined. He ran his thumb across her palm, and felt her tense and try to pull away. He held her hand firmly and his pulses raced when he looked down and saw the nervous excitement on her face.

She, too, was breathing fast, and his guard dropped further. When the musicians began to play and couples moved on to the dance floor, he slipped his arm around her waist, and they joined the dancers. When his arm tightened, pulling her against him, he ignored the alarm in her eyes.

'Simon, don't— Please, no—'

But it was too late for that. She was stiff and awkward at first, tight-lipped; but he held her tighter and felt the forbidden glory of her body moving against him. He quickly became oblivious of everything else in the room as they whirled in time to the music. His lips were against her hair, and the soft scent of violets drugged his mind. Gradually he sensed her body's resistance melting under his persuasive pressure.

'We mustn't,' she whispered, but he could no more have stemmed his reckless passion now than he could have walked on water. She closed her eyes, and he read her capitulation as she sighed. Dizzy with champagne, they danced into a world of their own, a borrowed world that she seemed now as loathe to leave as he was.

They slipped out of the saloon and ran up the companionway leading to the aft deck, where they clung together, and his lips met hers with a desire deep enough to drown them both. They paid no heed to the moon playing games with the phosphorescence glowing in the ship's wake, until Simon pressed one last, lingering kiss on to her lips.

'Anne, Anne,' he choked. With his chest heaving, he crushed her against him, his face buried in the curve of her neck. At last his arms slid away, and he turned from her. 'Oh, God! Forgive me for being such a damn fool.' His voice was dry and thin. 'For your sake, Georgina, and for mine, I pray Richard soon comes back into your life.'

In tears, she went back to her cabin and he stayed out on deck. For a long time she lay awake, waiting to hear him come to his bed in the adjoining room, but it was almost dawn before sleep overcame her. It was late in the morning when her breakfast tray was delivered and she woke to the sound of Simon's voice in their sitting-room. Pushing aside her tousled hair, and in her night-gown, she ran to the door.

'Good morning, dear,' Simon looked up and said with his usual cheerful-ness. 'Sleep well?'

She grunted a bleary affirmation as she watched him tie a shoelace, while a steward stood by, waiting to help him on with his cream linen jacket.

'The Captain has invited me on to the bridge to see us entering the Canal. Would you like to come?' His jacket was on now, and the steward handed him a Panama hat.

She made another grunting sound and shook her head. The steward held the door for him, and on his way towards it, Simon stopped and dropped a quick, friendly kiss on her cheek. 'See you this afternoon,' he said.

Georgina thought Erik was particularly tense when she joined him and Natasha in their stateroom at lunchtime. After her late breakfast, Georgina wanted nothing, but her mother, she was glad to see, was eating well.

'Natasha, I'd like to stroll on deck with Georgina. Should I call a stew-ardess to sit with you?'

'Don't be silly, darling,' she said. 'It's about time I started to read this dear little story Georgina borrowed from the ship's library.' Georgina looked away and stopped herself from saying that she had already read the novel twice to her mother.

Out on deck, Georgina took Erik's arm and they paced the length of the ship and back, before he stopped and faced her with an anger she'd rarely seen.

'Your husband came to see me last night,' he said without preamble. 'Very late indeed. He asked me to help him.'

She bit down nervously on her bottom lip.

'We talked, and he did me the honour of confiding to me certain matters which I'm disappointed did not come to me directly from your own lips.' Erik's voice shook with hurt. 'He says you have given your heart to Richard Eldridge. Your child is Richard's! Your husband says that when Richard comes, he will step aside and permit you to end the marriage.' He refused to allow her interruption.

'Georgina, how could you sink to these depths? How could you use a generous man who loves you – a man whose love for you can bring him

150

nothing but distress—' His voice was near breaking, and his glasses slipped down his nose as he shook his head at her.

She waited until she was sure his outburst had finished, and fought to remain calm. 'I'm glad Simon has told you everything, and he was right about most things. Richard will always be the love of my life, and I lie alone at night aching for what we briefly found together. Yes, I am carrying Richard's child. That was *my* mistake, and mine alone, but I don't regret it.' She slipped her arm back through his and they started to walk again. 'I could have told Richard about the baby, but I chose not to. Maybe *that* was my biggest mistake.'

'Simon is certain that Richard will come back into your life, and he seems prepared to step aside,' Erik said, in a tone of disbelief.

She stood with her hand on her stomach, thinking about it all as the ship passed slowly between the yellow sandhills cut by the canal. Every day the distance from Richard grew longer.

'Who knows when – if ever – I will see Richard again,' she admitted. 'The only thing I know for certain is that I will never, *never* walk away from this marriage. I couldn't submit Simon to the public humiliation of a divorce,' she said, and the hot desert wind dried the tears on her cheeks. 'I could never do that to him now.'

Once Richard was promoted and appointed to the staff at Intelligence Headquarters, he was allocated a pleasant little hillside bungalow on the outskirts of Simla. His bearer unpacked his belongings, and the unopened brown envelope lying amongst the box of shirts was unquestioningly placed with them in the new drawer.

Richard wrote to his mother and told her of his promotion, and of his house in Simla. He even suggested that his sisters might enjoy a summer visit to this most English of all towns in India, knowing that neither of them would dare anything so adventurous.

The quiet little hill town of Simla, set amongst groves of stately deodar trees, and flaunting its magnificent backdrop of Himalayan peaks, served as the year-round headquarters of the Commander-in-Chief of the Indian Army. However, once the summer heat on the plains below became uncomfortable towards the end of March each year, the Viceroy and his Council, accompanied by all the staff and trappings of administration, left Calcutta and travelled across India to settle in Simla for seven months.

Apart from a pleasant climate, Simla had strategic advantages for the government as well: it had quick communication by road and by telegraph to the vulnerable borders to the west.

The general population swelled dramatically during the summer months, with English families escaping the furnace of the plains to party and dance in the bracing climate, listen to band concerts in the rotunda, to hunt and ride, play tennis and polo, to attend the English church and the English playhouse, be invited to garden parties and picnics and viceregal balls, and to shop and gossip.

Richard very soon discovered that, as an unattached male, he was offered other diversions as well; and he felt no reason to refuse them. Georgina had found herself a husband, so why should he not enjoy a little flirtation with some of the eager young ladies who made themselves available?

He was entertaining and attentive, but none of his affairs lasted long. Besides, he was frequently forced to send apologies and cancel social arrangements when an order came. Within hours he'd be on his way to investigate men and events in far-flung regions or across borders.

He often told himself that this life suited him perfectly. He had everything a man needed, and it was only when his concentration occasionally lapsed that he recalled a time not long ago when Richard Eldridge was a man who had dreams.

He still sometimes had dreams at night of Georgina. He never dreamed of the lovely, widowed Pamela Barwick, who was going to invite him into her bed again, after they had dined tonight at the Viceregal Lodge.

He knew as little about Pamela Barwick as she knew about him. Through her late husband's family, she had connections with the Viceroy, and had come out to visit India even before her period of mourning was over. Richard had met her at a polo match, and was immediately attracted to the witty, sophisticated Pamela, as she was to him.

There was a recklessness about the way she attacked life, which stirred his blood. She'd made it clear at their first meeting that she wanted him as a lover, and it had excited him to play her game. Pamela was not a woman who wanted any man to woo her gently in the drawing-room; she wanted Richard to take her into the mountains to hunt. She climbed and stalked and shot with skill – hares, birds, antelopes, a leopard. And when their bearers carried her trophies back to camp, she shed her clothes and they made love on the grass, with a savage intensity that left them both shaken.

They met frequently and openly at parties and the theatre. They met frequently and secretly whenever an opportunity came, joining their bodies in a shared emotional hunger that was never expressed in words.

It was always like that. He didn't ask who she lay with when he was sent away. It was him she wanted when he came back, even though she sometimes called him Stephen when she cried out in the throes of ecstasy.

They'd dined well at the viceregal table tonight, and when the other guests rode off, Richard waited under the trees. At her signal, he swung up on to the balcony, entered her bedroom, stripped off his clothes and tumbled into the bed.

'You've been avoiding me all night,' he said, burying his face in her breasts. 'I haven't had a chance to tell you that I'm heading off over the border tomorrow.' He worked his lips up to her neck to nibble on her ear.

'Damn you! I don't want you to go, Stephen. I don't want you to leave me again.' She turned her head and her teeth clamped on to his shoulder. Hard.

He rolled her playfully, and the palm of his hand connected sharply with her bottom.

'So that's the way you want it, is it?' She panted loudly and clawed her nails across his shoulders, pinched his nipples, tried to slip down and nip him between the thighs.

He struggled with her. 'Shhhhh! You'll wake the household,' he whispered. He pinned her under him and caught her flailing hands as he slid into her silky fire and their passion mounted, then exploded, leaving them both breathless. And adrift in their loneliness.

'Richard, is Georgina dead?'

His heart lurched at that name, and for a moment he was speechless. 'No,' he said at last. 'She married someone else. I'm sorry – did I?'

'Yes, you often call me Georgina.' She ran her hand gently through his hair. 'Poor Richard, she's still part of you, isn't she?' He suddenly had to fight to hold in his emotions, but he was not completely successful.

'Let it out, my dear,' she said, continuing to stroke his head with a gentleness he didn't know she possessed. 'I understand why you feel so angry. It's a year now since Stephen died, and I still can't believe I'll have to live the rest of my life without him.'

'I'm sorry, Pamela,' he whispered. 'I thought if anyone could make me forget Georgina, it would be you. But I think we've both discovered that, despite all this, you and I can't really help each other to forget what we've lost, can we?'

'At least we tried, Richard,' she said, and tried to laugh and sniff at the same time. 'And, by God, we've had some times to remember!'

'Thank you, Pamela, we did indeed!'

'I won't be here when you get back from wherever it is that you're going this time,' she said, with a touch of sadness. 'This is goodbye, my dear.'

They lay quietly in each other's arms for a little longer. Then he kissed her, dressed quickly, and was gone.

*

The Davenport house in Bloomsbury had been built by Simon's father, and little had been changed in it since that time. It was large and gloomy, and filled with heavy, dark furniture standing forlornly about the rooms. As the house had been leased several times over recent decades, there were no personal touches remaining, no little treasures displayed in cabinets, no family pictures on the walls.

The staff of elderly servants had aired it thoroughly and filled vases with flowers from the garden, but they couldn't completely dispel the dismal atmosphere.

Erik had been adamant that he and Natasha would accept Simon's invitation to stay only until they could find a small house of their own to lease. Natasha's fragile health had improved during the sea voyage, but they had all seen how she had been alarmed on the drive to Bloomsbury by the unfamiliar noise and bustle of London streets. Now she clung to Erik tightly as they stood in the dimly lit hall of Simon's house.

'There's a room waiting for you upstairs, Natasha,' Simon said reassuringly. 'Rest today, and tomorrow I'll take you and Erik to find a nice little place, somewhere not too far away from us here.'

When Erik and Natasha and their luggage had been taken upstairs, Simon looked at Georgina and lifted one brow. 'Are you brave enough to come and see the rest of the house?'

He opened the double doors into the drawing room, and as soon as they crossed the threshold he gave a groan. 'I usually stay at my club when I'm in London, and I'm afraid I'd forgotten how dreary this house is.' He looked at Georgina apologetically. 'All the way back on the boat, I kept remembering the very happy childhood I had growing up here. I thought this place might do until. . . .'

She was sure he was about to say, '. . . until Richard comes.'

'Simon, it's the finest house I've ever been in,' she said quickly. 'I'm just rather overwhelmed by it, but if you were happy growing up here, I don't see why the next Davenport child shouldn't feel just as happy.'

From the corner of her eye she saw him swing on his heel to look at her with surprise, while she continued to speak.

'Don't you think that if the walls were a lighter colour, and those big curtains were pulled away to let in more light. . . ?' She walked to the window and tugged at the swathe of green velvet edged with heavy gold fringes. Immediately, the rays of the midday sun streaked across the shabby, faded room, and she and Simon were confronted by a large stuffed owl under a glass bell sitting on the ornate mantelpiece, glaring at them accusingly with his glittering yellow eyes.

They exchanged glances and laughed.

'There, now you can see how truly depressing the room is, m'dear!' he said with a wry grin. 'This won't do at all.'

'It's the *people* in a house that make it a home, Simon, and you've just told me there are happy memories here for you. We can find them again, I'm sure. Walls can be painted, chairs and curtains can be changed, carpets mended. Come along now, Mr Davenport, I'd like you to show me the rest of the house.'

'Then follow me, Mrs Davenport, and let me have your opinion,' he answered in the same tone. 'Perhaps the rooms upstairs overlooking the garden could be made comfortable for you, with a complete refurbishment.'

She murmured approval as they walked about. 'Is this where you were born?' she asked as she stood by a high, old-fashioned bed and ran her hand over the faded cover.

He inclined his head.

'Then this is where *your* child will be born, too.'

For a moment he stood rubbing a finger along his lower lip, while he studied her standing there with one hand on the bedpost.

'Georgina, I think Richard has a right to know that you're going to bring his son or daughter into the world,' he said evenly. 'if you won't write, will you allow *me* to get in touch with him?'

'No, Simon, this isn't the right time. He's still on duty somewhere— Oh, Simon, please don't.'

'I don't agree with you, m'dear. He'd *want* to know, wherever he is or whatever he's doing. We both know how deeply Richard feels for you.' Simon's voice was tight. 'I realize full well that it wasn't your intention to have a child, but nevertheless, a child *is* going to be born. It's his, and his child should know its father.'

There was no censure in his tone, but she flushed, and shook her head adamantly. 'You and Erik and I are the only ones who ever need to know that, Simon, because this child is going to be born here in *your* house and it's going to carry *your* name.' Her heart was racing and her voice was unsteady. 'I am your wife, and I intend to remain your wife. We *can* share a happy life here, Simon, and we can make sure our child grows up with happy memories of this house, like the ones you still have.'

He moved towards her slowly, until he was close enough to reach out and stroke the back of his hand down her cheek. 'You're a young woman, my darling. It would be foolish for us to make any commitments that can't – perhaps let's say that can't be *amended* some day.'

'Simon, I meant what I said! I will never leave you! Divorce is out of the question.' She smiled tremulously, but it was a smile warm with grateful affection. 'We *will* be happy together, I promise.'

He studied her closely for several moments, and a tiny muscle pulled at the corner of his mouth. 'If that's what you've decided, my dear, then I thank you from the bottom of my heart.' His voice was low and very much controlled. 'And if that's the case, we need to put our house in order without a moment's delay.'

As they walked downstairs again and through the conservatory, Georgina knew she'd made the right decision. The ambiguity about her life with Simon had at last been cleared, and her memories of Richard were now caught in time like a fly in amber, treasures to be kept locked safely away and sometimes viewed in private. She sniffed, and found that if she blinked fast enough, she could keep the moisture in her eyes from escaping on to her cheeks.

At the luncheon table, Natasha and Erik listened with interest as Simon talked about the changes he planned for the house. 'I agree with Georgina that we must get rid of the dark colours and let more light into the rooms. We'll order new curtains and have the furniture reupholstered immediately.' He encouraged her nod of agreement. 'The work must be finished by the time the baby arrives.'

Simon and Erik also wasted no time in making an appointment with a well-respected doctor to examine Georgina, confirm her robust health and agree to attend her confinement in three months' time.

Through Simon's business connections, the Larssens found a pleasant little house only ten minutes' walk from the Davenports, and Georgina spent the first days there, helping her mother settle into her new surroundings. The vast city and its ways were a far cry from the life they had known in Kashgar, but Simon appointed a cheerful woman named Mrs Flannery as housekeeper and companion for Natasha.

Mrs Flannery insisted that Natasha should begin immediately to sew baby clothes for her new grandchild, who, she was shocked to hear from Georgina, had no layette at all yet. Mrs Flannery took Natasha to visit a small drapery shop nearby to buy lawn and lace for little garments, and the outing proved to be a successful step towards repairing some of Natasha's confidence.

'I had to do it for Georgina,' Natasha still said sometimes when she met people, but Mrs Flannery was a down-to-earth woman who explained that Mrs Larssen meant she had to do a large amount of sewing for her daughter's new baby, because the poor bairn had barely a stitch to wear.

After a month, it was only Erik who remained unsettled in London.

Simon soon had a team of craftsmen at work refurbishing the house, while he was busy attending to a backlog of business matters, attending dinners and receiving awards, and having discussions at the Royal Geographical Society about a new series of public lectures.

Newspapers reported his return from Central Asia, and public interest was sparked in the wall painting of a golden pagoda, which was to be put on exhibition at the British Museum, along with a number of other artefacts he had collected along the Silk Road of Chinese Turkestan.

'My publisher thinks I should write a book about the pagoda,' he said, while he and Georgina were unpacking the boxes of Davenport silver that had been brought back from the bank to grace the house once more.

He had also bought several splendid oil paintings, which were now hanging on the walls, and the stuffed owl on the mantelpiece had been replaced with a pair of large Minton vases. It seemed a day rarely passed without Simon bringing home some lovely object to add to their growing collection. Or something he thought would please Georgina – a book, an ornament, or a necklace.

He bought a fine carriage and took her driving; occasionally they dined with his friends; sometimes they went to a play or a concert. But as he became busier with his engagements, he was often away from home, and when his crates from China finally arrived at the museum, he frequently worked there into the night.

Natasha's health continued to improve and she formed a firm bond with Mrs Flannery while they sewed baby clothes and read novels borrowed from the lending library. She was delighted when Simon asked if she would do a little secretarial work for him. 'Nobody's handwriting can equal yours, Natasha,' he'd said, and they arranged for her to come to the house two afternoons a week to begin the daunting task of transcribing his notes.

As the weeks passed, Georgina grew heavier and more restless. The wives of Simon's colleagues were pleasant middle-aged ladies who invited her to their lunches and tea parties, where she sat and unsuccessfully tried to contribute something appropriate to their drawing-room conversations.

'They think I'm terribly dull,' she confided to Erik. He was turning the soil to make a vegetable garden, while Natasha was out shopping with Mrs Flannery. 'I've tried to tell the ladies about my life in Kashgar, but they usually look appalled and say they feel sorry for me having had to live in a country so far away.' She sat down on a garden bench and made a huffing sound. 'Well, just look at me now! I live in the most exciting city in the world, in a grand house with a generous husband who will cheerfully give me anything I ask for – and yet I keep longing for what I used to have in Kashgar.'

Erik leaned on his spade and frowned at her. 'Admit that what you're longing for is Richard Eldridge.'

She bit down on her lip and thought for a moment. 'That's a big part of it, I'll admit, but out there I had dreams that, despite being *only a woman*, I'd be able to do something useful with my life.'

He began to dig again.

'When I went out into the desert with Simon and Richard, I met a truly independent woman – a botanist, who was quite famous in Russia. Irena was a wicked woman – and she's sure to be dead now – but she did make a contribution to science, and her husband was proud of her.'

Georgina stayed with her own thoughts, gently stroking her stomach. 'I'm certain there is a baby girl in here,' she said. 'I may have achieved nothing in my life, but I know Simon will allow my daughter to follow her dreams. This little girl will be able to study whatever she wants, and one day she'll have qualifications that will open the doors of the world to her.'

Erik threw down his spade and came to sit beside her. 'Stop this naïve nonsense before your frustration turns you into a bitter, controlling woman! You can't live your life through this child.' He gave her an affectionate, no-nonsense look. 'Anyhow, I'm prepared to wager that in a few weeks' time you'll be holding a baby *boy* in your arms.'

CHAPTER TWENTY-ONE

A nursemaid was engaged for the Davenport baby, and the nursery drawers were stocked with a layette that impressed even Mrs Flannery. Georgina's doctor arranged for a midwife to move into the Davenport house several weeks before the expected date of the delivery.

Georgina continued to grow more uncomfortable and restless each day. 'I'd love to go to the museum and watch Simon's treasures being unpacked, but he's sure I'd trip over something there,' she said to Natasha when she called. 'He's probably right.'

'Why don't we take a drive down to the river after lunch?' Natasha suggested. 'There's always something happening on the Thames to while away an hour or so.'

It was an effort to get Georgina comfortably settled into the carriage, but once Natasha and Symes, the driver, had tucked a rug around her knees and put a cushion at her back, the carriage moved off sedately.

Richard's child rolled and kicked impatiently inside her, sometimes with a strength that made Georgina catch her breath. A dozen times a day the baby forced her to think of him, and each time she remembered the promises they'd made in front of the Golden Pagoda. It gave her a strange feeling to think that soon the whole of London would be looking at that mural, and never knowing. . . .

'I don't think you've heard one word I've been saying!' Natasha scolded when their carriage reached the Embankment. 'This outing was supposed to lift your spirits. I think we should stop here for a moment to watch the antics of those two boatmen crossing the river.'

A cluster of men on the bank had apparently placed wagers on the rowers. When the first boat reached the opposite shore, a cheer went up and some of the spectators slapped each other on the back.

The crowd eventually dispersed, and other craft sailed past while Georgina and her mother sat idly watching the river. They paid little attention to the trickle of pedestrians walking past the carriage, until one young woman, huddled in a ragged shawl, rested her shoulder against a lamp post while she coughed deeply.

Through the carriage window, Georgina saw her struggle to catch her breath, then straighten. She'd taken only a dozen steps before her legs crumpled and she pitched forward, hitting her head on the ground.

Ignoring Natasha's plea to stay in the carriage, Georgina opened the door and scrambled clumsily on to the road. Natasha and the coachman were only a pace behind her when she reached the unconscious girl and turned her over.

She seemed little more than a thin, shabby child, burning with fever. Several people paused to look, then walked by, shaking their heads when Georgina asked if they knew the girl, or where she lived.

'Get her into the coach,' Georgina said to Symes. 'We'll have to take her to a hospital.'

'Don't reckon there's a hospital round here that would be inclined to take the likes of this one, ma'am,' he said as he placed the slight, malodorous figure on to the soft leather seat of the new barouche.

'This young lady must be seen by a doctor quickly,' Georgina called to the group of people gathering to watch. 'Where can she be taken?'

That question was also met by a number of shaking heads and shrugged shoulders, until someone at the back called: 'Doctor Thompson's charity clinic, down near the docks, might take 'er in, I suppose.'

'Wapping Lane,' another voice shouted.

'Do you know the direction?' Georgina asked Symes, as he and Natasha helped with the difficult task of assisting her back into the carriage.

He nodded, with a clear lack of enthusiasm. 'Have to watch they don't steal the nails out of the 'orses' shoes down in them parts, ma'am.'

'Just find the place quickly,' Georgina panted as she placed the pillow under the head of the barely conscious girl, covered her shivering body with the knee-rug. Natasha took the seat opposite, and held a lavender-scented handkerchief to her nose.

They set off with a clatter of horses hoofs towards the docks, but before long the driver had to rein in and ask directions as he took the carriage through noisy, narrow streets, and past dark, crowded buildings where poverty hung like banners in the breeze, and pale, pinched faces turned with suspicion towards the elegant vehicle invading their domain.

'I can take the carriage no further, ma'am,' Symes called down. 'The place yer lookin' for is down that alley a-way, so best put the girl out now.

Someone's sure to pick 'er up and take 'er there.'

'Certainly not!' said Georgina. 'We'll get down and take her ourselves. Come on, my man, look lively!'

'Madam!' He'd jumped down from his seat and looked at her in dismay through the window. 'The master would skin me alive if the 'orses was left unattended in this den of thieves.'

She opened the door, reached for her purse, and called to a thin youth sprawled on a step, watching them intently. 'Do you want to earn a gold sovereign? Hold these horses for a few minutes – and make sure no one puts a hand on the vehicle, remember!' She tossed the coin into the air and caught it again as the lad ran forward. 'It will be yours when we return.'

'Yes, m'lady,' he said, and threw a worried glance over his shoulder at the weaselly faces peering from corners and doorways, waiting to snatch his good fortune.

When Georgina had heaved herself on to the cobbled lane, and the coughing girl lay in the coachman's arms, the trio set off to find Doctor Thompson's clinic in the squalid alley.

At the door they were met with pandemonium and the overwhelming smell of human wretchedness and carbolic. Men, women and children, some angry, others sullen and tearful, clogged the benches near the entrance as the trio pushed their way in.

'What has happened?' Georgina asked a haggard man leaning against the doorpost.

She read resentment in the red-rimmed eyes that swept over her. 'I suppose the noise of the explosion in the fireworks factory this morning failed to reach Mayfair, did it, my lady?' he said with undisguised insolence. 'Them what wasn't killed in the blast was buried under the building when it collapsed.'

'No more, no more!' shouted a burly young woman, pushing through the throng, holding a tray in one hand and waving the other at the girl in Symes's arms, as if brushing away a swarm of flies.

Crying children, rattling buckets, raised voices, groans and the sounds and odours of the place, quickly drained the colour from Natasha's face.

Georgina's cheeks, on the other hand, grew flushed. 'I must speak to Doctor Thompson, just for a moment,' she called to the woman with the tray. 'Please, we need him to see this young lady urgently.'

The woman glared; her face was grey with exhaustion. 'Wouldn't we all like to see Doctor Thompson, dearie? When you find him, you tell him that for me, will you?' she said as she pushed by and swung open the door into a ward they could see was jammed with beds and straw mattresses on the floor.

Several women wearing aprons were weaving amongst the patients.

'Just leave the lass here now, and let's be on our way, madam,' Symes pleaded. 'Gawd knows what them thievin' types out there will be doin' to the master's beautiful coach!'

'Bring her in here, Symes,' Georgina said, heading towards the ward and indicating for him to follow with the girl. Natasha trailed behind them, looking about in dismay at the state of the injured lying on the floor or propped up against the walls.

When the burly nurse with the tray saw them walk into the ward, her face coloured with anger. Before she could order them to leave, Georgina called to her over the noise: 'If somebody will bring a mattress for this girl, I'll stay and help you here. I've had experience as a nurse.'

The astonished staff turned their weary faces towards her, as she took off her hat and passed it to Natasha, then untied the strings of her short cape and began to roll up her sleeves.

'Have you taken leave of your senses, Georgina? You can't stay here in your condition!' Her mother was now near to tears.

They saw the red-eyed nurse about to produce an automatic objection, until she met Georgina's determined expression. 'Get that mattress and bring it over here,' the woman shouted to a male attendant.

'Now tell me quickly about Doctor Thompson,' Georgina said. 'Have you any idea where he is?'

'I imagine he's at the bottom of a gin bottle again, though God knows whereabouts this time.'

They watched the mattress being flung into position and then the harassed coachman placed the girl on to it. Georgina gave him the sovereign. 'Pay the lad waiting with the horses, then drive my mother home.' She halted Natasha's protest. 'Tell Doctor Larssen there's been an explosion, and bring him back here immediately with his instrument bag.' The nurse looked on in disbelief. 'My father is an excellent doctor,' Georgina said, and turned back to Natasha. 'Please wait at the house, and when Simon comes home, tell him where I am.'

'I don't know how I'll ever be able to face your husband after allowing you to become caught up in this predicament,' Natasha said shakily.

Georgina wasn't listening; she was already at the basin, washing her hands and preparing to dress the wounds on her first patient.

In little over an hour, Erik arrived at the clinic and quickly summed up the situation. 'Well, here we are, doing just what we used to do together at the Mission,' he said, and they exchanged a smile.

Georgina held back from telling him that tonight's work would be nothing like anything they'd experienced in Kashgar. Her waters had just broken, and the niggling pains in her lower back were telling her the baby was not going to wait.

Doctor Larssen's presence at the overcrowded, ill-equipped little clinic created some degree of order in the chaos. 'Doctor Thompson should be horse-whipped for abandoning the clinic at a time like this,' he growled, and sent a young porter out to find Doctor Thompson, with instructions to drag the doctor back without delay.

If Erik wasn't able to help, many of these victims would have little chance of survival, Georgina thought, as she stood beside him, assisting as he probed a man's chest for the fragment of metal embedded there. Together they'd sewn up gashes, set broken bones and dressed burns.

'Are you all right?' her father asked several times. 'Sit down. Don't over-tire yourself, my girl.'

As the hours passed, she was glad to be walking about because the pains were growing more severe. She understood a little more now why the Kirghiz women of the mountains kept working with their animals until their gods decreed it was time for a child to be born. There was one awkward moment when a contraction forced her to grasp the edge of the table and she had to wait for it to pass before her hands were sufficiently steady to remove a splinter of wood embedded close to a woman's eye.

When she'd put a dressing over it and led the woman to her waiting children, she leaned against the wall, put her hands to her waist and stretched to ease the ache in her back. The clock on the wall said it had just gone eight, and her pains were sharper. The contractions were coming every fifteen minutes now.

The ward became less crowded when Erik allowed some patients to be taken home, and the young porter returned from his search for Doctor Thompson. He was pale-faced and almost incoherent as he told how he'd seen the doctor's body being carried away from Mrs O'Brien's brothel down by the river.

The head nurse threw up her hands. 'Lucky the Devil took 'im tonight, for I'd cheerfully have killed him meself tomorrow for leavin' us in this pickle. What's to become of this place?'

'One thing at a time, Miss Pettigrew,' said Erik, with more enthusiasm than Georgina had heard in his voice for a long time. 'First, I think it's high time my daughter told me how often she's having her contractions now.'

Nurse Pettigrew, sagging with fatigue, looked at Georgina and shook her head. 'What a time you've chosen!'

The table used for surgery in a cramped, untidy backroom, had been pushed aside, and a bed, ready with reasonably clean sheets and towels, stood waiting under the lamp. Erik held out his hands to Georgina.

'Don't be frightened, my dear,' he said. 'I'll be with you.'

After he had rushed Doctor Larssen to the clinic, Symes, the coachman, took it upon himself to inform his master of the afternoon's events. But by the time he reached the museum, Mr Davenport had already left his work there for the day and had gone straight to a meeting with the Committee of the Royal Geographical Society, which was to be followed immediately by his speech to the members crowding into the lecture hall.

'Can't open the doors and interrupt the proceedings once they've started,' the dour-faced hall porter informed Symes when he arrived. 'I'd lose me job if I did that, unless you can swear on the Bible that it's a matter of life or death.'

For a moment Symes was tempted, but as a man of good conscience, he shook his head.

And so it was almost nine o'clock when, after the ovation following Simon's speech had faded, Symes had an opportunity to inform his master of Mrs Davenport's whereabouts.

Simon ran to the coach and sat on the perch beside the coachman to hear the events of the afternoon while Symes took the horses as fast as he dared through the thickening fog rolling in from the river. Several times he lost his way and took a wrong turn in the darkness.

'The clinic is not much further on now, sir,' he said, when the carriage had gone as far as he could take it. 'Go straight down that alley on the left there, and you'll find it a little way along.'

'You have a pistol?'

'Aye, sir.'

'Good. Keep it in your hand.' Simon sprang down and, as soon as he moved away from the coach, he saw two figures appear out of the fog, then sink back into it as they followed him into the alley. His senses were alert, and when he heard muffled footsteps behind him, he slipped the blade from his silver-handled sword-stick. As the first arm came to snatch him, he slashed it with a punishing stroke and turned to face the second assailant. At the sight of the long blade pointed in his direction, the man quickly disappeared back into the fog.

Simon returned the sword to the stick, retrieved his silk hat from the muddy cobbles, and picked his way through the squalor to the lamp shining over the clinic door.

His stomach clenched with apprehension as he stepped inside and was confronted by the sights and odours of the dimly lit ward. Groans, snores and an occasional cough and muttered word reached his ears, and his heart raced as he saw no sign of either Georgina or Erik. Light shone from under a door at the far end of the ward, and he almost ran to it.

Without knocking, he turned the handle and flung the door wide. Georgina, her tangled hair spread about her on the pillow, lay on a narrow bed, gazing with rapture at a child in her arms. Simon's throat closed over as he looked down at her, and at the baby, and his eyes filled with tears of joy, and relief, and wonder.

Erik, sitting beside her, smiled up at him. 'All is well. You have a fine son.'

He stood and shook Simon's hand, then left the room and closed the door behind him.

Georgina held out a hand to Simon. He came slowly towards her, and the tiny creation in her arms.

'Come and greet your son,' she said, and he sat beside her on the bed while she pulled away some of the towel wrapped around the newborn.

His fingers trembled as he brushed the baby's cheek. 'So beautiful.'

'Hold him, Simon. He's strong and healthy, and we'll make sure his memories of growing up are happy ones.' She put the baby into his arms. 'I'd like to name him after his two grandfathers – if you agree. We'll call him Mark, after your father, and Erik, after mine.'

'Mark Erik Davenport,' Simon said, when he could find the voice to speak. 'Splendid.' He held one tiny hand in his own and bent to kiss it.

But when it came time to register the baby's birth, Simon wrote three names on the official form. The records showed that the Davenport son was named Mark Erik Richard.

CHAPTER TWENTY-TWO

The arrival of the baby into the Davenport household brought changes to all their lives. Motherhood filled Georgina with a new sense of contentment, but always hovering at the edge of her mind was the charge that she had deliberately locked Richard out of his beautiful son's life. What would she do if she ever saw Richard again?

Simon was a doting father. 'What a commotion you've caused, little man,' he said fondly to the baby lying in his lap, while his own work lay unfinished on the desk. 'Perhaps I should have handled the whole business differently, though under the circumstances facing your mother at the time, God knows how.' The baby gave a yawn. 'You'll never know, young Master Davenport, how hard I try to ignore the shards of guilt I feel when I remember that a man named Richard Eldridge still knows nothing of your arrival in this world.'

He bent his head to kiss the baby's sweet-smelling cheek. Richard might not know of his son, but enough time had now elapsed for him to have heard from Kashgar about Georgina's sudden marriage. Richard must still be smarting.

He looked down at the tiny fingers gripping one of his, and gratitude filled his heart. For the thirty years since Anne's death, he'd lost all hope of holding a child in his arms. 'One day, young Master Davenport, I'll tell you all about the myth of the Golden Pagoda. They say it brings hope, when all hope seems lost.' He held the baby tightly against his chest. 'Who would dare to scoff at that myth now?'

'I never knew this joy when you were so tiny,' Natasha said to Georgina, when she held her freshly bathed grandson and rocked him to sleep. 'I had to go back to work in the mill when you were a few days old.'

'You were the best mother – you *are* the best mother anyone could wish for.'

'You'd do the same for your child,' Natasha said, locking her gaze with Georgina's.

She nodded. 'Of course.' But how much courage would I find if Richard stood on our doorstep now? she wondered.

Erik visited the Wapping Street Clinic each day, doing what he could to help there, and Simon, generous as always, gave a donation that allowed the struggling charity to buy medicines and dressings and keep its doors open a little longer.

'It's not enough, though,' he said to Georgina after they returned from an evening at the theatre with a party of his friends. 'I had an idea tonight when I looked at the people around us: we need to raise public interest in the clinic and organize a fundraising committee with some titled person as chairman. I'll introduce you to the right people in society, and you, Mrs Davenport, can pluck at their heartstrings.'

Georgina looked appalled. 'I could never do it. I'd be quite out of my depth.'

'Look at yourself, my dear.' He turned her to face the mirror over the mantelpiece, and stood behind her to study the reflection. 'We both know that underneath tonight's satin and sapphires, there is still the independent woman who never once allowed herself to be daunted by the people and the customs she faced in a faraway land of mountains and deserts.'

Georgina flushed and bit her lip. 'And now you want the missionary's daughter to learn all about the customs and rituals of the tribe who inhabit the drawing-rooms of Mayfair?'

He laughed fondly. 'I think you'll be surprised at the number of ladies who might share your views, and who might even be looking for just the kind of opportunity you're going to present to them.'

Two weeks later, Georgina and London society met face to face at the official opening of the Golden Pagoda exhibition at the British Museum.

'I hope the guests can tear their eyes away from the sight of you and spare a glance at the Pagoda this evening,' Simon said as he helped her down from their carriage.

'Simon, I'm quaking,' she whispered, and lifted the hem of her white and gold brocade gown as they walked up the broad steps. 'Please stay close by me tonight.' Her palms were damp, and her heart pounded, half in excitement, half in dread, as Simon led her towards the exhibition hall, and she caught the looks of interest turned towards her.

'You look absolutely stunning,' he whispered. 'You've made me the proudest man in London tonight.'

'I'm glad you can't see the shambles I am inside,' she said, then took a deep breath and lifted her chin, smiling as they walked into the exhibition to the sound of applause.

With the centuries of dust and sand cleaned away from it, the Golden Pagoda glowed, towering at one end of the hall. For a moment Georgina's breath caught as the sight of it brought an avalanche of memories. She was grateful for Simon's steady hand under her elbow.

He kept her by his side throughout the evening, moving through the crowd, greeting acquaintances, gracefully acknowledging their congratulations. 'I'm fortunate to have married a lady of many talents,' he said each time he made an introduction. 'Georgina was with me in the desert when I first saw the cave of the Golden Pagoda.'

'How very exciting!' said the stately Lady Morley, one of London's most influential hostesses.

'I'm sure you'd be interested to hear some of the tales my wife has to tell about her experiences in Chinese Turkestan,' Simon added. 'And with a little persuasion, she might reveal her plans for something quite adventurous in London, too.'

'Oh, yes indeed, my dear Mrs Davenport,' Lady Morley said, with heartening enthusiasm. 'I would be delighted if you could join a small luncheon party at my house next Tuesday.'

'How very kind, Lady Morley,' Georgina said, with an appropriate deferential bow. 'I'd be delighted.'

'Beautifully handled, my love,' Simon whispered as they moved away. 'If you can persuade Lady Morley to support your cause, success will be guaranteed.'

At that moment the Prince of Wales arrived, accompanied this evening by the Princess, and all conversation ceased while Simon met the royal pair and their entourage, and Georgina made her well-rehearsed curtsies.

'I did so want to be amongst the first to view your exhibition, Mr Davenport,' said Her Royal Highness, and the crowd parted as Simon escorted the Princess across the room.

'So, Mrs Davenport, we meet at last,' said the Prince of Wales with an approving nod, which was noted by the cream of London society. 'Now it's clear why your husband waited so long to make his choice.' His hearty laugh was picked up by those around them. 'It was archaeology that brought you together, eh?' There was more polite laughter in the hall. 'Well, I'm sure half the ladies in London would have been racing off years ago to dig holes in the sand, if they'd realized that was the way to entice Simon Davenport to the altar.'

It seemed to Georgina that the attention of the whole room was focused on their conversation, and nervousness addled her brain.

'It would have made no difference to me, Your Highness, if Mr Davenport's interest had been in horseracing or bridge-building.' She fluttered her ivory fan. 'I think my good fortune in becoming Mrs Davenport had much to do with the quality of the moonlight in the desert.'

The pert response slipping so easily from her lips startled her, and to cover her embarrassment she laughed and gave the Prince a dazzling smile. He swiftly returned it, and the group around them joined in the good humour of the moment. Her cheeks flushed and she struggled to give the impression that she was enjoying this attention. It was a relief when Simon and the Princess rejoined them.

Alexandra placed her gloved hand on Georgina's wrist. 'My dear Mrs Davenport, your husband has told me a little of the extraordinary life you have led. I'm sure my daughters would be delighted to meet you one day soon.'

'I suppose your days of desert travel have come to an end now you've settled into domesticity?' the Prince said with a significant lift of his brows.

'I'm afraid, sir, we archaeologists are a fiercely competitive breed.' Simon's laugh didn't quite reach his eyes. 'There's a city called Niya waiting under sand, and I'd hate to think of any German or Frenchman or Russian getting there before I do.'

'And will you go exploring again with your husband, Mrs Davenport?'

'Ah – no, Your Highness,' Simon said quickly. 'Georgina has committed herself to a charitable cause here in London. A clinic for the needy.'

'How splendid,' said the Princess, while the Prince nodded in agreement.

Georgina's knees had barely enough strength to perform a deep curtsy as the Prince and Princess moved away. The school's charity-child, the missionary's stepdaughter, was now basking in the reflection of her husband's fame, and society had just witnessed royalty bestowing its approval on her.

The formalities of the night passed in a blur. Speeches were made, praising Simon's work, but she heard little, other than her own pulses pounding with pride.

It was late when they returned to the house. 'What a marvellous night it's been, darling! You were brilliant,' she laughed as they walked into the hall. 'And Lady Morley wasn't the only hostess to issue an invitation.'

'I said you'd be the toast of London.'

'How am I ever going to live up to the image you painted of me tonight?'

'You could never disappoint anyone.' His voice was warm and ripe with emotion.

'Simon, you mentioned tonight about going back to dig at Niya, and I dread that day. Must you go?'

He nodded slowly and let out a long breath. 'I won't go anywhere while you need me.'

It was a dangerous moment as they stood in the hall, both elated by the success of the evening, and now suddenly lost for words. Georgina could read her own aching needs reflected in his eyes, and she moved towards the stairs.

Since the night when they had allowed desire to overwhelm them on the deck of the ship, they had been careful never again to place themselves in any situation that could bring nothing but distress.

'Goodnight, Simon.'

If only – just once in a lifetime – it could be possible to share her love with him, this would have been the moment. She blew him a kiss.

He said nothing as he watched her slowly climb the staircase to her own bedroom, and her heart bled for them both.

CHAPTER TWENTY--THREE

The deep silence of the Taklamakin Desert was broken by the sound of an approaching horse. Simon looked up from his papers, and through the door of the tent saw the messenger from Kashgar ride in through the ruined gateway of Niya.

He carried a thick pouch of mail, and Simon swept aside his work and emptied the contents on to the table, rifling through the envelopes until he came to the one addressed in Georgina's hand. His heart turned over when he tore it open and saw the photograph of Georgina and Mark, taken on his third birthday, three months ago.

The boy's resemblance to his father grew more striking each year – the shape of his head, his colouring, the sweep of fair hair that fell determinedly across his forehead. And Georgina's smile was one he knew so well – that unique combination of serenity and determination.

He propped the photo against a pottery bowl which had been excavated that day, and felt a desperate longing to leave this desolate region behind and be back in London with them again. He opened Georgina's pages and held them to his face, hoping to catch one hint of her scent on the paper, before he began to read.

My darling Simon,

Your colleagues tell me that what you are finding at Niya will throw a whole new light on history, and we are all terribly proud. But really, all I can think about now is how wonderful it will be to have you home again with us by Christmas! Please, please don't let anything delay you, because we are planning to have the happiest Christmas ever, I promise.

He sat back in his chair, smiling as he read her descriptions of Mark's play and

171

his quaint sayings. The family was all well, she assured him, and she gave him news of their acquaintances, and the dinners and concerts she'd attended. Funds for the charity clinic were flowing in satisfactorily, and they had a new lady doctor to assist Erik, as well as two nurses trained by Miss Nightingale. She was delighted to tell him about a benefactor who had just donated a building for a new clinic, and Lady Morley's committee was planning a ball to raise money for more equipment. Georgina herself was working at the clinic two days a week, and other ladies with whom she'd become acquainted had volunteered to leave their Mayfair drawing-rooms and give their time also.

So, you see, my dear Simon, your grand scheme to transform me from a jellyfish is having consequences which I see gradually spreading amongst the female population here. Ladies are now saying to their husbands: 'Simon Davenport permits *his* wife to go about independently, so it *must* be an acceptable thing to do.' Believe it or not, my love, I think I'm starting to change the culture here faster than I ever could in Kashgar!

Come home quickly.

All my love, Georgina.

Simon picked up the photograph and walked outside his tent, past the excavation sites that were giving up the secrets of long-dead men and women who had once lived and loved in this place.

Did any of that really matter now? He looked around at the crates filled with ancient treasures destined to be opened on the other side of the world, and sat on a crumbling mud-brick wall to study the picture in his hand. Mark and Georgina.

It was time to go home now. He was ready.

When Major Richard Eldridge, tired, dusty and in ill-humour, returned to Lahore after his mission through the Punjab, he chose to ignore the invitation to stay again at the Residency. Instead, he walked into the Gymkhana Club, situated a few hundred yards further down the road.

'Of course, Major, we have a veranda room available,' the steward at the desk said, carefully avoiding more than a cursory glance at Richard's face. He called a porter to carry the baggage, while he personally escorted the Major upstairs.

'You would like your bath brought in immediately, sir?' he asked as Richard stood irresolutely in the middle of the room. A servant entered and began to unpack travel-worn clothing to be taken away for washing and repairs.

'Yes, yes, a bath, thank you. And send up a large whiskey and soda – a bottle,' Richard said, and walked to the French doors that looked out to the polo field. 'Oh, and I'll take my dinner in the room tonight, too.'

'Certainly, sir, I'll send the menu.'

'God dammit, man, don't bother me with menus! Just send up food on a tray! Anything.'

Richard cringed at the tone in his voice, and stood with his back to the room until he heard the tin tub being carried in, followed by boys with buckets of steaming water. At the same time a steward from the bar arrived with the tray of drinks, and placed it on a table.

'Thank you,' Richard said, without turning. He was in no mood to catch any further looks of sympathy or curiosity at his face. 'Just leave me now. I'll see to myself.'

He undressed, avoiding a glance in the mirror, poured himself the largest measure of whiskey he'd ever drunk, and slid into the bath to gulp it. Christ! He dreaded the scene he was about to experience when Rosemary Sutcliffe saw the damage done to the left side of his face four weeks ago by the blade of a desert thug's knife. The havoc that had then been compounded by a villager's rough stitching technique.

He swallowed the rest of the whiskey, dropped the empty glass on to the floor and rested his reeling head on the high back of the tub. Bloody hell! What sport the gods had played with the life of Richard Eldridge in the last five years. They'd flung Georgina Larssen into his arms, then torn her away again, and refused to cover the footprints she'd left on his heart. And now this!

Bloody, bloody hell! He was almost thirty-three, and he was still behaving like a lovestruck schoolboy over her. Love! Damn Simon Davenport for taking Georgina the moment the opportunity had presented itself. But why had she allowed herself to be persuaded by him?

Richard climbed out of the bath, picked up the empty glass, and dripped water across the floor as he went to pour another drink, adding a little more soda this time.

Back in the cooling water, he set about congratulating himself on the fact that, two months ago, he'd at last been able to push thoughts of Georgina *Davenport* out of his mind long enough to propose marriage to Rosemary Sutcliffe, daughter of the Resident of Lahore.

He closed his eyes; his head was spinning. It was difficult to remember why – just as he was preparing to set off on another mission – he'd chosen to ask sweet, pretty little Rosemary to share his life. The romantic setting that night of moonlight and sparkling fountains in the Shalimar Gardens couldn't be overlooked, of course. Neither could the frequent brush of her fingers across his hand, or the lovelorn smiles she'd thrown him.

He gave a short, bitter laugh. Of course! He'd asked her to marry him because he'd just admitted to himself that he was tired of this lonely, unsettled life, moving constantly about the damn country on shadowy business, arriving, departing, rarely lingering more than a few weeks in any one place. Except for that period in Kashgar nearly five years ago.

Lord, how much alcohol would he have to drink to forget that he'd felt so despondent on the night he'd proposed marriage to Rosemary Sutcliffe, that if she'd turned him down, he'd probably have asked for the hand of any other woman within a ten-mile radius?

Why the hell had little Miss Sutcliffe rushed to accept him? Why had her fastidious parents permitted their only child to promise herself? She was a sheltered eighteen-year-old virgin, and he a battle-hardened man of thirty-three, whose reputation with the ladies was no secret. Oh, Rosemary was eager for him, all right; and she knew how to tease. Involuntarily, Richard smiled at the recollection. Aaargh! That movement hurt his face!

How the gods must be laughing now. He gingerly ran his fingers down his left cheek, from the corner of his eye to his chin, tracing the livid, puckering scar that would be with him permanently, according to the army surgeon he saw last week.

He'd give himself a day or two here at the Club before he presented himself at the Residency. First, he'd send a note to Rosemary's parents explaining the situation. That might be the best way to prevent a fit of hysterics when the young lady herself sighted the long, disfiguring gash down the length of his cheek, pulling at the corner of his eye, constricting movement on one side of his mouth. His letter must assure them all that he already regarded Rosemary released from her promise to marry him, and there would be no necessity to discuss the matter further.

Richard drained his glass, and tried hard to think of ways to avoid presenting himself at the Sutcliffes', but it had to be done. As a gentleman, he had to grit his teeth and get on with it. Wherever he went now, his scarred face was going to raise comment, or pity. He'd wait another day or two before he called on Rosemary, then he'd make his way immediately back to Simla. And after that?

'Nasty business, nasty business, indeed, Major,' said the Colonel bluntly when

Richard reported to his Commanding Officer. 'But at least you can be grateful the knife didn't take your eye.' His bushy white eyebrows snapped together as he peered at Richard's scar closely. 'Probably fade a little in time, I imagine,' he said, then tapped his forefinger on the report lying on the desk. 'So, the Sikhs have finally decided to give up the idea of a revolt, have they?' He gave a grunt of satisfaction and leaned back in his chair.

'Yes, sir. We're still holding Maharaja Duleep Singh under arrest in Aden, and he'll never be allowed back into this country. The plans for an uprising collapsed when the other leaders in the Punjab realized that their Messiah was not going to materialize,' Richard said, and relaxed a little. 'The Russians have certainly lost interest in using a Sikh revolt for their own cause, and that should be an end to the whole business now.'

The Colonel steepled his fingers and nodded. 'Good work. Good.' He looked at Richard, then reached for an envelope on his desk, and pushed it towards him. 'Read this letter from the Foreign Office, Major, and give me some indication of your feelings about their offer. They want your answer by the end of the month.'

Richard picked it up and skimmed the page. 'A posting to London, sir?'

The Colonel seemed surprised by his lack of enthusiasm.

'Surely it's been obvious that Whitehall has had its eye on you, Eldridge? A man with your background in this region would be very useful at the Foreign Office. Perhaps the diplomatic corps? Give it some serious thought.'

Richard took the official letter, went back to his bungalow, and walked up the steps to the veranda. Could he go back and settle in London, knowing Georgina and Simon were living there?

He picked up the pile of letters and London papers waiting for him on the hall table. But he barely had time to open one, before the first caller arrived at his door.

'Major, we were so distressed to hear. . . .' He cringed at the pity he saw in their eyes.

The trickle of friends coming to commiserate about his injury continued through the day.

'Richard, my poor dear, I couldn't sleep when I heard what happened. . . .'

'Bad luck, old boy. . . .'

The following day, he woke in a black mood and told his servant to inform any visitor that he was not at home. He carefully shaved his disfigured face, ate breakfast, and ensconced himself in the sitting-room with his letters and newspapers. He needed time to think rationally about the Foreign Office post. As restless as he was to move on from the field-work he'd been doing for the last six years, what would he be stepping into if he went to Whitehall?

He sorted through his mail and set aside his mother's letter until he'd first dealt with other matters. This hesitation to open correspondence from his mother had started when she had begun to mention the name of Georgina Davenport.

That was another laugh the gods must be having at his expense. Who would ever have supposed that Prudence Eldridge would have become acquainted with Georgina at social gatherings in London? Some time ago his mother had written that she'd met the daughter of the doctor who had cared for him in Kashgar, and she considered Mrs Davenport 'a most pleasant, refined young woman, quite devoted to her husband and child'.

When he'd read those words, Richard had felt as though his heart was being torn from his chest. He'd never considered the possibility that Georgina and Simon might one day produce a child.

Today's letter from his mother was concerned mostly with a description of Bertie's wedding to Miss Edith Montgomery, whom Richard faintly remembered as a colourless girl with a predictably impeccable background.

Prudence Eldridge concluded her letter by listing her social engagements for the month, and mentioning a banquet being held by Lady Morley to welcome home Simon Davenport from his latest expedition to China. 'I'm sure his wife and child must have missed him most dreadfully while he was out there digging in the desert all that time.'

Richard dropped the letter on to his lap as a surge of anger hit him. He closed his eyes and saw Simon setting out with an expedition from Kashgar yet again, to search for a few bloody fragments of ancient history under the sand. Was the man mad, leaving his wife – leaving Georgina and their child for all those months – merely to go off into the desert and gather even more professional acclaim for himself? Why, in God's name, had she been so eager to marry a man who was prepared to abandon her so readily?

Richard's head pounded, his cheek throbbed, and bitterness, anger, envy and resentment all rose like gall in his throat. He poured another stiff drink and held it in a trembling hand. For a moment he gazed at the movement of the liquid in the shaking glass, then thumped it back on to the tray. The answers he wanted would never be found in the bottom of a bottle.

He turned and paced the room, once, then twice, while he cleared his thoughts. Right! The time had come for him to acknowledge two regrettable, but irrevocable, facts. Firstly, for the rest of his life he was going to live with a disfigured face, and secondly, although Georgina was married, he would never be able to stop loving her, or keep her out of his thoughts.

He walked to the open window and looked across his own well-ordered garden to the permanently snow-capped peaks of the distant Himalayas. When Fate had initially thrown them together in Kashgar, he'd found Georgina Larssen as cold and distant as those mountains. She'd kept her private self well protected behind an icy reserve, and he was going to have to learn to do the same, to hide the gut-twisting anger he experienced each time his face attracted attention.

He took three deep breaths and walked to his bedroom mirror to confront the ugly scar that had caused both Rosemary Sutcliffe and her mother to rush from the room in tears when he'd presented himself.

Well, he'd survived that little drama by giving the impression that their reaction was of little concern to him. He'd made damn sure that the misery he felt inside was hidden by a quickly constructed shield of indifference. He'd make damn sure now that the shield became permanent and impregnable.

Richard left the house immediately, and gave his decision to the Colonel. 'I'll take the Foreign Office offer,' he said, 'and I'd like to leave for London as soon as it's convenient, sir.'

He spent the rest of the afternoon in the Officers' Mess, receiving congratulations on his new appointment. He paid social calls the next day, and accepted several dinner invitations before he left Simla.

'What a terrible thing to happen to such a handsome man,' he heard ladies whisper behind their fans as he passed. News of his broken engagement to Rosemary Sutcliffe appeared to have raced across the country ahead of him, and Simla expressed its collective sympathy, frequently.

'But see how bravely the Major is keeping up his spirits!' they gossiped when they saw him riding out to hunt leopards in the hills with fellow officers.

As Richard prepared to leave his old life behind, and while his insides crawled with anger, the shield around his emotions grew thicker with practice. Only on one occasion did he feel it all about to come crashing down around its heels.

'Major-sahib, this envelope lying in the drawer with shirts. Should it perhaps be packed in trunk with books and papers, sir?'

His servant was methodically emptying drawers and bookshelves, packing his belongings for London into two large travelling-trunks. The little man held up the unopened envelope addressed to Miss Georgina Larssen at the Kashgar Swedish Mission. Richard cursed himself for not having had the courage to toss the damn thing – the lace veil – away years ago. Then he cursed himself for not finding the courage to do it now, and told the servant to pack it with his shirts.

Why, in God's name, was he holding on to it? Could he really pretend to himself that he was saving the veil for some niece on her wedding day? He got up quickly and walked out on to the veranda, to gaze for one last time on the changing colours of a glorious sunset turning the distant white peaks to a soft, creamy pink that melted to salmon, then to purple, as dusk fell.

He continued to stand there, recalling every detail of Georgina's features, while his head pounded and his cheek throbbed. Measured in hours and days, the time they'd shared had not been long, but there had been a depth and purity in their loving that would live with him for ever.

Long after the sun had set and the sky over the mountains was filled with blazing stars, Richard came to understand the reason he would never part with that envelope – and never open it.

When he'd sent it to her from Peshawar, every fibre of his hope and love had been sealed inside it. Now, like a child, he was refusing to open the packet and be forced to confront the empty place where that hope had once flourished.

One day he'd decide what to do about that envelope. Perhaps.

By the time he'd dressed for his final dinner at the officers' Mess, all sentimentality, along with any outward sign of his burning anger and resentment, had been safely tucked away behind a façade of dignified reserve. That was how he wanted Simla to remember Major Richard Eldridge.

And that was exactly what London was going to see when he arrived there.

CHAPTER TWENTY-FOUR

Settling into London was much as Richard had expected. No better, no worse. He lived quietly, and much of his time at the Foreign Office was spent assessing reports that were coming in about the faint stirrings of independence movements in India. How seriously were they to be considered?

The rooms he took near St James's were comfortable enough, and whenever he could get away from Whitehall for a few days, he caught the train to Hampshire and stayed with his mother. His father had died, unlamented, two years before.

Bertie and his new wife, Edith, were well matched, Richard decided, after he had spent a dreary weekend staying with them at their mother's house in the country. Edith rarely drew breath, and Bertie hardly spoke at all as he nodded and smiled at his blue-blooded wife's inane prattle. After that weekend, Richard ensured his visits did not again coincide with theirs.

Prudence Eldridge had long given up riding, and as there were no hunters remaining in her stables, Richard bought a big chestnut to leave there and ride into the New Forest when he came to stay. He needed this escape to solitude after living and working in the claustrophobic atmosphere of London. There were many times there, on the crowded streets and in busy office buildings, when his utter loneliness threatened to overwhelm him. Sometimes, lying awake at night, his fingers curled and the nails bit into his palms as his fantasies took him to Bloomsbury – oh yes, he'd discovered the address! – to confront Mrs Davenport with the lies and deceptions that had scarred him even more deeply than the would-be assassin's knife through his cheek.

'I've barely caught sight of you today, Richard,' his mother said from her end of the dining-table, as they faced each other along the length of polished mahogany. There was concern in her tone, not reproach. 'Are you unwell?'

'No, thank you, quite the contrary,' he said, and gave a fleeting smile before he returned his eyes to his dinner plate. They continued eating in silence, and when he looked up again, he found his mother sitting motionless, watching him. Her handsome features maintained their regal composure, but, with a pang, Richard realized tears were welling in her eyes.

'Of all my children, Richard, I'm sad to find that *you* have become the one most like me – and I wish with all my heart it wasn't so. I hate to see what you're doing to yourself.'

He froze and said nothing, while she left her seat and came towards him. He stood to take her extended hand and slipped it through his arm as they walked together out on to the darkened terrace. For some time they stood against the balustrade, wrapped in their own thoughts, while a thin line of clouds drifted across the full moon.

'Do you think a scarred face will change the way your loved ones view you, my dear?' Her tone was gentle. 'But it's more than that troubling you, isn't it? A woman somewhere who's hurt you? Is that why you've shut us all out of your life? It won't work, you know. If you continue to live behind this prickly armour, the outcome will be far worse.' Her voice rose shakily. 'I know all about keeping the world at a distance, Richard. For years I did it successfully, but now I'm paying a high price for lacking the courage to face my demons. My pride stopped me from openly admitting years ago how much your father had hurt me. Instead, I kept up the pretence that it was of no concern, and now I'm ending my days alone, still hiding my mistakes.'

Richard realized his mother was crying, and when he put his arm around her she didn't pull away. Her head was on his shoulder, and the scent of violets in her grey hair stirred memories of a red-haired woman who had once loved him.

'It's too late for me, Mother. She married another man.' He felt his own throat closing over. 'I don't doubt she loved me; but apparently she didn't love me enough.'

'Oh, my poor dear. How impossible it is to measure love,' she said. 'But promise you won't keep the world at a distance, as I've done. Don't leave yourself with nothing but your pride and a mountain of regrets.'

'Do you truly believe I could leave the memory of her behind, and move on?'

'Yes, you must. You've never lacked the courage to climb a difficult path.'

'I've tried that path several times already, and failed.'

She sighed and straightened. 'Then you must try again, and again, Richard, until you do find the happiness you deserve.' She ignored his grunt of cynicism, and presented her cheek. 'Goodnight, my dear, sleep well. And remember this discussion we've had.'

*

When Richard returned to London, he visited Savile Row and ordered new evening clothes, as well as a smart grey suit and a black suit, and hats and ties and several pairs of shoes. He also bought new shirts, which his servant folded and put away carefully in the drawer where a brown envelope addressed to the Swedish Mission in Kashgar still lay underneath the other shirts.

He'd fully intended to take his mother's advice about moving on with his life, and it occasionally annoyed him to think of the envelope there still, an irritation, a useless fragment of lost hope which he should never have brought to his new life in London.

On one occasion, a dismal Sunday afternoon when his mood was even darker than the weather, he had a sudden impulse to rid his life for ever of that envelope and all it stood for. He pulled it from the drawer, shoved it into the pocket of his overcoat and set out for the river.

He stood for almost an hour on Westminster Bridge, thinking of Simon Davenport's wife and watching the ebbing tide of the Thames swirl beneath him, eager to suck his disappointment and anger down into its depths and carry it away for ever. By the time he was chilled to the bone, he realized he was quite unable to bring himself to reach into his pocket and throw the damn thing down into the waiting, murky water. He could no more cleave Georgina from his heart than he could make the scar on his face disappear. He buttoned his coat again, walked home, and slipped the envelope back into his drawer, under his shirts.

To any observer, Major Eldridge began to live a full life. The novelty of his scarred cheek dimmed somewhat as he became a familiar guest at dinner parties and joined friends at the theatre. He gambled heavily at cards and developed an interest in horseracing, all of which should have lightened his pockets considerably. It didn't. In fact, with his winnings he went to an art auction and was quickly caught up in the bidding for a Gainsborough portrait of a young lady with glorious chestnut hair.

At the last moment he pulled out of the bidding, when common sense suddenly alerted him to the madness of bringing a reminder of Georgina into his sitting-room. Instead, he bought a Landseer painting of two appealing spotted retrievers to look down on him from his wall.

It was about time he bought himself a dog, he decided, as he walked into his club and crossed to the cloakroom with his coat and hat. A dog would be company on the long walks he took each day through the parks—

'I say, Richard! Glad I caught you here,' a friend called from across the hall. 'We've taken a box at Covent Garden on Tuesday night to hear that Australian soprano they're all talking about. Care to join us?'

Richard accepted, and joined a group of ladies and gentlemen with whom he had little rapport. Still, conversation was not the primary object of the evening, he reminded himself as he performed the social duties required. He retrieved a fan that was dropped, and looked for opera glasses that had been lost behind a chair, and read the entire programme to the fluttery woman next to him because she refused to wear her spectacles in public.

'Don't you think *Romeo and Juliet* is just the most romantic opera ever written, Major Eldridge?' she said to him breathlessly. 'I just wish Mr Gounod had given it a happier ending, don't you? Wouldn't it be so sweet if neither Juliet nor. . . .' Richard heard no more. His whole attention was drawn to a movement below in the stalls, where Simon and Georgina were walking down the centre aisle towards their seats, their progress slowed as they paused to acknowledge greetings from acquaintances seated on either side.

Richard's breath caught in his throat; he leaned forward and his heart thundered. She was there, just yards away from him, radiant in cream satin, with her husband's hand under her elbow. Richard was aware of nothing but her smile, as the Davenports were led to their front-row seats just before the lights dimmed and the overture began.

He sat back in his chair, closed his eyes, powerless to quell the tension that was making breathing difficult. The last five years had been good to her, that was clear. And Simon, damn him, must be getting close to sixty now, yet tonight he looked as handsome as ever.

The curtain went up, and the stage lights illuminated the faces of the people sitting in the front rows. He watched the profiles of Simon and Georgina throughout the performance, noticing how they occasionally whispered to each other and exchanged affectionate smiles. He prayed they didn't turn their heads and notice him in the box.

The longer he watched, the lower his spirits slid, seeing them so obviously content in each other's company. One part of him hoped initially for some sign that the marriage had proved to be a mistake, but that seemed far from the case.

During the intervals, Richard made an excuse to drift from his group and avoid any possibility of meeting the Davenports. When the performance was over and the last curtain call taken, he urged the party in the box to leave the theatre promptly before the congestion of carriages at the entrance made them late for their supper engagement.

They were almost to the street, when the lady who had his arm, uttered a shriek. 'My earring! Oh no, Major, I've lost my earring!'

The others in the group stopped, recalling just when they'd last seen her wearing the jewel, offering suggestions and blocking the doorway.

'Allow me to run back to the box to look for it, while you all make your way to supper,' Richard said firmly. 'I'll follow on shortly.'

He turned to edge his way up the stairs, against the downward flow of people, and when he reached the box, the woman's earring was on the floor beside her chair.

He put it in his pocket and joined the last of the audience slowly moving down the staircase towards the exit. Looking over the banister he caught sight of Simon and Georgina, moving in the sluggish tide, drifting away from him across the vestibule. On their present trajectory, Richard calculated, there was no chance of their paths crossing.

But, unexpectedly, Simon's head turned, and their eyes met. There was a look of anticipation on Simon's face, and for several moments he stood where he was, holding Richard's gaze, as Georgina and the throng passed through the foyer. Then Simon began to shoulder his way across the current towards the foot of the stairs, where he waited.

Richard was breathing heavily and too angry to speak when they faced each other on the bottom step.

'I caught sight of you in the box, Richard, and I've been hoping we'd find an opportunity to talk,' Simon said in a low voice, aware that he was being recognized by people passing.

'Indeed,' Richard said thinly. 'I don't think I have anything at all to say to you.'

'That's understandable. But there are some other matters that I think you should be made aware of.' They were both jostled, and moved to stand against the wall, which provided even less privacy for conversation. Someone called Simon's name, and he could see an acquaintance approaching.

'I want you to come and see the Golden Pagoda at the museum, Richard,' he said firmly, and pulled a calling card and pencil from the gold case in his pocket. He wrote on the back of the card and held it out.

'Surely you joke, Simon? I beg you to remember that I've already seen the Golden Pagoda. It was burned into my memory five years ago.' Bitterness clipped Richard's words, and he made no attempt to take the card.

'I've not forgotten that, but I'm sure you'll still find much about it to hold your interest,' Simon said, casting a quick look at the friend who was about to interrupt them. 'Come to the museum early tomorrow, before the public arrives.'

Richard shook his head. 'I don't think so. And anyhow, I have an appoint-ment in the morning.'

'Then come before you go to your meeting. Any time. I'll arrange to be there from eight o'clock onwards. Hand this card to the doorman and you'll be brought straight along to the Silk Road exhibition.'

Richard still hesitated. The tension in his chest tightened. 'Will *she* be there?'

'Absolutely not, I assure you.'

'Will you tell her we've met like this tonight?' As the words left his lips he half-hoped Simon's answer would be yes, and his own stupidity shook him.

'No, Richard. I'll say nothing to her until you and I have had a chance to make some decisions about – well, whatever it is we have to make decisions about.'

Richard's hand was damp as he took the card and slipped it into his own pocket. 'Nine o'clock,' he said hoarsely, and walked away before Simon had an opportunity to introduce him to his friend.

CHAPTER TWENTY-FIVE

Richard slept little that night, and woke next morning with a heavy head and a conviction that it was madness to rush into a reunion with Simon Davenport. He rose an hour earlier than usual to shave, and had difficulty in choosing an appropriate tie to wear with his new grey suit. He didn't want to give Simon the impression—

Every ounce of remaining commonsense told him to send a messenger immediately to the museum with his apologies, but instead he looked at his watch, picked up his hat and went out to hail a hackney cab.

When he arrived at the side door of the museum and presented Simon's card, the porter on duty was ready to escort him through the empty, echoing halls and to direct him to the entrance of the Silk Road exhibition.

The door stood slightly ajar. Richard's mouth was dry as he pushed it open and stepped inside. At the far end of the long, high-ceilinged hall stood the breathtaking image of the Golden Pagoda. The drumbeat of his racing heart filled his ears; his throat closed over. One morning, on the other side of the world, he'd woken with Georgina in his arms and looked up to see this golden image watching over them, listening as they shared their love, and their promises.

He swallowed hard and took a deep breath, then noticed Simon sitting casually on the plinth of a statue to one side of the mural, talking to a small fair-haired boy on his knee.

The child looked towards the door, then smiled shyly. Simon turned and acknowledged Richard's arrival with a nod, placed the boy on the floor and stood holding his hand, watching Richard's face as he walked hesitantly towards the pair.

Richard's head swam. The significance of meeting the child here in front of the Golden Pagoda was not lost on him; it needed no more than one glance at the boy's features to understand whose son he was.

'Richard, I would like to introduce Mark, who's now four years old,' Simon began, then corrected himself, with a smile down at the boy. 'Apologies, four and a half years old.'

Richard cleared his throat, desperately searching for a response, but was rendered speechless by the child who was looking up with curiosity at his scarred face. 'Mark, this is Major Richard Eldridge, who's come back from India. Remember, I told you about the tigers and elephants who live there in the jungle?'

'How do you do, sir?' the child said, stepping forward to hold out his hand in a well-rehearsed performance of good manners, before asking eagerly: 'Did you ride on elephants in India?'

Richard bent to shake the warm little hand, then crouched to bring his eyes level with the boy's. 'Yes, I sometimes rode on elephants.' It was hard to find the breath to speak, and he was barely aware that Simon had left them and walked to the far end of the hall.

'And did you have a gun and hunt tigers?'

'Yes, sometimes I did that, too.'

'And did a tiger put that scratch on your face?' The question was asked with the innocence of childhood, and Richard's heart melted.

'Yes, something like that happened to my face.'

'Did it hurt?'

'Yes, it hurt a lot at the time, but not any more.'

'It must still hurt a little bit, because I can see some tears in your eyes,' Mark said, nodding at Richard with the understanding of one wounded man to another. He sat on the floor to pull down his stocking and displayed a thin white scar across his knee. 'See, that's where I fell over and Grandfather Erik sewed it up. It hurt, but Papa kissed it better for me.'

Richard hastily reached for his handkerchief. Mark watched, then leaned forward with a concerned frown. 'Would you like me to put a kiss on your scratch and make the hurt go away?'

Richard swallowed hard. 'Thank you, I'd like that very much.'

Soft, warm lips touched his cheek damply for two seconds, then lifted. 'There, that's better now,' the child said with confidence, and sat back to pull up his stocking, while Richard floundered in his own emotions.

'Thank you, Mark,' Richard said, with a catch in his voice. 'You have indeed made the hurt go away.' Instinctively he reached to push back the sweep of fair hair falling across the child's forehead, just as his own mother had done to him throughout his childhood. He stood unsteadily, and held out his hand. 'Let's catch up with your father, old chap. He and I have a lot to talk about.'

186

Simon watched them approach. 'Like to postpone your appointments today? We can have a message sent to Whitehall.'

Richard nodded, and Simon arranged it with the head porter as they left the museum. Without discussion, they walked towards Russell Square, two tall, silent men, each holding a hand of the little boy skipping along between them.

They paused when they reached the square; Simon and Richard faced each other while Mark fidgeted impatiently and tried to pull away.

'My house is just a few streets away,' Simon said. 'We can talk privately this morning, if you'd care to. Georgina and Erik will be working at the clinic till late this afternoon. Natasha is transcribing my notes, but she won't arrive before lunchtime today.'

Still holding Mark's hands tightly, they turned several corners and came to the steps of the tall house, where a maid appeared as they walked in the door. While she was taking their hats, Mark ran to the stairs.

'Manners, my lad!' Simon called. 'I didn't hear you say goodbye to . . . er?'

'To Uncle Richard?' Richard's voice was tight.

'Of course. Come along, Mark, and say goodbye politely to Uncle Richard.' There was a twinkle of mischief in the child's big blue eyes as he threw back his shoulders, marched to Richard and stood stiffly to attention. 'Goodbye, Uncle Richard,' he said, then made a bow and burst into giggles.

'Off to the nursery with you, you rascal,' Simon laughed, and they watched him bolt up the stairs. 'We'll be in my study,' he called to the maid. 'Please make sure we're not disturbed.'

Suddenly, the child had gone, the house was still, and the men were alone in Simon's study, facing each other in buttoned green leather chairs on either side of the fireplace, each draining a glass of brandy.

'Why wasn't I told?' Richard said unsteadily, after a few moments of tense silence.

'Georgina has made a few unwise decisions in the last five years,' Simon said quietly, 'but always with the best motives.' He nodded sympathetically at Richard. 'She should have told you that she suspected she was carrying your child before you rode out after the Russian woman. And back here in London, she should have gone ahead with a divorce, as we'd planned in the beginning.'

Richard's jaw sagged as he listened, then he shook his head, as if to clear it. 'Do you mean to tell me that she knew she was carrying a child when we first stumbled on to the Golden Pagoda? How – I mean, she couldn't have known at that time. . . .'

Simon shrugged. 'She was nearly three months advanced by the time we got back to Kashgar.'

Richard frowned in disbelief as he tried to make the calculations. 'But that means ... dear God! She told me she was absolutely sure. ...' His face flushed. 'Dammit, why didn't she tell me she'd made a mistake with the dates or whatever, and that she'd conceived? And why didn't she wait until I came for her? We made promises.'

'Did you go back to Kashgar?'

'I wrote, but my letter was returned, with the news that she'd married you.' His old anger resurfaced and grated in the heated words.

Simon heaved a heavy sign. 'She planned to wait, I assure you. She was going to stay at the Mission with Erik and her mother – have the baby there and wait for you, till Judgement Day if necessary.' He stood and walked to the door opening on to the garden, leaned against the frame and scrubbed his fingers across his forehead.

'However, it wasn't as simple as that, you see, because when we arrived in Kashgar she was confronted by a chain of events that altered everything.' He swung on his heel to face Richard and his voice rose. 'Erik and Natasha were no longer at the Mission. They'd rushed off to India ten days previously and that left Georgina alone, with no money and no one to look after her. I thought we might catch up with them if we left immediately, and to cover any, er ... well, *embarrassment* for a single, pregnant lady, we married, with the understanding that I'd provide grounds for a divorce when – well, whenever.'

Richard sat with his head in his hands and uttered a bitter expletive. 'Yes, but once you'd married her, you were quick to change your mind about *that*, no doubt. Of course, what man in his right mind would willingly throw away the pleasure of lying with Georgina as a wife?' He looked up, about to fire more resentment, but a glance at the expression in Simon's eyes stopped him.

Simon returned to the chair opposite Richard, and sank forward with his elbows on his knees, twisting the gold ring on his finger. 'Unfortunately, that's not quite the way it was: Georgina and I can't share a bedroom. She married me, knowing that however deeply I loved her – and indeed I do' – he added with emphasis, quickly looking up into Richard's eyes – 'she knew before she accepted my proposal that since I survived the Mutiny in '57, it's been impossible for me to be physically intimate with any woman.' A tiny nerve jumped at the corner of his mouth. 'Unfortunately the yearning remains, and sometimes the hell of it all becomes, er – difficult.'

The tightness around Richard's mouth softened as his mind absorbed the significance of Simon's words. 'Good God, Simon! What can I say?'

'Erik is the only other person who knows the situation. Sometimes I need his help to sleep at night.' Simon's husky voice broke.

Richard looked at him with compassion, and Simon eased the tension by walking across the room, unlocking a drawer in his desk and taking out Mark's birth certificate. 'You were never overlooked, Richard. See? Your son carries your name, along with my father's and Erik's.'

The lettering blurred before his eyes as Richard scanned the document. 'Thank you, Simon,' he said simply. 'That means a great deal to me.' He handed it back, and climbed to his feet with his hand extended.

Simon took it in a crushing grip. 'I'm sorry this moment has taken so long to eventuate, Richard. I would have wished it otherwise, but, for Georgina, the time was never right.' He lifted his shoulders. 'I saw an opportunity last night at Covent Garden, and seized it.'

'She knows nothing about this morning's arrangement?'

Simon shook his head. 'At the moment she's totally unaware, but before our chatterbox upstairs gives her the news, I'll tell her myself.'

Richard blew a silent whistle. 'She might not be happy about it.'

'That's why you and I need this time alone, to discuss the future for both your son and his mother.'

'Yes, of course – calmly and rationally.'

The words had barely left his lips before they were interrupted by a burst of sound outside the door – Mark's high-pitched, excited voice, accompanied by several adult tones, and the clatter of shoes running across the tiled hall.

The study door swung open and Mark stood beaming at them. 'There you are, Grandmama, I told you Uncle Richard was here.'

'Mark!' Simon scolded as both men scrambled to their feet. 'How many times have I told you? Parkins, take my son to play in the garden, immediately!'

Mark looked quite unabashed. 'See, there he is!'

His flush-faced young nursemaid scooped the boy off his feet and fled with him from the scene.

Richard was only half aware of the episode; his attention was concentrated on Natasha's mounting distress as she stared at his scarred face and took two faltering steps into the room.

Simon hurried to close the door. 'Natasha, my dear. I didn't expect you so early today.'

Richard moved towards her with his arms outstretched. She flung herself against him and he held her tightly. 'It's all right, Natasha, truly,' he murmured, and saw Simon's anxious frown.

'Oh, Richard, I'm so sorry. Did Suvorov do that to you?' She stroked his cheek. 'Oh, I'm so sorry that you were the one he punished. It's all my fault.'

She lifted her head and what he saw in her eyes sent a wave of shock through him.

Richard held her face between his hands and looked directly into her eyes. 'Listen to me, Natasha. I was stabbed by a *dacoit* in Rajasthan – a robber did this to my face.'

She appeared not to understand him. Simon was already sitting behind his desk, writing. 'We need Erik here,' he said, without looking up. 'Natasha was very ill when they left Kashgar. Perhaps her recovery hasn't been as complete as we thought.' He went to the door and called for the maid. 'Take this message immediately to Doctor Larssen at the clinic.'

She was ashen-faced and trembling, seemingly about to swoon, when Richard picked her up. 'Carry her upstairs quickly,' Simon said. When he placed her on the bed, Richard felt as distraught as Simon looked.

'She's paid a high price for what happened in Kashgar.' Richard listened, scarcely able to believe Simon's outline of the events involving the Russian Colonel. 'It seems Natasha stretched herself until her mind snapped.'

'You and I must make sure that Georgina never feels herself stretched – pulled in any way between you and me, Simon,' Richard said. 'You have my guarantee that I'll respect your marriage.'

'We'll both tread carefully.'

When Erik was heard arriving at the house, Simon met him on the stairs while Richard withdrew and waited by a window in the hall. In the garden below, he saw Mark's worried nursemaid vainly trying to persuade him to come down from the branch of the old elm tree where he was perched precariously, and attempting to climb higher.

'Erik has calmed Natasha,' Simon said, coming to join Richard at the window, 'but he wants to take her home. She has an excellent companion called Mrs Flannery who has helped in the past, so if you'll excuse me, I'll send for the carriage and go with him.' He put a hand on Richard's shoulder. 'Can we meet again? Tomorrow?'

'Of course,' Richard said, then glanced again into the garden. 'Would you object if I spent a little time down there now with Mark?'

'Spend all the time you need, my dear fellow,' Simon said, and for a moment their eyes locked. 'All the time you need.'

Richard felt as if a huge weight had lifted from his heart as he ran down the stairs and found his way through the conservatory, into the long garden.

'Here comes Uncle Richard!' Mark squealed. He was now lying with his arms and legs twisted around a thick branch, vigorously resisting the maid's efforts to reach him.

Richard pulled off his coat and threw it on to the grass, loosened his tie to undo his collar, and swung himself up on to the branch beside his son. 'This is a splendid lookout,' he said. 'What can we see from here? Pirates on the horizon?'

'No. You can't see the pirates from here. You can only see them from up there.' The boy pointed up through the branches to the top of the tree, and, below them, the little maid whimpered.

Richard grinned down at her, unconcerned that only one side of his face had the capacity to smile. 'Don't worry, lass. Go off and find something else to occupy yourself. Master Mark and I will sound the warning if we sight pirates heading this way.'

While the girl ran towards the house, Richard surveyed the branches above them and plotted their route skywards. He climbed from one foothold to the next, heaving Mark up behind him until, a little way from the top of the tree, he judged they had reached their limit.

'We'll have to wait for those branches to grow a lot stronger before we can go any further, old chap,' he said, and noted a shadow of petulance sweep across the child's face.

'How long?'

Richard's arm around him tightened. 'The tree will take as long as it needs to take, Mark. Everything happens in its own time, and we'll only make ourselves unhappy if we become too impatient.'

'But will you climb up to the top with me when the tree is strong enough? Will you be here then?'

Richard was saved from thinking about his future by the sight of both the maid and the cook coming across the garden to spread a picnic rug in the dappled shade. 'The master said we was to bring lunch for you both,' said the cook, depositing a tray with two bowls of barley broth, two beef pies, and apples, while Richard and Mark swung down cautiously from their roost. Even so, they each collected a tiny splinter.

'We fired our cannon and frightened the pirates away,' Mark called cheerfully to the servants as he settled himself on the rug. 'Uncle Richard is going to stay until the tree grows strong, and then we can get to the very, very top one day.'

Richard dislodged the splinter from Mark's finger, then studied his son. His heart filled with wonder, and he stroked a hand lightly, lovingly, across the young fair head bent over the lunch bowl.

Twenty-four hours ago he'd had no inkling that Georgina's child carried his blood, and his likeness. The old embers of anger smouldering inside him flickered into life again. Damn her for refusing to tell him about her baby. His beautiful baby.

While Richard watched, the child attacked his food single-mindedly, and ceased his chatter until the bowls were empty. Richard sighed, and pulled his son against him when he saw a weary yawn signal the approach of rest-time in the nursery. He kissed the top of the boy's head. 'We'll play again another day, Master Davenport.'

'I don't want you to go,' the child said, dragging on his hand as they walked to the house. 'Promise you'll come back? Soon?'

Richard saw his son settled into bed, then left the house. There were matters in Whitehall waiting for his attention, people who expected him there this afternoon, but he pushed them from his mind as he walked down Kingsway and along Aldwych, to weave his way through the narrow, twisting streets, past Temple Bar towards the Tower and beyond. His purpose? To find the mother of his son and confront her at the clinic located down here somewhere in the slums.

Why was he rushing to see her today? What was to be gained now? Nothing could be done to change the present situation. Nothing! Any hint of scandal would inevitably rebound on to Mark, yet it had been Simon who had triggered it all.

In any case, whatever Simon's motive had been in introducing him to Mark, it was too late for Richard to turn back now. He stopped to ask directions as he trudged past cramped houses lining the miserable alleys that reeked with the clinging odour of poverty and, the closer he came to the woman who had borne his son, the longer and faster his stride became. But the closer he came to her, the more unsure he grew about his purpose.

Then, around a corner, he found himself at the door of the clinic, and steeled himself to walk into a waiting room. A woman and a coughing child sat on a long bench, beside a workman whose unshaven face was grey with pain as he held one arm tightly against his chest.

A small, well-scrubbed young woman in a spotless white apron and nurse's cap looked surprised to see Richard hovering inside the door as she bustled towards the woman with the coughing child. 'Here you are, Mrs Postle, give Molly four spoonfuls of this mixture every day, and keep her warm.' She handed a brown medicine bottle and a clean blanket to the mother, and turned to Richard. 'Sir?'

'Er – yes, Mrs Davenport. I'd like to see her, if she's. . . .'

'Take a seat, sir, I'm sure she won't be long,' the nurse said brightly, before turning to the workman. 'Oh, Alfred, what have you done to yourself this time? Come along now, and Doctor McPherson will see to you.' The man mumbled. 'No good grizzling, Alf, you'll be seeing the lady doctor today, or no one.'

Richard sat on the end of the wooden bench, and tension knotted his stomach. For years, the memories of Georgina had lived with him, tormenting him, distorting his perceptions. A thousand times he'd rehearsed this moment of confrontation, and now it was here, he was startled to find his heartbeat skipping out of rhythm at the sight of her. She came through a door, her arm around a young woman in a torn dress, whose bruised eye and swollen, cut mouth gave evidence of a beating.

'My Bert's a good man, really, Mrs Dav'port. It's jist the grog that gits the better of 'im at times.'

'If that's the case, Polly, you'll have to learn to run faster, or soon you won't have any teeth left at all,' Georgina said warmly, and the girl giggled.

'Aw, Mrs Dav'port, Bert won't do it agin. It'll be all right now, you'll see.'

Richard had climbed to his feet and his palms were damp. Every rational thought evaporated as she turned and saw him there. For a moment her jaw dropped while she stared in white-faced disbelief, slumped against the wall, her breasts heaving under the starched white apron. A smile started, then wavered. She spread her arms in a gesture of helplessness. 'Oh, Richard! You're here!'

He tried to speak, but found no words. He could only stare at her.

'What happened?'

'A *dacoit*'s knife – but you would have done a neater job with the stitching.'

She nodded. 'It doesn't matter.' She took a step towards him. 'I heard you had come back to London, and I wondered when our paths would cross.' A nervous flush crept up her throat. 'I even thought of calling on you at the Foreign Office.'

'What stopped you?'

'I didn't know what to say.'

'I've been angry with you for a long time,' he said thickly. 'I thought I had every reason to be, until this morning.' He saw in her eyes that she didn't follow his meaning, but he was at a loss for the right words to explain it. He only knew that if he held her in his arms, neither of them would need words.

'I would have come back a lot sooner if I'd known about Mark.' He saw the colour leave her face and curbed his tongue. 'Sorry, Georgina, I didn't come to scold you. God help me, I'm not even sure what I'm doing here at this moment. I had an overwhelming impulse to see you, because Simon introduced me to Mark this morning and' – he shook his head – 'when your husband explained the chain of events that led up to your marriage—'

'He told you . . . everything?' Her voice was a thin whisper.

'Yes.' When her chin trembled, it took all his resolve to stop himself from reaching out to her. 'And while I was with Simon, your mother arrived at the house unexpectedly.' He covered his cheek with the palm of his hand. 'She saw this and imagined the damage was Suvorov's work, and that upset her.'

'Oh, Richard, what can I say? What can we do? It's all too late, and I'm so terribly, terribly sorry that everything we planned came to nothing.' She seemed close to tears. 'There's no way now we can turn back the clock.'

'Would you, if we could?'

Her expression tore at his heart. 'You don't need to hear my answer to that, just as you know that we'd be fools to start playing the "what-if" game: "What if a child hadn't been conceived? What if my parents hadn't fled from Kashgar? What if Simon hadn't been there to carry us all away on his magic carpet?" ' She looked into his eyes unwaveringly. 'I love him deeply, Richard.'

She stopped abruptly when the nurse came back into the waiting-room and looked from one to the other, with barely disguised curiosity. 'Should I register this gentleman as a patient, Mrs Davenport?' she asked, sitting herself behind the desk, pen poised.

Before Georgina could gather her wits, Richard spoke. 'Yes, yes, I'm here for treatment.' He gave his name and address. 'It's my hand, er – injured it tree-climbing this morning.' He turned his palm and searched for the tiny splinter hiding under the skin. 'See? Here,' he said with a note of relief when he located it.

'Oh, yes indeed,' Georgina said, looking up from the hand he thrust towards her, and giving him a wavery smile. 'Come with me.'

She led him into the treatment-room, slid the bolt into place, picked up the tweezers, and took his hand to pull the splinter. It was a five-second procedure.

The contact of their hands lingered much longer. The first touch had ignited all the well-remembered passion, and sent it searing through their veins, while their gazes remained locked and their fingers slowly slid against each other's, intertwining with steadily mounting pressure. He lifted her hands, first one and then the other, to his lips.

She smiled at him; he thought she had never looked more beautiful. 'A thousand times I've dreamed of this moment, Richard, and now that it's here, I'm terrified. Hold me quickly, kiss me now, just once, I beg you.'

Against every ounce of common sense, he crushed her against him and brought his mouth on to hers in a shared hunger. For a few moments they clung to each other, drowning in a river of kisses, before they dragged themselves to the surface, panting, fighting to rein in their emotions before facing the world that was waiting for them beyond the locked door.

She reached out and tenderly touched the ragged scar on his cheek. 'I've never for one moment stopped loving you, Richard, but I can never, knowingly, do anything that would hurt Simon.'

She stepped back from him and smoothed her hair with unsteady hands before pulling the bolt. He placed his fingers over hers before she turned the doorknob.

'I've already assured your husband that I'll respect his marriage, Georgina. But don't forget that it was Simon who insisted on my visit to the Golden Pagoda this morning, specifically to meet my son.'

Her face revealed her confusion.

'By the way,' he said, and his gaze softened, 'I've become Mark's Uncle Richard.'

CHAPTER TWENTY-SIX

Georgina marvelled at the ease with which Richard Eldridge – Uncle Richard – eventually slipped into the Davenport family circle. But it didn't happen on that first evening when he escorted her home from the clinic.

Simon invited him to stay for dinner, but she had few recollections of eating the meal, floundering as she was that night in an atmosphere of unreality, finding herself seated at the table between her husband and her lover, unsure whether her appetite had been lost because of nervousness, or utter joy.

There were times during the meal when her throat closed over and tears threatened; she lacked the concentration to follow the men's seemingly relaxed conversation flowing up and down the table. They were discussing property. Buying and selling. Simon mentioned tenants who were leaving Hollywell, the house he owned on the Dorset coast; perhaps now was the time to sell it. Richard said he thought he might buy a place in the country and try farming one day. Probably Devon. Perhaps Somerset. He had friends with a pleasant little estate there.

'Stop it! Oh, please, stop it, both of you, and tell me what is going to happen to us?' Georgina gripped the edge of the table as she looked from one man to the other. There was a catch in her voice. 'Everything has changed between us now.'

For a moment there was silence, and Richard looked expectantly towards Simon.

'Yes, life is always full of changes.' Simon spoke quietly. 'But someone very wise once said there are two things that can never be changed: one is the *past* and the other is the *inevitable*. In the past, we all did what had to be done at the time, and somewhere ahead of us is the *inevitable*.'

She felt herself flush. 'No, Simon! You sound like those tribesmen who believe their lives are ruled by the mountain gods.' She couldn't bring herself to look at Richard.

Simon put his hand over her clenched one, and stroked his thumb across her knuckles. 'It's all right, my dear. I promise.'

She had no response. Surely he realized what shape the inevitable would take if Richard became part of their lives again?

'Georgina, you have my word that I'll never ask for more than the opportunity to play some part in Mark's life,' Richard said, as though he'd been reading her thoughts. 'Mark is Simon's son, you're Simon's wife, and that's the way it's going to stay.'

She let out her breath slowly. She believed his sincerity. But he'd always been stronger than she was, and it was her own frailty that frightened her.

Simon's hand was still on hers, and he pressed it harder. 'Georgina, none of us can change the inevitable.'

She didn't believe him, but as the weeks passed, Georgina realized that the family's relationship with Richard was actually working well.

When he was with Mark, Richard was careful not to encroach on Simon's paternal role, and his visits to Natasha and Erik helped to reassure her that Suvorov's shadow had disappeared. Before long Natasha had recovered sufficiently to take up her work again on Simon's new manuscript.

Even Mrs Flannery was full of praise for his attentions to the family. 'Such a fine gentleman,' she commented, 'and so fond of children, too. Why no young lady is sensible enough to see beyond the scar on his face is a mystery to me. If ever a man should be married, it's that one!'

Georgina was often with Erik at the clinic when Richard called at the house to see Mark. If the weather was poor, they played in the nursery, otherwise they went to the square. Sometimes Richard took him to fly a kite in Kensington Gardens, or hired a pony to ride in Hyde Park. He had his own chestnut mare sent from Hampshire and stabled in London.

Whenever she and Richard were together, Georgina was careful not to crack the fragile crystal barrier she wore around her yearning for him, but, without her being aware that it was happening, Simon's goodwill and Richard's common sense soon slipped that barrier away. A sense of happiness she'd never thought possible settled over the household.

Richard called frequently. He lost interest in the racetrack and the gaming-tables, as well as the furnishings of his own rooms. He brought the Landseer painting of the spotted retrievers to hang on Mark's wall.

'Perhaps your parents will let me buy a real puppy for you one day,' he said, and Mark immediately went off to persuade them.

At Simon's invitation, Richard often accompanied the Davenports to the theatre and exhibitions, sometimes with Natasha and Erik as well. Major

Eldridge was seen by others to become almost part of the Davenport family. On occasions, Simon found he had last-minute work which couldn't be postponed, and it was Richard who escorted Georgina to entertainments.

At these times he made no attempt to push the outwardly comfortable boundaries of friendship, but when he had gone and she was alone in her bedroom, she was left aching for the *inevitable* moment when they'd no longer be able to resist the pull of their mutual desire. It was a feeling that was never voiced when they were together, but it was alive in each glance, each touch.

And Simon, she knew, understood it well.

Prudence Eldridge was not a good sailor, and she stepped off the steamer from New York vowing it would be a long time before she had the strength to face the Atlantic again to visit her two daughters in the United States. She had never approved of them both marrying Americans – although Eleanor's wealthy in-laws appeared to be well placed in New York society, what there was of it.

It was young Sophie's marriage that concerned her most. Her husband might be handsome, wealthy and devoted – but, for goodness sake, the man had a silver mine in some place called Nevada, and he had taken her darling girl out there into the wilderness to face wild animals and Red Indians! Well, Sophie couldn't say her mother hadn't warned her!

Now, if only Richard were settled.

Richard had been surprised to hear from his mother that she was coming up to London to stay with her friend, Lady Fitzwilliam, especially to attend the ball being held to celebrate her daughter's engagement.

'I'd like you to be my escort, Richard,' she'd announced in her note. It made him smile; his mother was usually more subtle than this. But, of course, there would be a splendid selection of unattached young ladies dancing tonight in Lady Fitzwilliam's ballroom, and Prudence clearly held hopes that at least one of them would look beyond her son's damaged face and find it in her heart to love the man behind it.

Richard smiled to himself as he waited to meet his mother's train. He rarely thought about his scar now – the tiger's scratch, which Mark had kissed better. Georgina no longer noticed it, and nobody else was important.

Prudence Eldridge, regally gowned in cream lace and diamonds, stood with her son in Lady Fitzwilliam's drawing-room, acknowledging acquaintances and introducing Richard to those with presentable, available daughters.

Richard made an effort to be affable to them all, but at last the lady he was waiting for came into the room on the arm of her husband. Her glance quickly swept around the faces until she found him; and when she smiled it was for him alone.

He thought Georgina had never looked mare radiant than she did now in russet taffeta, the colour of her hair. Simon had told him that he was going to surprise her with pearls, and here they were tonight at her throat and wrists and woven through her hair.

'Oh! Mr and Mrs Davenport, how very pleasant to see you again.' Prudence took Richard's arm and crossed the carpet with her hand extended. Simon lifted it to his lips.

'I hear you've been visiting New York, Mrs Eldridge,' he said, edging her away from Richard. 'While you're staying in London, I hope you'll give me the pleasure of showing you the museum's exhibition of my most recent discoveries.' Simon had her full attention as they moved further away.

'Help me,' Richard whispered. 'Tonight my mother is determined to entice some poor unsuspecting female into believing I'm the answer to her dreams.'

'Perhaps then – to keep you safe – we should flee to the ballroom?'

He held her tightly as they joined the crush of waltzing couples. She held him just as tightly.

'Do you know,' he whispered, 'I used to lie in the Mission hospital and wonder what would happen if I took the doctor's daughter into the shrubbery one evening after a ball.'

'You know the answer to that as well as I do, Richard.' She angled her head so that her breath warmed his neck. 'But I'm no longer just the doctor's daughter, am I? I'm the archaeologist's wife, and a coward who's afraid that if she went into any shrubbery with you she might never want to come out again.' She spoke lightly, but her grip on his hand tightened. 'We just have to keep on dancing. And dancing—'

As he turned his head, his lips brushed her forehead, as if by accident. 'And dancing—' he murmured.

Simon, always the ideal guest, danced with young and old alike during the evening, but when supper was announced it was Prudence he led to the table to join Richard and Georgina.

'By the way, old chap,' Simon said when they were settled, 'has Georgina mentioned that I've decided not to sell Hollywell House in Dorset?' He made sure Prudence was listening. 'We're thinking of spending the summer down there.'

'I'm sure Mark will love it,' Richard said.

'Yes, indeed. I've very fond memories of childhood holidays in that old house. You must come down and visit us, Richard. There's a pretty little cove below the house, with a strip of white sand at one end. Not a safe bay for bathing, I'm afraid, but the chalk cliffs along there are a fossil-hunter's delight.'

'How well I remember your extensive fossil collection in Kashgar, Mrs Davenport,' Richard said with an easy familiarity that sent a questioning look into his mother's glance. 'What was your total at that time? Two? Three?'

She nodded.

'Oh, I promise you'll find many diversions apart from collecting fossils.' Simon spoke insistently. 'The house isn't at all grand, but it's large and comfortable enough. Georgina and I would be delighted to have you there.'

'Would there be room for a new puppy?' asked Richard, trying to ignore the flush that had swept into Georgina's cheeks.

'Thank you. I'm sure Mark would love one,' Simon said.

Richard hoisted Mark astride the grey pony he'd hired, and holding a leading rein, swung on to his own saddle. 'Good boy. Now, sit straight, loosen the reins a little and keep your hands down.'

The child's face was tight with concentration as they clattered from the mews and rode to Hyde Park. 'Now, we'll practise the trot,' Richard said, and watched Mark's effort to find the rhythm. 'Splendid, keep it up. That's the way, old chap,' he said again. 'We'll go around just once more.' Perhaps, next year, he'd talk to Simon about buying the boy a pony of his own.

While Richard's attention was occupied with the small rider at his side, a carriage passed them, then pulled up a little distance ahead. As he and Mark drew abreast of it, he glanced across and saw his mother's pale face at the open window.

He reined in, and with a defiant set to his jaw, swung from the saddle and led the grey pony towards the coach. 'Good afternoon, Mother,' he said with a coolness he didn't feel. 'May I have the honour of presenting Master Mark Davenport?'

Prudence Eldridge's shocked gaze flew from one face to the other and back again, and one hand clutched her throat. The resemblance between Richard and the boy was unmistakable. 'So *this* is Georgina Davenport's child.' It was not a question. 'Oh, my dear . . . Georgina!'

'Master Davenport, let me introduce my mother, Mrs Eldridge.' Richard's tone was defensive.

With great solemnity, the small figure on the pony doffed his cap with a theatrical flourish, and bowed his head till it almost touched the pony's mane.

'How do you do, Master Davenport?' Prudence Eldridge said tightly. 'What pleasing manners you have learned.' She glanced quickly, knowingly at Richard, and back to Mark. 'And may I ask how old you are, young man?'

'Five next birthday, ma'am,' he said, replacing his cap and returning her scrutiny. 'And Uncle Richard said he might give me a puppy.'

For a few moments she seemed deprived of words, then rallied. 'Yes, I think that would be a splendid gift for Uncle Richard to give a young gentleman on his fifth birthday.' She swallowed hard. 'And perhaps, when the puppy arrives, Master Davenport, you would allow me to present him with a collar?'

'Thank you, ma'am,' he said brightly. 'And, if you like, you can come and play with him, too.'

Prudence Eldridge inclined her head stiffly, then looked at her son. Her chin quavered and she appeared to fight for breath. 'So, this is Georgina Davenport's child, and he's almost five years old,' she struggled to say, and before she gave way to tears, called for her driver to move on.

Once Simon had decided to open the Dorset house for the summer holidays, his agent in Dorchester arranged for repairs and hired local staff. The Bloomsbury household geared itself for change, and Georgina arranged for volunteers to carry on her work at the charity clinic while she was away.

It wasn't easy to persuade Erik to take a holiday, but eventually, under pressure from them all, he agreed to spend a month with them at the house. Natasha was eager for the holiday, but was adamant that she and Simon must keep working on his manuscript while they were on holiday.

'Tell your publisher we will have it completed by the time you come back to London. I promise to give you no peace till it's done, my dear!' she threatened, with a smile.

CHAPTER TWENTY-SEVEN

Simon and Mark set out with the trap from Hollywell House to meet Richard at the station. It was almost a month since they'd said goodbye in London, and until now his work had delayed a visit.

Georgina climbed over the low dry-stone wall surrounding the house nestled into the fold of the hills, and strode to the edge of the chalk cliff overlooking the scalloped Dorset coastline. Breathless, she sank on to a thick cushion of turf, relishing the warmth of the afternoon sun lying across her shoulders like a friendly arm.

Richard was coming!

From this vantage-point she could look back to see the trap as it came along the narrow lanes leading from the village, past copses of silver birch and scrub oaks, little farms and the square-towered church half a mile away. Her heartbeat quickened.

Richard was coming!

She drew up her legs and wrapped her arms around them, hugging her happiness close, sniffing the salt-laden air, watching white clouds billow across a bright blue sky, and seabirds wheel past the cliff-face with barely a flap of their wings.

Richard was coming!

Below, the steeply shelving cove sparkled and, beyond the rocky headlands, the sea was intensely blue and flecked with white-caps. Each day it presented a different face – sometimes inviting; other times threatening. Yesterday, the thunder of the waves had been continuous, with breakers hurling themselves against the rocks and sending explosions of water flying high into the air, while the surf sizzled like soapy foam, creaming up to the shore, then drawing away again with an angry, hissing sound.

Erik and Mrs Flannery were down there now, paddling through the rock pools at one end of the little cove, investigating the variety of sea-life that had been hurled up by yesterday's storm. They spent a great deal of time together, engrossed in their study of natural science. Already they'd uncovered an interesting collection of fossils in the chalk cliffs, while Natasha's determination to complete Simon's manuscript on time kept her busy in the morning-room.

And now Richard was coming!

The surface of the water was glassy today, and lazy ripples spread behind the fishing boat heading towards the beach. Georgina watched the man pull hard on his oars, then raise them and run the little boat up on to the sand. He jumped out, heaved it further from the water, and secured its painter to an iron ring set into the foot of the cliff. People from the village left their boats here on the beach, and, when Mark and Georgina came down to play on the sand, they provided an irresistible invitation for pirate games.

She saw the fisherman hail Erik and Mrs Flannery, who picked up their shoes and stockings, and went to examine his catch. Several silvery shapes were put into the bucket they invariably carried when they went exploring, and then, with his fishing bag and rods slung on his shoulder, the man followed them to the steep track leading up from the cove. Halfway along it branched, and the fisherman took the path towards the village, while the others continued to zigzag their way up to the house.

Georgina closed her eyes and lifted her face to the rays of the afternoon sun. Richard was coming, and soon her happiness would be complete.

She looked away from the sea, towards the village, and shielded her eyes. Yes, the trap was already passing the church, and within a few minutes it would turn into the lane leading to Hollywell House. She began to run, almost skipping, down the hill to meet it, and the breeze coming up from the valley sent her skirt ballooning around her legs. Her eyes brimmed with laughter as she hurtled towards the house, and Richard sprang down from the trap to take both her hands in his. She lifted her face and he kissed her cheek.

'Mama, look what Uncle Richard has given me!' Mark cried as he was lifted down from the trap. Simon unloaded a basket and lifted the lid. 'Look, Mama! I've called him Wags and the lady sent a collar for him.'

Georgina looked puzzled. 'Who did?'

'My mother thought he should not arrive improperly dressed,' Richard said with a grin. 'She approves of the pedigree, you'll be pleased to hear.'

The Dalmatian puppy's excitement level was as high as Mark's, and the spotted tail wagged furiously as he tried to scramble out of the basket.

'Welcome, little Wags,' Georgina laughed. 'He's beautiful. Thank you, Richard.'

Natasha, Erik and Mrs Flannery came hurrying out to greet Richard and, amidst the flurry of handshaking and cheek-kissing, the luggage was unloaded, and the stableboy led the horse away.

Georgina's smile grew wider. Richard was truly here at last.

'Come along with me, Mark,' Simon said, scooping the wriggling puppy from the basket. 'We'll let Wags play in the walled garden. He'll be safe there.' They went off together, discussing a water-bowl and a bone from the kitchen, while the others swept Richard into the rambling Portland stone house.

'This is the oldest part,' Georgina said as they walked through the hall into the big drawing room, where tea was waiting. The room was warm and welcoming, with sunshine streaming in through tall windows, and under the beamed ceiling the curtains and chair-covers were well-worn and faded to soft hues. The walls on either side of the massive fireplace were lined with high bookcases, and big vases which Georgina had filled with fresh wildflowers stood about on tables.

Natasha fussed around Richard, and Georgina poured the tea. Excitement made her hands shake as she passed the cups. Erik talked about the flora and fauna he and Mrs Flannery had discovered in the surrounding countryside, and Natasha announced the extraordinary amount of work she'd done on Simon's manuscript in the last few weeks.

'It's good to have you here, Richard,' Simon said warmly when he joined them at last. 'I want you to make this a memorable holiday; this is our own private world.' His tone was heavy with meaning, and he smiled at Georgina as he took the cup she passed to him with an unsteady hand.

He sat back in his chair with an air of contentment and looked about at the room. 'This old house has weathered many a storm, you know,' he said, and spent the next hour entertaining them with anecdotes about some of the characters who had previously occupied it.

At last he glanced at the tall clock. 'Now, my dear, why don't you take Richard to see the rest of the place, before we change for dinner?'

'Come with me,' she said, trying not to appear too eager to be alone with him. 'The library is through that door, and see, here's the morning-room where Mother is working on Simon's notes.'

He was walking very closely beside her, and it needed no more than a simple twist of her wrist to touch his hand and lace her fingers with his. 'That corridor leads to the dining-room, and. . . .'

His hand tightened its grip as they walked up the stairs and wound their way along twisting hallways, past bedroom doors, some open, some closed. At the far end, she led him into one where his clothes had been unpacked and his silver-backed brushes were set out on the dressing-table beside the flowers she had arranged.

'You can catch a glimpse of the sea through this window,' she said. He came to stand behind her, and put his hands around her waist. She was breathing fast. 'Tomorrow I'll show you the path down to our little cove, and from the top of the cliff. . . .' Her words faded; she leaned back against him and felt his lips brush her ear.

For a moment they stood as they were, then he kissed her quickly on the neck and turned her to face him.

She was flushed as she gazed up at him. 'Dear God, Richard, how I've missed you.'

He frowned a little, and hesitated before he responded. 'I could have come sooner,' he said at last, and she looked at him in disbelief. 'I even thought that perhaps I shouldn't come at all.'

'But you *have* come. I think I would have died if you hadn't.' There was a catch in her voice, and she stroked her hand over his scarred cheek. 'Hold me, Richard, just hold me and touch me and feed my hunger for you. I love you; I ache for you.' She slid her arms around his waist and pressed against him.

He drew a slow, deep breath. 'Simon once said that none of us could change the past, any more than we could stop the inevitable from catching up with us. You know as well as I do, Georgina, where the inevitable is leading us.' He held her face between his hands and kissed her forehead lightly. 'Please God, we never allow ourselves to fall into some kind of furtive, backstairs liaison that would surely rebound one day on to Simon, and Mark.'

She gave a huff of frustration and pushed herself away from him, shocked to find her vision suddenly blurred by tears. 'Oh, damn all honourable men!'

Her words clearly startled him.

'And, of course, you're perfectly right, Major Eldridge,' she fumed. 'My husband must not be embarrassed by his wife's behaviour; and I must not besmirch your honour as a gentleman. I must be made to pay for the mistake I made five years ago, and I must continue to live as a nun because one man I love *cannot* love me, and the other is about to *refuse* the opportunity.'

Her words were like sharp-edged swords; her fists were clenched; she seemed about to vent her despair on to him physically when he grasped her wrists and held them tightly. His expression raised the heat of her anger.

'Look at me, Richard, damn you. Open your eyes and look at me! Can't you see that nature created me as a woman, and you were the one who taught me how to feel as a woman! I've been aching for you, every day and every night since we lay together before the Golden Pagoda, and Simon has brought you

205

back into my life – brought you here now – because he understands how much I need you.'

She began to shake and he wrapped his arms around her. 'Mistakes, mistakes,' she mumbled into his shoulder. 'I was the one who made them all, wasn't I?'

He drew breath to answer, then seemed to think better of it. She felt him hard against her, breathing fast, felt his hunger soaring to match her own.

'Please, Richard, oh – please, please, please.'

She knew she might be about to make another mistake, when she fell on to the bed with him in a tangle of fumbling hands and discarded clothes. But the fire was unquenchable and, if it was a mistake, it was a glorious, soaring, savage mistake that swept them away to a place that was theirs alone.

Afterwards they lay together, repleted, joyously damp-eyed and silently caressing, until it was time to re-enter the real world and return to their own rooms to dress for dinner.

So, Richard and I have met the inevitable. Georgina looked hard at her reflection in the mirror while the maid helped her dress in a green silk gown, and brushed her hair. Was any of her inner glow visible? Surely what she and Richard had shared just an hour ago was more than the start of a tawdry, back-stairs affair? *But where was it destined to lead them?*

She gave the outward appearance of serenity at dinner. But, as she sat at one end of the old oak table, she had the strangest urge to confide her confusion to Simon. Or Erik. Or even to her mother. Who here would know more about the tides and undercurrents of physical passion than Natasha?

The dinner was excellent, and Georgina appeared to enjoy it; the conversation at the table was light, and she gave the impression of taking part in it. She was very aware, though, that Simon's gaze drifted to her frequently, tenderly. When the servants had cleared the plates, and the party sat with their port and strong Blue Vinney cheese, he surprised her by climbing to his feet and calling for a toast.

With the expression of affection she knew so well, Simon looked at the faces around the table. 'First, I want to welcome Richard, whose arrival has made our little family complete. I hope – no, actually, I *insist* – that you, my friend, will always regard this house as you would your own.'

They drank to Richard, and Georgina bit her lip when Simon smiled directly at her. He knew! Somehow he knew that she and Richard had already met the inevitable, and no knight at the Round Table could have displayed greater chivalry than Simon was doing tonight. She inclined her head, and raised her glass to him and pursed her lips in a tiny kiss.

He acknowledged the gesture, then continued: 'And now I'd like to propose a toast to the remarkable Natasha Larssen, who has transcribed my manuscript into a work of art which I refuse to delay a moment longer in presenting to my publisher. I'm taking it to London in the morning—'

'No, no!' Natasha interjected. 'No, Simon, I haven't yet completed the footnotes, or even started the bibliography. Wait, just a few more days!'

'It's all right, Natasha,' he said firmly. 'We can finish that when I come back from London.' He wiped the serviette across his lips and looked down the table to Georgina. 'Delicious meal tonight, m'dear. Do you think we could manage lobster for dinner again when I return next Wednesday?' He held her gaze, and waited until he saw she clearly understood that it was his intention to stay away for a week.

That night when the house was quiet, Georgina lay in bed unable to sleep, unsettled by Simon's determination to step aside and give her the opportunity to spend this time with Richard. On impulse, she slid her feet on to the floor, wrapped a shawl around her shoulders and walked softly to Simon's bedroom at the far end of the corridor. She tapped tentatively, and at the sound of his voice, turned the knob and opened the door.

He stood in his robe beside the dressing-table, holding a small, empty glass. Nearby, she recognized a bottle of Erik's potent sleeping-draught. He smiled at her, and shrugged.

'May I come in for a moment?'

'Of course.'

He put down the glass and held out his hand. She flew to him and pressed his fingers to her cheek. 'You are the most generous man in the world, Simon. I love you.'

He ran his free hand through the russet cloud falling on to her shoulder. 'Yes, I know you do, my love, and I want to make sure you find all the happiness you deserve.'

'But must you rush off to London tomorrow? There's no need.'

'Perhaps,' he said with a shrug, 'but I'm going nonetheless.'

'And will you come back to me? Promise me you'll come back!' A sudden fear shivered down her spine.

'Just think, my dear, how much simpler life would be for everyone if I went back to live in London. You and Mark could make this your home, then—'

'Stop it!' she said with anger and indignation. 'Don't even suggest it! I'll never let you leave me, Simon, and I'll certainly never leave you. Never!'

She saw the emotion in his eyes, and the next moment found herself in his arms. His face was in her hair, he drew her closer to him and she felt his chest heave.

'The draught I've just swallowed will take less than an hour to work,' he whispered unsteadily. 'My darling, will you lie beside me and let me hold you, just this once, until I fall asleep?'

'Oh, yes, yes,' she breathed, and dropped her shawl, slipped the nightdress over her head, and climbed into the bed.

They needed no words when he turned out the lamp and slid hesitantly on to the pillow beside her. He knotted her hair through his fingers and shifted to feel the length of her against his body. His sigh was warm against her cheek as he slid his palm along the softness of her skin, tracing her contours. She turned her head and their lips met, and met again.

When she sensed the opiate taking its effect, she cradled him in her arms and held him against her breast. 'Anne . . .' he murmured. 'Anne. . . .'

Tears slid down her cheek, and she stroked him tenderly until he fell into a heavy sleep.

'I don't know what lies ahead – or how strong I'll be – but I never want you to be hurt by something I might do,' she promised, and stayed close beside him until the first rays of dawn crept into the room.

Erik drove Simon to catch the early train, and when he returned, he stayed in the house with Natasha, instead of joining the others at the cove. Natasha was still cross because Simon had refused to wait for her to complete the last few pages of the work.

'I will not put down my pen until the task is completed,' she said to Erik as he settled beside her and opened a newspaper. 'I don't understand Simon's ridiculous haste to get the manuscript to London today.'

Erik pursed his lips, and kept to himself the confidences that Simon had shared on the way to the train. 'I'm leaving to allow Georgina the opportunity to make her own decisions in this matter. I beg you, Erik, don't try to influence her,' Simon had said as he climbed aboard. 'She's a young woman and Richard is a fine man, who can give her what I never can.'

And Erik prayed that a kindly, guiding God had not entirely forgotten his daughter, because he himself could offer no fatherly advice. After all, it was his own flight from Kashgar with Natasha that had triggered the complications in Georgina's life.

The shore of the cove this morning was littered with flotsam left by the night's high tide, and it provided an endless source of interest to the puppy when he grew tired of the pirate game that Mark and Richard were playing in the beached boat.

Georgina and Mrs Flannery scrambled up on the rocks, and with makeshift digging tools, worked together to extract a fossilized sea creature from the cliff.

'It's an ammonite of some kind, I'm sure,' Georgina said as she scraped at the crumbling limestone.

Mrs Flannery looked at it carefully, and gave a murmur of agreement.

'Then at least I'm sure of one thing in my life,' Georgina muttered.

Mrs Flannery gave her a knowing smile, and passed Georgina the smaller trowel she needed.

She stopped her work and they both looked down at the beach, where Richard and Mark were attempting to catch the puppy, who was running along the sand with seaweed trailing from its mouth.

'You have a most understanding husband.' Mrs Flannery's tone carried no censure.

Georgina jammed her hat back firmly on her head, and scratched deeper around the fossil. Simon had made it so simple for her to take a lover. People did it all the time, and she'd had some vague, stupidly childlike feeling that once Richard was here, a clear answer to all this would emerge –just like this little ammonite shell coming out of the limestone. But it hadn't happened that way at all.

On the other side of the cove, Richard and Mark, who now had the puppy in his arms, sat watching a fisherman rowing strongly against the outgoing tide as he rounded the headland and pulled towards the beach.

Richard offered to help the man pull his boat up on to the sand. 'Thank ye, sir, them currents is surely getting stronger every day at this time o' the year,' he said gruffly. 'Floodtide is due next week, and that's when we'll see some even bigger rips on the ebb.' He heaved his heavy basket on to the beach. 'Now, sir, can I interest you in a couple of these?'

Daily life in the house while Simon was away continued in its familiar pattern – energetic morning activity outdoors with Mark and Wags, and rambles through the countryside, followed by lazy, companionable afternoons, reading in the warmth of the walled garden, with the exhausted puppy curled up asleep in his basket.

In the evenings, the family played cards or sat around the piano while Mrs Flannery entertained them with music-hall songs, and Richard and Erik sang duets. Georgina insisted her only talent was listening, but Natasha astonished them by lifting her skirts to perform impromptu, nimble-footed dances that hinted at past brilliance.

When Mrs Flannery's music stopped, she sank into a bow, and Erik led their applause. She was somewhat out of breath, but when Natasha smiled, Georgina sensed that her mother's dark clouds had vanished at last.

'What a life I led as a girl in St Petersburg!' she said archly, as she took a seat beside Erik and took his hand. 'I thank the angels every day for sending dear Doctor Larssen to find me.'

Sunday morning's sermon at the little church stretched Mark's patience and, to everyone's relief, Natasha took him outside to play around the gravestones until the service was over and the others came out, after shaking hands with the vicar at the door.

Mark waved to a village boy who sometimes came down to the cove to go fishing with his father. Mark was puffed with pride to have a friend who was eight years old and who, on occasions, could spare time to play with a boy more than three years his junior. 'Tom! Do you want to come and see my new puppy?' Mark called.

Tom pulled a long face and glowered at his mother. 'I'm goin' to spend the rest of the day locked up under the stairs,' he whispered as they passed. 'She caught me dippin' me hand in the collection plate.'

At that moment, the woman gave her son a clip around the ears for good measure. 'I declare you're more trouble than you're worth, Thomas Williams!'

The lad turned to wink at Mark, who was regarding the whole incident with awe. 'He didn't even cry,' Mark said, as he told Erik about it on the way home. 'I think he's very brave about being locked up in the dark, and not allowed to come and play with Wags.'

On the walk home, Mark received clarification – in no uncertain terms – on the subject of good and evil and crime and punishment, from his grandfather as well as from Mrs Flannery.

Georgina and Richard followed slowly behind them, arm in arm. 'I'm sure Mark is already wishing he hadn't mentioned the topic,' Richard said with a grin, then he stopped in the middle of the lane and faced her, suddenly serious. 'You and I are still avoiding the most important topic, aren't we?'

She nodded. 'I don't know what to do, Richard. It's ridiculous, isn't it, for a woman like me who always wanted to change the rules – to find that now I've been given complete independence here, it confuses me even more?' She ran her fingers softly along the puckering scar showing white against his tanned cheek. 'The only thing I know is that these few days with you have been everything I've ever longed for, and I'll always love you. But when we go back to London – I don't know—'

'Then let me tell you what is going to happen,' he said, and took her firmly by the arm and started to walk again along the lane leading to the house. 'I can't stop loving you, but neither can I go ahead with anything that might rebound on to Simon – and Mark.' He didn't look at her. 'So, Mrs Davenport, we must all return to the *status quo*, where Uncle Richard visits his nephew in Bloomsbury, and comes to dine with his friends from time to time.' His voice was flat. 'I intend to leave here before Simon comes back on Wednesday.'

'Only one more day together after this?'

'And two more nights. Let us never forget the nights we've shared, my darling!'

Before he left her room at daylight on Tuesday, she took her talisman – the little piece of the Golden Pagoda she kept amongst her most precious possessions – and put it in Richard's hand. He turned its painted surface to catch the light, and ran his thumb across it.

'Hope?' he asked.

'Perhaps just a memory.' She held him close. 'Perhaps just a beautiful memory for you to keep.'

CHAPTER TWENTY-EIGHT

'Richard was called back to London suddenly?' Simon raised his brows in surprise when Georgina and Mark met him at the door and told him the news.

'Yes, Papa, but when we go home again, Uncle Richard is going to come and teach Wags some new tricks,' Mark added. He was on his knees, vainly trying to train the puppy to sit.

Georgina and Simon exchanged an amused, affectionate smile. 'I must make it clear, Simon, that the puppy is the only one in this family who is learning to do things differently.' Her voice was low and warm and confidential. 'I've found it impossible to change anything in my life; I'm far too set in my ways, you see.'

For once, he seemed at a loss for words, and she held out her hand to him. He squeezed her fingers tightly, and in her heart she thanked Richard for having had the strength to make the decision she knew was the right one.

'I have to confess, Georgina, that I was anticipating – I don't know – a *compromise*, perhaps?' Tenderness deepened his smile.

'No, no compromise.' She thought for a moment. 'Richard and I are everlastingly grateful that you were brave enough to allow him into Mark's life, but I think we discovered while you were away that we are two simple souls, who see things in black and white. Neither of us has the ability to deal with any kind of grey compromise.'

'What can I say?' There was a keen, watchful expression in his eyes.

'There is nothing left for you to say, my love. I've told you the way things stand, and now, do come along, because the others are waiting for us in the garden.' She slipped her arm through his, and led him through the house.

Mark and Wags scampered past and ran ahead to announce Simon's arrival home, the tea-tray was placed on the table, and the household again picked up the comfortable threads of holiday life, exchanging snippets of Dorset and London news.

'Quite a to-do in church on Sunday when that Williams lad was caught with his hand in the collection plate,' Erik reported with a grin.

'It was a *bad* thing to do!' Mark joined in, with emphasis. 'Grandpapa told me it was.'

'Quite right, my lad.' Simon returned Erik's grin, and reached for another slice of plumcake. 'Now, do you have anything planned for tomorrow, Georgina?' When she shook her head, he said: 'Then I suggest we set out early and have an expedition to Corfe Castle. I used to love playing around the ruins there when I was a boy.'

Their days passed in easy fellowship; sometimes the party set out together, sometimes one or two embarked on individual pursuits. Once a week a cheerful letter from Richard arrived, addressed to them all.

Music and card games filled their evenings, and when Simon had kissed her cheek and they'd said goodnight, Georgina went alone to her own bedroom. While thoughts of Richard were never far away, she was determined not to make herself or Simon or Richard wretched by trying to solve the insoluble.

It became a mantra she repeated as she stood at her bedroom window, watching the moon's silver face change as the nights passed and listening to the sound of the tide against the cliffs, sometimes a whisper, sometimes a heart-pounding roar.

'I think we should spend every summer down here at Hollywell. Just like this, all of us,' Simon said idly as he and Georgina sat together on the cliff-top, watching the windblown sea birds wheel and call above them. Dark storm-clouds were gathering in the west, and in the cove below, the floodtide had covered the beach. A boat, tied to the ring in the rock, floated on the water rising under its keel.

The others had walked into the village with Mark to buy honey, but the storm coming in from the sea was still a long way off.

Simon picked a stalk of grass and put it into his mouth, then lay on his back with his hands behind his head, looking up at her. 'Do you know, sweetheart, I think I'd like to stay here for ever.'

She lay down on her stomach beside him, resting on her elbows, looking down at his face. There was more grey now in his dark hair, but the years had done nothing but add further distinction to his handsome features.

'If you'd like to stay in Dorset, then let's stay,' she said breezily. 'Why couldn't you and Mark and I live happily here for ever?'

'Richard?'

'Oh, don't complicate things! You know I can't answer you on the subject of Richard, because there *is* no answer.'

'When the day comes, and you do find the answer' – he reached out and ran the back of his hand down her cheek – 'you'll always have my blessing, you know.'

He heard her small, sharp intake of breath. 'Don't say anything further, because I won't listen. My life is joined with yours, Simon, and I'm truly content.'

'Content with the intimacy of companionship? No, you're too young for that, blossom.' His tone was teasing, but his eyes were serious. 'Don't leave it until it's too late.'

She shook her head at him in mock frustration.

'Y'know, Georgina, I have fond memories of riding through Kashgar with a young woman who told me she was determined to remain *unrestrained* by convention.' He raised an eyebrow at her. 'Has she really become as conventional as she now appears?'

'It's not convention that keeps me here with you, Simon. It's *love*.'

He sat up quickly and put his arm around her. 'Richard loves you, too.'

She put her head on his shoulder, and they sat for a long time, quietly wrapped in their own thoughts, huddled against the salt-laden wind, watching the floodtide turn and race out between the headlands of the cove. Gradually the sky became darker. A flash of lightning and a reverberating growl of thunder at last drove them back to the house as the clouds rolled in.

When the force of the storm hit, it whipped and cracked around the house, battering it with wind and rain all through the night, and in the morning the evidence of its violence littered the countryside. Although the rain had cleared, the wind still made outdoor activity uninviting, but Georgina went into the walled garden and busied herself repairing some of the damage done to some of the plants.

Mark and the puppy were permitted to romp inside the house, and spent all morning scampering up and down the halls, while the men sought quiet corners in which to settle with their books, and Natasha and Mrs Flannery worked on their embroidery. 'I don't think any of us slept well last night,' Georgina said at lunch. She tried to smother a yawn, while Mark's eyelids grew heavier by the minute, and Wags curled up in his basket.

Simon took Mark up to the nursery.

'He was asleep well before I finished the storybook,' he said on rejoining the others lounging near the fire in the drawing-room. 'Anyone interested in a hand of bridge? Chess?' He opened the card table.

'Simon, you know I'm hopeless at anything more complicated than draughts,' Georgina said, stretching as she crossed the room to join him.

'Then draughts it is, m'love.' He found the board, and they sat facing each other as the afternoon wore on.

'You're too good at this game,' Simon said at last as he packed away the pieces. 'Tomorrow, young lady, prepare yourself to learn the rules of chess.'

At that point, Wags woke from his long sleep and indicated it was time to hurry him outside.

'I'll go up and wake Mark now, too,' Georgina said, 'or he won't go to sleep at bedtime.'

When Simon came back inside with the puppy, Georgina walked into the room with a frown. 'Has Mark come down here? He's not in his room; I'll see if he's in the kitchen with cook.'

Simon opened other doors and called, but there was no sign of the child. Perhaps he was playing a game? Hiding behind curtains? He ran upstairs and called, searching in all the hiding-places he'd known when he was small. He pulled aside the curtain of an upstairs window, and in the distance, saw a boy running from the cove.

He looked hard, and recognized young Tom Williams, the lad who'd been caught with his hand in the church collection. He was coming to the house.

Simon ran downstairs and opened the front door, sending a blast of cold wind into the hall. Tom Williams halted when he saw Simon and started to back away, but not before Simon had noted the lad's water-soaked clothing.

'What is it?' he called to the retreating figure, and began to run towards him. The frightened boy took to his heels and waved his arms towards the cove, yelling words that were blown away by the wind. All Simon caught was '. . . boat. . . .'

'Erik! Erik! Come quickly!' he shouted, and raced towards the path leading down to the cove.

Georgina and Erik ran from the house together, in time to see Simon reach the edge of the cliff and disappear down the track.

Terror lent speed to Georgina's legs, and she lifted her skirts to outpace her father in the dash to follow Simon. And when she reached the cliff, the scene on the water below chilled her blood. She ran down the path, stumbling, tripping, falling to her knees; for it was impossible to drag her eyes from the sight of Mark alone in the fishing boat, drifting into the middle of the cove, rocking, tossing in the current, sweeping towards the rocky headlands on the rush of the ebbing king tide, out towards the cresting sea beyond.

'Simon!' The scream tore from her throat. 'Simon!' She kept running. His jacket was on the sand, he'd pulled off his shoes. Now he was wading into the angry water; throwing himself into it and stroking strongly out through the waves towards the drifting boat.

She was at the water's edge, wading into it until it reached her waist, and the surge of the swell dragged on her heavy skirts, threatening to pull her down. Erik was beside her, holding her. She clung to him, scarcely able to breathe, while they watched Simon struggling to reach the boat. He was closing the distance. Soon, soon— Only another twenty yards— Closer, closer—

Then to her horror, his strokes slowed, and slowed further, and his head slipped below the surface. She could no longer see him. It happened so quickly, she refused to believe her eyes. He wasn't there! Where was he? Why couldn't she see him? Oh, dear God! He'd gone! 'Simon! Simon!' she screamed, but all she could see was the lonely, unforgiving dark water with its swirling currents that had dragged Simon into its depths.

'No! No! No! No!' she cried, and seemed about to throw herself after him, when Erik pulled her back towards the beach. Mrs Flannery and Natasha were there, their arms reaching out to her, shocked, looking helplessly towards the little boat drifting towards the waves surging and foaming around the rocks on the northern headland.

Georgina pushed the women aside and, almost choking on her own fear, she ran along the beach with Erik hard on her heels, and the others trailing behind him. She splashed through the rock-pools, then started to scramble and claw her way over the boulders lying at the water's edge under the northern cliffs, desperate to reach the headland before the boat was inevitably dashed on to the rocks there.

Through the noise of her own ragged sobs and the thunder of the waves, came the distant sound of men's voices. She turned her head, barely pausing a second, and saw a group running towards the beach, shouting at her, waving their arms. Her hands and legs were scratched and bleeding, and her desperation mounted when she was confronted by a wide, seemingly bottomless gully of foaming water in her path. Frantically, she looked up at the cliff wall, searching for some foothold to grasp, some way to climb and work her way up and around the barrier.

The shouting voices continued, and when she quickly glanced again, she saw several men scrambling across the rocks on the other side of the cove, waving at her. Erik was still in her wake, but he was also now signalling for her to stop.

She began to sob. Why was nobody trying to help her save Mark? A villager had caught up with Erik, and he, too, was calling for her to come back.

Rage threatened to sap her last drop of energy, but when she turned to watch for the impending disaster on the rocks ahead, she was astonished to see that the direction of the little wooden boat had changed, and it was now swirling towards the opposite headland, where the men had gathered.

All strength left her legs and she sank on to a spray-drenched rock to watch a rope being tied to one of the men, who threw himself into the waves and struggled out to reach the boat with a grappling hook.

Slowly, experienced hands hauled the boat towards the opposite shore, and through a numbing haze of grief, she saw Mark lifted to safety and carried towards Mrs Flannery and Natasha, who were running back along the beach towards him.

A violent trembling overtook her. It was impossible to move, and she sat staring at the place where she'd watched Simon be stolen by the cold, black water that now refused to return him. How could it be true? This must be nothing but a terrifying dream. Shock swept over her in great, numbing waves. Come back, come back, Simon! If she closed her eyes and counted to ten, he'd be here beside her, vowing to teach her to play chess tomorrow.

She turned her face to the sky and sobbed, deep, racking cries of despair, refusing to contain her grief and her burning anger at the injustice of the fates that ruled men's lives. Dear God, why *Simon*?

Now Erik was beside her, holding her in his arms. 'Mark is safe, dear. The local men understand the ways the currents run, you see, that's why they went straight to the other side.'

She struggled to understand.

'It seems Mark and Tom Williams came down here to play in the boat, and when the tide took it out, Tom ran home to tell his father. That's the reason the men from the village appeared on the scene so quickly with their ropes, and so forth.'

'Tell them to look for Simon,' she said through chattering teeth. 'Please, please, quickly they must find him. I'll wait here until they find him. I can't leave him alone out there. I *won't* leave him all alone.'

'No, dear, you must come with me. They'll keep searching, but it may take some time to find him in these waters.' Erik was weeping, too. 'Come home, my dearest girl, there's nothing more we can do now.'

CHAPTER TWENTY-NINE

The news of Simon Davenport's death was quick to reach London, but even before it appeared in *The Times*, Richard was on his way back to Dorset.

'Come as quickly as you can,' Erik's urgent message had concluded. 'Mark needs you.'

When Erik met him at the train, he clasped his hand. 'Thank God you're here. This is a dreadful business, Richard, dreadful. We've just received word that Simon's body was found this morning, and they're bringing him back to the house now. Will you take Mark off somewhere and talk to him? The lad is taking it badly.'

'Of course I will, but – Georgina?'

'The last days have been difficult for everyone, but especially for her.' Erik described the tragedy in detail, and Richard shook his head.

'Good God! Who could have imagined where a spot of childish mischief would lead?' He looked at Erik with a frown. 'Mark blames himself?'

Erik pushed his spectacles further up his nose. 'I fear I must bear some of the responsibility there.' He tut-tutted, and shook his head. 'I've been preaching to the lad so hard lately on the topic of right and wrong, that the poor boy has taken it to heart, and blames himself for going off to play without permission.'

Richard gave a groan. 'What about Georgina? Surely *she*'s not blaming Mark?'

It took a few moments for Erik to gather his thoughts. 'From the day we met fifteen years ago, I've felt as close to Georgina as any father could. But since Simon drowned, she has cut herself off from everyone. Apart from Natasha. It's her mother she wants with her in her grief, not me.' He glanced quickly at Richard. 'Frankly, I have never seen Georgina so – so devastated. So utterly vulnerable.'

'And how is Natasha?' Richard couldn't hide his concern.

'She's remarkable. Yes, I feared what her reaction might be, but she's been the one that Georgina has wanted to cling to throughout this ordeal. I sense that – in a strange way – Natasha feels closer to her daughter at this moment than she ever did when Georgina was growing up.'

'I know what it is to grow up finally and see a parent in a different light,' Richard said. 'It took me thirty-three years to know my own mother.'

When they reached Hollywell House, Mrs Flannery's strained, pale face showed her relief as Richard followed Erik into the drawing-room. 'Ah, here you are at last, gentlemen. May I introduce you to these neighbours, who have so kindly come to express their condolences? Unfortunately, Mrs Davenport is unable to receive callers today.'

Two men and three women, all dressed in their best Sunday clothes, sat tense and upright with teacups in their hands, and soberly acknowledged the introductions before continuing their commiserations.

Richard quickly excused himself and went to find Mark. Erik had said that the child had scarcely been out of his room in the last two days. And Georgina was still unwilling to leave hers.

Richard ran up the stairs and turned first into the corridor leading to Georgina's room. He tapped on the door, and after a pause, Natasha opened it. Her anxious expression instantly broke into a smile.

'Georgina, Richard has come!'

She was standing at the window, motionless, staring out towards the sea, and didn't move.

'May I come in?' he asked, and Natasha bit her lip as Georgina looked over her shoulder at him. She had not yet dressed, and her disordered hair hung around her shoulders. Her white, grief-ravaged face shocked him, and every impulse was to rush to her, but she shook her head.

'I'm waiting for Simon. He is coming home soon,' she murmured, and turned back to the sea.

Richard's eyes smarted. He didn't move. 'May I see Mark? Perhaps take him for a walk?'

She nodded.

Natasha touched his hand. 'Yes, yes, please care for him, comfort him.'

He kissed her cheek and, with one last glance at the desolate figure silhouetted against the bright noonday sun streaming through the window, he closed the door and left the room.

His stomach churned with anxiety as he hurried up the stairs to the nursery, where the door stood open. Before the boy was aware of him, Richard had a moment to observe the uneaten meal on the table, and his son listlessly playing a board-game with a rosy-cheeked young housemaid, who was trying very hard to be jolly.

'Hello there, Master Davenport!' he called, swallowing hard. 'I've come down to see if Wags has learned to *sit* yet.'

Mark leapt from his chair and bounded into Richard's arms, clinging tightly and burying his head into the curve of his neck. 'Papa's not here. He drowned.'

'Yes, old chap, I know. Let's go for a walk, and you can tell me all about it.'

He carried Mark down the back stairs and, with the puppy frisking at his heels, they went out through the kitchen garden. That way they were able to avoid a fresh influx of callers coming to the front door, as well as the sight of a wagon trundling up the lane towards the gate, carrying what he surmised was Simon's body.

With Mark mounted on his shoulders, Richard marched into the village and straight to the bakery, where the smell of fresh pies proved irresistible. They sat on a stile while Mark ate ravenously, and a little colour crept back into his sallow cheeks as they talked. They fed their scraps to Wags, and walked to a farm to buy mugs of milk, and found apples to crunch as they tramped companionably across the fields, hand in hand, and talking of this and that.

At last, Mark mentioned the afternoon he'd woken up to see Tom Williams heading towards the cove, and had run out after him. 'I forgot to ask Papa if I could go out to play.' Little by little the floodgates opened, and the terror of the events of that afternoon came tumbling out in a jumbled, often illogical, sequence of childish impressions. Richard lay stretched out under a tree with the child's head resting on his shoulder, listening to the flow of talk.

'Nobody is to blame, Mark. I know it's hard, but we have to accept that sometimes accidents do just happen.'

'Like the time the tiger scratched your face?'

'Yes,' he said, and ruffled his son's hair affectionately, 'something like that. Things happen that make you sad, but you'll find there are always a lot of good things waiting ahead.'

Mark started to chat about other days at the cove, times that brought back sunny memories, and Richard was sure the child's mood was lifting, until the boy startled him by suddenly starting to wail.

'Papa's dead and now Mama's going to die, too. She's going to die!'

Richard sat up quickly and turned Mark to face him. 'What do you mean?

She's not going to do any such thing. Where did you get that idiotic idea?'

'They won't let me see her, but I peeped in her room and I saw her lying on the bed, and they sent me away and wouldn't let me in the room again, so I know she's going to die.'

Anger hit Richard like a fist in the solar plexus and he scrambled to his feet. This was too much! If Georgina was falling apart with grief at this time, there was absolutely no excuse for allowing their child to be punished with fantasies of doom.

'Here, dry your eyes, lad,' he said, mopping the wet face with his handkerchief. 'We're going home right now, and you and I will have a stern talk with your mama, whether she wants to or not.'

'Can you stop her from dying?'

'I have no intention of allowing her to die,' he said fiercely, 'because, one of these days, she's going to decide to marry me.'

Mark's jaw dropped, and Richard cursed his own lapse of discretion. 'Of course, old chap, your mama doesn't know that yet, so it has to be our secret. Will you remember not to tell a soul about what I've just said?'

The boy looked at him in awe and nodded. Then they grinned at each other, and set out hand in hand on the long walk back to Hollywell House.

By the time they arrived, Richard was clear in his mind about how he would confront Georgina with his concern regarding Mark, but all thought of that fled when they walked into the hall, holding hands tightly, and with the puppy tucked under Richard's free arm.

She was coming down the stairs. Her face was white and there were blue circles under her eyes, but when she saw them, her expression lit with delight, and she ran down the last few steps and came to them with her arms open.

'Thank you for coming, Richard,' she said, then crouched in front of Mark and hugged him. 'You didn't eat your lunch. You must be very hungry.' She kissed him, then stood to kiss Richard's cheek also, while father and son assured her they'd eaten pies and apples and were not hungry at all, though they both continued to regard her with astonished relief.

In the time that Richard and Mark had been away, Georgina had dressed in black and styled her hair. Although her face retained a gaunt, strained look, she was again the woman of strength he knew so intimately. The beautiful woman he loved.

'Mark, my love,' she said softly. 'Papa has come home, and he's waiting in here. Would you like to say goodbye to him?'

The child looked up into Richard's face. His father nodded and together they followed Georgina into the morning-room, where Simon lay. Erik and Natasha sat beside him, and when Mark came close, Richard lifted him to see Simon.

'Would you like to kiss Papa?' he whispered, and the boy's lips trembled as he nodded.

Richard watched closely as his son studied Simon's strong, gentle face, then kissed his forehead. 'See, he's not cross with me, Mama,' Mark said as he looked up at Georgina.

'No, darling, he'd never be cross with any of us.' Her eyes were damp, but her composure didn't slip. 'Now, perhaps Grandmama will take you up for your bath before supper? Uncle Richard and I will be up later to see you.'

Erik followed, blowing his nose as they left the room, and closing the door behind them.

For a few moments Georgina continued to stand where she was beside Simon, then she moved closer to Richard and slipped her hand into his and held it tightly. She rested her head against his arm and sighed.

'I'm sorry I gave way so, but I couldn't bear the thought of him out there under that deep, dark water – alone all that time – and there was nothing I could do to find him. He was lost and I was frantic, so frantic, but—'

She took a deep breath. 'Look at his face, Richard. Don't you see that he wasn't lost and alone at all? He found Anne out there; she was waiting for him, and now they're together. I didn't realize that until they carried Simon home this afternoon, and when I saw his face, I knew that he'd gone to where he always yearned to be. He's with Anne again.'

Richard held her while she wept into his chest, and his own tears fell to dampen her hair.

Simon Davenport was buried three days later in the little churchyard at the bottom of the lane leading up to Hollywell House. Friends who had rushed from London expressed some surprise at the simple country funeral arranged by his widow, but she was adamant that it was Simon's expressed wish to remain near Hollywell.

Richard stayed close beside Natasha, watching Georgina hold Mark's hand tightly as they left the flower-filled church and stood by the graveside. Erik was at her side throughout the service, and although she was pale, Georgina maintained her singular composure. Richard's heart swelled with pride as he watched her acknowledge the stream of condolences with a quiet dignity, before they walked back to the house.

When the last of the mourners had gone, the family continued to sit, emotionally drained, in the drawing-room, reminiscing fondly about Simon.

'I don't want to go back to London – at least, not yet,' Georgina announced suddenly. 'I'd like to stay here with Mark and see that Simon's affairs are completed as he would have wanted.'

Erik and Natasha expressed concern about her living alone in the house.

'I can't stay any longer, my dear,' he said with a frown. 'I promised the clinic I'd be back at the end of the month.' He looked towards Natasha.

'Mother, I insist you go home with Father,' Georgina said, with gentle firmness. 'I assure you all that I will be perfectly content to live here alone while I'm in mourning.'

She turned to Richard. 'I do hope that you'll be able to take leave from Whitehall and come down to visit Hollywell whenever you can. Mark will miss Simon very much, but if he knows you're still part of our life, both he and I will be content.'

'Yes, of course I'll come down.' He felt his heart turn over. 'Often,' he added.

Natasha and Erik heard the invitation and, by their murmurs, it was clear they were also delighted that Georgina had left nobody in doubt about what she wanted.

Richard travelled to Dorset each month, and when he judged the time to be right, he took the unopened envelope from the drawer where his shirts were kept, and presented it to Georgina as soon as they were alone in her bedroom.

She read his letter and fingered the fine lace from Peshawar, and wept. 'Oh, I'm so sorry, Richard. What complications I created for us all! Yet you waited for me.'

She clung to him and he comforted her. And they made love.

'Do you remember the night we found ourselves in the cave of the Golden Pagoda?' she said later as they lay snugly together in her bed, listening to the winter wind fling itself against the stone walls of the old house. 'Remember the feeling of hope it left with us?'

'How could I forget?' He was near to the edge of sleep.

'I won't repeat the mistake of keeping secrets from you this time.'

It took several seconds for the meaning of her softly spoken words to reach his consciousness, then an immense, delighted joy came welling up in his heart. He lifted himself on one elbow and peered through the darkness at the pale shape of her face on the pillow. 'Are you saying—?'

'I'm saying, my dearest, that I now have a beautiful wedding veil waiting to be worn,' she whispered, 'and, as I'm certain there's another baby on the way, I would be much obliged if you would be so kind, on this occasion, as to marry me without delay.'

He held her close and they kissed and laughed and kissed again. 'Choose the day, Georgina – any day, any day at all.' Then he kissed her again. And again.